CARNIVAL OF MANIACS

Pamela Voorhees's son Jason now lies dead. Of course, that's never stopped him before, but now his power is all but gone. Unless he can kill someone on Friday the 13th, he will never rise again.

When a travelling Carnival of Terrors discovers Jason's body, Alice, the Ringleader's ambitious daughter, sees the monstrous killer's corpse as a great crowd puller. Of course, Pamela wants nothing of this, and possesses an unwitting girl in order to be reunited with her son. She is going to have to hurry though, because Alice has just put Jason's body up for sale on an Internet auction site.

With the FBI on Jason's trail, his mother following fast behind and a crazy rock star set to win the bid on his body, Camp Crystal Lake's favourite son must respond the only way he knows how – raise the bodycount!

FRIDAY THE 13TH

CARNIVAL OF MANIACS

A NOVEL BY
STEPHEN HAND

BASED ON CHARACTERS FROM THE
MOTION PICTURE FRIDAY THE 13TH
CREATED BY VICTOR MILLER

BLACK FLAME

A Black Flame Publication
www.blackflame.com

First published in 2006 by BL Publishing, Games Workshop Ltd.,
Willow Road, Nottingham NG7 2WS, UK.

Distributed in the US by Simon & Schuster, 1230 Avenue of the
Americas, New York, NY 10020, USA.

10 9 8 7 6 5 4 3 2 1

ISBN 13: 978 1 84416 380 9
ISBN 10: 1 84416 380 6

A CIP record for this book is available from the British Library.

Printed in the UK by Bookmarque, Surrey, UK.

Dedicated to Reginald Aubrey Wootton – a master storyteller.

PROLOGUE

"Come on, give me another chance. Stay a week. Help get the place ready. By Friday, if you're not happy, I'll put you on the bus myself."

Those four simple sentences kept spinning through Alice's mind as her face was slammed into the dirt for the second time.

It seemed impossible that her thoughts could take a time-out like this. Perhaps it was the shock of the impact—of her nose almost breaking against the damp, compacted sand. She hoped to God that wasn't it; the last thing she needed now was concussion. Now that she was fighting for her life.

Grunting at the weight of the assailant pressing down on her back, Alice lay flat out on the ground. She was so close to the lake she could almost touch the water. Above her, the full moon cast a razor-sharp light that left no place to hide.

It bathed her in a cold gleaming light that was perfect for murder, yet she couldn't help noticing its beauty. She'd never seen a moon so big; it almost filled the entire night sky. So bright, so clear, so hypnotic, so easy just to surrender to it and let it all…

"No!"

Alice was shocked to realize the cry had been her own.

She struggled and kicked beneath her attacker. But her efforts were for nothing. She was lying face down on the shore of Crystal Lake, pinned down by a full adult body's weight on Alice's slender teenage form.

A powerful arm snaked around her throat, tugging into her neck with all the wrenching power of a hangman's noose. Alice retched at the kick she felt in her windpipe. She tried to wriggle out, to roll, to turn, anything, but the forearm was locked too tightly around her neck. She could see the strangling limb clad in thick, pale blue wool—a hardwearing sweater worn by the maniac who was trying to kill her. Alice sank her teeth into the course knit and bit hard. It was her last chance.

Her attacker cried out in pain and suddenly Alice could breathe again. But she knew she couldn't keep it up for long. Her pursuer seemed to have limitless energy, an unending capacity for violence, but Alice wasn't a fighter. She was just a mixed-up girl from California who liked working with kids. That's why she'd come to Camp Crystal Lake: to help teach valuable life skills to little boys and girls. Life skills such as how to defend yourself against a raging psychopath.

Alice heaved with all her might. Somehow, she managed to push the powerful but wounded foe off her back. Then she scurried out from underneath—suddenly, she was free again, but for how long? Her desperate act had used up almost every last ounce of strength in her body. The slim blonde was practically exhausted. But her attacker?

Alice knew her hunter would never give up. Once the pain of the bite subsided, the murderous onslaught would continue. Alice made for easy prey because she abhorred violence. She didn't have any real fight inside her, and each time she'd felt the physical impact of striking her attacker—even in self defense—she'd wanted to throw up. All this punching and kicking, and her crawling along the sand, was coming from the pure animal instinct to survive.

It was a pity that damn instinct hadn't kicked in when the camp owner, Steve Christy, had asked Alice to stay. What was it he'd said?

"Come on. Give me another chance. Stay a week."

Those words again, so calmly persuasive. He'd spoken them only that morning, while he and Alice had been fixing up one of the cabins. Now she cursed whatever it was that had made her agree. If she'd gone back to California, as she'd planned, she wouldn't be running and screaming through a forest of dismembered human remains. She'd have been spared the gut-shuddering terror of seeing all her campmates slaughtered one by one in the space of a mere few hours.

It had taken just one day for the silent killer to creep into the summer camp and butcher all six camp counselors: Annie, Ned and Jack had all had their throats slashed; Marcie had taken an axe to the face; Brenda's dead body had been trussed up and thrown through a window, and Bill—oh God, Bill!—had been pinned to a cabin door with arrows. And not one of them was much older than Alice.

As for Christy, he'd worked hard to restore the summer camp founded by his parents in 1935—the camp all the locals said was cursed, that had been shut down in 1962, following five years' "bad luck." And the killer had rammed a knife into his gut. Great going, Mr Christy; the camp hadn't even opened for business and already everyone running the place was dead.

Everyone, that is, except Alice.

Through a process of elimination, Alice Hardy—the girl who didn't even want to be at Camp Crystal Lake—had found herself alone against the maniac.

The full horror of that night had crept up on her slowly: people had started to disappear; the power kept cutting out; the phone lines went dead; then Alice thought she heard somebody scream. Everything was confused. But it was only when she discovered the stabbed, abused, mutilated corpses of the others that Alice realized there was a killer in the woods. And that she would be the final victim. Twenty miles from the nearest town, she was being stalked by a predator with only one thought in mind: Kill. Kill! *Kill!*

And so here they were. Grappling by the boat dock. Fighting on a shore that was no more than a sliver of sand beside a vast lake—a carcass of water enclosed by an impenetrable body bag of trees.

Alice lurched to her feet and readied herself for the next deadly attack. She still could not believe that the killer was a woman.

Dressed in a powder blue sweater, work boots and dark jeans, Mrs Pamela Voorhees cut the figure of a woodsman—a hunter. She wasn't particularly tall nor in any way brawny, but her average frame exuded extraordinary physical power. Her whole body seemed coiled tight to kill, and it was clear she'd let nothing and no one stand in her way.

Moonlight sparkled over her crop of permed blonde hair, and made her demented rictus grin appear even more deathly and deranged. But although the wild, dark eyes of Mrs Voorhees were turned in Alice's direction, they were staring through the girl; seeing beyond to the waters of Crystal Lake, back to a time when her only child had drowned in its depths.

Over two decades had passed since that terrible day in '57, when all the other little brats staying at the camp had tormented her poor, poor boy. They had teased him. They had made fun of him because of his... Because his appearance was special. They had chased Pamela's son, and he had run away. He was crying as he fled along the boat dock, where he'd stumbled and fallen.

If the camp counselors had been doing their job, the boy would have been saved. But no, they were too busy playing and screwing around, and they left her poor boy to drown. The counselors had let Jason Voorhees die, and for that they too had to die. Every counselor, every wretched teenager and meddling do-gooder who came to Crystal Lake— they all had to die.

Pamela had succeeded in keeping the camp closed for over twenty years; a little fire here, a poisoned well there—nothing anyone could pin on her. But that fool Christy—Steve Christy, whose parents went bust wasting money on this place— had thought he could start it all over again. He thought he could just forget about the past, reopen Camp Crystal Lake and put more children at risk; more little ones who might fall into the water and drown, just as Jason had.

So Pamela was really saving people's lives. She had to deal with these teenagers, in order to save the lives of infants. Innocent children with warming smiles. Children who were still alive. Still alive, like the voice she could hear calling to her from the bottom of the lake. The voice of her son Jason. Speaking to her. Talking into her mind...

"Kill her, Mommy! Kill her! Don't let her get away, Mommy. Don't let her live!"

Pamela almost choked with rage as she answered the sickly tones of her split personality with a voice completely her own:

"I won't Jason, I won't."

She reached a hand down to the leather sheath hanging off her belt, before remembering she'd left her knife buried in the gristle of Steve Christy's sternum. That's right, and then she'd hung his body out to dry. No, no, that was the first knife. It was her second knife she wanted, the knife that bitch Alice had knocked out of her hand with a poker. Oh, that girl—Christy—those filthy screwing teenagers! Didn't they understand? This place was Pamela's hunting ground.

"Kill her, Mommy! Kill her!"

Alice could see Mrs Voorhees steeling herself for one final attack.

When Alice had first met Pamela, less than a quarter of an hour ago, she'd thought the woman had come to save her. Pamela was around fifty, for God's sake! Psychos were meant to be young men; sinister assassins veiled in dark hoods, not middle-aged widows wearing sensible shoes. It didn't seem possible that Mrs Voorhees could be the killer. Even when she'd told Alice some crazy story about her dead son, and had come lunging at the girl with a hunting knife, Alice still couldn't believe it was happening.

But then they'd fought—a brutal, desperate struggle for life.

Alice had hit Mrs Voorhees time and again, but the indomitable old witch had just kept coming. Thrusting, stabbing, punching, slapping, throwing the girl to the ground. Alice had run for her life, but couldn't get away—the automobile was out of action, the camp was littered with bodies, and worst of all, there was no place to hide.

Pamela knew the layout of the camp better than Alice. And then there was the full moon, opposing all concealment and urging Mrs Voorhees to ever darker deeds of lunacy.

If Alice still needed persuading that Pamela had killed all her friends, then the woman's dummy-free ventriloquist routine was it. She heard Mrs Voorhees speak to herself in that freaked-out baby voice:

"Kill her, Mommy! Kill her!"

There then followed a visceral game of cat and mouse; ten nightmarish minutes that led to this final confrontation at the boat dock on the shores of Crystal Lake.

Pamela had aimed a deadly machete blow at Alice, only for the girl to deflect it at the last instant with a canoe paddle. After a few more wild swings, the oar had been broken in half, the machete bashed out of Pamela's hand, and the maniac had dived on the girl from behind. They'd wrestled and grappled on the sand, Pamela grabbing hold of Alice's hair and repeatedly shoving the girl's face into the dirt, once, twice—which was when Alice found herself despondently recalling Steve Christy's words, asking her to stay.

But here, now, standing but a few yards away from her deadly opponent, Alice could see Pamela was no long bothered by the teeth marks in her arm. Mrs Voorhees was ready. She was coming.

Omigod!

Alice looked left—the broken paddle.

Right—the machete!

The long, narrow blade was almost dazzling in the moonlight, a vicious slash across the sand that sent a message that needed no voice: use me.

Alice bent down, seized the machete in both hands, and went rushing forward in denial of every civilized code she had ever learned. She broke through all moral restraints and ran screaming toward Mrs Pamela Voorhees with only one outcome in her mind.

Pamela, for so long the hunter, was now facing an impossible truth.

Her mouth sagged in horror, her eyes opened wide. This could not be. She was the predator, not the prey. She was the one who dealt the red hand of death. She would decide when...

Alice snarled, lashed out with the machete, and lopped the head of Mrs Voorhees clean off its shoulders. Over and over it turned: a ball of severed arteries pitching with ragged lines of skin until, frozen in an expression of fear, finally hitting the sand in a puddle of blood-slush. Pamela's hands clutched at the air, driven by willpower but ultimately defeated by the spurting stump of her neck. Slowly, like the falling of rotted timber, her headless corpse dropped to its knees and then pitched forward, spewing chips of broken spine into the dirt.

Pamela Voorhees was dead.

The voice in her mind—the voice of eleven year-old Jason, calling to her from 1957—had been silenced. But at that moment, in the light of the full moon, something that no one ever could have expected took place.

There was a shifting in the darkness: not the dark of the night, but the darkness of the soul. When Alice shuddered, she thought it was with the release of someone who had stared into the gouged eyes of Hell and had somehow pulled through. She had no way of knowing she had just unleashed a monstrous evil. But two months later, that same evil would come back to destroy her. Two months from now, Alice Hardy would be dead.

For this was an evil that would never die. Here at Camp Crystal Lake—Camp Blood—Alice had unwittingly set in motion a spear gun of bloody slaughter that would shoot its way through hundreds of victims over an unimaginable number of years. Because tonight, beneath the bloated moon, Mrs Voorhees would learn that her boy hadn't drowned at all.

Yes, he had fallen in the water. Yes, he had nearly died. But he'd survived. Damaged, frightened, confused, the retarded boy had crawled out of the lake and spent his whole life scavenging in the woods. But now that Pamela Voorhees was dead, she'd discovered something that would make things much better for her poor, sweet boy. Mommy had found a very special gift for her son—something that would change his life forever—and this was the perfect day to give it to him.

Because the date of Pamela's death was Friday the 13th of June, 1980.

Jason's birthday.

CHAPTER ONE

Erwin pressed down on the gas as the gleaming eighteen-wheeler began its long, slow drag up the hill. The gradient at Danver Rise wasn't much to shout about, but it went on for a couple of miles in one continuous haul; so it never hurt to give the four stroke a little more juice. When the engine struck the right note, Erwin snatched at the manual gear shift, causing the high cab to lurch with the sudden bite of transmission.

The gentle rocking brought on a smirk. What with the punch of the gears and all the bumps along this stretch of road, the driver knew exactly what he was doing. Because the more his truck rattled and rolled, the more he felt the girl's leg brush against the denim on his thigh. And she was wearing black fishnet pantyhose.

You see, Bill Erwin was on day two of his weekly run to a chemical plant over in east New Jersey.

There, he'd fill his trailer with some good, honest produce of the Garden State, and then turn around and bring the shipment back to a distribution center some place near his home town in Illinois. And that's what he did fifty weeks of the year—fifty-two when they let him.

Trucking was good. It paid well and Bill enjoyed the freedom of driving through hundreds of miles of countryside. He knew the journeys would go quicker if he kept to the Interstate, but then he wouldn't get to see pretty areas like this remote lake region in Wessex County. There was so little traffic on these roads, he could relax and have a smoke or play some music. If he was real careful, he could even sneak himself a beer.

Sure, he spent most of his time alone—and that's not everybody's bag—but Bill enjoyed his own company. If he ever did get lonesome, he could pull up at a diner or a gas station, or talk to some hitchers like the three kids he'd picked up late this afternoon.

He'd found them outside a general store some miles back and they'd been striking out big time all day. No one wanted to stop for three high school Goths dressed head to foot in black; they were just way too weird. But it was precisely because of the way they looked—well, one of them at least—that Erwin had put on the brakes and offered them a ride. He knew four upfront would be a tight squeeze, but that was all part of the game plan.

You just don't see black fishnet pantyhose in Wessex County; In fact, you don't see any black in Wessex County outside a burial. And the girl who was wearing them? Sweet Christ, she was hot.

Her boyfriend, some loudmouth who called himself Trick, had tried to get on board first, but Erwin had pushed him back down and reminded him of his manners. "Ladies first, son."

Give the kid his due. He'd apologized and stepped aside to let the girls on. That was "girls," plural. Two of them: the tall, slim goddess with the fishnet legs and some dumpy little pig with a face like a pitcher of phlegm. Guess which one Erwin helped up first?

The trucker had reached his hand down to the pretty young lady like he was the perfect gentleman. He'd even formally introduced himself. "My name's Bill Erwin. Pleased to meet you, honey."

In return, the punk bride of Dracula had lit his fire with a funereal parting of her lips, and told him to call her Z-Moll. Then she'd snuggled up real tight beside him.

Z-Moll. What kind of name was that?

But then what kind of kids were these? No transportation? Stuck outside some poky old store in the ass end of New Jersey? They'd just been sitting in the dirt, baking in the early evening sun like three barbecue briquettes: black hair, black clothes, black makeup, black everything—even the polish on the boy's nails. Oh, and don't forget the boy's eyeliner.

Regardless, Erwin was happy enough to have them along. Even though these three charcoals of the "whatever" generation had been hitting him with some serious adolescent 'tude, it meant he could sit by the tall girl with the legs.

For their part, the kids' gratitude totally clashed with their undead image. Trick, in particular, was suffering from verbal diarrhea. Despite letting the girls on first, the boy somehow got himself planted on the other side of Z-Moll, and over the last ten minutes he hadn't shut up once; Bill wondered if he was high on something. But the other girl—Glo—had hardly said a word. The grumpy little stump-butt had just crushed herself in between Trick and the passenger door and had spent the entire journey staring out the window. Fortunately, conversation wasn't Bill's main concern.

He shot a glance down at Z-Moll's thigh. It was long, slim, and crisscrossed with webbing. Bill had to call on sheer strength of will not to place an oily hand on her leg.

Just then Z-Moll turned and caught him.

She was wearing a black padded jacket, with black feathers on the collar and cuffs. It shone like it was made of satin. Underneath, she wore a black tank that had been torn along the hem to display her pale, narrow midriff. The tank had a print on it, which Erwin quickly turned his attention to in a bid to play a save.

"What's that on your tee?" he croaked in a voice trained at the Tobacco School of Elocution. "Slapnut?"

The boy sitting on the other side of Z-Moll howled with laughter.

"Slapnut?" Trick spluttered. "Slapnut?"

Then all three of them broke up, even Glo.

Erwin scowled and returned his eyes to the road. He didn't see what was so damn funny, but they just kept laughing and repeating "Slapnut" over and over. He was about to tell them to quit it, when Z-Moll raised a hand up to her beautiful, kissable, BJ-able, black lips, then pulled back her jacket to show him the full logo.

"It's Slipknot, stoopid."

Z-Moll could have said almost anything, and Erwin would have melted. But Trick was only just getting started.

"Hey... *Slappy*!" roared the boy through his tears. "How's it going... *Slappy*?"

Erwin shook his head. "Don't smudge your mom's mascara, boy."

Trick writhed in his seat—this was getting funnier by the second. He mimicked the threatening lowness of Erwin's voice. "This ain't like dusting crops, Slappy." And then, "Slappy... I am your father."

Seeing the cloud descending over Erwin's alcohol-creased brow, Glo swiftly nudged her friend in the ribs, "Come on, Trick, hit the mute button."

Z-Moll laid a soothing hand on the trucker's knee.

"Ignore him," she said playfully. "He's only jealous 'cause you wanna hump my legs."

The truck swerved, making Trick laugh even louder, "Slappy's gone cardiac! If you think it's guilt, press one. Sexual arousal, press two. Slapman, you dirty old fuck!"

Erwin tugged at the wheel and got the semi back under control. He shouldn't have lost it in the first place, but the boy was right: he'd been made to look like a pervert by a girl not even half his age.

How old was she? Fifteen? Sixteen? Sure, she was over six foot—all the girls are these days—but Christ, she was probably illegal. If Bill wasn't careful, Z-Moll could land him in a whole world of trouble.

"Hey, honey," he growled, "the last thing I want is to look at your legs."

"Oh, that's right," she smiled mischievously. "I forgot. It's my vest you're interested in."

Z-Moll laughed and suddenly lifted the hem of her tank to expose a black leather bra wrapped tight around her breasts.

Trick cheered her on. The boy didn't seem to mind that his girl was putting out for the trucker. Glo, however, groaned and sunk her head in her hands. Bill was beginning to understand why the half-pint always looked so miserable.

Z-Moll cupped her leather-clad breasts in her hands, doing her best to catch the driver's attention, but Erwin just kept watching the road—despite the temptation.

"Great," he sighed. "Jailbait."

Z-Moll leaned forward to look Erwin in the eye. She couldn't believe what a cliché he was: the plaid work shirt, the baseball cap, even the thick mustache—he was totally homo. She blew him a kiss.

"It's only jailbait if you touch, breaker-buddy."

The trucker tightened his grip on the large steering wheel. "Are you crazy?"

"No," purred Z-Moll. "I'm from Seattle."

"That's a heck of a long way to hitch," said Erwin, blowing the horn of his truck as if to let some pressure out of the cab.

Trick shouted over the noise, "What you waiting for, Slap-attack? Go on. Take a look. She can't hold out like that all day."

"Who says I can't?" snapped the girl.

"Well, what about Frink Park?" whined Trick accusingly.

"It was January!" she shouted.

"I had a thermal blanket," the boy protested.

As the two of them bickered, Erwin peeked at Z-Moll's punk bra—just like she'd invited him to do.

Sweet almighty Christ.

Even through the leather, he could tell she had nipple-rings.

"All right, that's enough," she said, lowering her tank. She must have seen him out the corner of her eye. "That's for the ride, okay?"

Erwin cursed under his breath and returned his attention to the blacktop. Maybe he was getting old after all. Thirty-eight, and these kids were killing him. This was all just fun to them, and now he had a hard-on he didn't know what to do with.

"You can look at my dick, if you want," offered Trick.

That did the job.

Bill's pants tent hit the deck.

Half an hour later, and the rolling plains had been replaced by miles of dense forest, a body of trees dissected at crucial points by dirt tracks leading to places of threatening seclusion.

They lumbered past road signs Erwin knew by heart, but which led to townships and settlements he had never been to; their names were merely measuring points along his regular route beneath the shadowy green canopy. To the kids, however, the signs spoke of locations that suggested pumpkin-headed knifemen committing slaughter to heavy metal music.

Bennington Glen. Boring.

Newhope. Not bad.

Millwood. Perfect. The Millwood Maniac. The Millwood Machete Killer. Like Trick said, "The places gotta have rhythm or they don't work."

It was clear to Erwin that the boy was never going to shut up. He looked ridiculous in that outfit: long cotton duster, frayed jeans, a torn tee, and a pair of knee-high combat boots with side buckles and front padding—all black. His head shaved but for a black buzz up top. Trick seemed to see himself as fifty per cent Jesse James, fifty per cent Count Dracula, but to Bill he was one hundred per cent prick. The kids were pierced as well. Brows, tongues, noses, ears, Z-Moll's nipples...

"How far is it?"

The abrupt question startled Erwin out of his black leather daydream.

"Whassat?" he mumbled.

It was Glo. She'd taken a map out of her backpack and was studying it.

"How far to the crossroads?" she asked. "We must be getting close."

And they were. Erwin had picked the kids up some time around five, and it was now—he glanced at his clock—twenty before six. Funny how one noisy kid could make forty minutes seem like four hours.

Z-Moll grabbed the map out of Glo's hand and started to fold it back up. "Ignore her," she told Erwin. "She's just having a Velma attack."

"Hey, fuck no," Trick countered. "If we're close, I wanna know. I've waited all my life to come here."

"Where?" asked Bill. "Camp Crystal Lake?"

The kids fell silent and glanced nervously at one another.

Again, Bill couldn't help but be in awe of how fantastic Z-Moll looked. Okay, she was a little too Addams Family, but with her long black hair flowing down to her waist...

"How d'you know we're going to Crystal Lake?" asked Glo hesitantly.

For the first time since he'd taken the three smart-mouths on board, Erwin sensed he had an advantage. Payback time.

"So you think you're the first set of Boris Karloff rejects to come sniffing round old Camp Blood?"

"What's he saying, Trick?" whined Z-Moll.

"Don't worry, babe," answered the boy. "Slappy's just yanking our chain."

"No way," said Erwin, shouting the boy down. "I've seen it all before. Kids like you, with your Charlie Manson tee shirts and this whole undertaker deal—I bet you got a mountain of videos back home—tapes on the Crystal Lake Massacre, Jason Voorhees. I bet you got all the books and periodicals."

"Don't forget the action figures," quipped Trick, but his joke fell flat. Besides, he really did have a Jason Voorhees action figure; it was standing right next to his plastic models of Jeffrey Dahmer, John Wayne Gacy, and good ol' Eddie Gein—and each figure had an amazing thirty-six points of articulation.

Glo, on the other hand, wasn't so ready to ignore Bill's sarcasm.

"It's not what you think," she replied.

"Is that so?" said Erwin. "Twenty-five years ago a a whole lot of people got killed and you come here, dressed like Count Dracula in diapers, looking for where some innocent folks got slaughtered? You got your camcorders with you? Got your cellphones with your digital zoom?"

Each and every one of Erwin's bullets found their mark. He could see Glo getting more and more riled. For a moment, it seemed she was about to erupt; instead she just sat back and muttered, "You wouldn't understand."

Bill understood all right, but there was something about Glo's manner that made him think twice. Because the minute he'd mentioned Crystal Lake, she had come over all serious; she seemed nothing at all like her friends and Bill got the distinct feeling she was holding something back.

He took a closer look at her.

Her skater pants had enough cloth in them to roof Soldier Field; how the hell didn't she trip up in them? But at least she had the sense to be wearing a decent pair of trail boots. Her beat-up biker's jacket was a good call too, but her hair? A crow's nest of bottle black, with long, mousy roots hanging down from the kind of center parting normally reserved for mental patients.

"Come on, Slap-fest," Trick reached over and patted the driver on the shoulder. "Don't kill the atmos."

* * *

There was a metal squeal and a sudden hiss of air pressure, as the massive wheels of the semi rolled to a halt. It was a couple of hours before sundown and the truck was now deep in the heart of the woods. The junction wasn't marked—there were no signs or directions of any kind—there was just the road they'd come in on and a dirt trail heading north and south; everything else was forest.

They'd arrived at the crossroads.

The last part of the journey had passed in uncomfortable silence, but that didn't stop Bill helping the kids down from the cab.

He reached up for Glo and almost got tangled in her pants as he clumsily lowered her to the ground. Then he went back for Trick, but the boy giggled and jumped straight out of the truck. However, it was only when Bill took hold of Z-Moll—and felt the way she was snaking her hips—that he realized what an idiot he'd been. Although Z-Moll in sneakers stood taller than any of them, she was still only a dumb school kid. They were all only dumb school kids. And now they were about to go off on some lunatic pilgrimage.

Bill considered the situation for a moment, and then came to a decision. He knew they wouldn't listen but at least he had to try.

"Listen," he said earnestly, "I don't live round here, but I know the people of Wessex County are sick of freaks and wackos coming out and treating the whole goddamn forest like a Jason Voorhees theme park. If the cops get one look at you, they'll run you outta the county. And if they do, you'll be lucky because if the locals find you—I swear to God, they'll beat the crap outta you."

"Great pep talk," answered Trick, lending a hand to Z-Moll as she put on her backpack. "Well, here's the headline, Slappy, we're not going anywhere near town. This is a woods-only operation."

"Dressed like that? Do you know how cold it can get out here?" Erwin tried to reason with Z-Moll. "Are you gonna go walking through the bushes and all the scrub and poisonous plants in that mini?"

Z-Moll sniggered and latched on to Trick's arm.

It was Glo who answered the question. "I've taken a course in outdoor skills. We…"

"I don't care if you've joined the fucking SEALs," snapped Bill. "This forest covers hundreds of square miles. Hardly anyone lives out here. There are bears, snakes—you're just three kids fooling around without proper equipment. Now if you'll listen to me, you'll get back in the truck…"

Trick raised a hand, "Don't be a Slap-o-phobe. We're not as dumb as we look. We know what we're doing."

It was obvious Bill wouldn't get through to the boy, so he looked at Z-Moll. She just buried her face in Trick's shoulder and giggled. As for Glo, she wasn't paying attention to any of them anymore. She just stood by the edge of the road and gazed into the woods, preoccupied.

"Well," said the trucker, giving up, "don't say I didn't warn you."

"I'll give Jason your regards," laughed Trick.

Bill stopped and looked the boy straight in the eye, "I really hope you do, son. I really hope you do."

Then he walked back round to the driver's side of the cab and climbed back up behind the steering wheel.

Outside, Trick and Z-Moll burst out laughing. The boy began to jeer at the gleaming chromium tractor, "Jason's gonna get me! Jason's gonna get me! Screw you, Cluster-Slap!"

Erwin slammed the door and ignited the engine. He peered through the windshield: nothing but trees, and a long empty road. He looked back through the mirrors: nothing but trees, and a long empty road. Not another vehicle in sight.

"Dumb kids," he muttered, then put his foot on the gas.

The rumble of the diesel-powered machinery echoed one last of civilization as the vehicle pulled away, severing the umbilical cord between the city and this wild wood of isolation. A few seconds later and Trick, Glo and Z-Moll were alone: three tiny figures standing shoulder to shoulder, stranded in the sylvan gloom.

"Thank fuck he's gone," said Trick.

Deep inside those same woods, a fawn nervously tiptoed into a small clearing and then stopped: there was an unfamiliar scent in the air. The young deer raised its head to see whether the odor indicated any kind of threat. Unfortunately, this was the first time the creature had come into contact with the stench of human excrement and, yes, the odor did indicate a threat—a very real threat.

"Get him!" yelled a rasping, high-pitched voice, and two figures burst out from their hiding place behind a clump of bushes.

Even if the deer had seen humans before, it would never have seen anyone like Francis and Enoch Grissom. These two filthy, inbred brothers—aged somewhere between thirty and a hundred and thirty—wore their shit- and piss-stained rags like a second skin. We're talking about two guys who never undressed, never took a wash, who didn't belive in shaving and who sucked the tart shit-juice out of their dental cavities on religious grounds. And they never combed the head lice out their hair because the itchy critters made a tasty snack twenty-four/seven; the little bastards just kept multiplying, and you didn't have to pay a cent for 'em.

It was Francis who'd shouted out, the short, thin, wiry one. But you wouldn't belive he was the younger of the two brothers, it was because he was mostly bald; a beat-up astronaut's helmet of long brown pubes that seemed to float two inches away from his scalp.

Francis moved with the poise and sophistication of a lobster that'd just been thrown into the boiling pot. He dived forward, arms akimbo and flailing, but the fawn easily leapt out of harm's way and Francis got himself a face full of leaves. And some raccoon shit.

"God fuckin' damn fuck God damn!" He beat the dirt with his fist.

"Don't you'n go worryin'," called his brother as he moved to cut off the deer's escape.

The elder Grissom was just as wretched as his brother but easily three times the weight. Wherever Enoch went, his hooch gut went first, wobbling inside his filthy burlap shirt like a hot sack of puke. He too was bald, but only on top; everywhere else, his hair was as thick and as dark as a squaw's bush—at least, that was how he liked to describe it. He could grow a real beard too; he didn't have a sow's pussy full of face-fuzz like his scrawny kid brother.

Francis crawled to his feet and shouted some encouragement, "Don't let'n him get away, man-tits."

Enoch stopped reaching for the deer and stood upright. "How many times have I got'n to tell ya, don't call me man-tits."

"Well, you lose'n the fuckers and I'll shut'n the fuck up, man-tits."

"Don't call me man-tits!"

"Man-tits, man-tits, fuckin' man-tits!"

"I told you," Enoch ran forward to grab his younger brother by the throat, but stopped when Francis pointed over his shoulder and cried out.

"Bambi! He's fuckin' hoofin' it!"

Quickly, the two of them set aside their differences and lurched in chaotic pursuit. They should have been no match; the fawn was young, nimble and frightened, but it didn't know the terrain and mistakenly went springing out onto the open shoreline of Crystal Lake.

Behind it were two slabs of human detritus out foraging; in front was a lake where, almost fifty years ago, a young boy nearly drowned.

"Gotchoo, you little furry bastard!"

Enoch wrapped his big hands round the willowy stalk of the deer's neck. The fawn struggled and grunted. It kicked in terror, desperate to be set free, but Enoch wrestled the creature to the ground and used his obese, sweating flesh to keep it there.

"Well, go on," he called up to his brother. "Kill'n the fucker."

Francis, named by Ma after the patron saint of animals, scratched one of the boils on his pale scalp and licked the running sores on his lips. This was the part he enjoyed most: the bit where he got to kill stuff. It was even better if he could scare the little bastard in the process. Slowly, he stepped forward and placed a foot on the side of the young deer's head.

Enoch looked up, "What'n the fuck are you doin', Francis?"

His brother smiled, "Look 'n' learn, man-tits. Look 'n' learn."

Then he placed the sole of his battered leather shoe directly over the creature's temple and pushed—hard.

Down, down, down, Francis Grissom trod on the squealing animal's face. The louder the yearling cried, the harder Francis laughed.

Enoch labored to hold the thrashing fawn in position—it was a real fight—but when he heard the moist cracking of its skull, he had to look away. He'd rather have put a knife to the creature's throat and have done with it, but his crazy brother...

Francis screeched maniacally at the red liquid brain-jelly shitting on his shoe.

"Who's laughin' now, Bambi? Who's fuckin' laughin' now?"

"Hey, Glo, wait up!"

It was the second time Trick had called to her, but the girl still wouldn't slow down. What was wrong with her? The truck had barely started moving when Glo had just taken off, marching straight into the woods.

Z-Moll had tried walking with her arm linked with Trick's, but it had been impossible. There was too much green stuff and the ground was totally up and down, so she just did her best to stick close.

"Let her go," she said dismissively. "I don't want her around when we fuck."

"Oh?" laughed Trick. "When's that?"

"As soon as I get my clothes off," smiled Z-Moll and she immediately came to a halt.

"No, don't." said Trick, grabbing hold of her hand and pulling her along. "We've got a long way to go and we'll never make it without her. She's got the whole fact thing going on."

But Z-Moll wasn't done.

"That driver said the lake's hundreds of miles long," she moaned. "That doesn't work for me."

"Square miles, math queen!" shouted Trick, but his answer only made Z-Moll frown. It was bad enough she had to concentrate on where to put her feet; with all the roots and plants, she'd already stubbed her toe on a rock, and they'd only been walking ten minutes.

Trick ran forward, took hold of Glo's shoulders and spun her around. He was surprised by the stern look on her face, her shoulders all bunched up.

"Hey, Glo, whassup?" he asked. "Where you going?"

The short girl seemed confused. She just stared at Trick in silence. He tried again.

"You're not even using a map. We made a plan, remember?"

Which would have astounded anyone who knew these kids back home. Not even their parents would have credited them with being able to put any kind of strategy together—unless it meant skipping school or fooling around. But it was because Trick and the two girls had made the painful effort to do things properly that they'd had to hitch all the way over from Washington. They couldn't afford plane seats because they'd sunk all their money into equipment: a stack of USGS maps, a digital camcorder, three flashlights, new cellphones, a handheld GPS receiver, a first aid pack, and a heap of other useful stuff that had been shared out across their three backpacks.

They'd also pooled their allowances to pay for Glo to take an outdoor skills course, all of which—if her behavior right now was anything to go by—she'd completely forgotten.

"You can't just go out there," said Trick. "Slapmaster Flash was right; it's dangerous."

No response.

"Glo!"

Suddenly the tension seemed to pour out of the girl's body. Her shoulders relaxed, her brow lifted, and she offered an apologetic smile.

"Sorry," she said, cutely biting her bottom lip. "Brain fade."

"It's that fucking truck of Alcatraz," smiled Trick. "It did me too."

"So which way now?" asked Z-Moll. "I need to go for a leak."

Glo took off her pack and pulled out a map. 1:24,000 scale was absolutely essential for this kind of walking; but when Z-Moll glanced at the unfolded sheet, all she saw was a large square of green print.

"Useful much," she sniped.

"Leave the navigation to the experts, babe," bragged Trick. "Me and Glo have got everything covered. She's got the contours and I," he said, pulling a small blue gizmo out of his pocket, "got the GPS. No fucking Blair Witch for us, man!"

Enoch trudged along the footpath, dragging the dead fawn behind him. He'd tied some twine round its front legs and was holding it in his coarse right hand; the creature's back legs were left to slip and buckle in its cadaverous wake.

A few yards ahead of Enoch was the big oak, where earlier he and his brother had left their sacks—just before they'd spotted the deer. Francis was there now, rifling through the rough bags, checking on the day's kill.

"Don't fuckin' leave me'n carryin' everythin'!" shouted Enoch.

"We don't got'n enough meat," answered Francis.

Enoch let the fawn drop and stomped over to take a look. Both of the sacks were filled with

snuff wildlife: birds, rodents, raccoons—
everything they'd collected from all their snares
and traps, along with a poisonous snake Francis
had bitten.

"What'n the fuckin' fuck do you mean?"
snapped Enoch. "The bags are full. Anyways," he
nodded in the direction of the skull-crushed fawn,
"I thought you'd wanna spend some time with
your new friend."

Francis sprang forward, whipped a knife out
from under his rags and pushed the tip of the
blade up into Enoch's jaw. The knife was made of
hand-carved bone.

"Whatchoo talkin' about, man-tits?" he snarled.

But Enoch was unimpressed. "You got'n yourself a Bambi to fuck. Don't think I don't know
what you're thinkin'."

"Why," Francis pushed the knife tip further but
still not piercing the skin, "I'm thinkin' I oughta
cut'n you right open."

"Yeah?"

Enoch head-butted Francis square in the face
and sent his brother reeling backwards. As he
stumbled, Francis slashed at the air with his
knife, making it easy for Enoch to reach out and
grab hold of his brother's arm, bringing it down
hard on his knee.

Francis dropped the blade and yelped. "You're
not fightin' fair, you dirty fat fuck!"

"Fight fair?" huffed Enoch, grabbing his spindly
brother in a headlock. "You wanna fight fair?"

The two of them were grunting and panting,
Enoch forcing his brother's head lower and lower
until it was held down by his waist. Suddenly

Francis shifted his weight, unbalancing his older brother, and dived forward.

Enoch released his brother and screamed. "Bastard! You gone bit'n me in the fuckin' cock!"

Francis laughed, reached down for a handful of dirt and threw it in his brother's eyes. Then, while Enoch was blinded—unsure whether to rub his stinging eyes or grab his aching nuts—Francis looked for the thickest branch he could find and then whacked Enoch hard on the back of the head. Enoch dropped to his knees and Francis got ready for a second strike.

"Scream for me, man-tits!" he raved.

But his older brother wasn't done yet. His eyes weeping, his balls smarting, Enoch stood up, threw his arms wide and bellowed: the noise reverberated through the trees with primeval stupidity.

"Oh shit," Francis intoned with a look of panic in his eyes. "Enoch gone get'n the red fuckin' haze."

Francis was about to run for his life when he saw something on the ground—something they hadn't seen earlier—and stopped. But Enoch was still in the grip of an unquenchable fury. He bellowed a second time and ran forward for the kill.

"No!" cried Francis.

Too late.

Enoch crashed into Francis and slammed him into the trunk of an ancient pine.

"God damn it, Enoch!"

The pain in Francis' ribs was unbearable, flecks of blood appeared on his lips. But Enoch was beyond reason. Completely berserk, he threw

Francis down onto the ground, the impact causing his brother to cry out even louder. More blood trickled out of Francis' mouth. But now he had a chance, because his brother had body-slammed him down next to...

Francis held out a shaking hand, fingers stretched wide to stave off the blow.

"No," he whimpered. "Look, Enoch, look!" He pointed to the ground. "Footprints, Enoch. Human footprints."

Enoch—his chest rising and falling, his fists held ready—stood over his beaten brother. His mouth was filled with the saliva foam of hyperventilation, his eyes almost completely white, but slowly, finally...

Francis could see the change; his brother was calming down.

"Look," he said pointing again at the tracks. "There's somebody out here with us."

"All I'm saying," said Trick again, "is that if we find an original Camp Crystal Lake sign, it's mine. End of story."

"And all I'm saying," said Glo, "is you can have it. I don't want any of that junk. I just want to see where it all happened."

Trick couldn't believe what he was hearing. "Don't you even want any pictures for your website?"

"Well, sure," answered Glo hesitantly. "But look, you're the boss here, okay. If you want stuff, it's yours."

"All right," said Trick making her a final offer, "fifty-fifty. But I get the sign. Okay?"

Z-Moll sighed. "What the fuck is wrong with you, Helen Keller? She said you can have it all."

"You don't get it, babe," he explained. "Any time Glo agrees with me, it means she's totally up to some serious mind-juju."

They'd been walking for a couple of hours now and the sun was getting low. Worse, Z-Moll's feet ached and she was sick of the smell of pine. But what really got her pissed was the humidity; all that plant vapor caused by the warmth.

"Are you sure you know where we're going?" she asked for the thousandth time.

Glo double-checked her map against the GPS Trick had given her.

"I'm absolutely positive. I got the location of the original camp from an old promotional brochure—that stuff's worth a fortune now—and I've checked with dozens of other sources. I know exactly where I'm going. A lot of people get confused between Camp Crystal Lake and Camp Forest Green, but I've taken care of that."

"Yeah, right," mumbled Z-Moll, puzzled.

"It's easy." It was Trick's turn to strut his Voorhees stuff. "After Pamela went nuts in 1980, they closed the old place down. But in '85…"

"'87," corrected Glo.

"… the local economy was so fucked, they built another camp close to the original. And the new camp was Forest Green."

"'Cause no one wanted their kids to vacation at the scene of a blood bath?" guessed Z-Moll.

"Absolutely," Glo confirmed. "But then Jason attacked Forest Green in '88, so they tore the place down in '93."

"After the CIA..." said Trick.

"The FBI," amended Glo.

"... fucked up their ambush."

"But the original camp is still out here some-place," Glo continued. "A construction company was hired a few years ago to pull it down, to make way for some luxury apartments, but guess what?"

"The Man came along," answered Trick in awe, "and wiped every fucking hard hat off the face of the planet."

Z-Moll stared at the self-satisfied pair with a deadpan expression, "You two should get married."

"No, listen," said Trick hurriedly, "Jason Voorhees is the ultimate killing machine. Forget Zodiac, forget DeSalvo; Jason's the man. He's a megaton psycho-bitch. No one can stop him. They've been trying for years but he just keeps coming back, waiting until he's ready to strike, and then *wham!* Twenty, thirty, forty dead moth-erfuckers all in one night."

"And we're looking for him?" gulped Z-Moll.

Glo shook her head. "Don't listen, Z. I've read everything that's ever been written about Jason and the only thing people know about him is they don't know anything. No one knows what's real and what's bullshit. I've got a book full of copies of official reports released under freedom of infor-mation, and even they don't make sense."

"Yeah," laughed Trick. "Only because every cop who goes after Jason winds up dead before they can fill the fucking paperwork. You try filling a rap sheet when some fucker's got his machete up your ass."

"Is Jason really that powerful?" asked Z-Moll, trying to mask what looked like a horny grin.

"Way beyond!" beamed Trick. "Jason is the big bad you do not fuck with. He can snap your neck with a click of his fingers and you wouldn't know who the fuck he was because of his hockey mask. You'd just hear his breathing—like this..."

Trick's heavy breathing sounded more like an obscene phone call.

"Wow," gasped Z-Moll. "Look, I uh—I really have to go for a leak."

The girl skipped away, searching for a bush large enough to give her some urgently needed privacy. While she was gone, Trick nodded at the USGS map in Glo's hands. "Is the camp on there?" He asked.

"No. I tried to get an older edition, but no joy. But I know where it is. I got it marked."

"You really are the fucking queen, you know."

Glo blushed. "Thanks."

Trick quickly changed the subject. "What kind of name is Voorhees, anyway?"

"Dutch," said Glo. "They were the first Europeans to come to New Jersey. Early seventeenth century."

"Wow. Cool. And how far are we from the camp?" The sun finally dipped below the mountainous horizon.

Glo checked her map. "I'd say another couple of miles."

"Come over here."

"What for?" asked Glo.

"What?" said Trick.

"You just told me to come over," said the girl.

"Bullshit. I just asked how far away the camp is."

Glo frowned and called over to the bushes. "Want something, Z?"

"No! Quit it," came the impatient reply.

Glo looked all around, but saw nothing except dense woodland taking on a darker hue with the gradual onset of night.

"Well, fuck me, fuck my dog," declared Enoch, rubbing a grimy hand through his beard.

"Whatchoo reckon?" asked Francis, kneeling beside the tracks and dabbing them with his fingers. "Two thirty?"

"Two forty at least," said Enoch.

Francis stood up, "Big fucker."

The footprints seemed to go only a few yards before heading into a carpet of stinging nettles.

"I reckon," said Enoch, glancing furtively in the direction of the prints, "I don't want no folk snoopin' round our house. They ain't got'n no business with Ma and Pa."

"What'n if it's the law?" asked Francis.

"You know better than that," said Enoch. "Those cops'n too chickenshit to come out here. Reckon it's a fuckin' tourist. Huntin' or somethin'."

"Huntin'." Francis nodded his head. "Ain't no hunters round here 'cept you an' me," he continued. "But I ain't goin' through no fuckin' stingers."

"Shhh!" his brother warned, putting a filthy finger to his lips.

Even with the taste of blood from his last defeat still fresh in his mouth, Francis wasn't about to start taking orders.

"Don't you fuckin' shush me, you man-tit fuck."

"Quick! Down!" hissed Enoch.

Francis stooped low and tried to see who or what his brother had spotted—which was just where Enoch wanted him. He pulled his leg right back, aimed his foot, then attempted a fifty-yard field goal straight up Francis's ass.

Francis screamed and went flying forward into the vast bed of nettles, where he abruptly vanished from view. He didn't even cry out in pain.

"Francis?"

Silence.

"Quit foolin' round now."

Nothing.

Expecting his brother to get up and attack him at any moment, Enoch took a cautious step forward. He could see the footprints, he could see the nettles, but…

"Enoch!" came an urgent voice. "Get'n the fuck down here!"

It was Francis, but where the hell was he?

Enoch ran straight into the bushes and suddenly, he found himself falling down a steep embankment into a pit formed during a recent landslide. Over the previous week, torrential rains had turned most of the area into a quagmire. The ground had hardened since then, but in some places the earth had given way.

Enoch landed with a dull thud at the bottom of the newly-created basin, his head banging against a peak of hardened mud.

When the stars cleared, Enoch saw that his brother was still on all fours, gawking like a dog at the very same slope they'd both just fallen down.

Because there, standing upright in the sunset gloom, trapped half in and half out of the solidified dirt, was the giant body of a man; his legs and hands poked through the mud face in a cartouche of defiance.

"Musta been caught in the landslide," whispered Francis.

"Yeah," hissed Enoch. "Looks like he tried'n claw his way out."

"Big fucker, ain't he."

But the figure's astonishing height—easily approaching seven feet—wasn't his most distinctive feature. Nor was the fact he must have been incredibly strong to have stayed on his feet beneath the cascade of sludge. No, the most remarkable thing about the dead man locked in the earth was that his face was completely hidden behind the mud-stained plastic of a hockey mask.

CHAPTER TWO

"This is bullshit! Whaddya mean, we're lost?"

The light in the forest was fading fast and Trick was close to boiling point. His irritability centered on the girl with the map, but Glo was just as concerned as he was.

"The GPS," she said, "I can't get a signal."

Glo sounded rattled, more like the nervous kid they all knew back in Seattle. Not a good sign.

"Okay," said, Trick, trying to calm things. "What about your cell?"

"Already tried," answered Glo as she continued stabbing buttons on the useless navigator.

"Z?" For all the focus his girlfriend had, Trick would have fared better talking to the trees. "Z-Moll!" he called again.

"Fuck you!" she exploded. "I knew I shouldn't have come here. I told you this was bullshit!"

"You're bullshit!" he raged, getting in her face. "If you stopped thinking with your fucking pussy for one second, you might not be such a fuck-tard!"

"Yeah?" she reached inside her jacket pocket. "Well, you can just forget about 'fucking' and 'pussy.'"

She took out her phone and jiggled it in front of him.

"Oh, look—no fucking signal," she said. "No fucking signal!" she repeated herself, shouting.

Glo couldn't understand what had gone wrong. She'd planned it so that, even at their lame-ass pace, they should have reached Camp Crystal Lake by now. Yet somehow, they'd drifted off course. Sure, she'd been distracted by the voice she'd imagined hearing, but not enough to go making stupid errors. Now, without the GPS, the map was useless and without the map… Glo didn't even want to consider that possibility. They were carrying enough food and water for only two days. Their whole plan had been about getting into the camp, staying the night, and then getting straight back out again. Anything else and they were in deep trouble, survival course or not.

Total nightfall was still over an hour away, but Glo decided to try her flashlight. She didn't know why, because the problem with the GPS was signal not power, but she tried all the same—oh, who was she fooling. She knew exactly why she'd turned on the harsh white beam. She was checking to see that some malevolent force wasn't screwing with their equipment. Which could only mean that Glo was losing it.

"Hey!" called Trick. "Batteries."

Funny, Glo noticed, how the boy could break off from his argument with Z-Moll to bitch about energy conservation.

She turned off the lamp, put it away, and tried again with the navigator.

"Over here!"

It was that voice again. The one she'd heard earlier.

Glo glanced over at her friends; they were still arguing furiously—just like they always did before a fuck.

"This way," said the voice.

Glo slapped her ears, shook her head. She turned to look every which way, trying to see who was calling her, but all she saw was the forest. The air was still, there was no breeze, nothing moved. Was she going mad?

"Over here!"

"Shut up!" she cried, dropping the GPS to the ground.

"Why don't you butt out?" spat Z-Moll, thinking it was aimed at her and Trick's bickering.

"Don't talk to her like that," shouted Trick. "We can't do any of this without the Glo-ster."

"Well, for your information, dickweed, Ms fucking Inch High just got us all lost in the middle of fucking nowhere!"

The two of them started fighting again. Their yelling dissolved in Glo's mind as she concentrated on listening out for more hallucinations. Maybe that was it. Maybe Rickster the Trickster had spiked her water bottle. Whatever the cause,

Glo didn't have to wait long before hearing the voice again.

"Come this way, dear."

The voice wasn't like anyone she knew and there was something about it that was persuasive; reassuring; compelling...

Glo left the GPS lying in the dirt and calmly walked away. She'd gone twenty paces before the others even noticed she'd moved.

"Hey!" Trick hollered. "Wait up! Glo!"

But the girl wouldn't stop.

"Now look what you done," said the boy, turning on Z-Moll. "Your cocksucking mouth wins again. If we don't stop Glo—if you don't apologize to her, we're screwed."

Suddenly, unexpectedly, Z-Moll began to cry.

"Oh, Trick, you know I only wanna be with you. I don't understand all this Crystal Jason stuff!"

"Shit," the boy sighed.

What should he do? Stay there and comfort his girl, or go after the only one among them who had any idea how the hell to get back to the road?

"Glo!" he shouted, setting after the receding figure. "Wait up!"

But Glo wasn't stopping for anyone. Not Trick, not Z-Moll, no one. Because the voice was still calling to her, leading her on. Only now it was calling her by name.

"This way, Gloria. This way."

And suddenly, Gloria Sowici knew where she must go.

Through inexplicable means, this place—this whole forest—had become intimately familiar to her. She no longer needed any map or bullshit gadgets to reach her destination.

The girl walked on.

Francis and Enoch were bushed.

The Grissom boys had just spent a big bunch of minutes digging that huge sonofabitch out of the dirt, and all they'd had to work with was their picky little killing knives. Now Enoch had such a sweat on that his butt reeked of ass-crack vinegar.

"He's in pretty good shape," he said, mopping his brow with a shirt sleeve.

"Considerin' he's a gonner," agreed Francis, eyeing the petrified corpse. "Don't think I ever seen anyone so big."

The two of them were sitting on the trunk of a tree that had fallen, with the landslide into the crater and were taking a short break from their labors. Jason was still standing in the near-vertical mud face. Most of the earth around him had been chiseled away, as if Francis and Enoch had been working on a sculpture, but some of the soil clung to his back, keeping him upright. Strangely, Jason's arms remained outstretched, even though there was no longer any dirt to support them.

"You know'n who I think he is?" said Enoch thoughtfully.

"Don't be a streak o' piss," whined Francis. "It's patent who he is. It's that nut, Fourtrees."

"Sure is," nodded Enoch appreciatively. "Jason fuckin' Fourtrees. All these years, I ain't never seen him. Musta taken the heat for a dozen of ours."

By "ours," Enoch referred to those victims he and his brother truly deserved credit for; tourists and woodsmen who, over the years, had wandered off the beaten track and found themselves in the bloodstained grip of these twisted hill folk. The Grissoms knew for certain that at least three of their victims had been attributed to Jason by the authorities. Well after all, there couldn't be more than one psycho roaming the woods of Crystal Lake, could there?

Through the failing twilight, Enoch could see Jason was wearing some kind of jacket made from sackcloth, along with a pair of heavy work pants, a dark shirt and black leather gloves. Everything was torn and beaten, the whole cheapjack ensemble mottled with a layer of baked mud. And then there was the hockey mask.

That ugly piece of plastic had seen some real bad shit. It was scratched, some pieces had broken off, there were cracks, a couple of bullet holes—how many beatings had this boy taken?

Enoch got up off the log to take a closer look.

The mask was decorated with three red triangles: one between the eyes, pointing down to the nose, and the others one-a-piece on each cheek. And the whole plastic dish was pocked with air holes.

Enoch stood up on his tiptoes and tried to see inside.

"What you doin'?" called his brother.

"Gonna see what'n he looks like." Enoch raised his hands to lift the mask off Jason's face.

"Don't you fuckin' touch that thing," warned Francis, stepping forward to stop his older brother from going any further.

"Why'n the fuck not?" moaned Enoch, his fingers hovering over the straps fastening the hard white oval shape to Jason's head. "Look at him," continued Enoch. "Look at his fuckin' skin. He's black and wrinkled as a fuckin' skunk turd. He ain't goin' complain none. He's fuckin' dead. D-ceased!"

But Francis took hold of his brother's arms and pulled them away.

"I don't care if'n he's d-ceased, d-licious or d-fuckin' lovely, man-tits. You leave that faceguard where it is until we get'n the fucker home. Ma an' Pa'll wanna see when we take it off. This mad dog's their fuckin' hero."

"They weren't so fond when he killed the Hubbards," Enoch protested. "The Hubbards were our friends."

"Man-tits, you unholy streak of ignorant piss! The Hubbards was one of them copycat murders. Now stuff a cock in your trap and help me get this fucker down. I don't wanna be here all fuckin' night."

Enoch thought about smashing his brother in the mouth, but decided to let that one go. Time was getting on and lugging the big bastard home wasn't going to be easy. So, instead of jawing, the brawny redneck clamped his strong hairy hands around Jason's wrists and pulled.

"Harder, you faggot!" barked Francis. "He ain't even movin'."

But struggle as he might, Enoch could not separate Jason from the remaining sheet of filth that clung onto him.

"Grab the fucker's legs," he panted.

Francis just stood back and watched. "I ain't takin' your orders."

Enough was enough. Enoch grabbed his puny brother by the scruff of the neck and shoved his maggoty little face all the way down into Jason's crotch.

"All right, all right, I'll do it!" coughed Francis, almost choking on the stink of dead man's balls.

A few moments later, the two of them were working as a team. Francis grabbed Jason's legs, while his much stronger brother took hold of the masked maniac's shoulders. Then together they pulled until slowly, inch by resentful inch, the body of Jason started to come loose. Corpse-skin grated on dirt, a sound broken with deadly intent.

A wiser man than the Grissom boys would have left Jason just where he was. An even wiser man would have filled in the rest of the hole, and buried the killing machine forever. But no. Like so many idiots before them, Francis and Enoch Grissom had a better idea.

When the last claw of soil finally released its grip, the lifeless body of Jason Voorhees toppled forward and crashed to the ground. The two brothers jumped out of the way; if they hadn't, Jason would have crushed them.

"He ain't gon' fit in any damn sack," Francis observed.

It was only now that Enoch remembered the sacks full of fresh meat they'd left up by the oak. They'd have to go back and fetch them. But first…

"You grab his legs an' I'll take his arms."

Francis was on the verge of saying that *he* wanted the arms, and that Enoch should take the legs, when he saw the murderous look on his brother's face, daring him to open his mouth. So Grissom Junior kept his thoughts to himself, and wrapped his arms around Jason's ankles.

"You ready?" asked Enoch. His brother cleared his throat and spat a greenie in confirmation. "Okay then." Enoch counted, "One… Two… Three!"

They heaved the unmoving hulk up off the ground almost giving themselves a hernia.

"Jesus H!" groaned Francis. "This boy's got bigger man-tits than you."

Francis waited for the blow to land on the back of his head, the punch never came, but his brother had just taken to wondering how the heck they were going to haul the hockey-masked mother-frigger out up the steep side of the basin. There was only one thing for it: start climbing.

Bill Erwin flicked the headlamps up to high beam and lit himself a cigarette.

At long last, the trees were starting to make way for open fields, but the sun was almost completely gone now, making the lamps a necessity.

He'd passed through the small town of Crystal Lake a few hours ago. If you didn't know anything about the history of the place, it seemed just like any other rural one-street. It had a couple of stores, a diner, a white clapboard church, a sheriff's office and some historic houses built in the colonial style. But Bill wasn't much on archi-tecture; so he'd just followed the road straight through town and out the other side, where a neon sign had diverted him with the irresistible promise of burger and fries.

Inside the diner, he'd found he was the only customer. The waitress wasn't much on talk either. Two pots of coffee later and he was back on the road, still just inside the easternmost limit of Wessex County.

Suddenly, he was thinking about the kids again. In fact, he hadn't stopped thinking about them since he'd left them behind at the crossroads.

"Slappy," he chuckled.

For all their BS, he hoped nothing bad happened to them, and he now regretted mouthing off at the boy. After all, what was the point of picking up hitchers if they didn't add a hint of uncertainty to life?

Bill sucked on the cigarette and blew the rich smoke out through his nose. Everyone said it was a bad habit—his pop had even died of throat cancer—but then who the hell lives forever? And if you took a wider view of things, who the hell wanted to live forever? Turn on the news and you've got the Middle East, terrorism, people losing their jobs, crime getting out of hand, corruption, the environment's a mess, the economy's screwed...

Suddenly Erwin was in the mood for some country. He had a CD already in the player. All he had to do was—

"What the—"

Bill noticed a short convoy of vehicles coming towards him on the other side of the road. The first two trucks were motorhomes, roomy but shabby with overuse. The third truck was a fully-loaded pickup—so far, so ordinary. But the fourth vehicle was a semi almost as long as Bill's, and both sides of the trailer were covered by the same massive piece of airbrush art: a montage of comic book monsters—Dracula, the werewolf, Jack the Ripper—all striking scary poses beneath a blood red banner that read, "Doktor Geistmann's Carnival of Terror."

It was this last truck that made Erwin pause. He couldn't believe it. A sideshow of horror? Going to Crystal Lake?

Bill's shoulders twitched. Then his chest. Then his stomach. Then suddenly his entire body convulsed with laughter. Tears rolled down his cheeks, his sides were aching, but he just couldn't stop.

A carnival of terror goimg to Crystal Lake? You couldn't make up that kind of crazy shit.

"I know where I'm going," said Glo. She shook off Trick's hands and tried to get by him.

"Well, I'm glad that's your delusion," replied the boy, holding on to her again, "because from the outside your eggs look *completely fucking scrambled!*"

His sudden burst of shouting caught Glo off guard, and she shook her head as if coming out of a daze. Z-Moll just stood and watched. It made her horny to see her man treat other girls like shit.

"Kudos to the captain," she said, giving Trick her best "screw me" eyes. Unfortunately, now was neither the time nor the place.

"What's happening, Glo?" he demanded.

"I... I don't know," she stammered. "I'm sorry. But... I know... I know where we are."

"Oh, that's bullshit!" Trick was losing it. "And where the fuck's the GPS?"

Glo ignored the question and pointed at a beech some way ahead of them.

"Just through there, past the tree," she said hurriedly, "there's a footpath. A few yards on and you reach a pile of stones where the path takes a fork."

"Why are you doing this?" Trick was doing his damnedest not to blow his stack. "Just tell me where the fucking navigator is."

"I..." her chin fell to her breast. "I don't have it."

"What?" Trick threw his hands in the air. "Tell me I'm not hearing this."

"I'm sorry. I dropped it."

"Well *where*? Fuck, Glo, I thought you were the brainiac. You were supposed to get us to Camp Crystal Lake and now we're bodycount one, two, and fucking three."

"I'm sorry," she pleaded.

"Well we're going to have to find it," he said. "Let's go back."

But then he suddenly noticed Z-Moll was missing.

"Fuck." His shoulders drooped. "I'm through with this shit."

For a moment, it seemed as if the boy was going to strike out on his own, before Z-Moll appeared from behind the same tree that Glo had indicated.

"She's right," said the tall girl.

Trick was confused. "What?"

"The path," replied the Goth babe, sounding more than a little spooked, "and the fork by the pile of stones—it's all there."

Now it was the boy's turn to be fazed.

"But we haven't been there yet. You sure?" he asked.

Z-Moll nodded. Suddenly, the two of them regarded Glo with trepidation; though in Trick's case, the feeling of uncertainty turned swiftly to excitement.

"Fuckin' A!" he beamed. "Glo's gone Carrie on us! Come on, Glo, how d'you do it?"

Somehow, she was even less sure of herself now that her friends seemed to believe in her—a belief which, in her confused state, she couldn't share. Nor could she handle the Uzi-style grilling Trick was giving her.

"Have you been here before—as a kid maybe? Or—oh, I know. Were you adopted? Or were you born near here? Maybe you've recovered a lost memory? What about your folks? Did you see this place in a dream? Come on, Glo, open up!"

The questions kept coming, forming a whirlwind in her mind. She could vaguely hear herself say "no" to everything Trick asked her, and was relieved when Z-Moll inadvertently came to the rescue.

"Hello," Z-Moll waved a hand in Trick's line of sight. "I found the path, remember?"

But the boy only had eyes for Glo. "Can you get us there?" he said. "Camp Crystal Lake?"

Glo nodded mutely.

"But how?" pressed Trick. "What's going on?"

"I don't know," murmured Glo. "It's just that—well, there's this voice."

"Oh oh," interrupted Z-Moll ruefully before singing a bad rendition of the *Twilight Zone* riff.

"I can hear someone," Glo continued absently, "a woman… calling me."

She started to walk away again. Trick was about to follow, but Z-Moll pulled him aside.

"Don't go," she said. "She's a mentalist!"

But Trick had made up his mind, "You told me yourself she got it right."

"Only because she forgot to take her medication," sniped Z-Moll.

"Hey, look, maybe she's playing a joke on us, I don't know, but I've always gone with the Glo-ster."

"Well maybe you should go with the 'Glo-ster' next time you get an itch in your pants," huffed Z-Moll. It was she who then turned to line up beside Glo.

Trick laughed and hurried after the two of them, shouting, "Flashlights on, Trickettes, and if you find a river, just follow the fucker!"

But Glo didn't need any river to help her find the way; she knew exactly where Camp Crystal Lake was. And she had no intention of going there.

Someone was watching the teenagers as they blundered their way deeper into the woods. For over twenty years the watcher had lain dormant, relying on Jason to do all the hard work. In truth, taking out the trash should have been the watcher's responsibility. But soon the two of them would be reunited.

None of those other girls—the ones from before, who'd gone out on the lake—had been suitable. They had dismissed her voice as a figment of their imagination, or half-remembered it as part of a nightmare of someone jumping out of the water at them—or had been driven insane. But Gloria was different. Gloria was receptive, impressionable, and so very, very rare. The watcher had been able to reach out to the girl over thousands of miles; calling to her, bringing her to this place for this very special occasion. The watcher was speaking to the girl even now, making sure that she kept along the right track. The watcher had waited a long time for this moment.

"This way."

Glo stopped and turned to look straight at where the watcher was observing her. But the girl's flashlight revealed nothing, save for a few gently waving branches.

There was no wind.

Soon the watcher's years of solitude would be over.

When Bill Erwin drove past the traveling sideshow, he'd had no idea what an awful week they'd been having. Atlantic City, Trenton, Middleton, Edison—all the major towns of New Jersey had been complete blanks, and in Newark they'd been busted for not having a license. If they'd had the money, they could have sent a patch to sweeten things with the local authorities. But, as always, they were broke; and so they'd upped sticks and scurried out of the city before the law got wise and came to collect.

If it had been up to Doktor Geistmann, aka George Arthur Witney, they'd still be there now, digging into their pockets and scraping up a cap full of dimes.

Fortunately, his daughter had more sense. Alice Jane Witney had told her people to get the trucks loaded and then they'd sneaked out of town, giving the Interstate 80 a miss and taking all the godforsaken back routes. Basically, it was business as usual for the sideshow, and Alice was sick of it.

All her life, all she'd ever known was bumming from town to town with no money, no education and no prospects. Her itinerant lifestyle had even stopped her having a regular boyfriend. She'd just mooched around with her father, grinding through the states with a truck full of wax effigies put on display by five dummies of the human variety. And every leap year they managed to sell a few tickets.

Yet here she was, the dutiful daughter sat behind the wheel of the motorhome at the head of the convoy: still driving, still cussing, still determined to take charge of the carnival, just like she'd been every day for the last five years. The only good thing about being on the road was that it gave Alice plenty of time to reflect, especially on out-of-the-way routes like the one they followed now.

It was her father who'd suggested trying some of these smaller places up in the lake region. "There probably won't be so many people there with video games," he'd said. "People in rural areas—they'll respect our work. They'll understand traditional entertainment. They won't be young hoodlums or drug addicts like those wretched New Yorkers."

All the years he'd lived in America and George still sounded British; but then he was seventy-two.

Alice, no suprise, didn't agree with her father, but they sure as heck couldn't remain in Newark. Besides, Wessex County was probably as good a place as any to lose money. Good a place as any to take your life and flush it down the john.

The young woman was grinding her teeth again. Bad habit. She needed a drink.

Dad didn't approve of her drinking, of course; in fact, he didn't approve of anything she did these days. But then maybe he needed to take a good, long look at himself. It was okay for him just to fill time until his appointment with God, but what about the rest of the show people? What about Alice? Would she still be here, forty years from now, wheeling a dilapidated model of Franken-stein out on some garbage-strewn parking lot, putting up with threats and abuse from a bunch of unruly brats for the sake of a few lousy bucks?

No. Something had to change.

She didn't want to hurt Dad. Sure, they fought all the time—in fact they never stopped fighting— but she still had a spot for him. Love? She wouldn't go that far, but Mom had died when Alice was only very young, and George had raised the girl all by himself; at least when he could fit her in between Dr Jekyll and Jack the Ripper. That's why Alice couldn't just push him aside and take over. Mom's death had left George a broken man. He'd retreated more and more into a world of spooky castles and eerie graveyards, almost as if the wax show was his cocoon from reality.

Alice turned to look at the old man asleep in the passenger seat beside her. God, he was thin. Thin and immaculately attired, in his British flat

cap and casual cotton clothes with their needle-
sharp creases. The gray-haired gent even wore a
tie.

She reached over and caressed the stubborn
old mule's cheek. How was she going to tell him
that unless business picked up after the very
next show, she was going to take charge? How
could she tell him she'd already discussed it
with the others? It would break his heart.

Just then George began to rouse from his
slumber.

"Where are we?" he yawned.

"Nearly there," said Alice.

It was dark outside. George looked at the
clock; it was after nine.

"Where are we stopping?" he asked, his short
tongue splicing the sibilants of an enunciation
that was otherwise gentle and measured.

"Dunno," she replied. "See what turns up."

"Well, we need to restock with some—"

"I know, I know," cut in Alice impatiently.
"We need water."

George brushed his trim white moustache
with his fingers and briskly inspected his only
child. The show had aged her. She was thirty-
three and yet she looked fifty-three. He was
pleased she never wore cosmetics, but he would
have preferred her to wash her hair more often;
brown and lank, it flopped about like a greasy
horse's tail. He wasn't particularly fond of her
arms either. Her muscles weren't particularly
large, but he could see them and they were
made of granite. As for the tattoos, why did she
have to have so many? She didn't cover herself

to the extent that he could exhibit her—"Come see the Tattooed Lady!"—but there was still enough ink visible to make conversation with strangers difficult.

About the only part of her appearance George did approve of was the long, sleeveless floral dress he'd handed down from Ellen, her mother. Alice had made a mess of the hem, but she'd told him it made the dress more fashionable. Like the brown engineers' boots she clomped about in.

"That's odd." Alice was staring at something revealed in the headlamps.

"What is?" her father asked.

"That road sign. Coming up."

George squinted; at his age, it was a miracle he didn't need glasses. "Crystal Lake. Two miles. What's so unusual about that?"

Alice frowned, "Well, there's no Crystal Lake on the roadmap."

The first thing that struck visitors to the Grissom home was that it stank like a septic tank full of dead rats. The house was four walls of landfill under a roof of shit. Everything inside the hovel was flea-bitten and buckled. The floor alone was a minefield of rusty tools, animal remains, a gramophone with an axe buried in it, scraps of half-eaten food, an old sneaker with a dead mouse tucked in the toe, some girly books with jizz on them, and two dozen pints of homebrew in bottles scattered around the room, so that no matter where you stood, all you had to do was hold out your hand and some hooch would be there. You could even take a swig while pissing in the massive fireplace.

One corner of the room was taken up by a cast-iron range, where all the food preparation was done, and opposite was where the family did their relaxing—in four easy chairs arranged in a semicircle round the hearth. But mostly the room was dominated by the family table: an oak slab big enough to give most senior vice presidents boardroom envy. When you came in through the front door, the family table was the first thing you saw, and the Grissoms always kept it clean.

Right now, the interior was lit by a single kerosene lamp. It hung from a bent nail that had been hammered into a beam running the length of the low ceiling. Scorched moths had glued themselves to the glass shield, turning the lamp into a magic lantern of suicide. The tiny flame didn't do much to lighten the gloom, and nothing to break the total silence that Ma and Pa so much enjoyed.

Mr and Mrs Grissom were like two cadavers dressed in nineteenth-century formal wear, reclining in their bug-infested seats with every semblance of waiting at a chapel for cremation. They didn't talk, they didn't move—they just sat there, wasting every precious remaining second of their lives. They couldn't even remember the names they were born with.

Suddenly the door was flung open. The cabin was dragged back to the land of the living by the sounds of Francis and Enoch, returning from the day's forage. The boys were trying to haul something inside but they were struggling, their steps as heavy and uneven as a spastic hoedown.

"Watch his head," shouted Francis, followed by a loud thump as Enoch bashed Jason's skull into the door frame.

"Now look what you made me do," moaned Enoch, shifting the blame.

Lifting Jason out of the pit and carrying him all the way back had been exhausting. It was Enoch, the strongest of the brothers, who'd had to do most of the work. Francis, by comparison, seemed to have sunk all his effort into aggravating Enoch's tinnitus, and if Enoch wasn't so whacked he'd have killed his idle brother there and then.

A strange gurgling sound came from the far corner of the room. It was Ma trying to get her throat to work.

"Whatcha—got?" she drawled through her desert dry lips.

"We got'n some fuckin' meat, Ma," answered Francis, grinning like a fool.

"Now don't you go'n take all the credit, Francis," warned Enoch.

Ma tried to get up out of her seat, but fell straight back on her ass. Grey linen really suited the decrepit old bitch.

"Now, you hold on, Ma," called Francis. "I'll come get you soon as me an' man-tits are done. I got a real surprise for you an' Pa."

The old man still hadn't moved a muscle. Enoch's muscles, on the other hand, were screaming with pain.

"Quit flappin' and help me get Fourtrees up'n the board," he groaned.

"Don't you go disrespectin' the family table," croaked Ma with what, for her, passed for an animation.

"Shut'n the fuck up, Ma." Enoch was in no mood for her griping.

He gave his younger brother the nod and they hoisted the body of Jason onto the tabletop. The limbs of the hockey-masked killer were no longer stiff; so when he hit the wood, he lay perfectly flat on his back. He was utterly lifeless.

"Look what we got, Ma!" yelled Francis, having enough energy left to break into a jig.

Enoch just leaned forward, gripped the edge of the table and tried to get his breath back. His clothes were soaked, especially round the pits.

"We got'n us a whole lotta meat," snickered Francis. "We got Jason."

"Who?" scraped Ma.

"Jason Fourtrees." Francis was upset. He couldn't tell if Ma was deaf, senile or just being a dumb ol' whore.

"Who?" repeated Ma.

Francis punched the wall, "Hell, Ma! We got Jason fuckin' Fourtrees! A whole lotta fuckin' meat!"

"Meat?" asked Ma, her voice like cancer.

"Meat!" bawled Francis. He ran outside to pick up the two sacks he and his brother had managed to drag along while struggling with Jason.

"Meat, meat. Fuckin' meat!"

Francis was ranting now. He jumped up on the table, stood astride Jason and emptied the two bags of dead critters all over the killer's massive body.

"Get off the family table!" squawked Ma.

Enoch started to laugh. Even Pa was beginning to stir; all the shouting was reminding him just why he hated his family so much.

"Meat!" bellowed Francis.

Then he pulled out his bony knife and knelt down over Jason.

"Disrespectin' the family table," said Ma yet again. "Tell him, Pa."

But her dandruff-encrusted skeleton of a husband was too busy wishing her dead to do anything else. As for Enoch, he just couldn't stop giggling; his brother was acting like a girl.

Francis slapped a furry bastard chipmunk off of Jason's chest, then stabbed the big freak right below the collar bone. But the notched blade went in so deep that the knife became stuck. Enoch laughed even louder as Francis—snarling and gnashing—tugged the knife loose, and then started sawing until he'd succeeded in cutting out a cube of festering, black Voorhees flesh.

"MEAT!"

Francis held the wet morsel out, so that those three ungrateful shits could see it, and then he popped the dripping tit-steak plumb into his mouth.

CHAPTER THREE

Three fireflies were dancing in the night. At first their luminescence was dwarfed by the blackness of the forest, but, as they zigzagged their way forward through the trees, the pinpoints expanded into discs of blinding white. One of these discs remained fixed on the ground but the others—the beams from Trick and Z-Moll's flashlights—moved in a sphere of unpredictable tangents.

Z-Moll noticed that the rays were becoming diluted; the moon had risen and, with its ascent, the sky had become a cyclorama of steel. The day-dreaming teen had never seen a moon so full—so large.

They were walking single file, the trail so narrow that they didn't have any choice. Glo was leading the way; Trick stuck to her back like super adhesive, with Z-Moll stumbling and bellyaching at the rear. Now that they were no longer using the map, or the GPS that they never recovered, Trick kept testing Glo to see if her weird shit was still working.

"What's next?" he called.

"A ditch on the left with a sweet gum tree wrapped in poison ivy," she replied uninterested.

A few yards on and Trick's flash confirmed her prediction.

The boy had been running this question-and-answer shtick all evening. It provided him with a minor comfort zone; Glo had scored ten out of ten, and that had to count for something. It also confirmed Glo was still alive because outside her answers the moody little girl had nothing to say.

"What was that?" Trick had heard a splashing sound. "Shit!"

He'd just stepped into a deep puddle that spanned the width of the track. His combat boots kept out the water, but the jolt had shocked him all the same.

"Quality heads up, Glo!" he moaned, but she just kept walking without even acknowledging his gripe. Unfortunately, the boy had stopped so abruptly that Z-Moll plowed straight into the back of him. She screamed.

"Fuck!"

The water drenched her fishnets, and the sudden cold around her ankles made her drop her flashlight. The lamp fell into the puddle and promptly went out.

"Shit!" Trick shouted. "The flashlight! Save the fucking flashlight!"

He bent down and swept his left hand through the water, splashing Z's legs.

"Stop it, stop it!" she shouted and she slapped him on the back of his long coat.

"But we need it!" he protested, still waving his hand around. How big was this damn puddle?

Glo didn't pay the two of them any attention. She continued along the trail until she saw something—and then stopped.

Z-Moll put her hands on Trick's side and tried to push him over. The boy fought to keep his balance but was soon occupying a front row seat in the filthy water. Z-Moll's flashlight was pressing into his left buttock.

"This is so fucking the end of our relationship!" he shouted as she stepped over him to put her feet back on dry dirt. "You fucking skank witch reject!"

Z-Moll turned, flipped him the finger and headed off after Glo.

Thoughts of Jasonesque homicide ran through Trick's mind as he crawled to his feet, retrieved Z-Moll's flashlight and clicked the switch. Nothing. The bulb was dead.

"Fucking… fucking…" he couldn't even bring himself to finish the insult. He hurled the device into a rock where it shattered in a cascade of plastic. Suddenly, he heard Z-Moll call his name.

"Trick! Over here! Come quick!" Was he imagining things or did the girl sound happy?

He turned his light on Z-Moll. She was pointing at something ahead of her and, yes, she did look excited. She'd caught up with Glo, yet wasn't remotely aware that their mysterious friend seemed to be in some kind of trance. But then neither Trick nor Z-Moll had noticed that Glo hadn't moved at all since first catching sight of whatever had Z-Moll so keyed up.

"Trick!" shouted Z-Moll a second time.

He ran over to join her and saw they'd reached the end of the trail. "Where the fuck's Crystal Lake?" he asked indignantly.

"Fuck Crystal Lake," Z-Moll replied. "This is our ticket home."

Glo had led them to a clearing far from any beaten track that side of the lake. The glade was of considerable size, yet was made to feel oppressive by the overhanging of dead leaves; leaves that paved the area between the edge of the clearing and the rundown shack that nestled in its center.

It was immediately obvious to Trick that the building wasn't a cabin from the old summer camp. Nor was it a vacation lodge near the water's edge. No, this ramshackle dwelling was a low hut hidden from prying eyes, and its assembly spoke of savagery. Discarded boards, sheets of corrugated metal, broken window panes, warped plywood panels, torn measures of tarpaulin, old ropes and fastenings—the lair had been built by a scavenger.

Trick rubbed his chin and considered the situation. "And I'm excited because…?"

"They'll have a phone," Z-Moll contended.

"See any lines?" asked Trick.

"All right, Captain Happitude, we'll borrow a car."

Trick leaned back and gestured for Z-Moll to take a good, long look at the luxury estate that only she could see.

"And which one would that be?" he asked, sweeping an arm in the direction of thin air. "The sporty Ferrari, or the safe but comfortable four by four? Or would Madam Fuckwit care for the stretch limo? Oh, and while you're making your choice, perhaps you'd like to me show a power line or a generator or a *single fucking light bulb!*"

Now it was Z-Moll's turn to be upset by the way Trick punctuated his sentences with shouting.

"Screw you!" she cried. Then she turned on her heels and made for the shack.

"Don't," said Glo. It took the girl to speak in order for her friends to notice how silent she'd been.

"Whassup, Glo?" Trick laid a hand on her shoulder.

"Don't go in there," was all she said.

Glo could hear the voice all the time now. It was constant; encouraging her, urging her forward. With every step Glo had taken, the words had become louder and more distinct. They had led her through the woods, and gained strength with each passing yard until now. Glo knew that this glade had been her destination all along. This shack was where the voice wanted her to be. And yet, despite surrendering to the voice—and leading her friends on with easy little lies about moving closer to the lake—Glo's instinct now was to turn back, to run. To get away from this evil place.

"Come along, dear," said the voice, as clearly as if from someone standing beside her. "I'm waiting for you."

Glo gripped her temples and wailed, "Get out of my head!"

"But we've become such good friends," said the voice persuasively.

Z-Moll smiled at her boyfriend. "She's out of her head, all right. Come on. Let's go find a door."

Even though it was almost impossible for Glo to hear past the voice, she had to warn her friends. She had to fight. But how much determination did a fifteen year-old have?

Enough.

She stood fast against the floodtide of spectral delusions and managed to disgorge a single word of caution.

"Don't."

But how much trust and loyalty did the two other fifteen year-olds possess? Could they even begin to empathize with, or understand, what Glo was going through?

"You're a freak," said Z-Moll. When they got back to Seattle, she'd be filing Glo under "ancient history."

Even Trick wasn't sure anymore that the girl wasn't just an oddball. Okay, her Ghostly Positioning Sense had brought them here, but now she was behaving as if she was having a bad substance reaction. And what if Z-Moll was right? The shack didn't look much, but what if there was some slappy old hick in there who could help them escape the forest?

The boy was still unsure what to do when Z-Moll saw something that made his mind up for him.

"Look at that," she said, indicating part of the wooden patchwork.

"Can you be any less specific?" asked Trick.

She grabbed his flashlight and shone the beam over by one of the cracked windows, a point where the wall appeared particularly clumsy in construction.

"They're all parts of bunk beds," she said.

The light played over the area Z-Moll was talking about.

"Oooh, there's a sign on my back saying 'KICK ME,'" answered Trick sarcastically, but then he took a closer look.

His jaw dropped. Z-Moll was right.

The section of wall next to the left window was definitely the side of a cot. And that part near the corner—Trick snatched the flashlight out of Z's hand—was a door lying on its side. Then he saw an old notice board made of cork. And a strip of white slats that could only have come from a boat dock. Suddenly it hit him. The shack had been assembled from the remnants of Camp Crystal Lake. There couldn't be any doubt.

"Fucking A!" he cheered. Then he grabbed Z-Moll by the hand, "Come on. Let's do it."

Glo tried to stop them but it was no use. They ran off round the side of the hut and swiftly disappeared from view, in search of a door.

Behind them, Glo was racked with anxiety. The voice was too strong to resist, and it was telling her to put one foot in front of the other—and then the other—and then the other. The girl tried everything she could to stop herself from walking, but the shack loomed larger and larger. She was succumbing to an amplification of madness brought on by the full moon, and only now—when it was almost too late—did Glo realize she was fighting for her very soul.

Alice helped her father down the folding steps of the motorhome. The elderly man had to take one cautious step at a time; Alice was sick of doing the same thing day after day, and wondered if her role shouldn't be changed to unpaid care worker.

For his part, George seemed most grateful for his daughter's assistance.

"Thank you, my dear," he said tenderly—though Alice didn't know if this was a mark of honest gratitude or merely an expression of his usual impeccable manners.

Indeed, no sooner had the soles of his shoes scuffed the asphalt than the old man, walking cane in hand, tottered off in the direction of the long trailer that stored virtually the entire show. The wax models, the banners, the scenic backcloths, the electrics, even the diesel generator—if anything ever happened to the eighteen-wheeler, the carnival would be finished. They weren't even insured.

Alice sighed and shook her head.

They'd pulled up at a neglected RV park on the edge of a small town called Crystal Lake. She never did find it on the map, but its self-evident reality meant she needed to buy a better road atlas—that is, when she could afford one.

There were no other vehicles in the park; as a matter of fact, the place looked like it hadn't been used in over a decade—but that's exactly why Alice had chosen it. She hoped there wouldn't be any attendants around to come take their money, and the site had the additional advantage of being hidden from town by a low hill and a band of trees. If nothing else, they should be able to get a good night's sleep. Best case, they'd announce their presence to the locals in the morning and maybe do some business.

Alice picked up a voltmeter, along with the RV's heavy-duty power cord, and walked round to the AC hookup on the other side of the truck; she wasn't optimistic, but the coach battery needed some juice.

By now, the other showmen had also got out of their vehicles and one of them, Judge, was helping her father unlatch the massive doors at the back of the semi.

Alice was the only woman with the show, but as far as the other carnies were concerned she was one of the guys—except, of course, when she wanted to get one of them in the sack. She didn't know if having sex with the other showmen was a good idea—these people were practically family—but they all seemed to enjoy it and it never caused a problem. After all, it was only for fun. The guys knew from the outset that the occasional drunken hump with Alice meant nothing; there was no jealousy or commitment. It was just life on the road.

It always amazed Alice how easy it was to recruit new people to the carnival. It wasn't a big show—just ten dummies, a few lights, a public address system and Doktor Geistmann's pitch— and they never made any money. But whenever anyone quit, her father couldn't keep the kids from wanting to join up. Four of the five guys currently with the show were younger than Alice. They all had this crazy, romantic idea about touring high grass places like Crystal Lake with a carnival of horror, as if they were living the dream of a black and white monster movie. None of them particularly cared about a salary or a career. They just wanted a roof, some food and a rush of nostalgia: which pretty much put them in the same camp as the rubes they were meant to be bilking.

Alice took time out to see how everyone was coping after the long day spent snaking through the backwaters of New Jersey.

Judge was the juice man. He drove the semi, maintained the generator, wired up the show and had recently sunk all his savings into a laptop computer. These past few weeks, Alice had been talking him into building a web site for the show. He was almost finished, but his desire to learn everything about HTML meant that he never worked quickly enough for her. Judge was one of those guys who had to master the nuts and bolts of everything. When he'd successfully uploaded their home page for the first time, he felt like the guy who split the atom.

Vincenzo and Sparx, on the other hand, were pure manpower. Between them, they had the arduous task of setting up and tearing down the show. And when they weren't moving the displays, they were maintaining or fixing them—or even improving them. In his downtime, Sparx fooled around with special effects and makeup; stuff like fake wounds and rubber masks. If you wanted a head to explode in front of a live audience, and you wanted the chumps to go screaming into their cell-phones for the police, Sparx was your man. It was partly because of the boy's astonishing talent that Alice knew the show could be so much better.

Vincenzo too was totally reliable, but only when Alice gave him a thorough brief to work from. Self-motivation was not a specialty. On the plus side, he seemed to know every dealer north of Mexico, and whenever she needed any beanies to get through an all-day stint, she went straight to Vincenzo.

Finally, she looked across at Minter.

Heck, she loved Minter. He was the show's muscle. Sometimes he used his brawn for lifting, but most times he used it to flatten faces when business got rough. Two other qualities in Minter's favor were that he could hold his liquor against Alice any time, and he was like a jackhammer in the sack. More importantly, he had an ocean of a heart. He was always around to help, and the way he fussed over her father, he behaved more like a Witney than she did—though his Afro-American origin was one indication that he might not be George's son. But it would have been a mistake to dismiss Minter as the clichéd gentle giant. The man had a brain well in proportion to his six-four body. Point of fact, Shawn Minter was the sharpest guy Alice had ever met.

The fifth showman, however…

Kenton Freely was the only member of the carnival who'd joined before Alice was born. Now in his fifties, and with a fashion sense to match, it was Kenton's job to sell tickets—whose crazy idea was that? Every time Alice followed him into town, to check how well he was promoting the show, she found him propping up a bar. Every time she watched him take gate receipts, she saw him issue tickets to only three out of every four townies.

Everyone else in the group doubled up and helped out wherever they could; odd jobs, fetching stuff, managing the public—you name it—but Kenton never lifted a finger. He just went where the money was, and Alice was certain he was raking oats in addition to the hard cash he pocketed from withheld tickets.

On top of which, the guy was a total creep. He only had to speak and Alice's skin crawled. And she wasn't the only one. Freely swaggered around like he owned the place, when the truth was that everyone else—Alice especially—wished he would just go suck on an exhaust pipe. Why her dad didn't just get rid of the goldbrick was a mystery to all of them.

Just now, Kenton was standing by his pickup. That truck was the only piece of carnival equipment that didn't belong to her dad, and Kenton literally lived in the rust heap. He carried supplies and equipment in the back and drove, ate and slept up front. After all, Alice sure as hell wasn't going to let him sleep in her and her dad's RV. Likewise, the three beds in the other motorhome were reserved for Sparx, Vincenzo and Minter; the amount of physical work those guys did, they needed quality rest. And it made sense for Judge to use the sleeper in the eighteen-wheeler because he drove the thing all day. So poor little Kenty was forced to sleep all by his shitty little self.

Alice plugged the voltmeter into the park's electrical outlet and was amazed to find it still working. Whoever it was who'd closed the place must have forgotten to turn off the juice; she wondered if they were still paying utility bills.

She called across to Vincenzo and told him to hook up the other RV. Then she plugged in the cord and went to look for her dad.

George was inside the long trailer and was checking to see if the models had survived the journey intact, a process of inspection he carried out immediately after every ride. Judge had helped the old man climb inside the truck, but now Witney was completely alone. Lamps had been fitted along the length of the ceiling, and he'd switched them on so that he could carry out his examination.

He leant forward and stared into the eyes of Dracula, shaking his head.

"What's wrong?" a voice came from behind, making the old man jump. "Too scary for ya?"

George turned and saw...

"Kenton!"

"That's Mister Freely to you, George."

Kenton was standing just inside the open doors. His slicked back hair clung to his head like a skullcap of leeches, while his shirt and pants looked like they'd been stolen from the set of *I Love Lucy*; smart casual threads for the out-of-touch hepcat on a budget.

"I was just thinking," commented Witney, turning back to study the model, "that our Count here is looking somewhat anemic. He could do with a fresh lick of red paint."

No response.

"I said," repeated George, "the Count could do with some paint."

Witney turned and saw that Kenton was staring out of the trailer. But he didn't know that Kenton was leering at his daughter. Kenton liked the way she manhandled those thick power lines, and when she bent down to plug them in, seeing her dress fold round her body like that made his cock tingle.

"Freely!" barked the old man.

A snarl cracked the corner of Kenton's mouth. He turned on his heels, bowled forward and seized Witney by the lapels of his jacket.

"Don't you speak to me like that, you old bastard," Freely kept his voice low so that no one outside could hear him.

The old man shivered but held his ground.

"W—we need s—some paint," he said, trembling.

Freely liked that. He liked to see Witney shitting bricks. Suddenly he released his grip and pushed George back so that the elderly showman almost crashed into Dracula's outstretched claws.

Kenton sniggered, "Gimme the money and I'll send someone for your goddam paint."

"Don't bother," said George, collecting himself. "There'll be nowhere open till morning anyway. I'll send Alice."

Freely took another step forward. George took another step back, and found himself standing next to a wax rendition of the Frankenstein monster.

Kenton ran a finger over the blood on Dracula's fangs.

"A can of paint?" his threats were like silk. "Oh, I'd say that's at least a Benjamin."

"A hundred dollars!" gasped Witney. "Don't be absurd."

Freely laughed and continued his menacing advance.

"I love that British short-tongue thing you do. A hundred dollarth!" he mimicked. "Don't be abthurd."

Witney raised his walking stick as if preparing to strike the weasel across the face. "Don't come any closer."

"Don't come any clother," mocked Freely. "George, do we have to go through this every time? You know I always win."

"Now you listen to me, Freely..." But Witney had barely begun to reassert his authority when he was caught short by a pain in the chest. He started to cough.

"I'm listening, George." Kenton smirked, "but all I'm hearing is an old man having a heart attack."

"What's going on?" it was Alice.

"N—nothing, dear," coughed the old man.

Alice grabbed on to one of the metal latches and pulled herself up into the trailer. Kenton Freely stood back, moving away from her father. Then he looked Alice up and down.

"I'm sure I've seen that dress before," he said slyly.

Alice pushed right by him, knocking him aside with her shoulder.

"Freely, you're so fucking predictable. This is the bit where you remind me I'm wearing my

dead mom's clothes and how she died in a carnival accident when I was only four years old.
Boo fucking hoo."

Kenton tried not to show pain, but he knew
he'd bruise where she'd knocked into him. Bitch.

Alice placed an arm over her father's shoulders
and began to escort him in the direction of the
door. The old man's walk was no more than a
shuffle and he was coughing uncontrollably.

"Dad?" Alice looked concerned.

"The old man can't hack it," said Freely,
enjoying the moment. "Maybe it's time he made
way for young blood."

Alice whipped her head in Freely's direction,
"Young blood? An oily old fuck like you?"

"Alice," her father spluttered, "leave it, child."
He raised a hand to silence her.

"But Dad!"

"You heard Daddy," smiled Freely. "Now be a
good girl and get off my case." He turned and
jumped down from the trailer, leaving George
and Alice Witney alone with their mannequins.

Hell, the dummies looked so cheesy, Alice
could have wept. She swore that if she ever
found one—just one—person who actually found
any of this crap scary, she'd take a vow of
celibacy, give up Jack Daniel's, and go join the
nearest convent.

"I don't get it, Dad," she said.

The old man's coughing fit had subsided, so
she took her arm off him and moved round to
look him in the eye.

"The guy's a freeloader," she went on. "Why
do you take so much crap from him?"

"Please," her father begged, "change the subject. You wouldn't understand."

"I understand when some loser is trying to fuck you over."

"I won't discuss this any further," answered George firmly. He began to walk to the door, even though he had no way of getting down from the trailer without her help.

But Alice stayed right where she was.

"What is it with you and Freely?" she persisted, talking to the back of his head. "Every time I mention him, the same old wall keeps coming down. 'You wouldn't understand, Alice.' 'I don't want to talk about it, Alice.' Well, make me understand!"

Witney kept his back turned towards her. When he spoke his voice was unnaturally calm, almost as if he were struggling to control it.

"Perhaps if you weren't always so rude—so confrontational all the time—you and Kenton might get along."

Alice turned George around and the whole carnival heard what she had to say next.

"So that bastard corners you. He threatens you. He tells you to hand over the show. And then he—he talks about Mom like it's a fucking joke! And it's my fault?"

"I'm just saying that perhaps if you spent less time fraternizing with the more junior members—and maybe less time drinking…"

"I was wondering when you were going to bring that up."

George could always tell when Alice was really angry, because her voice would suddenly drop to a low monotone and she clipped every syllable. Just like she was doing now.

"Please, Alice," he said. "Let's not fight."

Alice walked forward and jumped down onto the asphalt.

"Get someone else to fetch you down," she snapped, storming off and leaving a tearful old man in her wake.

Kenton stood by his pickup and watched the hardnosed bitch march in the direction of her RV. And look at George: the stupid old bastard couldn't get down from the truck. He just had to stand there and cry like a baby until somebody fetched him. Well, Kenton wasn't going to play wet nurse: not until Witney stumped up his hundred bucks.

Freely always parked his truck a little away from the others because that was how he liked it. It made it easier for him to keep an eye on everyone, and it made it harder for them to come snooping through his stuff.

"Well, would you look at that," murmured Kenton.

Shawn Minter was "running" to the old man's aid, but the big lunk was so muscle-bound it was like watching a buffalo tottering in high heels. As if playing the Witneys off against each other wasn't already funny enough, he now had Queen Kong prancing on his pointy little toes, coming to the rescue!

Freely burst out laughing—only to hear someone laughing along with him.

Kenton had parked near the edge of the lot. There was someone hiding in the surrounding bushes.

"Who's there?" Kenton challenged.

The only answer he got was more inane giggling.

"Come on out," he tried again. This time he was successful. A bedraggled mess of a man fell through the bushes and landed with a thump on the asphalt. He was clutching a bottle of single malt in his left hand.

"Jesus," said Kenton. "The town drunk. That's all I need."

If winos had a union, and there were regulations governing the appearance of its members, Jonah would have been fully compliant. The matted hair, the missing teeth, the grime—it was all textbook stuff. And he insisted on singing every single word.

"Ohhh, brothers a-coming to Crystal. Camp Blood here to die. Gonna cut your fucking throat, friend, and stick a chopper in yer eye."

Kenton hiked his thumb at the inebriate, "Go on. Beat it."

The wino snickered and rose shakily to his feet.

"Take a drink, good friend of Jonah," he held the whiskey bottle out to Kenton. "A last request before you die. 'Cause Jason is a-coming, oh on that you can rely. So take the whiskey bottle up and driiiiiiiiiiiii…"

Kenton punched the bum in the mouth and brought the sustained note to a sudden finish. Then he snatched the bottle from Jonah's hand and threw it on the ground; the glass shattered with threatening clarity.

Still reeling from the blow, Jonah spun like a confused tornado before finally rebounding off the side of the pickup and falling on his ass.

"You're gonna die for this," he drawled.

"Think so?" Freely's eyes were like needles of ice. He bent down and picked up the broken bottleneck.

Jonah took one look at the jagged cylinder and knew exactly what Kenton planned to do with it. Quickly, the wino dragged himself over to the bushes.

"You're gonna die," he ranted, diving for cover through the leaves and then fleeing for his life. "All of you. You shouldn't 'a come here. This is Jason's town. Jason's!"

"Yeah?" shouted Freely. "Well, send this 'Jason' my way and I'll kick his frigging ass as well."

Francis Grissom spat the chunk of prime Voorhees out of his mouth. Strands of black slime hung from his teeth and dribbled down his chin. There were lumps in it.

"Tastes like shit!" announced Francis, no longer raving.

He'd calmed down just as quickly as he'd lost his temper, because now he had culinary concerns on his mind.

"Get off the family table," wheezed Ma pathetically.

Francis ignored her and gave more thought to the problem of what to do with Jason.

"Still," he said, weighing up the possibilities, "with'n the right seasonin'… after all, there's a lotta meat on the boy."

"Let me try," suggested Enoch, who had finally stopped laughing.

Now he too wanted to see what raw zombified psycho tasted of. Pork? Chicken? He leaned over

Jason's body, then dug his fingers into the open wound, hooked his nails under a soft ridge of flesh and pulled.

Francis jumped down from the table and looked on as his brother tugged at the weeping injury.

"Tough, ain't it?" he commented, as if in revenge on Enoch for laughing when his knife had become stuck.

Enoch ignored him and continued tearing at the meat until eventually a scrap came loose. He raised the piece and turned it in his fingers: it looked bad. He held it close to his nose and sniffed it: it smelt bad. He put the revolting chunk of flesh in his mouth and chewed it.

"You're right," he said to his younger brother. "It does taste like shit."

"But I can do somethin' about that," boasted Francis.

Then he set about hacking more gobbets out of the hole in Jason's chest, so that he could toss them over for Ma and Pa to try. The first piece landed in Pa's lap. When the old raw-bones saw it, he lifted the black strip of Jason up against his mouth and slowly swiveled his head, so that his lips crawled along the meat like a masturbating tapeworm.

But when Francis threw a sample at Ma, she just let it bounce off her face and fall to the floor.

"Get off the family table," she whined.

"Ma!" screamed Francis. "You blind fuckin' whore! I am off the family fuckin' table."

"Now don't you go disrespectin' the family table," chided Enoch, as he sucked on the dark Voorhees sludge coating his teeth.

Francis slammed his knife into the tabletop, the blade stabbing the wood mere inches from Jason's right hand.

"Shut your mouth, man-tits," he shouted. "If anyone's disrespectin' the family table, it's you. You were the one who put Fourtrees on it. You're treat'n the family table like it's a fuckin' chopping board. You're gonna get a pail of fuckin' water and wash off all the blood like it's Thanksgiving. You got no fuckin' respect!"

Enoch slowly curled his hands into fists. "Don't go makin' me get the red fuckin' haze again."

But Francis was too angry to give a damn.

"You know what I think of your red haze, man-tits? I could fuckin' shit the fucker. Now get the fuckin' stove on 'fore I lose my patience."

The older Grissom boy considered killing his lazy loudmouth of a brother, but he was caught short by a rumble in his stomach. Seemed like it really was time to get dinner going after all. With Jason Voorhees as the main item on the menu.

Enoch piled some logs on the range and started banging about with pots and pans: all too small. He went outside and found the old tin bathtub they used for skinning, but it was still too small—unless they cut Jason up first.

It was getting pretty dark out now. Full moon in the sky.

The Grissom brother dragged the tub back inside the cabin and lifted it onto the range. Then he set about filling it with water; a tedious job that meant taking a pot back and forth to the faucet. However, a few minutes later a tub full of water was gently on the boil. Which meant it was time to get the meat ready.

Enoch took a cleaver down from the knife rack and went over to where Jason lay on the family table. Ma was fast asleep and Pa was still chomping away on his piece of Voorhees, only now the senile old bastard was sniggering too. Enoch sniffed and raised the cleaver, ready to bring it down across Jason's neck.

"Whatchoo doin'?" It was Francis. He had been spending all this time flicking through a recipe book.

"Gettin' him in the pot," said Enoch, lining up the blow.

Francis threw the book aside, grabbed his knife from the family table and thrust the festering blade into Enoch's right arm.

Enoch howled and let go of the cleaver. The bone knife had penetrated at least an inch beneath the skin and blood was pouring into the sleeve of his shirt. He gripped the wound and backed off. There were a whole lot of weapons on the knife rack. Or maybe he could just whack his lunatic brother with a skillet.

"Why d'you do that for?" he shouted, stalling for time. "You told me to cook the fucker, so I'm puttin' him in the pot! I'm gonna boil him."

But Francis was beyond reason. He just stood holding the knife, livid with rage, his whole body an expression of feral hatred.

"You ain't boilin' no one!" he hissed. "Jason Fourtrees is gonna be spit roasted!"

* * *

Trick rapped at the door a fifth time. Still no answer.

"Trick, honey!" moaned Z-Moll, worried that the shack was going to be yet another dead-end, but desperately hoping it wasn't.

"Babe, what am I supposed to do?" Trick was just as anxious as his girlfriend.

"You're the captain," she said. "Do something."

"Like what?"

"Go inside."

"I can't do that."

Trick shone his flashlight back over the clearing. The place was a dump; there was garbage and scraps of wood everywhere. But the one thing Trick couldn't find was any sign of life. There was no light, no sound, no movement, nada. On top of which, the boy was concerned that all the windows had been boarded from the inside. Sure, there were gaps in the makeshift shutters—enough to see it was dark in there—but that kind of interior design hardly inspired confidence. And Glo still hadn't joined them. In fact, Trick hadn't seen the girl since he and Z-Moll had come round looking for the door.

He knocked again.

Z-Moll was growing irritable. "You really need to go in. If there's no one in there, no one'll find out."

"Nice equation, Einstein. But if your logic is so fucking true, I'll let you take the props for proving it."

Trick posed like an usher and stood aside so that his girl could make the grand entrance.

"You want me to do it?" she tried to sound argumentative, but came across like a finalist for Miss Yellow Streak 2005.

"Yep," answered Trick. "And I'll just wait out here. And when I hear someone rev up their fucking chainsaw, I'll run so fast you better be Flo Jo to... uh, maybe someone who's still alive might be a better starting point."

Z-Moll fired a loud tut and folded her arms, "Can I interrupt the meeting, *Norman*?"

"Don't you fucking Bates me, Z-ro!"

But her insult had served to shift the subject away from Trick entering the shack. Z-Moll opened her mouth to retaliate, when she heard a twig snap behind her. Trick heard it too. They whirled round and he aimed his flashlight to reveal...

"Glo!" shouted the boy, scared out of his skin. "Creep factor ten! Jesus!"

Both he and Z-Moll sagged with relief. But their comfort evaporated when they realized Glo wasn't paying them the slightest attention. They were even more freaked out by the song she was singing. It sounded like a nursery rhyme.

"This is the house that Jason built, Jason built, Jason built. This is the house that Jason built on a warm and bloody evening."

Trick shook his head, "All right. This has gone on way long enough. We surrender. Joke over. Call out your friends." Then he cupped his hands over his mouth and shouted, "Hello-oo! Game over!"

Z-Moll tried to shut him up, while Glo slipped between the two of them and reached for the handle of the cabin door.

"Don't!" shrieked Z-Moll.

Too late. Glo turned the handle, pushed open the rickety door and stepped inside. The girl didn't even have her flashlight on. Trick leaned forward to see what he could but the door swung shut in his face. Glo had gone in there alone and she'd closed the door.

Trick looked at Z-Moll. Z-Moll looked at Trick. They didn't need to say a word. Friendship decreed they should go inside, but fear made the tentative suggestion that it just might be preferable for them both to wait outside the door. Trick could almost hear his old man back in Seattle...

"Well, Richard, my boy, you go sneaking off across the country searching for serial killers. What do you expect? An afternoon in Disneyworld?"

Z-Moll was having exactly the same experience. It was as if the two of them were at some halfway house along the roaf to having their enitre lives flash before their very eyes. Z-Moll was imagining what her mom would say if she could see her daughter right now.

"What-*ever!*"

But suddenly the image was shattered by an unmistakable sound tearing through from the other side of the closed door. Trick and Z-Moll recognized it at once: it was the sound of Glo screaming.

Ma slithered out of her armchair, and shuffled over towards the kitchen end of the room. If there was any cooking to be done in the Grissom household, she'd be the one to do it; she wasn't so old that she didn't know her obligations. Besides, now that her sons were fooling around, no one was watching the pot.

Francis with the knife, Enoch with the cleaver—the boys had gone crazy, a-snarling and a-fighting, trying to kill each other like they'd got nothing better to do. They were always the same. Maybe Ma should have listened to Pa when he'd told her to strangle the boys at birth. But then if she had, who'd bring home the meat?

Ma picked a dead raccoon off of Jason's belly; she could tell it was one of Francis's because two of its legs had been pulled off. Then she went over to the range. The water in the tub was good and hot now—it was all bubbles and steam. She tried to tell her boys to shut up, but they kept hollering and yowling. If they carried on that way, she'd send them to bed with no food.

Enoch swung the cleaver and caught Francis in the thigh.

"Boys are like your Pa," drawled Ma to no one in particular, and then she lifted the 'coon, fur and all, and dropped it into the boiling pot. Still breathing and wriggling.

Stunned and near to extinction, the raccoon was shocked into its final death throes by the unbearable heat of the water. The critter screeched and, with its remaining limbs, kicked a wave of scalding liquid all over Ma's face. Her leathery skin blistered as she went prancing around the room, wailing, barely avoiding the knife and cleaver as they swung around her like a cloud of flies.

What with the kids fighting, and Ma burned and crying, her face like a red balloon, Pa snickered so much, he gone let out a real tight fart.

Trick kicked open the door and burst into the shack. He was holding the flashlight forward in both hands like a gun. Z-Moll huddled up close and peered over his shoulder, as he aimed the light all around the room.

The inside of the cabin reminded him of TV footage he'd seen of houses in the Middle East after the wire-guided missiles had done their job, the only difference being that none of the domestic debris in this hovel was less than thirty years old.

Straight across from the door was a crudely made cubicle containing a disgusting toilet. To the left Trick saw an empty cupboard, and beyond that some planks had fallen to the ground. There were a couple of windows, all nailed up, but no real furniture in the small room, no attempt at decoration, and the floor was just a layer of dirt strewn with garbage and scraps of old newspaper. The hut looked like a tree house built by a lobotomy patient.

"There!" Z-Moll pointed across the room.

Over in the far corner, to their left, was a doorway; Trick didn't know how he'd missed it the first time—maybe because everything was brown and gray, and it was too damn dark!

The door was no more than a thin sheet of iron fixed to a wooden frame. There were two large holes in the metal, at around head height. The punctures bent inwards as if someone had

attacked the door with a pickaxe. It couldn't
have been done while Trick and Z-Moll were
outside, or they would have heard it.

The ajar door opened inwardly, giving access
to another room. Quickly, Trick ran his flashlight a second time over the walls, but the
half-open door was definitely the only other
way out.

"Come on," he whispered, taking Z-Moll by
the hand. The poor girl shivered with fear.

"I'm not sure this is a good idea," she hissed.

Trick smiled, trying to reassure her, and then
took his first step into the shack. He stopped,
almost as if expecting to fall through a trap
door. But nothing happened and the hut was
deathly silent.

"Let go of me," said Z-Moll, trying to shake off
his vise-like grip.

"You wanna wait out there without a flashlight?" he asked, waving the beam. "Alone?"

Z-Moll bit her lip. She had to admit to herself
that he had a couple of very good points.

"All right," she whispered. "But be careful!"

Trick turned the light back towards the metal
door and tiptoed across the room. He couldn't
hear a single footstep behind him, but Z-Moll's
sweet breath wafted over the back of his neck;
that's how close she was.

Using me as a shield, Trick thought.

His heart pounded as he crept up to the door
and eased it wide open. But he almost puked at
the smell that came out to meet him. The air
from the inner room was foul, like something
had died and then died again. But there was no

sign of Glo's flashlight. If she was in there, she had to be standing in the dark.

"Glo," he called gently, still reeling from the stink.

He waited a moment but there was no reply.

"Let's get out of here," urged Z-Moll, but Trick had already made up his mind to go further. Money couldn't buy moments like this; it was like living in one of his favorite slasher movies. Only Crystal Lake was real. But he still had to find Glo, the messed-up little screwball.

Trick covered his nose with his left hand and then shone his flashlight into the room. Glo was the first thing he saw.

Despite her earlier scream, the girl seemed unharmed. She was standing beside a heap of rubble that lay just in front of the door—it looked as if part of the ceiling had caved in years ago. Trick called to her again but she didn't budge. She just kept staring, transfixed, looking towards the far side of the tiny, windowless room.

Afraid of what he might be about to see, Trick slowly angled the light in the direction of his friend's gaze.

"Holy shit!" He almost dropped the flashlight.

Z-Moll screamed.

On the other side of the room stood a round table with three rotted corpses lying at its feet. Trick was no expert, but he guessed the bodies must have been there for decades. Their eyes were completely gone, and the skin beneath their clothes had shriveled back to the bone. As for the table itself, it was weird enough to disturb Trick and Z-Moll far more than the sight of the decomposed remains.

It had been set up like some kind of shrine. Its round surface acted as a dais of spent candles, while the corpses on the ground comprised an offering; the whole forming a temple dedicated to an unholy relic that had remained here, forgotten and unworshipped, for almost twenty-five years. For there, sitting on the table amid the melted stubs of wax, was the severed head of Mrs Pamela Voorhees.

CHAPTER FOUR

Jason pulled the machete out of the head of the midget, and then stabbed the Hell's Angel through the stomach. The biker fell back—disbelief etched on his every feature. And then froze. While everything around him continued to move, the biker remained suspended in a snapshot of recoil: body arched, arms flailing, head thrown back, hair floating yet motionless. His immobility defied the laws of physics.

Suddenly there was a flash of lightning, and the entire image rotated ninety degrees. It jittered. It blurred. It flew across the chest of the motionless victim and zoomed in on Jason's hockey mask. The faceguard was flecked with arterial spray, but the plastic was so slick that the blood just ran off it and dripped onto Jason's tanned breasts—breasts that had been pumped up with silicone to an alluringly spherical 34E.

A white micro bikini barely covered "Jason's" nipples as she wriggled and sashayed from one victim to the next. A pump jockey, a preacher man, a snake oil salesman—they all fell under her machete. And as each man died, he too was frozen just like the biker in mid-spasm, until "Jason" had converted the whole cemetery into a maze of twisted pain.

Ladies and gentlemen, step inside Jack the Stripper's Graveyard of Go-Go: A two-dimensional landscape of deadwood, headstones and hookers. A neon-lit burial field, where manmade angels fought against one another in a display of German expressionism. And where open graves lay scattered like roadkill.

Clouds of dry ice coiled around "Jason" as she pole-danced on a hangman's gibbet. Save for the hockey mask and the bikini, the young woman with the long blonde hair was butt naked, and her porn star body was drenched with blood.

A dead man sat up in his coffin. "Jason" saw him and, keeping to the beat of the music, ground her spandex-clad Brazilian in his carious face. The sky rippled with CGI menace as "Jason" faked her orgasm. Then she positioned the machete behind the zombie's neck, took the blade in both hands and slowly pulled it towards her, guillotining her undead victim. The ghoul opened his mouth to scream, but all "Jason" could hear was the heavy metal soundstorm of "Frightday 13," the latest single by horror-metal legend Ross Feratu. Because this was a music video and renowned Hollywood porn star, Jaomi Marantez was the main attraction.

While Feratu sang, Marantez was dressed like Jason. Dressed to fuck and kill…

"Hack the motherfuckers
Fuck the motherhackers
Hack the motherfuckers
Yeah. Yeahhhh!
Frightday 13, thirteen die.
Hey yeah, here's blood in your eye
First you're gonna run, then you're gonna cry
Frightday 13… DIE!"

The track burst into a guitar solo that wailed and screamed over a doom-laden riff, the barrage of sound leaving spaces for audio samples of actual TV news reports from the old Crystal Lake murders:

"Eight corpses have been discovered in what is already being called the most brutal and heinous crime in local history."

"Bodies were found literally strewn over the four square-mile campground."

"The person responsible for the Crystal Lake horror remains at large."

The end of the final sample was repeated over and over, increasing in distortion as the solo built to a finger-blistering climax.

"At large… at large… at large… AT LARGE."

Jaomi threw the machete aside, jumped down into the desecrated grave and started to make out with the zombie. Suddenly the whole image was a mess of celluloid scratches and color turned to black and white, before the screen was taken up by the man himself: Ross Feratu—singer, songwriter, millionaire, obsessive fan of Jason Voorhees, and the legal, wedded husband of one Jaomi Marantez.

Feratu was the kind of performer kids loved and parents switched off. Every song he wrote was a paean to the Crystal Lake massacres, and every video he made was an essay in unease. Although Ross didn't know it, his number one fan was a kid from Seattle who owned every one of Ross's seven platinum-selling albums. The kid's name was Trick.

Ross growled the chorus into a vintage microphone while aiming a spear gun straight at the audience: the video was being shot in 3D.

His trademark look was based on that of the vampire Graf Orlok, from the 1922 classic movie *Nosferatu*. Just like Orlok, Ross shaved his head, but unlike Orlok, who was almost completely bald, Ross had left a few strands of hair dotted erratically across his scalp. The hairs didn't form any pattern and they were far too long; they just hung down his back and made him look retarded. But, according to some reports, that was exactly how Jason Voorhees looked. And Jason Voorhees was more than just Feratu's hero. Jason was his god.

When Ross was working, he also put on special makeup that gave him a bat-like appearance. His eyes were hollow, his ears pointed, he built up a hook nose, wore black contacts, and his fingers were elongated into talons. On video shoots he also wore two rows of fangs—but for live appearances, forget it. He'd tried singing with them once and had sounded like an asthmatic duck.

His costuming was equally dramatic. The centerpiece was a period gray long-coat, with thirteen embroidered fastenings running down his torso like massive sutures. Beneath the coat he wore pants put together from different scraps of cloth. Take the left leg: part of a Texan flag had been sewn next to some frayed denim, the denim sewn next to a square of leather with a hand-painted skull motif, and there were holes all over—the broken thread was clearly visible—but it was all fake. Ross had paid an LA designer over two grand to get that homemade grunge look, and the kids loved it.

Throughout his career, Ross had looked pretty much the same. With increased sales there had been an upgrade in quality—especially with the bat makeup—but the core concept hadn't changed much since he'd invented it back in '96. Occasionally he used props—skull-topped canes, top hats, diaphanous shrouds and all the usual horror paraphernalia—and his skin was a shifting mess of studs, rings and other jewelry, whether he was performing or not. But for "Frightday 13," Ross had decided to keep it simple, because Jaomi was the star of this video. If his wife's "nekkid," man-killing, psychopathic butt couldn't shift units of his new single, nothing could.

"D'you see that?" Alice pointed at the picture on her portable TV.

She was sitting in the RV with her father, watching Jaomi Marantez lick the blood off her machete.

"That's what kids want," Alice continued. "Tits and gore. They want serial killers like Jason Voorhees—hey, didn't he come from New Jersey someplace?"

"My child, we've had this discussion a thousand times," replied her father as he sipped on a mug of tea. "The carnival is a waxwork of horrors, not a traveling burlesque. I've seen rock concerts on the television—the crowds are full of delinquents."

Alice gave up trying to remember what she'd heard about Jason, and reached for her coffee. She knew her father could smell the whiskey in it, but what did she care? It was late; she needed to come down from a day behind the wheel.

"They're not delinquents, they're just kids," she replied.

George forced himself to glance at the video a second time, and was appalled by what he saw. Jaomi was rubbing her crotch with the handle of the machete.

"Filth!" he spat and turned the portable off.

"Dad, audiences have changed. Shitty old puppets don't cut it any more. People want sex. They want blood and gore. Kids are more sophisticated now."

"Sophisticated?" he struggled through his lisp. "Is it sophisticated to behave like an animal?"

Alice groaned. She could tell the old man was working up to a speech.

"That's the problem with the world these days. Everything's for sale and the customer is always right. Drugs, guns, prostitution—and with the technology available, people expect instant gratification. But if you say that what someone is doing is wrong or immoral, people stare at you as if you're some kind of lunatic or a Nazi. It doesn't matter if someone's an ill-mannered drunkard addicted to pornography. All people care about is whether or not his credit rating is good."

"You finished?" Alice knocked back the rest of her drink. The hot coffee helped get the booze into her veins faster; give it ten minutes and she'd be ready to hit the hay.

They'd not been parked outside Crystal Lake for long, but already the carnival was set for the night. Some of the guys had mentioned going into town, but Alice had talked them out of it. She wanted the show to keep a low profile at least until they'd had a chance to rest.

"Dad, when did you forget what the sideshow business is about?" she asked, stifling a yawn. "We're here to take money off marks, not make friends with them."

"Frankenstein and Dracula are timeless," he persisted. "People love the classic monsters."

Alice rose to her feet, "That's the problem. They love them but they're not afraid of them. We've got no reputation. I've spent my whole life working this show and I've never had a new dress."

George rested his elbows on his knees, clasped his hands and lowered his head, "Alice... I've always tried—"

"I know," she interrupted, "but trying doesn't pay the bills. Look, Dad, if you seriously want this show to have a future, you've got to try things my way. We need to find a new audience—maybe become a vampire circus or a murder show. I've been speaking to Sparx and he...

George reacted sharply, "You've what?"

Alice realized what she'd done. She'd just let slip that she'd already spoken with the others. She'd undermined her father's authority. So now she could either bullshit her way out of trouble, or she could come clean and force him to hand over the show. She was still wondering what to do when a brick came crashing through the RV window.

It had taken two seconds—two ticks of realization—before Trick's fear had been kicked into touch by sheer excitement.

"Sweet jumping Jehoshaphat!" he whooped. "We've hit the fucking mother-lode!"

Glo said nothing; she just stared at the shrine in a hypnotic stupor. Z-Moll, however, wasn't so quiet.

"Trick, this is so freakathon. Let's get outta here."

"Out of bounds!" he shouted. "This stuff's what we came here for. It's *beyond* triple fucking A."

"Well, I don't like it," Z-Moll scrunched her face.

"But look!" he trained his flashlight on one of the three bodies. "A black and white bathrobe—and that ice pick in her head—it's Alice Hardy. It's got to be. She's the only girl who survived the 1980 murders committed by Pamela Voorhees. She killed Pamela, but then she disappeared from her apartment two months later. There was blood everywhere, and her parents described this exact bathrobe. Everyone thinks Jason took revenge on Alice for killing his mom, but no one's been able to prove it until now."

He turned the light onto the remains of a second girl; a corpse dressed in old-fashioned jogging pants.

"Oh, this is too much," he babbled. "Jason went on his first killing spree in 1984. It lasted a week and in the first two days he killed seven people at a counselor training center. But two of the bodies went missing. The first was a girl named Terry—I don't remember her last name. Well, this is her. And that," he moved the beam to the right and illuminated the body of a cop, "is the second."

"I'm feeling nauseous," the stench was turning Z-Moll's stomach.

"She's talking to me," Glo murmured out of the blue.

"What?" asked Z-Moll. Her expression showed every sign that she was tired of the little freak.

"She's talking to me," said Glo again.

Trick ignored her and aimed his light straight at the severed head. Was this how those old guys felt when they'd opened the pyramids? Come to think of it, the head reminded him of an Egyptian mummy he'd seen in a museum one time. Skin like brown paper, wisps of white hair, exposed teeth, vacant eye sockets—jeez, Pam sure looked rough.

Z-Moll took the unused flashlight out of Glo's hand. Then she held it up close to the girl's eyes and turned it full on.

"No longer funny!" she spat.

Glo's transformation was so abrupt that it merely confirmed Z-Moll's suspicion that her friend had been faking it all along.

"What d'you do that for?" asked Glo, looking about the room in bewilderment. "Where are we?"

Z-Moll was about to reply but Trick did it for her. He hadn't noticed the change in Glo's demeanor at all, but once he heard her voice he just had to go fishing for Glo-ster Points.

"Glo, look!" he shouted. "Look at this! Pamela fucking Voorhees. Luck factor ten or what?"

For the first time since the girl had regained control of her faculties, she saw the head sitting upon the table. She saw the bodies. And suddenly everything made sense.

"We need to go," she said. Then she grabbed hold of Z-Moll's sleeve and began to pull the girl towards the door. "Trick!" she called.

"Oh, come on!" he whined. "Glo, I thought you'd be up for this more than any of us. You're the Queen of Crystal Lake!"

"Leave it," she repeated. "Those voices I've been hearing—it's her. Pamela Voorhees. She's been watching me. She lured me here."

"Fuck!" he roared. "Dead people don't talk! What's wrong with you?"

"Please, Tricky," begged Z-Moll. "Elvira's right. Let's go. We'll call the cops and they can CSI the shit out of this dump."

The boy didn't know what freaked him more: the fact that Glo wanted nothing to do with this awesome Voorhees collectable, or the fact that Z-Moll had actually sided with her on something.

"If you think," he started to pace, "I'm going to let Sergeant Dillweed come *here* and put *my* fucking head inside his bowling *bag*..."

Z-Moll wished she had a gun. When Trick got real mad, he went totally Jim Carrey.

"Listen to me," said Glo. "That fucking witch is taking over my mind. It's a trap. She wants out of here. I can hear her right now."

"Oh yeah?" Trick couldn't believe he was even having this conversation. "What's she say?"

Glo stared him in the eye and said, "She's saying, 'Kill the boy.'"

"That's it," said Z-Moll. "This is *so* yesterday." She made straight for the outer room leading to the exit. Glo went to follow her.

"No, wait!" called Trick.

He ran over to the table, leaned over the dead bodies, and lifted the head of Mrs Voorhees from its resting place. No sooner had he done so than both flashlights went out.

"What is the meaning of this?" George held out the brick that had just been used to break his window.

He was standing in the doorway of the RV, looking out at a mob of twenty to thirty locals ganging up in front of the truck. Most of them were armed: guns, baseball bats, wrenches, knives—one of them even carried an unlit Molotov. And they were in an ugly mood.

One guy shone a light in George's eyes while another blew a loud horn. Behind them was Jonah. The drunk laughed and danced, with a fresh bottle of liquor as payment for warning the townsfolk.

"Oh, I told the little bastard, I told him you'd all die. But he wouldn't listen, so now you're gonna cry-yyyyy."

The other inhabitants of Crystal Lake were far less poetic as they hurled a volley of abuse at Witney.

"Get out! Fucking perverts... Get out of town... Don't want your kind... This is God's country... Get the fuck out of town! Leave Crystal Lake... Go now... Break your fucking necks... Go back where you came from!"

A soda bottle smashed against the RV, a few inches to the left of George's head.

"Dad!" Alice was just inside the trailer behind him.

"I'm all right, dear," he replied. Then he faced the mob a second time. "We've done nothing wrong. You can't treat us like this. We have rights."

A man stepped forward and walked right up to the door. He had the build of a linebacker and the overalls of a mechanic. There was oil on his face and he was brandishing a tire iron. Suddenly the mob went quiet, so that they could all hear what the grease monkey had to say.

"You better leave, mister," he warned, shaking the iron. "People here have seen enough horror without trailer trash like you cashing in."

The crowd cheered and blew the air horn, and two more bottles were thrown at the motorhome.

"But I don't understand," said George, only now he was starting to cough.

"Shit," gasped Alice, smacking her forehead. "That music video. Jason Voorhees. Crystal Lake. Oh, shit!"

The mechanic nodded in her direction, but kept his eyes on George, "Your girlfriend understands.

Now go on, clear out before we throw you out!"

George stepped down on to the asphalt and raised himself to his full height—which was still some way short of the mechanic.

"How dare you!" fumed the old man, but then he was stricken with a pain in his chest. He staggered forward and grabbed onto the mechanic's overalls to stop himself from falling to the ground.

"Take your hands off me," growled the big guy.

George was so racked with hacking spasms that he couldn't have relaxed his grip if he'd wanted to. The coughing was growing much worse.

"I said, get your filthy hands off me," the mechanic raised the tire iron as if getting ready to slug the old guy.

"No!" Alice ran out and locked her hands round the man's wrist and elbow. Then she twisted his arm and bent it back against itself. The mechanic couldn't believe it; she was a stick of a girl, but her muscles were like steel. He cried with pain and the weapon fell out of his hand. Then she put an arm around her father and pushed the troublemaker away.

"Hit an old man, you filthy fucking coward!"

She looked around the RV park, but couldn't see any of the other carnies—except Kenton, parked away from all the rest, leaning against the hood of his pickup. Even from this distance, Alice could see the bastard was laughing, enjoying the fix she and her father were in. One day, she swore, she'd kill him. Now, however, the mob was closing in on her and she really didn't have any answers.

* * *

Ma lowered herself back into her easy chair. She was bleating like a weasel with a pineapple up its pussy, but too damn stale to shed any tears. Pa leaned over and sniffed the burns: boiled pork.

"For the sake of Ma's accident," said Enoch over by the range, "I won't break your fuckin' balls."

His arm was still bleeding and there were other fresh nicks dotted about his body. But Francis was cut just as bad—if anything, it looked as if Enoch's cleaver had won the argument. Nevertheless, Francis remained adamant that Jason should be put on a spit. And now it seemed his older brother was going to grant that one concession.

"Good," said Francis, nursing a wound in his side. "I'll go put'n my special blend of 'erbs and spices on the fucker."

He went and fetched an earthenware jar down from the shelf. Then he popped out the cork stopper and poured a heap of dried leaves all over Jason's body. No one seemed to care that Jason still wore his clothes.

Across the room, Enoch was contemplating the huge fireplace. They had a spit there permanently, but it was nowhere near big enough for Fourtrees, and turning the bastard was going to be a bitch. The inbred threw some wood on the fire and walked over to the family table. He reckoned he'd have to cut Jason up.

"Hey, upchuckfuck," he called to his brother, "help me carry Fourtrees over to the fire. If'n I slice him there, I won't have so far to go with the meat."

"Fuck, man-tits, can't you see I'm busy?"

Francis had started preparing some vegetables. He was bleeding all over the potatoes, but the tin tub was still on the boil. Francis dropped a couple of chopped carrots into the water, the orange segments bobbing against the raccoon carcass.

Cussing under his breath, Enoch grabbed hold of Jason's ankles and started to drag the killer off the family table. He pulled, and pulled, until suddenly there was a loud thump as Jason's head slid over the edge, plummeting to the ground.

While this was going on, Francis walked by and, without a word of warning, tossed a pail of cold water into Ma's face.

"That should stop your fuckin' squealin'," he shouted, but it only made her cry even more. When Pa saw Ma's soaking hair drooping over the blisters on her face, he broke out into giggles.

"Hey y'all," called Enoch, "I got an announcement to make."

"You an' Fourtrees gettin' hitched?" snickered Francis. That got a good family laugh—even from Ma.

"No, you piece of cock itch!" huffed Enoch. "I'm takin' off Fourtrees's mask. Y'all need to come and look."

Enoch finished dragging Jason's body down beside the fireplace. Ma and Pa cheered and clapped their hands like retarded kindergarteners. Even Francis was getting excited. Yellow light flickered across the hockey mask, but still Jason showed no sign of life. He just lay there, flat on his back.

"Okay, everyone," said Enoch flexing his fingers, "I want'n you all to give me a count of three. Ready?"

They nodded and then joined in a shambles of a countdown.

"Onnnnne... Twooooo..."

Enoch reached down and placed his hands on Jason's mask.

Alice took another step back. She had her arms round her father, who was still caught in a paroxysm of hacking coughs. Yet another bottle smashed against the RV. Two of the townsmen started to rock the motorhome while the others edged forward, tightening their noose around the Witneys.

"Leave us alone!" screamed Alice and she pulled her father close to her breast, expecting any second to feel the...

A siren tore through the air, and suddenly the crowd made like one of the soda bottles hitting the trailer. By the time the two patrol cars pulled up in front of the RV, there wasn't a single member of the lynch mob to be seen.

"Thank God," sighed Alice. She was surprised to discover she had tears in her eyes. "Come on, Dad," she said, rubbing the old man's chest. "It's okay now."

The other showmen began to emerge from their vehicles. They looked sheepish. Just the sight of them made Alice mad. When push came to shove, they'd been no help at all: not even Minter.

Sheriff Haslip got out of his car. He was clean-shaven, didn't have much of a paunch, and everything about the way he moved said he was a guy who was used to being listened to. He strolled over to the two deputies in the second car and sent them off to check the perimeter of the RV park. Then he came back to speak with Alice and her father.

"Officer," began the old man, fighting to regain his breath, "you arrived just in time."

Haslip raised a hand to stop Witney going any further, "Sir, I'm afraid I'm going to have to ask you all to leave town."

George reacted as if he'd been stung, "What, now? Do you know what time it is, officer?"

"S'nothing I can do about that. It's your truck see…" he nodded at the gaudy painting on the side of the semi. "The people of Crystal Lake are sensitive to this stuff."

"But can't we stay till morning?" George was almost pleading.

"No can do. The minute we leave, they'll come back and finish what they started. The way I heard it, one of your people hit crazy Jonah."

"One of *my* people?" Witney found it impossible to believe.

"Yeah, Jonah came into town and got everyone worked up. Look, I'm sorry, but I don't have the manpower to babysit you guys. You're going to have to leave. Immediately."

George bowed his head. "Very well, officer," he sighed. "Very well."

Alice, however, was tired of being messed around. She got between her father and the sheriff and started to bawl the cop out. Haslip thought the woman had a face like thunder and tattoos to match, but there was something about her sass that made him warm to her.

"… so tell me how you're any different from the vigilantes?" she shouted.

Kenton Freely had come over to listen, standing just a few yards away. He was enjoying the show Alice was putting on. Solely because of that, she suddenly felt the urge to shut up.

"Look, Miss, err…?" Haslip began.

"Alice Jane Witney."

"Well, look, Miss Witney, I'm doing this for your own security. I can't protect you from these people."

"You're supposed to be the fucking sheriff!"

"Please, Alice!" her father was appalled by her lack of respect. "Let's just pack up and go."

Haslip, however, wanted her to see sense. "Look, Miss Witney, I can't lock up half the town. My job's to keep the peace and the easiest way I can do that is to help you people on your way."

"Well thanks!" She turned on her heels and walked round to the power hookup on the far side of the RV. As she began unplugging the cord, she could hear the sheriff trying to explain to her father.

"Need help?" Kenton had snuck up behind her. "With the juice, I mean."

"Why don't you drop dead, Freely," she didn't even bother to look away from the outlet.

He lit up a cigarette, "Too bad. You look stressed. Maybe if you give me some sugar—slap me around a little—it could help ease the tension."

He exhaled his smoke into her hair.

Alice took the cable in her hands and looked Freely square in the eye.

"I saw you grinning back there when that mob was threatening us. And I'd bet on my mother's fucking grave you're the one who hit the town nut and got us into this mess."

Kenton smirked, "Who? Me?"

He blew more smoke in her face but she refused to flinch. "You better get back in your pickup and fuck the hell off. You're fired."

Freely laughed and took another drag on his high tar stick. "You can't do that, sugar. You know that."

"Dad will…"

"Your father'll do nothing. Now why don't you and I just patch up our differences with a good, long screw?"

Alice pushed Kenton aside, submitting a formal response to his proposal.

"Fuck off!"

Then she went back round to where her father and the sheriff were still talking. Kenton followed her.

"C'mon Alice," he teased. "Everyone else in the show's licked your pussy, so why not me?"

George's mouth fell open, while Haslip looked aside and shuffled his feet.

"Alice," lisped the old man as she walked past. "Is that true?"

But the young woman just climbed aboard the RV and slammed the door.

That flashlight stunt had been the final straw; Z-Moll and Trick ran out of the shack—the girl screaming, the boy laughing. Dark clouds had moved in across the sky, their tenebrous mass extinguishing the stars and confining the moon-beams to a tight circle over on the far side of the clearing. But Z-Moll ran the opposite way, making for the path they'd come in on, while Trick stopped dead in his tracks.

"The head!" he cursed. "I've dropped the fucking head!"

He must have let go when the blackout had almost made him shit his pants.

"Screw the fucking head," shouted Z-Moll, and she carried on sprinting in the direction of the trail.

Trick didn't want to go back inside the hut but he wasn't leaving without his star prize; so, with Z-Moll's footsteps fading in the distance, he reluctantly turned—and saw Glo calmly step out-side the door. The girl seemed strangely composed—another shift within her person-ality—yet Trick didn't notice. All he had time for was the severed head she was carrying in her right hand. She was holding the relic up high, like an old-fashioned lantern, and was moving towards the spot where the moonlight hit the ground.

"Glo!" shouted the boy. "Way beyond cool!" He ran over and snatched the head of Mrs Voorhees away from her.

Glo snarled wordlessly and shot a hand down to her left hip, as if she expected to find some-thing hanging off her belt. But there was nothing there. She hissed as the boy turned the putrefied body part over in his hands like a basketball.

"I can't see it," he whined, squinting. "It's too fucking dark."

"Then why don't you…" The girl's voice was laced with venom. She stopped and tried again, only now she sounded like a parody of Grandma Walton. "All right, dear, why don't you be a good boy and take it over there, where the moonlight's shining? Then you'll be able to see it as much as you like."

"D'oh!" he kicked himself. Then he lifted the head and held it like a ventriloquist's dummy, a little prop comedy for Glo's amusement, "Trigg, I tink dis is de geginning of a geautiful griendship."

Glo pretended to laugh, but when Trick turned away her face was consumed with hatred.

Ahead along the trail, Z-Moll was trying her flashlight, her cell, everything—but nothing worked. All the same, she wasn't going back to the shack. Uh-uh, no way. But she didn't want to get lost either; so she decided she'd go as far as the end of the trail and then wait there for the others.

"Fuck!" she'd just stepped in that puddle again.

Back at the clearing, Trick was about to walk beneath the shaft of silvery moonlight.

"That's right, dear." Glo purred. "Go on. You'll be able to see me—I mean the head, much better there."

The boy stepped into the light. For the first time in a quarter of a century, the head of Pamela Voorhees was bathed in the superlunary aura of the moon—a full moon, like that which had enshrined the moment of her beheading. Her every ghastly lineament was suffused with dark energy. She immediately channeled the power, and directed it to the one who needed it most…

Ch-ch-ch. Ah-ah-ah-ahhh.

Jason sat bolt upright, grabbed a blazing coal from the fireplace and thrust it into Enoch's mouth.

"Aghghhhgg!" Enoch clawed at his face, but the burning chunk was too large and too damned hot to pull out. Smoke poured through his blackening lips, his cheeks glowed from the fire within, and all he could do was scream and twist with pain. His face was being grilled from the inside.

Francis looked over at his sizzling brother and howled with laughter. "You gone get'n the red fuckin' haze now, ain't you boy?"

Jason smoothly climbed to his feet, seized the thrashing Enoch-o'-Lantern by the scruff of his neck, and then, keeping hold of the collar, drove his head through one of the cabin windows. There was an explosion of glass as the baked retard shone like a broken turn signal, before Jason snatched the body back into the room and slammed it down on the table.

Had Enoch not been so utterly consumed with suffering, he would have done his best to put up a fight—if only to delay the inevitable; but his brain was being toasted and he no longer had control over any part of his anatomy. The backcountry cannibal was now mere clay in Jason's hands. Just another victim.

Jason picked up Enoch's meat cleaver and brought it down through his neck. The blade buried deep in the wood, pinning the corpse by fibrous strands to the hard oak surface. Steam rose from the freshly stewed blood.

"Get off the family table," squawked Ma.

Jason turned and stomped towards her. Behind him, Francis finally got to thinking that Jason just might mean trouble. He grabbed a skillet off the range and came running to the attack; the pan was heavy enough to knock Fourtrees out cold. In theory, anyways...

"You leave her alone!"

Grissom swiped Jason around the side of his head, the skillet clipping the hockey mask with a musical clang. Jason spun and Francis, relieved to have distracted the killer away from Ma, hit him again and again like someone ringing a bastard bell at a funeral. But Jason barely flinched. As the flat iron bounced off his faceguard one more time, Voorhees grabbed a poker from the fireplace and rammed it clean through Grissom's left thigh.

"Oh, you cocksucker!" wailed Francis through clenched jaws.

He fell to the floor and grabbed his leg with both hands. If he didn't know better, with the aroma of cooked meat and the hiss of spitting fat it could have been breakfast time.

Now in command, Jason glanced at the crippled jackass, took in the dropped skillet and then went back for Ma.

Francis called after him in desperation. "Fourtrees, don't do it! You can join the family. Enoch was no use anyhow. We can be brothers! We can kill stuff. Francis Grissom and Man-tits Voorhees. It'll be like old times with you and your ma. Listen to me, you dumb sack of shit!"

Unmindful of his pleas, Jason carried on. He lifted Ma out of her easy chair and threw the old bitch on the fire. She squealed and howled, kicked flames across the hearth, and her bones snapped in the heat like so much kindling.

"You bastard son of a fuckin' bitch!" shouted Francis. He unsheathed his bone knife and struggled to get up off the ground.

But in one fluid motion, Jason lifted the flaming corpse out of the fireplace and threw it across the room. Francis screamed as the geriatric fireball crashed into him and knocked him back down. The knife went skidding out of his hands. He went scrabbling for it. Ma was lying on him, melting. His clothes were on fire. It was getting too hot. He was burning. He just needed to reach the damned knife. He crawled as fast as his blazing Ma would let him—until Jason stepped forward, placed a foot on the side of his head and slowly pressed down. Francis heard his skull crack and felt the bone cutting into his soft stuff. He was finished and he knew it.

"Who's laughin' now, Francis?" he sniggered faintly. "Who's fuckin' laughin' now..."

Then he was gone.

Fire was raging through the cabin, but there was still one victim waiting to be killed. Jason found Pa writhing in his chair—but it wasn't fear, or the heat of the flames, that had Grissom squirming: it was laughter. With each horrific murder the old bastard had choked on his spit, pissed his pants, and then blown his ass—all in that order. He'd never seen such quality entertainment in his miserable goddamn life. And now with Jason staring at him like that, Pa just pointed a finger at the hockey mask and laughed even louder.

Jason looked down on the feeble wretch. Then he glanced about the room, at the fire spreading over every surface, entangling the old man within an incendiary web. Jason stiffened his back, turned and promptly walked out of the building.

The grass beneath his boots was instantly familiar—as was the voice that suddenly called his name.

"Jason!"

He stopped. Listened. There it was again. Only the sound didn't enter through his ears; it came from within his mind. The voice was talking inside his head. And it was a voice he recognized.

Over his shoulder, the cabin was now a bonfire in the night. And as Jason followed the voice deeper into the woods, Pa Grissom's laughter turned into screams.

CHAPTER FIVE

Sheriff Haslip looked on as the last of the show trucks was made ready. He could see how angry Alice was, and didn't know if it was his fault for moving them on, or Freely's for being such a heel. Either way, the sheriff wanted to patch things up; if he could just get her to understand, then maybe—maybe what? He'd take her number and ask her for a date?

Haslip shook his head and sauntered over to the RV. Alice was sitting behind the steering wheel and did her best to avoid his gaze as he spoke to her through the open front-side window.

"Miss Witney…"

"What's the highest point around here?" she interrupted, still not looking at him.

"Uh—I'm, err—I'm sorry?"

"The highest point?" she asked again, her eyes fixed on the windshield.

Haslip didn't understand where the question came from, but, "Well, err, Horton Ridge, I guess.".

"Well," she said, turning to him at last, "why don't you just take yourself up Horton Ridge and jump the fuck off?"

She shut the window and gunned the engine to drown out any possible reply. Haslip shrugged—at least he'd tried. Then he walked down to the back of the long semi, where George Witney was checking to see that Judge had locked the doors properly.

"Not the best time to be setting out on a journey," commented Witney, pressing on one of the latches.

"No, I guess it is pretty late," replied the cop. He seemed genuinely concerned. "Look, I'm sorry for what happened here but…"

"No need to explain, officer," the old man insisted. "Once my daughter told me about—well, the murders—to be perfectly honest, I feel awful for even having stopped here. No, I'll be only too happy to leave you all in peace."

"Thanks," smiled the sheriff. "Now if you want my advice, your best bet's to head northwest. Just follow the road through town and go right through the lake area until you reach the north road to Reculver…"

"Reculver?" asked George.

"Small place like Crystal Lake," answered the sheriff. "But I wouldn't stop there either—too many hicks. Just keep going north till you get to Hunt Ridge."

"Is that a city?" lisped Witney.

The sheriff laughed. "Anything but. It's a farming town. But they have a lot of things going on: rodeos, circuses, stuff like that. I've posted deputies so you shouldn't have any trouble getting out of Crystal Lake."

"Thank you, officer," said the old man warmly.

Moments later, Witney was taking his place in the front of the RV—he seemed more dependent on his walking cane than ever. Alice watched her father buckle up and then she shifted into gear, dismayed to find herself once more at the head of a convoy going nowhere. Sheriff Haslip stood back as the vehicles rolled out onto the road, their tail-lights bright and then gradually disappearing. Doktor Geistmann's Carnival of Terror was leaving Crystal Lake.

Jason's stride was like a heartbeat on the earth. Step by step he pounded, ignoring the hiking trails that twisted and meandered, seeking to lead him away when the next scene of slaughter lay dead ahead of him; a raven slash through the nightmare of trees. The voice had told him there were intruders at Camp Crystal Lake: two teenagers who were snooping and prying where they didn't belong. Jason trusted the voice. It was familiar. It was someone from the past. He knew that if he followed the voice, he would find the two young interlopers. And then they would die.

"Didn't they know how to moisturize in the Eighties?"

Trick bobbed the head in his hands, completely unaware that he was toying with a desiccated kill-switch that had just caused the death of four cannibals. In truth, the boy no longer found the head the slightest bit scary—partly because he'd seen worse at the multiplex, but mostly because the head was "fucking awesome!"

He looked over at Glo. Her eyes were closed and she held her arms stiffly by her side, fists bunched, as if she were locked in concentration.

"Hey," Trick called. "Let's go find Z."

Glo didn't budge.

"C'mon!" he repeated.

"Nowhere to run," she said totally out of the blue. Her voice reminded Trick of games of hide and seek he used to play with his mom.

"Who's running?" he asked. "Oh, you mean Z! Yeah, she took off. But she won't go far. Not without her captain."

"She can't hide," hissed Glo. "No place to hide."

"Shit." Trick suddenly realized what was going on. "I get it," he said, pissed. "Voice number four." Then he bowed his head and pushed past Glo without even bothering to look at her. "If you do Kurt Cobain," he spat, "write me a fucking song."

Glo watched as he went back towards the trail leading out of the clearing.

"It's too late," she called after him. "Don't you see? You can't run."

The boy stopped to take one last look at his friend.

"Okay," he said, "either you come right now or you find your own way out—I don't give a shit."

But Trick wouldn't have been so ready to abandon the girl if he'd known that, ever since leaving Erwin's truck, she'd been straining to resist the power of the dead Mrs Voorhees—a power that had grown stronger as Glo had drawn nearer to the severed head, until finally, when the flashlights failed, the girl had been left alone in the dark with the object that had enslaved her. Glo's body was now in thrall to the psychotic spirit of Pamela Voorhees.

"He's coming," she said.

Suddenly Trick heard a strange rustling sound. There was something moving in the under-brush.

"Z-Moll?" he called. "Hey, Z! Stop kidding around!"

A wind was rising and the clouds were being blown clear out of the sky, but not even an unbridled moon could help the boy see what was making the twigs snap and the branches break all around him.

"Who is it?" he shouted.

But the sounds kept moving. One second they were in front of him, the next they were behind.

"Glo!" he ran up to her, grabbed her leather jacket and tried to shake some sense into her. "What's going on?"

But she just laughed in his face.

And then he heard it: the unmistakable sound of footsteps. Thump. Thump. Heavy. Thump. Thump. Coming closer. Thump Thump.

"It can't be, it fucking can't be," babbled Trick. "Z-Moll!" he shouted.

"Don't you see?" laughed Glo, her eyes following him with unflinching cruelty. "You should have saved my boy."

Trick darted about like a caged animal, but every which way he turned, the footsteps seemed to be in front of him.

"*You should have saved my boy!*" raged Glo, as Jason crashed into the clearing and hammered towards the two of them, with murder daubed on ever scratch and crack of his hockey mask.

The low lighting from the dash shone in George's face and was reflected in the windshield. Since passing the police roadblock on the edge of town, the carnival had entered a strange sort of limbo; a tunnel of impenetrable darkness where each forested mile seemed identical to the last. There'd been no other traffic to meet or overtake, no headlamps to dispel the soporific blanket of night, and only the full moon was watching as they slowly made their way northwest.

"Well?" asked George, staring through the side window at the monotonous wall of black. "Is Freely telling the truth? Did you seduce them?"

Alice's knuckles turned white as she gripped the wheel with irritation.

"For God's sake, Dad," she barked. "Stop using words with fucking 's''s in them. You sound ridiculous."

"You're changing the subject," countered the old man, ignoring her cheap shot at his speech impediment.

"No," she cut in, "you're the one changing the subject. This isn't about me sleeping around; this is about the carnival. We'll never make any money unless we modernize."

George sighed. "Please, Alice, not again. Now's not the right time."

"Bullshit, Dad, this is the perfect time! In case you weren't paying attention, we just got thrown out of town. Again. Another fucking blank."

"The show's fine as it is," Witney turned to look at Alice and saw she was frowning. "We'll make more money eventually. We just need a break."

Alice nodded rapid-fire, a shallow bobbing of her chin born from a fusion of anger and sarcasm.

"That's right, I forgot," she snapped. "Always the next fucking town."

"Well, what about that website you're building?"

George tried to sound positive. He would clutch at any straw if it meant stopping Alice from going through with her plan. The girl didn't have all the facts. She didn't know the danger of what she was proposing.

"Point of fact one," she replied, "I'm not building the website, Judge is. Point of fact two, it's nowhere near finished. And point of fact three, there's no point having a website if even we don't know what towns we're gonna play, and what towns we're gonna get fucking kicked out of."

"Alice, that's enough!" George banged his fist on his knee for emphasis. "I will not let you turn my show into a degrading spectacle for perverts. Doktor Geistmann's Carnival of Terror will remain a waxworks. That is my final word."

"No, Dad. This is *my* final word. You've been in the business over forty years and the last time you turned a decent profit was '62. You've had your shot. Now it's my turn. And I'm through with this bullshit penny-pinching."

A sharp bend in the road lay just ahead and George was worried his daughter would corner too quickly.

"Alice!" he warned, but she misunderstood his cry.

"No, I've had it!" she shouted, instinctively wrenching at the wheel. She'd been driving the RV for as many years as her father had been dozing in the passenger seat. "Crystal Lake was the limit. I'm taking over, Dad, whether you like it or not."

The old man shifted in his seat but said nothing. He couldn't let go of the carnival, not after so many years—it had been his whole life. And what about Kenton? What would Freely say if he discovered Alice's intentions? George shivered and began to cough.

"Save it for the rubes," Alice said flatly.

Any other time, Witney would have admonished his daughter for having the temerity to suggest his illness was an act. But now the old man was too worried even to talk. He'd known for years this moment was coming—the day when Alice would claim her birthright—and he'd dreaded it. For if his fears were correct, Alice was about to embark on a path that might not only destroy the carnival—it would drive a wedge between the girl and her father forever.

Jason had emerged almost halfway between the two teenagers, and seemed uncertain which one he should kill first. He looked at the girl; she was laughing and smiling at him—something he wasn't used to.

"Jason, my poor dear boy," she soothed. "Mommy's here. Mommy will take care of you."

Then Jason glanced over at Trick. The youth was terrified and fascinated in equal measure. He had worshipped Jason almost all his young life. He'd played with his Jason action figure, he'd worn his Jason mask every Halloween, he'd even written his own Jason stories. But—and only now did Trick realize this—he'd never truly believed Jason was real. It was like waking up one Christmas Eve to find Santa Claus fucking your mom.

"C… come any… c… closer," the boy stammered, "and your m… mom gets it!"

He lifted the severed head and shook it at Jason's face.

For the first time, Jason saw the withered remains of his mother. He immediately knew that she was the one who had brought him to this place. Now he stared into her sunken eyes and remembered…

Echoes of a distant past: a night much like this and the death of the nice lady. She'd fallen, been decapitated, and her killer had drifted away in a boat across the lake. Yet she had reached out to Jason, and had somehow made him special. He was only thirty-four then, and scared. He was retarded. He wore a sack on his head to hide his deformity from the world. But despite his fear of the girl in the boat, he'd crept out from his hiding place and recovered everything of value to him; the severed head, the murder weapon—he'd even removed the pale blue sweater from the nice lady's headless corpse. And then he'd brought these relics back to his home where he'd treasured them until, years later, some strangers came and spoiled everything. They'd forced Jason to leave his woodland sanctuary and in return he'd killed them. Jason hadn't seen the nice lady for a long time, but he still remembered her—and he wanted her back.

Jason only had to take one step for Trick to realize the killer's indecision was over—as was the spell that had been turning the boy's legs into stone.

"Shiiiiiiit!"

Trick screamed and bolted off along the trail. His pulse beat in his head as he ran, but no matter how hard he pushed, he couldn't escape the leaden footsteps closing in on him. And Jason was only walking.

Suddenly the ground fell away as Trick stepped into the deep puddle, yet somehow he managed to stay on his feet and keep running. Behind him, Jason splashed through the ditch without even breaking stride, while Glo cackled and cavorted in the monster's wake, her hips swaying with the clumsiness of a much older woman.

Not far ahead, Z-Moll sat waiting on a log stump. The skeletal arms of a dead maple reached sinuously over her head like a shadow of veins waiting to throttle her. A few minutes earlier she'd been scared, but now she was plain bored. Trick's "I'm being chased" act was textbook-pathetic, and his bogus cries only made her yawn. So when he came rushing round the corner, Z-Moll got up—eager to bitch at him—but he just darted straight past her and vanished through the trees.

"Run!" he shouted.

"Run?" she asked derisively. "From what?"

Z-Moll turned to look in the direction Trick had just come from—as Jason grabbed her shoulders, lifted her off her feet, and pushed her back onto the sharpest, heaviest branch of the old maple. She kicked and screamed as the wood drilled into her spine. Jason drove her forward, screwing the limb of the tree through her intestines. She heaved and punched, her mouth spat a plume of blood into the air—the droplets falling on Jason's hockey mask. He pushed harder. The bough poked out through her stomach, tearing a raised hole in her gut. She wailed and cried. For her mom, for her dad, for her sister, for her dog, for her friends, for her school: she was crying for her whole damn life, and she wanted it all back.

Jason spun her on the wooden spoke until her head was upside down and she was staring into his shins. Then he grabbed both her ankles and split her legs further than they wanted to go. Z-Moll retched and screamed as her body began to rip—it was just like pulling the legs off a roast chicken. Jason tore her groin apart, gashing her all the way down from her pussy to the wooden spear sticking out of her gut. But the most appalling facet of the murder was just how long the girl remained conscious before death finally seized her.

Jason stood back.

Z-Moll hung upside down in a broken V of scarlet. Her legs flopped askew and her eyes were like glass shining in the moonlight. Suddenly the branch cracked from the weight of the dead girl and then broke, dropping the whole bloody mess into the dirt.

"Oh, Jason, you're such a good boy. Mommy's real proud of you."

Jason turned to see Glo watching him; her face was flush with pride and she had tears of joy in her eyes. He started to make a move towards her when Trick burst into view.

"No... oh Jesus Christ... Z-Moll!" he cried.

The girl's screams had helped Trick overcome his momentary fear, only for him to find her lying in a mangled heap. He'd loved her. She was his girl. She'd been a pain in the ass. She was Z.

Glo stepped up to the boy and smiled in his tear-streaked face, "See? Look what he's done. Look what my Jason has done!"

"You fucking lunatic!" shouted Trick. He lashed out with his left fist and punched Glo in the mouth.

She grunted and fell on her back; and as her head hit the ground, she accidentally swallowed the tooth Trick had just knocked out—her mouth was a mess of blood. She sat up, dazed, and saw the broken corpse. Then she saw Trick swerving to avoid Jason's deadly onslaught. Suddenly, all the horror of the scene became clear to Glo, and she screamed.

Jason paused to look down at the girl. She was simply a frightened teenager.

"Trick," she cried, "what's happening?"

"Glo!"

This time Trick hadn't missed the change. He sidestepped past Jason, reached for the girl's hand and pulled her to her feet. Jason aimed a blow at the boy, but his fist went crashing into the bark of the dead maple.

"It's Jason!" gasped Glo in utter disbelief.

"You don't fucking say!" rasped Trick, as the two of them ran for their lives. But Jason wasn't finished with them yet.

The engine maintained a steady hum as the trailer wound its way through the hills. Though he hadn't stopped fighting with Alice for a moment, George had managed to rally his wits and he was no longer shaking. This was a war of words he had to win—had to—even if it meant saying things he would regret for the rest of his life.

"Alice," his voice was stern, "if you persist with this—this coup, then I'll have no choice but to leave the carnival."

"Sure, Dad," Alice snorted. "Seventy-two—no money—I can see you in Florida already."

Alice was tired. Her eyes were stinging and she wished she could concentrate on the road, but she was in too deep to stop now.

"Listen, Dad," she continued. "I'm doing this for your good as well as mine. We need the money."

"Have you…" he hesitated. "Have you spoken to *all* the others?"

"Let's just say if I were you, I wouldn't put it to a vote." Her simple reply upset the old man more than she could possibly have imagined.

"Even Kenton?" he gulped, choking back the emotion.

"I'm firing that bastard," she snapped. "If he wasn't like family, I'd have cut him years ago. But listen, Dad, you're a good barker… "

"Lecturer," he corrected. Alice was never good with carny slang.

"Lecturer, barker, whatever—you're good with your mouth. The show can still use you."

"I'm very pleased to hear it," replied George tartly. This confrontation was destroying him, but he built himself up for one last brutal assault.

"You know what I mean," said Alice, trying to be reasonable.

"If your mother were still alive…"

Alice groaned at her father's inevitable invocation.

"She would be appalled by what you've become. If your slovenly manner and your arrogance, your boozing and your cheap tattoos weren't enough, I now learn that you've been prostituting yourself solely as a means to replace me."

"Dad!" Alice was furious but she had to keep watching the road.

"Oh, I've known all along about your sordid sex life," he continued, quivering with nerves, "but I've always turned a blind eye. I consoled myself with the knowledge that at least you weren't a drug addict. But to use your body as a weapon against your own father!"

Alice hit the brakes and screeched the RV to a halt, not giving a damn if Vincenzo was awake enough in the following truck not to slam into her. Then she unbuckled her belt and directed her full wrath at the old man.

"If you're not happy with the way I am—*Dad*—maybe it's because you fucking made me this way! All my life you've dragged me around the country. I've got no education, no career, no real friends—I don't even have a fucking mom. She died in a carnival accident! This show killed her! Most people would have thrown in the towel at that point, but no, everyone has to come second to your fucking fantasy world. Do you know what it's like being a little girl who can't get her dad's attention 'cause he's too goddamn busy playing with his little fucking toys? Screw Dracula, Dad! *Screw him!*"

She pushed open the door and jumped out of the cab; she needed some air. Behind her, the old man dissolved in a flood of tears.

"Please, Alice," he cried. "Give me one more chance."

"Dad," she said pacing the asphalt, "I love you. But if you say another word, I'll fucking kill you."

"He's gaining on us," shouted Glo, looking over her shoulder.

She was spiritually battered and physically exhausted, but she had to keep running. Through all her confusion, one thing was clear: Jason Voorhees was alive, and he was coming after them with charnel determination.

Trick panted. "The bastard won't give up. Glo, you have to think of something."

They were running side by side through a dark confusion of bushes. The trail was already a mile or two behind them, but they were far from lost, as the very same knowledge that Glo had tapped into to find the dilapidated shack now served to chart their escape route.

There was a break in the trees no more than fifty

yards ahead of them, and on the other side of the gap lay a road. It was a different route from the one they'd set down on, and it was in the opposite direction to the town of Crystal Lake, but if she and Trick could reach it, they might just be able—even at this late hour—to flag someone down and hitch a ride to safety.

"Try your cell," she gasped, her legs scraping through the bramble.

"It won't work," he protested.

"Do it!" Glo shouted. The moon was throwing Jason's shadow across her footsteps.

Still holding the severed head, the boy reached his left hand into his duster, took out the phone—and fumbled it. The piece of silver plastic hit the ground.

"Shit!" he cursed, bending down and scooping it up just in time to stop Jason's foot from crushing it.

Glo screamed, "Trick!"

Jason reached out and grabbed the collar of Trick's coat.

"Fuck!" the boy shouted, as he swung Pamela's head at Jason with all his might. The corpse-ball hit against the hockey mask with a muted *thwack*, and suddenly Trick was free, the collar torn off in Jason's hands.

Quickly the boy tossed the phone over to Glo, "I'm no good with one hand. You try!"

Jason was right behind them. The girl pressed the power switch and...

"I've got a signal. Trick, I've got a signal!"

"Call 911!" the boy ducked to avoid a crushing blow aimed at his windpipe.

"No," shouted Glo. "I've got the local sheriff's

number."

"I don't care if you call the fucking President!" yelled the boy. "Just do it!"

The two teenagers were desperate. For all their agility and youthfulness, the lumbering mass of Jason Voorhees continually cast its shadow over them; their capture seemed only a matter of time. And yet, in defiance of certain death, Glo skipped over some rocks, hit the speed dial and prayed.

Sheriff Haslip took one last look around the empty office. It had been a crazy night and now he was calling it quits. He was looking forward to a late session of ribs, beer and HBO. Pity about the empty bed.

He stood up behind his desk, reached for his hat—and then the phone rang. He waited a moment to see how serious the caller was. Maybe if he ignored it long enough, he could take off without having a guilty conscience. But the phone wouldn't stop ringing.

"Shit," he sighed, lifting the handset. "Sheriff's office."

He listened. And groaned.

"Yeah, sure, Jason's back," he answered wearily, "and he's killing everyone in his path— yada, yada, yada—like I've not heard that one before. Come on, Alice, give it up. I know you're angry but…"

"Who the fuck is Alice?" Glo screamed down the phone.

"What's going on?" asked Trick, barely one step

ahead of Jason.

"I dunno," panicked Glo. "He thinks I'm someone…"

"Here," Trick snatched the phone out of her hand. "Sheriff? My name's Richard Willis, please—just listen to me…"

But in concentrating on the call, Trick had let himself be distracted just long enough for…

"Watch out!" cried Glo, but her warning came too late.

Jason yanked Trick off his feet and pulled him up close. Then he coiled an arm around the boy's throat. Trick struggled; he slammed his head back into Jason's chest, but the chokehold was as tight as an elevator cable, and suddenly the boy was struggling for air. He gagged. His tongue popped out. His mouth fell open. Jason used his free hand to wrest the phone from Trick's fingers and force-fed the plastic receiver into the boy's mouth.

Trick punched and screamed—his every muffled cry going straight down the line to Sheriff Haslip—but he was less than a child in Jason's grip. Jason rammed the phone all the way down to the bottom of Trick's throat, and held it there until the boy stopped moving. Snot dribbled from Trick's nose and ran onto Jason's sleeve. The boy's face was red and puffy with asphyxiation. Tears mingled with dirt on his cheeks. Jason tossed the body aside and it crashed into a bed of ferns.

A muted voice sounded through Trick's unmoving lips. "Making a false 911 call is against the law."

Then the line went dead.

"Ungrateful bitch." Sheriff Haslip slammed the

phone down in disgust.

Jason bent down and removed his mother's head from the dead boy's fingertips. He gripped it by the hair and lifted it to where he could see it through the sable hellholes of his hockey mask. Then he stared at her. The nice lady. Beheaded.

Glo jammed her fist in her mouth because it was the only way to stop herself screaming. She'd known Trick since junior high and she'd just watched him die. Both of her friends were gone now. Trick—Z-Moll—Glo was alone against the indomitable violence of Jason Voorhees, and she didn't even know why she had journeyed to Crystal Lake in the first place. Trick? Sure, he'd always had a thing about serial killers and crazy religious cults. And Z-Moll, she was like a chameleon taking on whatever skin got her close to her boyfriend. But Glo—she had spent all her life studying the Crystal Lake murders without ever fully understanding why.

Jason snapped his gaze in Glo's direction and, severed head in hand, beat a demolition march toward her.

Glo turned and ran.

"You've got the fucking head!" she screamed. "What more do you want?"

Unfortunately, the girl was sufficiently versed in the Voorhees case to know exactly what Jason wanted. She also knew that she was less than ten yards from the road.

Gathering what energy she had left, Glo put on a final sprint, ignoring every scratch and bruise as she hared through the bushes and broke out onto the blacktop. Suddenly free from entanglement, the girl was caught by a rush of momentum. She stumbled a few steps and then fell. For a moment, she lay sprawled beneath the moonlight. But then Jason reached down with one hand, grabbed hold of her biker's jacket, and hoisted her high into the air. Glo's feet weren't even touching the asphalt when Jason coiled back his other arm, preparing to administer the death blow using the head of Pamela Voorhees as his lethal weapon.

"Please, Alice," begged Witney. "You'll get us both killed."

The vehicle swayed as Alice took a swig from the bottle of Jack sitting in her lap. She'd opened an Old No. 7 as soon as she'd got back on board the RV, and already the bottle was half empty.

"But I thought Daddy liked his girl good and loaded," she laughed. Then she hit the gas even harder and knocked back another mouthful of liquor.

The old man hadn't driven in years, and yet some buried memory had him stamping on a non-existent brake pedal. Alice was going too fast. She was drunk. The branches of the midnight trees were flashing by in the headlamps.

"For pity's sake!" he shouted.

"Shut up!" she screamed, swinging the neck of the bottle to her lips.

Witney looked on, appalled, as his daughter took hit after hit. Just like her mother. Finally he could stand no more.

"You're a disgrace," he murmured.

She laughed—a barren, mirthless rattle, "And you're fired."

"Alice!" he gasped in shock.

The young woman turned to look at him, to finish this thing once and for all, but her father was staring through the windshield. And there was fear all over his face.

She followed his gaze. "No!"

There was someone standing in the middle of the road. It was late at night, in the heart of nowhere and yet there were people standing in the middle of the road.

Alice drew in her breath and pummeled the hell out of the brakes. The van skidded; she fought for control; her father was jerked forward into his seat belt; the tires screamed in protest at the unbearable load they were forced to endure.

The RV pitched and spun and plowed head-on into Glo and Jason Voorhees.

CHAPTER SIX

Imagine ten different aircraft from ten different nations and ten different periods in history. Now fill the planes with furniture from their respective zones of departure and crash them all on top of a single ranch house: welcome to the home of Ross Feratu.

It had taken six years for the rock star to finish designing his Beverly Hills pied-à-terre; a place where minimalism, medievalism, functionalism and any other damned ism he liked all combined to form the world's most expensive vomit. Ask Ross to name the concept and he'd have called it "European" even though he would be hard pushed to find anyone from Europe prepaired to live in such a tastless mishmash of crap. But then what did Ross care? If he wanted to spend a few hundred K on a piece of Chippendale to put next to his Elvis standee, then he would—he wasn't

asking anyone else to live there. And besides, his
place was no different from his neighbors', not
even those pretentious actors who insisted on
rhyming pasta with Costa. Anyone who was
anyone in town, they all lived in their own
grotesque versions of Fort Knox.

The upkeep of Castle Feratu, however, was left
to Jaomi. She handled the caterers, the chauffeur,
the pool boy—all that crap—and Ross let her do
whatever she wanted with the lawns. In fact, he
pretty much gave her the run of the place. The
only rooms she couldn't enter without his permis-
sion were the den where he chilled, the studio
where he rocked, and the office where he did
business. Two fiancées, a former wife and count-
less staff had all been kicked into touch for
breaking that one inviolable commandment;
Ross's unscheduled guest, however, had just been
asked to wait in the office by the singer personally.

Luke Veranti sipped at his bourbon and let his
eyes roam around Feratu's inner sanctum. The
place looked like an old-fashioned library; it was
all wood paneling, and brass desk lamps and fit-
tings. One wall was taken up by an overstuffed
bookcase, while the other three were covered with
framed photos, documents and front pages from
old newspapers. Luke noticed a 1984 edition of
the *Wessex County Register*, the headline reading,
"MASS MURDERER'S BODY MISSING." Then he
looked to the left and saw a smeary black and
white photo of someone wearing a hockey mask.
Next to that was a driving license belonging to
some guy named Charles McCulloch; the document was genuine, and it had what looked like

dried blood stains on it—but who the hell was Charles McCulloch?

Luke got up and went over to browse through the books. There were hundreds of them and they were all about murder, specifically the Crystal Lake Murders. On one shelf alone he saw:

Jason Voorhees—Fact or Fiction?
Camp Crystal Lake—The Bloody Truth.
The Man Behind the Machete.
The Springwood Copycat Killer.
Who's Afraid of the Water?
Mommy Made Him Do It.

Six other books had all been written by some cash-in merchant named Thomas Jarvis.

"Admiring the collection?"

Luke turned and saw Ross standing in the doorway.

"Fuck," squawked Veranti. "You nearly gave me a bypass."

Ross closed the door and helped himself to a vodka from the drinks table. In the flesh, Ross was surprisingly tall and attractive in a curiously dysfunctional way, like a police identikit picture with insufficient room for the features—though his hair, of course, was modeled on Jason circa 1984. Unusually for someone in his profession, he didn't have a single tattoo, and when he was off duty he didn't put on a lick of makeup—not even eye pencil. Instead, he just bummed around in what looked like shop clothes: tough khakis, like the kind worn by his screwed-up Crystal Lake idol.

Ross dropped some ice in his glass and sat down behind a massive antique desk. "And to what do I owe the pleasure of your delightful company?" he asked.

Luke pointed at the smudged photo of the man in the hockey mask. "I thought you said this was fake."

"It is. Tyrone Pooley, a farmer from Blairstown, New Jersey, but it looks kinda cool. No one's got any photos of the real deal."

"You don't say," snickered Veranti.

"Hey." Luke's skepticism never failed to annoy Ross. "I had tickets for the turnbuckle action at Staples tonight. So come on, what is it that can't wait?"

There were three plush leather armchairs angled in front of Ross's desk. Luke parked his ass in one of them.

"Okay," said Veranti, "do you want the shit news or the double-shit?"

"Nice suit you're wearing."

Ross wasn't enjoying Luke's attitude at all. The compliment was a not-so-subtle warning to Veranti that, before he opened his mouth, he needed to remember who was paying the bills.

"Wish I could say the same about you," Veranti shot back. "I could do with someone to check the fucking oil."

"Okay, it's a tie." Ross sipped at his white spirit; he should have known by now not to spar with Veranti. "So what's pissing on my parade today?" He stared across the desk at Luke and readied himself for the worst.

Veranti was five foot two of compacted bile. He never wore anything but black—black roll neck sweater, sharp black suit, patent shoes—he was never out of black sunglasses and his dyed black hairline was permanently sculpted in the shape of Ayers Rock. He was also President of Veranti Entertainment, Ross's manager, and one hardnosed son of a bitch.

"Okay. Bad news first. Your album's dead."

Ross choked and spat liquor across the mahogany, "What the fuck d'you mean? It's only been out a week."

"Trust me," Luke replied in an accent that had stepped off a boat halfway between Rome and Brooklyn. "The sales curve's fallen faster than the WTC. Internet, retail, mp3—you're fucked."

The news was so unexpected, Ross found himself giggling, "Okay, uh… sure… but uh… okay, well what's the really bad news?"

"I'm canceling the tour."

Ross stopped laughing. "You're yanking my chain," he hoped.

"No. I can't book you anywhere."

"But I've always been good for the arenas. My stage show…"

"Is a crock of Eighties horse shit where you go bumping around in the dark like some egg-faced prick—that's what your fucking stage show is. It's like your fucking albums—it's just one big crock of shit, like all this bullshit you got in here. It's all about your fucking egg-man with his big, fat fucking chopper."

Ross jumped to his feet, "Hey, don't talk about Jason like that!"

"Or what?" challenged Veranti. "You'll dress your wife like him and take her up the ass? Oh, I forgot, you already did that in your last promo video."

"'Frightday 13'…" began Ross.

"Sucks," finished his manager. "Half the stations won't carry it 'cause there's too much blood on her rockets, and the other half have buried it in the jack-off slot. We got zero uplift in sales. D'you hear that, Ross? Zero."

Ross hurled the tumbler across the room. It smashed against a life size manikin of Jason that stood over in the far corner, away from the light. The design of the effigy was based on the most reliable eyewitness reports.

"Wrong answer, Luke!" he shouted. "Do you wanna come with me to the studio—"

"I don't need to see your studio."

"Take a look at my gold fucking discs—"

"I'm not interested in your discs."

"Seven platinum…"

"I know a guy in the nickel who makes 'em twenty bucks a piece."

"A whole fucking wall papered in music industry awards…"

"My dog's got no nose. How does he smell? He doesn't. He just follows all the other bitches."

Ross walked over to look at his framed Voorhees memorabilia. For all his millions, all he had were newspaper cuttings, photos, stuff that everybody owned. He'd gotten into the collector's market too late, and about the only unique original he possessed was the McCulloch driving license. Big deal.

He kept his back to Luke as he spoke.

"I've had seven albums—they've all sold millions," he tried to sound calm but his voice was brittle with anxiety. "The eighth one can't just fall off the map. It doesn't work that way. I have an audience."

Luke laughed. Only he didn't laugh as most people would, because Luke Veranti had no humor in him at all. He just made a noise—a harsh rasping sound with all the joy throttled out of it.

"Hardcore fucking lunatics who go around wearing Timothy McVeigh T-shirts," he chuckled. "That's your fucking audience—a few hundred thousand, tops. With everyone else you were just fashionable. Times change. The new kids don't give a fuck about Eighties egg-men."

Ross turned and clenched his fists, "Jason—is not—an egg!"

"Ooh, scary," Luke sniggered. Then he nodded at the tall Jason dummy standing in the corner, "Gonna get your friend to do me over easy?"

Again, that rodent scrape of a laugh drove Ross crazy. He was desperate to throw a tantrum, but knew Veranti would claim it as another interpersonal victory.

"Okay," said Ross, trying a new angle of attack, "if you're not bullshitting—if the figures really are as bad as you say—then it's gotta be the marketing."

Veranti fixed him with a cold stare, "It's gotta be the what?"

"Weak management," Ross emphasized each syllable of his spanking new missile.

"Weak management?" Luke smiled with the charm of a mafia hit man.

"Weak management," repeated the Jasonophile, rapidly gaining confidence. "You need to use more force, Luke."

Veranti groaned. "I don't believe you just said that."

Suddenly the singer walked across the office, opened the door and shouted, "Jaomi!"

And now Veranti *really* groaned. "Just what I fucking need. Now you gotta call in Yoko for backup."

While they waited for Mrs Feratu to show, Ross sat down in one of the two vacant armchairs—the one facing Veranti, which left the middle seat free.

"She needs to hear this," said Ross with exemplary neuroticism.

"I'll tell you what she needs," muttered Luke. "You're so fucking obsessed with that egg-faced prick you even dress your wife like him. What the fuck is wrong with you? She's a top-class model. Why don't you fuck her naked like any normal guy?"

The subject of Luke's rant jogged into the room.

Jaomi Marantez was the kind of woman every guy imagined when whacking off, but would never actually meet in real life. She had a blank slate perfection that men could paint their fantasies on, giving her an almost interactive beauty. To see Jaomi was to buy into her, and no one likes to walk away from an investment empty-handed.

Much as he hated her, Luke gave her the once over as she traipsed in and took the middle chair. She was wearing a pink racerback bra top and black baggy workout pants with a white stripe and drawstring.

She flicked her long blonde hair and gathered her legs up onto the seat, "What's wrong, Dwayne?"

"Fuck!" Ross whined, "Jaomi! How many times?"

She immediately realized her faux pas. "Sorry—Ross."

Veranti squeaked in amusement, "Don't mind me. I write the contracts, remember? It's in black and white. Dwayne fucking Weintraub. Deceased."

"Deceased?" she asked. "What does that mean?"

"It means," said Ross, "that my wonderful, supportive manager here seems to think I can't sell records anymore. It means he's hero-to-zeroed my fucking ass."

"Hey!" snapped Veranti. "I've always supported you. You lose eighty per cent, I lose eighty per cent; that's how it works. My job's to manage your career and that's why I'm telling you to lose the fucking egg."

Ross threw back his head and placed the palms of his hands over his eyes. "He's killing me, Jaomi. He wants me to drop Jason."

"You can't do that!" She was shocked that Luke could even consider such heresy.

"I know," Ross displayed the kind of despair normally reserved for daytime soap. "Jason's my muse, my inspiration, my—I owe him everything."

"Then you better hope he's not real," cracked Veranti, "or he'll Chapter 11 your ass in unpaid royalties."

Jaomi was far from impressed with Ross's manager. "That's right, Veranti. You just sit there and make jokes. That's what we pay you twenty per cent for."

"We?" queried Veranti with a puzzled smile. "Funny, Jaomi, but I don't recall offering to represent you. Sure, I've seen your movies—*A-cock-o-lips Now* is one of my all-time favorites—but my operation doesn't have the facility to handle your level of talent."

"I said it from day one, Veranti." It was Jaomi who now got up to fetch herself a vodka. "You're a total spunk-nut."

Luke nodded. Then he glared at the floor, "You gonna let her talk to me like that?"

"Jason stays," answered Ross firmly.

"If the egg stays," threatened Luke, "I don't."

The two men stared at each other and Jaomi stared at the two of them: the good, the bad and the indifferent. It was Veranti who broke the silence.

"Then I quit."

Without saying another word, he knocked back his drink, got up and walked out of the room.

"You leave now," Ross called after him, "and you don't come back. Not now. Not ever."

"Let him go," sniped Jaomi. "I've seen this coming a long time. The guy's a loser. Just look at the way he dresses. He rolls around LA like a fucking SWAT munchkin."

"I mean it!" Ross shouted, ignoring her.

Luke slammed the front door on his way out.

Jason's body went rolling and sliding at incredible speed along the asphalt, his limbs flailing as if on the receiving end of fifty thousand volts. His mask slammed repeatedly against the paving, his torso bounced and kicked against the road, his neck jerked and snapped in three different places—and the severed head of Pamela was sent spinning out of his grasp.

When Jason lifted Glo off her feet, the girl thought it was going to be the end of her. But, paradoxically, it had saved her life. The RV had crashed into Jason and his colossal form had absorbed most of the impact, while Glo had merely been flung to one side, her body projected with such force that the only time she felt the ground was when she landed on it.

She came down in the undergrowth, just beyond the edge of the far side of the road. Luckily, the vegetation was so thick that it cushioned her fall; she didn't seem to have anything broken. All the same, when the girl tried to sit up, she found she could hardly move. Her head was aching, she felt dizzy and confused, and there was ringing in her ears. She guessed from the first aid module of her survival course that she most probably had mild concussion; so she followed what she could remember of her training and lay still for a moment. Then she took a couple of deep breaths and promptly passed out.

"Alice!" gasped George. A sheen of perspiration coated his forehead and he was shaking all over. "That was a man! You've just run somebody over!"

The accident should have worked on Alice like a cold shower but she'd had far too much liquor to think straight.

"Shut up!" she slurred, struggling to unfasten her seat belt.

"I warned you," the old man chided. "I told you you'd get someone killed."

Alice turned and slapped her dad across the face. "I thought I told you to shut up!"

The blow was weak and poorly aimed, yet it couldn't have hurt Witney more than if it had come from a heavyweight champion.

"You—you hit me," he stammered.

"There's no time for this," she fumbled with the door handle. "We have to go check." She pushed her way out.

The old man unbuckled and went after his daughter, only to find the convoy in disarray. Behind Alice, the other drivers had done their best to respond to her emergency braking, but it still resulted in an Olympian game of Jack Straws scattered along the road. On the plus side, none of the trucks had collided and it soon became clear that no one else had been injured.

"What's going on?" asked Sparx, the first of the showmen to clamber out of his vehicle. He headed towards Alice's trailer to see what had happened, but the woman quickly got in his path.

"I want you all back in your trucks," she called. Even so, the guys kept coming, gathering in a bunch in front of her.

"What's this?" she drawled. "Did you form a union or something?"

"We just want to know what happened," Sparx said in a nasal that could only have come from Boston.

"Is there a problem?" asked Judge nervously.

The poor lamb seemed terrified. In fact, the more time Alice spent with these guys, the more she realized they were just a bunch of college kids.

"No," said Alice. "No problem. We just hit an animal, that's all."

Judge took out his cell. "Maybe we should call a vet."

Alice ran a hand through her hair.

"No!" she shouted, louder than she meant to. "No…" More quietly now. "No vet. We just gotta drag it off the road."

Minter stepped forward, "Need a hand?"

The woman looked at his tall, muscular body but shook her head, "No, Mint. Look, all of you—just go back to your trucks and wait for my signal. Dad and I'll take care of it."

Minter was unconvinced and he wanted to help. "Your old man couldn't wipe a fly off a windshield. How's he gonna lift a bear?"

But for Alice it was one question too much. "Just do as you're fucking told!" she shouted.

Judge immediately mumbled an apology and sidled back to the eighteen-wheeler; Vincenzo and Sparx hung on and watched in embarrassed silence, as Minter tried to understand what was happening.

"Listen, Alice," said the big guy reassuringly. "If you're in any kind of trouble—or Mr Witney—if any of you need anything, I—"

"You'll what?" she cut in. "Hide like you did at Crystal Lake? You too, Sparx—Vincenzo—I didn't see any of you running out of your fucking trailers when me and Dad were surrounded by an angry fucking mob."

"I… I… let me explain," began Minter, but Alice had nailed him and he seemed to deflate in front of everyone.

"Goodnight, Mint."

Alice turned and walked back towards the front of the RV, where her father was searching along the path of the headlamps, trying—but failing—to find whoever it was they'd knocked down. The old man had been too distressed by the accident to pay attention to her clash with the others; nevertheless, when Alice glanced over her shoulder and saw Minter, Sparx and Vincenzo all returning to their trucks, she heaved a sigh of relief. But then she heard a voice.

"That was no animal."

Kenton Freely stepped out of the shadows. While she'd been fending off the mutiny, he'd snuck down the side of her motorhome and had been waiting for her.

"Not now, Freely."

She tried to ignore him and went to join her father a couple of yards in front of the truck. Kenton, however, held back, so that when Alice tried to look at him she was blinded by the headlamps.

"Manslaughter," said Freely with cool insinuation, "that's at least five years."

Alice stopped and turned. Her body, still clad in the long floral dress, was caught in the twin floods of the RV.

"You look good in lights," Kenton snickered. "Maybe we should start up a new routine—a skin show. What do you think, George?"

The old man didn't answer. He was too busy hunting for the inevitable outline of a fallen figure.

"I'm talking to you, George," Kenton iterated menacingly.

After Crystal Lake, a full bottle of Jack and now a dead body in the road, Alice was in the perfect mood to take Freely on. She shielded her eyes against the beams of the truck and walked over to square off against the creep.

"Freely, why don't you just fuck off back to whatever rat-shit stink-hole you came from?"

But Freely wasn't going anywhere. He'd been with the carnival over thirty years and most of that time he'd lived on Easy Street. The ride would have been even smoother, if it wasn't for Witney's roundheel of a daughter growing up and making all kinds of problems for "Uncle Kenty." For too long now, Freely had had to bite his lip and let Alice think she'd got the upper hand. But he'd just been biding his time. He knew the lousy bitch would slip up sooner or later, and tonight, she'd just slipped up good.

"I don't think you understand what's going on here, Alice." His whole attitude was slick with blackmail. "I'm putting you in my pocket. Right where you belong."

The woman was unimpressed.

"Kenton, I could argue with you, we could fight, or I could try to reason with you but, well, I just don't have the time. You're fired."

Freely looked over her shoulder and spoke to the old man. "Is that right, George?" he asked. "Is she firing me?"

Alice didn't know what the lowlife was up to, but suddenly, even through her drunken haze, she could feel the swirling of undercurrents. Kenton was playing some kind of game—a game involving her father.

"George," repeated Kenton. "I said…"

But the old man was oblivious to the dynamics of the moment. He simply stared down the road and said, almost absent-mindedly, "Go back to your truck, Kenton."

Freely took a lungful of air and was about to let loose, when suddenly he fell quiet. Alice could see there was something going on behind his eyes. He was weighing up the odds, wondering whether to go for the big one or not. But what stunt was the bastard going to pull?

"Okay, George," Kenton squeezed out a smile to show everyone who was boss. "It'll keep."

Then he gave Alice one final stare before slinking back in the direction of the pickup. Alice waited until Kenton was out of sight before going up to her dad. She wanted to ask the old man what was going on between him and Freely, but now was neither the time nor the place. They had to go find the guy she'd killed.

Glo murmured as she gradually regained a muffled form of consciousness. She needed help. She needed to see a doctor. She needed to go someplace. But why?

The girl tried to think. She tried to remember, but the concussion made everything seem distant and fuzzy. She had a vague memory of running away from someone. She was trying to get somewhere. She was trying to get to—the road! That was it. She was trying to get to the road because she wanted to get away from someone. But who?

Just then she heard two voices—an elderly man and a woman—coming from the blacktop. Glo tried to call for help but her voice was so pathetic she could barely hear it herself.

Haltingly, the girl got up and tried to walk, but almost immediately her head started spinning and her legs began to give way. She steadied herself against a tall pine, but even that didn't stop vertigo from overwhelming her. The ground swayed and pitched in all directions, and Glo knew she had no chance of making the simple five paces back to the asphalt.

Out on the road, the old man and the woman continued talking; they had no idea the girl was so close. And as Glo clutched desperately at the tree for support, a bank of cloud scudded across the moon and plunged the frightened teenager into even darker isolation.

"There!" Alice pointed out a shape lying in the road.

She and her father had walked an incredible fifty to a hundred yards before finding anything: it didn't seem possible anyone could have been thrown so far.

"Who is it?" George's cane tapped on the paving as he hurriedly limped along beside his daughter.

Alice looked back towards the carnival vehicles; their headlamps were only just useful at this distance, and now some damn clouds were blocking out the moon.

"I don't know," she answered, frustrated. "It's too dark."

"Wait," George reached into his jacket pocket. "I have my pen torch."

Then he hobbled forward and shined the light from his novelty key-chain down onto the split hockey mask of Jason Voorhees. The maniac lay in a misshapen tangle on the asphalt and was completely motionless.

"Omigod, omigod, Jesus," Alice said excitedly. Then she raised a hand to her lips and tried to stifle a spontaneous laugh.

"Alice, are you insane?" her father was outraged. "This is no laughing matter. Pull yourself together, girl."

But the woman couldn't stop at all, and very quickly she broke into laughter at the sheer incredulity of it all.

"Do you know who it is?" she spluttered.

"How could anyone possibly know?" replied her father, his whole body now a mass of anxiety. "And what difference does it make?"

"What difference?" she whooped. "It makes every damn difference! This is the break we've been waiting for."

She grabbed the small flashlight from her father's hand, bent down beside the spread-eagled body and turned the beam full on the hockey mask.

"Dad, it's Jason Voorhees. The Crystal Lake Killer. We're rich!"

Glo moved away from the tree and did her best not to trip as she stumbled through the bushes. The girl was still badly disoriented, but she had to get to the road. She had to do something, or say something, or warn someone about something—it was all muddled up, but she knew she had to go forward.

One foot, then another—Glo was only two steps away from the sunken verge when she saw the head of Mrs Voorhees lying on the ground in front of her. And it was then that the clouds parted, throwing moonlight on the head with all the willful guile of the Devil playing dice.

Sheriff Haslip was amazed to find himself still hanging round the office. He knew the phone call was a hoax, he'd taken dozens of them over the years and they were always the same. It was a Crystal Lake tradition. Every summer, the fruit-cakes came to town and suddenly Jason was alive again. Admittedly, the strangling act had been quite convincing—but then if carny people couldn't put on a good performance, who could?

For the tenth time since taking the call, Haslip kicked himself for misreading Alice so badly. Then he swiveled his chair round to look at the map mounted on the wall behind his desk. The sheriff wasn't born locally but he'd seen what was left of the old case files, so he knew where the murders were supposed to have taken place.

"Surprise, surprise." he muttered.

The road nearest to the abandoned camp just happened to be the one he'd sent the carnival along. It was definitely time to call it a day.

The sheriff crossed the room, flicked the light switch and walked out of the building. But back inside, the map on the wall stubbornly refused to comply with Haslip's cynicism. The old camp, the roads, the lake—all these places were clearly marked as undeniable facts.

* * *

"Just think about it," Alice spread her hands as if delineating a new banner over the gateway to the show, "Doktor Geistmann's Carnival of Terror featuring the Body of Jason Voorhees."

"This is lunacy!" gasped her father. "If what you said before is true, Voorhees would have to be sixty years old. The police would have caught him long before now."

The old man's logic sent an upper-cut crashing into his daughter's jaw, but she was already feeling punchy from the whiskey she'd knocked back.

"I don't know," she griped. "I'm not a fucking expert. But if some jerk goes stomping round Crystal Lake in a fucking hockey mask, that'll do for me."

"You're not making sense, child," the old man protested.

His fear-fractured mind could not understand how the scenario had shifted one-eighty from the two of them needing to save a casualty's life—or at the very least facing a prison sentence—to suddenly seeing this disaster as the salvation of the show, an opportunity lined with nothing but hot, fat greenbacks.

"I got it all worked out," Alice was almost breathless with excitement. "It's like you say—no one thinks he's real, so no one'll miss him!"

"But surely you intend to report this to the authorities?"

It seemed to Witney that the nightmare was growing in madness. And it was. Because as the clouds sailed clear of the moon, neither George nor his daughter noticed Jason sitting up behind them.

* * *

The voices had grown louder; not because Glo was any closer—truth was, she hadn't moved an inch since finding the head—but because the people who were talking had just started to shout.

Glo stared forward through the trees. Her concentration was shot and her vision kept going in and out of focus, but she could just make out this crazy farmwoman, giving a hard time to some dapper old guy leaning on a walking stick.

"We can have him ready for tomorrow's show," the woman shouted.

"Alice, I forbid it," the old man tried to sound equally angry, but was cut short by a coughing fit. "We need to call the police. Maybe Sheriff Haslip…"

"Forget it Dad. Jason's our property now."

Jason?

The name echoed and rebounded through the cobwebs of Glo's mind, distorting and resounding in an opera of bloodstained mortality.

Jason…

Jason…

"Jason!" she gasped and she looked over to see the supermaniac sitting upright in the road. He was getting ready to kill and kill again, and the two poor bastards standing right beside him were too caught up in their bitching to realize they were already dead.

Glo raised her arms and tried to cry out, but she barely managed a whisper before nausea overtook her and she dropped to her knees. A second later and she slumped forward, her breasts landing on the severed head of Pamela Voorhees and canceling out the moonlight.

Without making a single sound, Jason's upper body fell back down on to the asphalt and he was immobile once more.

Though every fiber of common sense shouted at him to walk away, George was gradually coming round to Alice's way of thinking. He had too much of the showman in his blood—and he didn't want Alice to know it, but his main worry now was making sure they wouldn't be caught.

"But what of the others?" he whispered. "What if they've heard anything?"

Alice shrugged. "What'll they do? Can us and cut off their dreams? I don't think so."

"Well, why don't we leave him here?" the old man felt compelled to play devil's advocate. "Go on and call from a phone booth. That way, they won't be able to trace us and you won't have to go to prison."

But Alice could see right through him, "Dad, look—the kids'll do whatever we tell them. We're so fucking under the radar, if one of them goes to the cops with some story about kidnapping Jason's body they'll laugh him all the way to the nut-house."

"And they'd be right to laugh," said her father stubbornly. "This man can't possibly be Jason Voorhees."

"Well, whoever he is," Alice could tell she was almost home, "fact, fiction or phony—he's part of the show now."

George tapped his foot on the hard surface of the road. He was undecided. Neither of them had seen

Jason sit up and sit back down again. They were totally unaware of the danger they were about to try to deal with. So for now, there was only one more test the old man could think of.

"Are you certain he's dead?" he asked timorously.

Alice laughed, knowing what was coming, "Oh, and I wonder who's the only one here trained in first aid."

"Well, I wasn't going to say anything," added George with a twinkle in his eye, and just for the slightest moment father and daughter shared in the warmth of good honest humor.

Alice took a moment to prepare and then passed Witney the pen torch, "Here—hold this while I lift the mask."

George took the light and tried to keep it steady as she knelt down on the road. She paused for a moment. Then she placed her fingers on the white plastic of the immortal face shield and slowly— ever so slowly—removed the puck guard from Jason's head.

"Christ."

The one word was so understated that George couldn't resist taking a look for himself.

"Good Lord!" he gasped.

Alice looked up. "Still want me to check for a pulse?"

Glo tried to move. She tried to get up and made every effort to call out, but she was too far gone. Still lying sprawled over the head of Mrs Voorhees, the young girl from Seattle slipped irresistibly into the comfort of sleep.

George lent moral support while Alice dragged Jason back towards the RV. She'd locked her hands under Jason's shoulders and was struggling to pull him inch by sweaty grunting inch. Jason's boots scraped noisily against the stony surface.

"Almost there," said the old man, rounding the sentence off with a couple of loud coughs as if to remind Alice of his unsuitability for physical exercise.

The woman shot him a dirty look, and wrestled Jason's bulk up on board the trailer. As she laid the killer out along the central aisle, her father resumed his place in the front passenger seat. The old man was flooded with doubt, and yet there was something irresistible about his daughter's proposition—his mind suddenly flashed back to the video image of Jaomi Marantez with a hockey mask on her face and stage blood on her breasts. But just as swiftly, he blanked his impulses and put the dark side of his imagination back in the cage where it belonged. The last time George Arthur Witney had given full vent to his baser instincts, it had ended in disaster.

Alice flopped into the driver's seat beside him.

For the first time in a long time, she felt almost optimistic. She'd successfully taken control of the show and she'd just hired its new star attraction. If her dad ever complained, she'd just remind him he was party to an unreported manslaughter and that, if she went down, he'd join her and would never smell the flowers again. No, for once, things were positively looking up. But then, Alice didn't know that Kenton Freely had been hiding in the darkness and had seen and heard everything.

Shortly the carnival was once more on the move. One by one the four trucks started their engines, and one by one they rolled past the broken pieces of hockey mask lying in the road.

CHAPTER SEVEN

The drums beat with a fervor that was turning the air into heat. Every note they played was urgent, every pattern they spun so complex as to banish all thought in favor of delirium. An uninformed listener would have dismissed the tropical rhythms as mere noise—a furious cacophony of random sounds—while someone with more catholic tastes would have hailed the performance as a virtuoso display in percussive world music. But to Special Agent Kyler, the breakneck interplay of the three handcrafted drums—the heavy manman tambou, the medium-sized segon and the small, high-pitched boula—meant only one thing: death.

She reached inside the jacket of her stylish mocha pant suit and took the GLOCK 22 out of its shoulder holster.

When she'd first joined the Bureau, the guys had recommended the GLOCK 23. They'd told her it was lighter and smaller than the 22, making it easier to conceal, but what they'd really meant to say was that a model with four per cent less kick was more "suitable" for a woman; just like the "small of the back" holster they'd offered her, because a normal side holster would probably ride up her hips. In response, Michelle Kyler had given her advisors a lesson of her own.

"Guns are for shooting, not hiding," she'd said, adding, "and, for your information, studies have shown that women can draw faster from a shoulder holster than men. The female rib cage has a natural slope better suited to shoulder holster design, and women have greater physical flexibility. But if you guys want to go on wearing cup-less bras because you think they look macho, don't let me stop you."

Then she'd proceeded to shoot perfect score after perfect score both on the range and on Hogan's Alley—the realistic training environment at the FBI Academy in Quantico. And that same deadly accuracy had served her time and again throughout her eight years working law enforcement. Kyler didn't have a name for her semiautomatic, but whenever she felt its stippled grip in the palm of her hand, it was like being in the presence of an old friend. The only difference being that the GLOCK 22 never let her down.

She stopped and listened to where the music was coming from; the condemned tenement block was vast, and any mistake now could be critical. But the bare walls gave off echoes that made exact determination difficult. Worse, the drums had just altered their tempo in a way that told Kyler she

was running out of time. Because just as the great
fictional detective Sherlock Holmes was suppos-
edly an expert in recognizing different varieties of
tobacco ash, Michelle Kyler was a very real
authority on the sinister music that was pounding
in anticipation of the imminent sunrise. Indeed,
she was so accomplished in her studies that she
understood the patterns racing off the goatskin
drumheads just as clearly as if they were in Morse
code.

The rhythms spoke to her of their origin in ani-
mistic religious ceremonies practiced in thirteenth
century Africa. They invoked images of traveling,
some three hundred years later, in French and
Spanish slave ships to an island which Christo-
pher Columbus named La Isla Española—an
island abundant with natural riches, but where
manpower was in short supply, after the native
population of two million Taino-Arawak people
had been all but wiped out under fifteen years of
brutal European rule. The drums also suggested
the bloody revolution of 1791, when the priest
Boukman Dutty set his African kinsmen on a violent path that culminated in a declaration of
independence in 1804; the victorious slaves
calling their new nation by the island's original
Taino-Arawak name of Haiti.

And now, in the year 2005, those same rhythms,
those same primal drums, were charging the night
with mystery. Still distant, still veiled in darkness
and spurring men on to deeds of fanatical devotion, still invoking the menace of the most feared
and misunderstood religion in the world. For
when the three *rada* drums spoke aloud, in this

derelict building on the northern outskirts of Buffalo, NY, Michelle Kyler heard the unmistakable
voice of vodou.

She tiptoed across the lobby to an old fire door.
The door was falling off its hinges, but the slim
brunette managed to squeeze through and,
without making a sound, came out at the bottom
of a concrete stairwell which, like the rest of the
block, was decorated with graffiti, stale urine and
trash.

Kyler glanced at her watch. The music was
already telling her that dawn was less than ten
minutes away but she had to be sure.

5:46.

The victim had approximately seven minutes to
live.

The federal agent wished she was wrong, but
the rhythms were specific: they were designed to
summon the *lwa*—the spirit—of Baron Samdi,
chief of all the dead. At five fifty-three precisely
the sun would break the horizon, the drumming
would reach its climax, and the third abductee in
four months would be killed in a ritual homicide.

Suddenly, no longer caring whether her shoes
made any noise, Kyler sprang up the steps two at
a time. It wasn't possible for the kidnappers to
hear her over the drums, so all she had to worry
about was whether or not they'd posted a lookout.
But by the time she'd reached the fifth floor—
where the music was loudest—Kyler had seen no
sign of anyone, which meant the killers were confident they wouldn't be discovered.

Gun at the ready, Kyler eased open the fire door
onto the main hallway through the level, and was

so deafened by the sharp increase in volume that she wanted to cover her ears. The drums were impossibly loud. Dust fell from the ceiling as the plaster vibrated with staccato insistence. The music was frenetic, overpowering, calling down the *lwa* of Baron Samdi, whose symbol was the cross and whose natural domain was the grave-yard.

Again Kyler paused, only this time it was to regulate her breathing.

Firearms 101: unless you can manage the physi-ological effects of stress in a survival situation, your complex motor skills deteriorate, your depth perception and peripheral vision are seriously reduced, and you may even experience hypervigi-lance—a stress response that will cause you either to freeze or to behave irrationally, as in a state of panic. Any one of these problems can turn a marksman on the range into a corpse on the streets.

A few seconds later, Kyler was perfectly calm. She flexed the fingers of her right hand round the grip of the GLOCK and raised her left hand so that she could check the time. 5:47. Six minutes left.

The musty corridor ran the entire length of the building, completely dark save for a few rectan-gles of pale gray where apartments were left open to admit the first feeble scrapings of dawn through broken windows. Kyler had left her flashlight in the trunk of her car, but the drums were leading her to the second door on the right as effectively as a neon arrow. And if that wasn't enough of a lead, the kidnappers had chalked a large death's head on the door—just like they had at the scenes of the previous vodou homicides.

There had been two murders in the series so far: computer technician Victor Carullo in February and personal trainer Saul Gulacy in March. Both men had been kidnapped early in the evening, both taken to abandoned properties on the edge of town—Carullo to the north and Gulacy to the east—and both killed at sunrise on the morning following their abduction.

Officially, the deaths were outside Kyler's jurisdiction. They had happened over in Buffalo, which had its own field office, while Kyler was based in a resident agency in Corning, NY—a small satellite branch that reported into Albany. But then, Kyler never paid any attention to territorial boundaries during her regular trawls through the National Crime Information Center database.

For as long as Kyler had been with the Bureau, she'd spent one night a week alone in front of a computer terminal, searching through hundreds of new cases added daily to the NCIC, banking on the rare instance that one of them might demonstrate the features she was looking for. It was on one such evening that she'd recently discovered the files on the unsolved Carullo and Gulacy homicides.

A consultant ethnologist had given his firm opinion that both men had been murdered as part of a vodou sacrificial rite. Crime scene photos showed both bodies lying gagged and bound in the exact center of a vèvè—a large symbolic drawing traced on the ground in cornmeal. According to vodou mythology, each lwa had its own vèvè, the symbol acting as the spirit's signature and used in rituals to attract the spirit to the earthly plane. In the case of the Buffalo murders, the vèvè used was that of Baron Samdi.

Autopsy reports stated that both victims had been sedated with a plant-based narcotic of unknown origin, both had been killed by a knife blow to the heart and both had undergone post mortem dismemberment during which the heart, lungs, liver and brain were all removed and taken from the crime scene. The whereabouts of these missing organs remained unknown. Furthermore, both bodies had been partially eaten; saliva DNA and bite mark tests had proved conclusively that those responsible for the injuries were human. Other trace evidence suggested there were three or four abductors, all Caucasian, working as a team.

Alone, none of these facts would have caught Kyler's attention—the history of crime was replete with homicides of a similarly occult nature. However, she was surprised to see no mention in the file of two other obvious features.

Fact one: both murders were carried out on the first night of the full moon in their respective months. Fact two: the killers were using the homicides to draw a giant cross—the symbol of Baron Samdi—over the city of Buffalo. Carullo was killed to the north, Gulacy to the east, and in April, the killers had failed to kill Bob Reed to the south.

Like the two men before him, Reed had been kidnapped and taken to a deserted warehouse, but somehow he'd managed to break free. In the ensuing struggle, Reed was stabbed three times, but survived just long enough to dial 911. His call had been recorded.

"Gotta help—please, I'm bleeding... They got me... Voodoo... Tried to kill me... Dead people... Zombies... They're alive."

A police dispatch found Reed's body lying outside a call booth, while an extensive search of the neighborhood uncovered the place of the intended sacrifice. But it was on reading a transcript of the man's dying words that Kyler had decided to get involved.

By rights, she should have gone to her boss, Landau, and offered Buffalo advice through the normal channels. But the killers were operating a monthly program, so Kyler simply didn't have time to follow correct procedure. She'd tracked the gang down solely by relying on hunches and her knowledge of vodou—a line of investigation that any decent defense attorney would have turned into a charge of harassment.

Also there was another reason—more important than her selfless burning of the rulebook—why Kyler had gone solo. Reed had mentioned zombies, the living dead. If such beings truly existed, Special Agent Kyler needed to see them. Needed to know. The only guaranteed way of doing that was to make sure she was present at their next scheduled appearance.

So here she was risking her career, her future, and even her life, drawn by the lure of vodou drums. Procedure demanded that she immediately withdraw and request backup, but Kyler wasn't listening. She crept forwards. One step, two steps—the music grew even louder. She pressed her back against the wall and breathed deeply, counting to herself in four-second loops. Her watch read 5:51.

Lifting the gun in both hands, she got ready to kick open the door. She decided to adopt the isosceles shooting stance: arms forward, head low, legs apart, shoulders hunched, chest turned to face the target.

Inside, the drums were locking astral thunder with the lwa of Baron Cimetière, the cemetery baron: Baron Samdi.

"Vodou…" they hammered. "Vodou…"

Suddenly, Kyler heard a faint moan. Muffled. Gagged. The cries of their latest victim. Her LED flipped to 5:52. Less than sixty seconds before the knife stabbed into a pumping, beating heart.

She breathed once, twice, tightened her hold on the GLOCK, then spun away from the wall and kicked the door wide open.

"Federal agent!"

Kyler had less than a second to make sense of the unreal tableau arrayed before her.

The door opened into a small living room. A naked man lay on the floor. He'd already suffered a number of superficial cuts, and his blood was mingling with the yellowish cornmeal of the *vèvè* to form a sickly paste. He was bound at the wrists and ankles, and a squat wooden phallus had been plugged into his mouth. As soon as he saw Kyler, the man tried to call out but his screams were muffled, leaving only the arching of his torso to convey the horror of his predicament.

Outside the *vèvè*, the floorboards were peppered with short black candles, the waxen stubs releasing a peculiar odor that reminded Kyler of incense, while standing in the corners were four electronic speakers whose ceremonial function was to blast a surround sound recording of vodou drums into the center of the room.

Kyler noticed two doors in the wall facing her. One led to the bathroom and the other opened onto a kitchen area. Both doors were ajar and someone could easily have been hiding on the other side of them; but of more immediate concern to the federal agent was the maniac dancing over the kidnap victim, terrorizing him with near-miss slashes of an ornamental dagger.

The killer writhed and chanted in time with the music, seemingly oblivious to Kyler's warning, and he was attired exactly as she knew he would be: black tuxedo, black pants, top hat. His face was daubed with white paint to give his already pale skin an even more corpse-like appearance, and his eyes were concealed behind sunglasses. To all intents and purposes this man, with his sadistic blade painting, was the living embodiment of Baron Samdi.

Special Agent Kyler, however, knew him by another name.

"Carlton Wallace," she shouted, struggling to be heard above the tribal cacophony, "I'm placing you under arrest."

And it was at that point that the zombies shuffled into the room.

Two came from the kitchen and one from the bathroom—three men dressed in rags, their skin unnaturally bleached and their eggshell eyes devoid of any color. Drool spilled from their sagging mouths

as they shambled forwards, their shocking appearance distracting the agent who had been awake all
night, and who was gradually succumbing to the
soporific effects of the drugged candles.

Baron Samdi spun on the ball of one foot and
howled with laughter as he prepared to flick the
dagger into Kyler's face.

Kyler made a tactical assessment. Four oppo-
nents all less than three yards away: she was in
the wrong stance and should have had the gun in
one hand instead of two. All the same, the Baron
posed the most critical threat, and there was
plenty of time to fire a bullet straight between his
eyes.

Michelle squeezed the trigger and—

The .40 caliber round exploded through the left
lens of Wallace's shades and drilled a hole through
to the back of his skull. The Baron was dead even
before he started to fall, and when his body hit the
deck it extinguished exactly thirteen candles.

Kyler was furious with herself for putting the
shot an inch to the left of where she'd aimed it.
Her poor choice of stance was about to backfire as
the zombies suddenly screeched into life and
came diving for her.

She tried to bring the gun around, but one of the
zombies grabbed hold of her forearm and pushed
it up into the air, causing both arms to snap vertical and her second bullet to hit the ceiling. And
while the shot was going wide, a second zombie
punched Kyler in the gut and the third landed a
crushing sidekick just below her right knee.

The agent cried out in pain and dropped the
GLOCK to the floor, just as the third zombie hit

her with another kick square across the chest. The blow sent Kyler stumbling through the open door and back out into the hallway, where she slammed against the far wall before falling down on her ass.

She shook her head and tried to regain some focus.

Her gun was back inside the apartment, resting on the floor. She could see the kidnap victim struggling against his restraints and Baron Samdi lying dead with a bullet in his brain. But the three zombies were coming out to finish her, so if Kyler was ever going to find out whether or not the creatures were real, now was the time.

Pretending to be more stunned than she really was, Kyler snuck a hand inside her jacket pocket and braced herself as the three undead assailants fell upon her. Their hands grabbed at her clothes—ripping, pulling scratching. She tried to shield herself, but the thirty shredding fingernails were coming in too fast. The drums built to a crescendo as the third zombie—the one who'd kicked her into the corridor—bent down, grabbed her shoulders and pinned them back against the wall. Then he leaned forward. His lips parted and his jaws opened wide, baring two rows of perfect teeth.

"Now!" shouted Kyler, pulling a hand full of salt out of her pocket and ramming it into the zombie's dripping maw. The tiny crystals were hardly standard issue but the traditional way to defeat a zombie, according to Haitian folklore, was to put salt in its mouth. This was the acid test.

The other two creatures stood back, trying to make sense of what Kyler was doing, but the zombie with the white powdered tongue coughed, choked, spat and then laughed.

"You stupid fucking bitch," he sneered, chewing on the salt, very much a human being and very much alive. Then he screamed at Kyler and all she could see was his open mouth hurtling towards her face.

As she came to, the first thing Glo noticed was a sharp pain in her ribs. She didn't know if it was bruising or just early morning stiffness, but it was all she could think of as she yawned, rubbed her eyes and climbed sluggishly to her feet.

She'd been sleeping on the forest floor all night. Her clothes were damp and now, in the early morning light, she could see just how dirty they were. But how did they get that way? Glo knew she'd come to Crystal Lake with her friends, but after that everything was hazy.

"Trick!" she shouted, her voice shrill against the chirruping of the dawn chorus. "Z-Moll!" she tried again, but there was no reply.

The girl massaged her aching chest and looked down to where she'd been sleeping. She expected to see a big rock lying there, but what she found was the head of Pamela Voorhees.

Suddenly her mind's eye was sent hurtling through a vortex of twenty-twenty memory. She remembered everything: the trucker, the voice in her head, the cabin with that horrible shrine, the death of her two friends, and Jason. Jason Voorhees was alive. He'd killed Trick and Z-Moll.

Their bodies were over in the other side of the woods.

Glo ran out onto the road and found herself standing in the middle of a spaghetti of skid marks. The final piece of the puzzle fell into place.

"The Winnebago!" she gasped, clutching her hair. "It hit me and Jason. And they—the morons. Oh God, they took Jason!"

Panic began to infect her voice as she flitted back and forth across the asphalt, trying to pluck key words from the fog of her previous night's concussion.

"There was a woman and a man, an old man— that's it! They were arguing about something. Now what was it—what were they saying?"

She knew the answer was buried somewhere in her mind and she could feel it getting closer. If only she could make the final synaptic connection.

"A carnival!" she shouted, shaking her head. "A freaking sideshow! The idiots! They're all dead!"

Glo looked up and down the road, but there wasn't a vehicle in sight, so she took out her cell-phone—her mind flooded by sudden memories of Trick dying, choking on his own receiver—and pressed the "on" switch. She hadn't used the cell once since leaving Seattle so the power had to be good, but would she still have a signal?

"Yes!"

Her first thought was to speed dial the local sheriff's office, but then she remembered how well that had gone last night and thumped 911. Her call was answered right away.

"They can't help you, dear," said Pamela Voorhees through the earpiece. "No one can. You're too late."

Glo screamed in shock and threw the phone to the ground. Almost immediately, she made a move to pick it up again, but the cell was broken. She turned and glared in the direction of the severed head.

"This is all your fault, you old bitch!" she snarled and ran back to where the head was lying, fully intending to stomp on Pamela until there was nothing left of her. But when Glo raised her trail boot, she caught sight of the shriveled eye sockets and was transfixed. Her foot hovered in mid-air as the cadaverous gaze held her against her will.

Back on the road, Pamela's laughter rang out of the shattered cellphone.

The kidnap victim wriggled across the bare floor and kicked his bound feet in unison, brushing the GLOCK 22 and sending it sliding out into the corridor.

Kyler was now lying on her back. One of the zombies was gripping her left calf and trying to bite it, another was clumsily sprawled across her body—his generous catsuit of fat helping to keep her off balance—and the third was still recovering from having four teeth broken by her head butt. The salt in his wounds just had to hurt.

But as soon as the gun skidded within reach, Kyler took hold of it, put it against the temple of the obese phony, and decorated the hallway with his rose drops. At the sound of the shot, the zombie who'd been struggling to get his teeth through her polyester cotton pants pulled away and tried to stand up. In doing so, he conveniently lined up for bullets four and five straight through the heart.

At this point, Kyler should have advised the remaining zombie—the salty kickboxer—of his Miranda right to remain silent. After all, he was no longer posing a threat, just holding his mouth and whining. He wept even more when bullet number six entered his right kneecap, and shut the fuck up when bullet number seven hit him between the eyes.

Four perfect shots from a reclining position, with Kyler straining to lift her head and shoulders off the ground while trapped beneath a dead whale. That took skill.

She crawled out from under the quivering corpse and checked herself for injury. There were scratches, bruises, some bite indentation but nothing serious. The kidnap victim called to her through the phallus and raised his limbs to suggest she might want to untie him. Exhaling with a sudden decrease in stress, Kyler walked back into the ceremonial apartment.

"And you can shut up."

She fired shot number eight into the CD player and, at last, the vodou drums were halted. The abrupt silence had an eerie effect; somehow the bodies of the Baron and his three lackeys suddenly seemed more real.

Again, the kidnap victim wordlessly urged her assistance.

Kyler smiled in apology and, returning the GLOCK to its holster, bent down to untie his wrists. Suddenly the apartment exploded with heavy footfalls, and Kyler found herself staring into the squat barrels of four Heckler & Koch MP 5 submachine guns.

"Put your hands in the air!" barked a voice.

Kyler looked back at the victim and shrugged. They'd just been "rescued" by a SWAT team.

It was shaping up to be a beautiful morning. The skies were blue, the temperature was perfect—warm with a cooling breeze—and the clean woodland air made for an invigorating tonic.

Glo sang as she marched along the side of the road, hands holding the straps of her backpack, her jaunty girl-scout demeanor at odds with her Goth styling. She'd been trying to hitch a ride for the last couple of hours, but so far there'd been no takers. One bastion of the local community had even gone to the trouble of winding down his window and calling her a "fucking weirdo" as he'd driven by.

There was another car coming right now—Glo could hear its engine rise gently behind her. Almost out of desperation, the girl extended a thumb. She wasn't optimistic, but there was somewhere she badly needed to be, and time was running out.

The metallic cerise Lexus pulled up a few yards ahead of her.

Hardly believing her luck, Glo ran to the passenger door just as the driver leaned across and pushed it open.

"Where you headed?" he asked.

The driver was a smoothly handsome man in his late twenties. Judging from his white Dior shirt, Italian cut pants and excessive hair gel, Glo guessed he was traveling on business—an executive of some kind.

"Hunt Ridge," she answered, placing one hand on the door and one hand on the chassis, to dissuade the man from pulling away. "That is, if it's not too inconvenient."

"Well, I can take you halfway," he offered. "If I drop you at Reculver—"

"Reculver will be just fine," Glo interrupted perhaps a little too enthusiastically, but then she noticed the driver was frowning. "Is something wrong?" she asked.

The driver eased back in his seat and grinned apologetically, "No... err... it's just... I don't do mornings."

How could he explain to the girl that the way she talked just didn't fit the way she looked? When he'd thrown open the door to the kid in the biker jacket and the black baggy pants, he'd expected to find her cool or full of snap; he certainly didn't expect her to act like his mom. And why was there blood on her mouth?

"Oh, I quite understand," answered Glo, lifting the backpack off her shoulders. "My son's the same. It's all I can do to get him started each day."

The driver tried not to show it, but Glo's reply knocked him sideways. Her *son*? She was only fifteen or sixteen herself. Quickly, he tried to get off the subject. He nodded at her pack.

"You wanna put that in the trunk?" he asked, trying to sound casual.

Glo snatched the bag close to her chest and a palsy of hatred spewed her face. But when she saw how oddly the driver was looking at her, she forced her mouth into a smile.

"No—no, thank you," she said, relaxing her grip on the backpack. "If it's all right, I'll just keep it on my lap."

"Suit yourself," replied the man warily.

Glo paused, half expecting him to change his mind about the ride. Instead, he held out his hand.

"The name's Elliot," he said.

The girl smiled and shook his hand, "Pleased to meet you, Elliot." Then she took her place in the passenger seat and reached for the seatbelt. "My name's Pamela."

Elliot watched as she finished buckling up. "Play basketball, Pam?"

At first, the possessed teenager didn't know what he was talking about, but then she saw him staring at the large, spherical shape bulging through her backpack and she began to laugh.

"Something like that," she chuckled, patting the severed head. "A healthy body makes a healthy mind, I always say."

With that she closed the door, and very shortly the two ill-matched traveling companions were putting Crystal Lake behind them.

When Kyler had parked around the corner from the condemned block, less than thirty minutes ago, the streets had been deserted; but now, as she stared out through the main door and squinted into the daylight, the area was swarming with emergency response units.

Police officers had set up road blocks at both ends of the street and were cordoning off the building. Crime scene investigators were working inside, busily recording the bloody aftermath of the federal agent's successful rescue operation. The SWAT team members had exited the building and were now getting ready to leave, visibly annoyed that some "breast-fed" had spoiled their fun. Next to the SWAT truck, a couple of forensic experts were donning protective overalls, getting ready to go inside the apartment in search of every minute piece of trace evidence they could lay their tweezers on. A police helicopter was making its presence felt on everybody's eardrums as it circled the derelict apartments.

Kyler stepped out into the open air and gave herself a moment to adjust. Across the way, two paramedics were trying to persuade the kidnap victim onto a gurney, but the poor guy had already spent all night lying on his back. Kyler herself had already been checked out and had been given the all clear: none of the zombie bites had broken skin and her other wounds were all small change. She wasn't even suffering from shock.

Unfortunately, that last fact left her open to grilling by local detectives. It seemed that senior figures from the city police were arriving every five minutes; each wanting to see that the vodou homicides really had been solved, and each wanting to talk to the federal agent who'd solved them. But, just as Kyler expected, her "from nowhere" investigation was kicking up a stink— so much so that she found herself wondering if her law enforcement peers wouldn't have preferred the murders to continue.

Whatever the problem, Kyler had been able to deflect their questions by saying she needed time to collect her thoughts; unfortunately, she knew any respite was merely a postponement. Two hours from now the FBI agent, who had single-handedly broken Baron Samdi's pattern of death, would be back in Corning getting ready to submit a full report. And that's when the shit would really hit the fan.

"Kyler!"

She turned and saw a familiar figure running towards her. He was around five eleven, medium build, clean-shaven, and wore a stiff navy blue suit and black shoes that shone from good, old-fashioned grooming. By and large, the man's appearance was indistinct, but his eyes were uncannily green—the irises almost uniform in color—and his face had a boyish quality that knocked five years off his actual twenty-four.

Michelle groaned. The last thing she needed was the puppy-dog yapping of her unofficial junior "partner," Special Agent Cory Tolleson.

"What are you doing here?" she asked, surprised to hear herself sounding so tired.

"More to the point," he replied, "what are you doing here? I can't believe you went in there without me. I thought we were a team."

"I received a tip-off…" she began.

"Bullshit," Tolleson cut in. "You've been working this case for weeks. And don't try to lie. I've been sitting outside your apartment, covering your back every night."

Kyler felt like one of the zombies had just punched her in the gut again. "You've been spying on me?"

"Good job I did," replied Tolleson without a hint of embarrassment. "As soon as I heard the shots, I called for backup."

"So it was you," she said with relief. "That question's been bugging me since the SWAT team showed."

"Whatever. Landau's going to want your ass over this."

The sudden mention of her boss caused Michelle to groan a second time, but just then she caught her reflection in the window of a squad car. Her face, hands and white blouse were all spattered with blood—she didn't realize she looked so awful. Then she turned to Tolleson and saw his young face lined with concern.

"They were just men in make up," she sighed, letting her shoulders fall. "I don't know if they believed in what they were doing or not, but I saw nothing to suggest paranormal phenomena."

"Does that mean we're friends?" asked Cory.

Kyler turned back to look up at the skeletal slab of brick she'd just escaped from. "I was sure I'd find something this time—some proof."

"You're making a lot of enemies," he said, whistling through his teeth. "One thing about being new is everyone gives you their advice."

"Oh?" she queried, lifting her eyes. "What do they say about me?"

"Nothing you don't already know," he answered, holding her gaze.

She rubbed a finger across the bridge of her nose. "I'm losing my perspective, right?"

"Right."

"Too much of a loner."

"Yep."

"I could have had a great career but I don't have the correct attitude."

"That's it."

"Well," she smiled and pointed over Tolleson's shoulder, "this should kill them."

Tolleson followed the direction of Kyler's finger and saw a news crew hurrying over to interview the hero of the hour.

As the hammer knocked another nail into the wooden board, its remorseless tempo beat in perfect time with the ache in Alice's head. The woman was no stranger to hangovers, but right then she could have grabbed Vincenzo's mallet and swung it into his balls. In fact, the only thing that stopped her was that she'd ordered him to carry out the work in the first place.

Both Sparx and Vincenzo—she'd grabbed them after breakfast and told them to get started on a new platform in time for tonight's show. She wanted a diorama based on the theme of a deserted summer camp. So that meant a fake cabin wall, some lights, a floor made from white slats like part of a boat dock, and a sign on which Sparx was currently painting the words "Camp Crystal Lake."

It was Sparx who'd suggested finding some additional props. He'd grasped the Jason concept immediately but didn't think the display would really come to life until they had all the fine details in place. Alice agreed and so she'd sent the excitable youth into town with just enough money to buy a paddle, a life preserver, a can of red paint—and a machete.

As far as Alice was concerned, Jason Voorhees was a license to print money, and now that she was running things, she'd be the one pulling the jackpot.

"Let the paint run a little," she told Sparx, "so it looks like blood."

"Gotcha," nodded the young man, and then quickly set about making the scarlet adjustments.

The carnival had reached Hunt Ridge in the early hours of the morning and had set up in Harper Field, a clearing just outside town. In the daylight, Alice could see that the place was a natural amphitheater ringed by hills and mountains, and there were two routes leading out: a trail of cracked asphalt that stretched back to the road and a dirt track that ran off up into the hills. For all her years behind the wheel, Alice didn't care for the high route at all; it was so steep and winding that the only truck in the carnival even remotely capable of taking it was Freely's pickup.

Suddenly a voice startled her out of her daydreaming.

"Alice," gasped her father, leaning heavily on his stick, "we need to talk."

Sparx and Vincenzo glanced nervously at each other. They half expected Alice to take the old man aside, where she wouldn't be overheard, but she remained firmly where she was.

"I'm busy," she snapped. Then she turned and shouted, "Okay, bring him out."

George looked round and saw Judge and Minter struggling to carry Jason out of the Witney motorhome. Neither man seemed particularly comfortable with the job, but at least they were prepared to do it—unlike Sparx and Vincenzo, who'd both refused outright to lay even a single finger on the corpse.

Revealing Jason to the company had been one of the most nerve-racking moments of Alice's life. She hadn't slept properly all night, and at daybreak she'd called a general meeting. It had never occurred to her to pretend Jason was an effigy, because she knew no one would have believed her. So instead she'd come clean and told everyone the truth, and either the showmen could accept the change or they could quit. Unsurprisingly, they all voted to stay—though Freely stormed out, pushing past her father, who'd spent the whole meeting staring gloomily at the floor.

Now Alice looked on as Jason was lifted onto the platform. Vincenzo had bolted a steel pole to the base of the exhibit, with the idea that they would tie Jason to the post so that he would appear to be standing upright.

"Alice!" pleaded George, grating on her headache. "You're making a terrible mistake. I've been thinking about this all night and I was wrong to listen to you. Please, I beg you—get rid of him!"

Alice shook her head, "Dad, we've been through all this. I'm running the show now, so

I'll give you the same choice I gave the guys.
Either do as you're told or fuck off."

Everybody froze.

"Look, Dad," said Alice more softly, "we need a
new pitch to open the show. That's your job. It's
what you're best at."

But it wasn't the old man who answered her.

"So you think you're in charge now?" Kenton
Freely strolled into view. "Well, I can't speak for
anyone else but I'm not taking orders from a tattooed slut."

Alice threw a punch at Freely but he caught her
wrist—and held it.

"If Pop's getting too old," he sneered, "there's
only one person taking over round here: Kenton H
Freely."

Alice tried to pull free but his grip was too
strong, so strong that it surprised her. And the
more she struggled, the more he smiled—his
greasy hair flicking in reaction to her every effort.

"I swear to fucking God, Freely," she growled,
"you're a dead man, do you hear me? A fucking
dead man!"

"That's it," he purred. "Gimme some sugar."

"I'll fucking kill you!"

"Look out!" shouted George.

Kenton turned and saw Jason toppling forward
off the platform. Quickly, he pushed Alice to the
ground and jumped back as Jason came crashing
down. The inert body landed suggestively
between her legs. Despite herself, Alice screamed.
She tried to push Jason off but he was too heavy,
his moribund knees pinning the fabric of her dress
like a couple of tent pegs.

Freely stood over Alice and licked his sweating lips as she lay cheek to cheek with the hockey mask. "Better get used to that position, sugar."

Glo waved the Lexus goodbye and took a moment to appreciate the picture postcard elegance of small town Reculver, basking in the golden sunshine.

Elliot had said the girl would have no trouble getting a ride the rest of the way to Hunt Ridge, but what did he know? Pamela had lived in this region her whole life; she didn't need advice from some smarmy little rat smothered in body spray. Why, if there hadn't been so many people around, she probably would have cut his...

Not yet, Pamela. Calm down.

Main Street, Reculver, was only eight or nine stores and a chapel, but there was a small gas station, a diner and even a hairdresser. As a matter of fact, the town had everything Glo needed and, thanks to Elliot's insistence on breaking the speed limits, she had a few hours to spare before continuing on her journey. That was plenty of time to make some preparations.

There were a few people on the street—a couple of kids squabbling over candy, a dowager in a blue dress posting some mail, and a waitress who was chalking the day's specials on a board outside the diner—and they were all looking at Glo in a peculiar way. However, it was only when the girl saw her own reflection in a window that she realized it was her heavy metal black and her bloodied mouth, from when Trick had punched her, that was making all the waves.

"Good morning," called the old lady tentatively.

But suddenly Pamela was gone, shocked out of Glo's body by the image of her real self in the glass.

Glo dropped to her knees and ground her fists into her temples.

"What are you doing to me?" she cried, her cheeks glistening with tears. "Get out of my mind, you witch! Get... out... of my... mind!"

She looked up to see if there was anyone who could help her, but the old woman across the road had been decapitated and was drenched in spreading pools of blood. The two kids, the waitress, a man driving by in a GMC—they had all been beheaded and now had gnarled, pitted stumps where their heads used to be. And even though the townsfolk were moving and seemed to be alive, their bodies were streaked with the indelible tarnish of blood.

CHAPTER EIGHT

Supervisory Senior Resident Agent Landau remained seated behind his desk, as Kyler was shown into his office. Since returning from Buffalo, she'd called at her apartment for a shower and a quick change of outfit; though, like Einstein, she kept a wardrobe of identical clothing—brown suit, white blouse—because that meant one less decision to waste time on each day.

Kyler sat down and waited for her superior to proceed.

"So where do we start?" he asked finally.

Landau was a sallow-faced man in his forties. The other agents in Corning found him easy to work with, but there was something between him and Kyler that had never quite gelled.

"How about," she suggested, "congratulations, Agent Kyler, on solving a difficult case."

"No," countered Landau, "how about you explain how you got involved in something you weren't assigned to? How about you tell me what gives you the right to cut out this office, Albany, Buffalo, city police—"

"I received a tip-off—"

"Credit me with some intelligence, Agent Kyler." Landau had seen through her ruse even faster than Tolleson. "Getting someone to leave a 'last minute' message on your phone is the oldest trick in the book."

"If I hadn't gone in, they'd have killed him."

"The abductee is corroborating your claim of self-defense, but you went into a critical situation making errors a rookie would be ashamed of. This one's not going to go away, Agent Kyler. I've already had calls from the OPR."

At the mention of the Bureau's internal watchdog, Kyler started to open up. "I had no evidence. I needed to catch Wallace red-handed."

"You could have arrested Wallace before the ritual even started," Landau barked. "But no, you had to go playing God because an earlier witness had reported some bunk about zombies."

Kyler lowered her head. Was it true? Had she really put lives in danger for the sake of personal motives?

Noticing her uncertainty, Landau piled on the pressure.

"Don't think I don't know what's going on here, Agent Kyler," he continued. "You've turned down two offers to join the firearms training team at Quantico. You keep applying for posts that get you closer to New Jersey. Every time a report mentions life after death you go running, even though it's damaging your career. You just won't let the Voorhees case go, will you?"

Kyler wanted to answer, but all she could manage was guilty silence.

Glo closed her eyes and tried to concentrate. The last thing she remembered was getting ready to stomp on Pamela's head. But that was in the woods near Crystal Lake, whereas now she had no idea where she was. As for the people…

"It's an illusion," the girl told herself through gritted teeth. "It's just an illusion."

"Are you okay?" asked the old lady with genuine concern.

Glo looked and saw the neck drip right in front of her face. Her rational mind knew the stump couldn't possibly be real, but her subconscious mind sent her fleeing down the street. For the first time since this whole nightmare had begun, the girl was starting to doubt her own sanity. Now, more than ever, she needed to call for help.

Finding no phones on the street, Glo ran back to the diner where she was met by the comforting aroma of a hot grill. The waitress turned her bloody neck in Glo's direction.

"Hey there," said the severed spine in welcome.

Glo forced herself to look at the damaged flesh and tried her utmost to pretend everything was normal.

"I… I need to make a call."

The waitress pointed to a payphone right next to the door. Glo mumbled her thanks and was about to use the phone when she noticed a small TV sitting on the counter. A newscaster was reading the headlines through a gaping wound across his neck. Glo shivered and turned away, only to catch sight of a mirror which, instead of her own features, reflected the living face of Pamela Voorhees, healed and restored.

"Hello, dear," grinned the psychopath.

Glo couldn't take any more. She dropped the phone and bolted into the restroom, where she cried her heart out.

"But for all the rumors, the stories and the legends," the voice boomed through the fifty-watt speakers, "one thing is sure. Jason Voorhees is dead."

"Horse—shit!" shouted Ross.

The rock star was sprawled over a black sofa in the middle of "the pit"—a sunken floor that occupied almost half of the massive living room—and he was watching the newest Voorhees DVD release on his eighty-inch plasma.

It was just after eight in the morning and Ross had been up all night. The split with Luke had seriously messed with his head, so he'd taken refuge in the world of his favorite serial killer. Somehow, immersing himself in all those familiar hockey-masked facts gave him comfort.

"Maybe you should get some sleep," Jaomi suggested.

While the pit was dark, plush and surrounded by concealed speakers, Jaomi preferred to sit in a brightly painted corner over by the French doors, where she made sure there were always fresh flowers, and where she sat at a table, typing on her computer.

"He keeps on about the FBI," Ross whined, "as if their records mean a shit. The FBI say they killed

Jason in August 1993, but then who the hell did hundred of kids see trashing a party outside Springwood ten years later? And if the Feds shot Jason in '93, who the fuck did the Wessex County cops bury at the Eternal Peace cemetery in '84? I'm telling you, Jaomi, it's all bullshit."

"I know the feeling," she sighed, tapping the keyboard. Suddenly she had an idea and her fingers worked even faster.

"I've read every book on Jason that's ever been written," Ross complained, "and not one of them has gone through all the facts. As soon as they hit something that won't fit their pet theory, they ignore it. You know, all these idiots, all they've gotta do is get some DN fucking A. Go to the cemetery. Trawl the bottom of the lake. That's where you'll find the answers."

Jaomi had heard this speech so many times she could have written it on her word processor.

"But no," Ross bellyached, "it's all *I saw this* and *I believe that*. Fuck, there's even one stupid bitch who says she beat him with psychic powers! Do you believe that? These people should be certified."

He stood up and pressed a button on his remote. In response, the plasma went blank and four large shutters rolled back to flood the pit with sunlight.

"Shit!" Ross flinched, shielding his eyes. "Got coke?"

The porn star was about to look in her bag when a gentle chime came from her PC. She clicked the mouse a few times and called Ross over.

"Look," she said excited, "there's a book about Jason Voorhees on ZingBid. I just did a search for you."

Ross scrunched his features. "What the fuck are you talking about?"

"ZingBid," she answered as if that explained everything. "You know? Coolest internet auction site on the planet? Someone's selling a Jason book, so do you want it or not?"

"Not, Jaomi, not, not, not! How many times do I have to tell you? I own every book on Jason that's ever been written. Which part of 'every' don't you understand?"

She folded her arms and pushed back in her chair. "Hey, if you don't want my help…"

"Just stop right there," he shouted. "I don't ever want to hear about BingBong, PingPang or ZitFuck again, you got that?"

"Not even if I find a collectable?" she teased.

"You won't," he replied with sudden intensity. "They've all been snapped up by that bastard Nathaniel Morgas. He was collecting before I'd even learned guitar. That's why my house is full of repros and his house has got one of the most famous private collections in the world."

"Have you ever met him?" she asked, almost interested.

"No," he frowned, "but if I do, I swear I'll kill him."

Jaomi sighed, disconnected her computer from the internet and took a sachet of top-dollar blow out of her bag.

Gripping the sides of the washstand, Glo raised her head to look at the mirror one more time: the bitch was still there. That square cut of blonde hair, that broad face and the dark inset of her manic eyes. There was a photo of Mrs Voorhees in one of Glo's true crime books, and it was indistinguishable from the woman now reflected in the silvered pane.

"Leave me alone!" cried Glo.

"I'm sorry, dear," smiled Pamela, "but I've grown rather fond of you."

Glo stuck out her bottom jaw. "If you don't get out of my head, I swear I'll kill myself."

"Don't be silly, child," Pamela tried to sound nonchalant. "There's no reason why we shouldn't get along just fine."

"I mean it!" warned Glo, and she started to remove her backpack.

"What are you doing?" A hint of fear entered Pamela's voice.

"I've got painkillers," answered the girl with grim determination. "A whole damn bottle full."

Then she threw the bag to the floor, looking on in amazement as the head of Mrs Voorhees rolled out onto the tiles.

"You!" gasped the girl.

And suddenly Glo found the answer she didn't know she'd been searching for. The hallucinations, the voices—it was all because of the damned head. She'd picked it up from the roadside under Pamela's influence, in just the same way that a nine year-old child named Gloria once developed an inexplicable fascination for a series of murders that had occurred on the opposite side of the country. Her whole life had been manipulated from beyond the grave.

"You need me," she whispered, thinking it through. "You could have called anyone but you called me. And the closer I get to you, the more powerful you are."

"That's nonsense, child," scoffed Pamela, only now her smile was replaced by an expression of sheer hatred.

"No," said the girl, gathering strength. "I can beat you. I'll take you back to Crystal Lake—back to the dump where I found you, and then I'll burn the whole place to the ground."

"I don't think Jason would like that," snarled Pamela.

"Oh really?" asked Glo. Then she stepped up and kicked the head square in the mouth.

Suddenly there was a knock at the washroom door.

"Are you okay?" It was the waitress.

Glo looked in the mirror and saw a girl with black hair, a missing front tooth, a delta of flooded mascara, and a godawful tired expression. It was the most beautiful face she'd ever seen.

"I'm fine," she answered, shaking with relief. "Really."

"I'll get you some coffee," called the waitress and then she walked away, leaving Glo to clean herself up.

The war with Pamela was far from over and yet this round belonged to Glo. Pamela needed Glo's body, which meant she couldn't harm the girl. Instead, she'd wait until she had enough energy to try and possess her again—and Glo had no idea when that might be.

She shoved the head into the backpack and hurried out into the diner. She was relieved to see that everyone had regained their heads. A few of the customers looked warily at her.

"Travel sickness," she shrugged with a forced smile.

The waitress had put some coffee on the counter, but Glo left it and went to the payphone. The mutilated bodies of her friends were still out in the woods, Jason was off traveling with some carnival, and there was every chance that destroying Pamela's head might not be the magic bullet she was hoping for. She needed help—badly.

Glo lifted the receiver and got ready to punch 911, when her eyes landed on the TV. The news was running an interview with a woman covered in blood, while a large caption along the bottom of the screen read: "NY FBI—ZOMBIE KILLER."

The paint was still wet, Judge hadn't yet wired up the lights, and the guys needed to fit some drapes in time for the grand unveiling. But Alice thought the Crystal Lake diorama looked pretty damn sensational. Jason seemed to be stalking through a dark corner of the infamous summer camp. He had a machete in his right hand and was closing in for the kill, just like he'd done hundreds of times in real life.

Alice turned and looked around the field. Since her confrontation with Freely, the other guys had spent all morning setting up the show—keeping out of harm's way until they knew who was going to come out on top. She guessed her dad had gone back to the truck, while Freely—she had no idea where he was skulking.

Just then a local boy, no more than eleven years old, came riding across the field on a pushbike. Alice watched as the sandy-haired kid pedaled towards her. Maybe she could use him for some word of mouth.

"Hi there," she waved.

"Hey," answered the kid flatly. Then he went to stare at the towering form of the serial killer. Jason's machete was daubed with fake blood, but his hockey mask was the very guarantee of death.

"Don't get too close," cautioned Alice with spookshow menace.

But the boy had already finished his inspection. He looked up at the expectant woman and dead-panned, "Jason sucks."

George watched through the window of the RV as the brat cycled away from his crestfallen daughter. Everything was falling apart just as he'd feared. If only Alice wasn't so much like her mother...

The old man shuffled over to the side door, only to see it thrown open before he could even touch the handle.

"Going somewhere, George?"

"Mister Freely!" Witney jumped in surprise and took a step back from the man deliberately barring his way. "I—I need to go out."

"Not now, George. We got business to discuss," Kenton entered the truck and closed the door behind him.

"It'll have to wait," Witney made a move as if to dismiss Freely out of hand, but Kenton just shoved the old man back down in his seat and helped himself to a beer from the cooler.

"What do you want?" George demanded.

"You know what I want. What I've always wanted. The carnival."

Witney tried to sit up "But I can't!"

Kenton pushed him down again and took a swig from the bottle. "I want it in writing," he snapped. "Legal. And after tonight's show, I want you to tell everyone I'm in charge."

"It's impossible. You saw how Alice treated me..."

"Why do you think I'm here?" Freely interrupted. "We had a good thing going, George. You did all the work, I took all the money. But now you've forced my hand."

"I tried to stop her," the old man pleaded. "You must believe me."

"Oh, I do believe you, George," said Kenton with a smirk. "You've got too much to lose. And unless you do as I say, you'll lose everything."

"Kenton, please..."

"You know what'll happen, George. Sign it over to me or..." he smiled. "Well, hopefully, it won't come to that. Will it, George?"

Witney said nothing.

"I said..." Kenton threw the bottle to the floor and shouted over the breaking glass, "will it, George!"

The old man stared despondently through the window towards Alice.

If Agent Tolleson needed any proof that light traveled faster than sound, he was just about to get it. He was kicking his heels outside Landau's office when a blur rushed past his eyes, followed by the sonic boom of a slammed door. Kyler was over halfway down the corridor before it dawned on him that she had just come from her meeting.

"I take it, it didn't go too well," he said, jogging after her.

"You could say that," Kyler's voice was bubbling with suppressed anger. "He's put me on administrative leave pending a Fitness For Duty evaluation."

"What?" Tolleson drew to a halt.

"The only thing he hasn't done is have me escorted from the building," she continued, striding into the open plan where she and Tolleson shared partitions with three other agents, none currently present.

Tolleson skipped after her, "But what did you say to him?"

Kyler went to her desk and started to gather a few personal items into her briefcase. "It's what he said to me. He said my obsession with the paranormal is affecting my judgment."

"Well," Tolleson said hesitantly, "I did warn you."

Michelle looked up from her open top drawer. "This is your first posting and you're giving me advice?"

"No, no," replied Tolleson hoping she wouldn't jump down his throat. "I don't agree with them— your record in violent crime speaks for itself—but it's what people are saying."

"Well, they'll have to find somebody else to talk about," she dropped a compact in her briefcase and closed the drawer. Cory frowned: he'd never seen Kyler wear makeup.

"For seeing who's behind me," she explained, catching his glance. "No one ever notices a woman powdering her nose."

Tolleson smiled and asked, "So what are you gonna do?"

"Calm down," she shrugged. "After that, I don't know. Think about my future, I guess."

"Just don't rush into anything," he counseled. "You're a great agent. This place needs you."

Kyler's anger melted a little. "I appreciate your support."

"Hey, don't thank me," he laughed. "I just want you around long enough to steal your methods. But I don't think I'll try the compact trick."

Kyler grimaced and took one last look at her desk. A framed photo of her mom sat next to the phone. The agent reached forward to take it when suddenly the phone rang.

"Leave it," Tolleson urged. "Go on. Get out of here. Take a break. You've earned it."

Michelle hovered indecisively as her voicemail kicked into action.

"Hello, this is Agent Kyler of the Federal Bureau of Investigation. I'm not at my desk right now, but if you leave a message, I'll call you back."

Beep.

"Go!" said Tolleson.

A frightened female voice crackled out of the handsfree speaker.

"Agent Kyler—are you there? My name's Gloria Sowici. I need to talk to you. It's about Jason—Jason Voorhees. He's alive."

Kyler's expression hardened into cold steel.

CHAPTER NINE

Glo pumped another four coins into the slot and continued talking, trying to cram as much information as possible into the shortest amount of time.

"The Winnebago knocked me unconscious," she prattled. "Jason too. That's how they got him. They missed me but he was lying in the road. I don't remember exactly but I think they were called 'The Carnival of' something."

Casting a quick look around the diner, Glo put the backpack down by her feet and opened it just enough to reach inside for the USGS map. Her hand brushed against the severed head, its parched, leprous skin making her feel instantly nauseous.

"The sheriff wouldn't listen," she continued down the phone, "but I can tell you exactly where the bodies are. So if you don't believe me, go look for yourself. The map reference is..."

The girl was cut short by the unexpected sound of laughter—a mocking, disjointed hysteria that could only be the renewed psychic blitz of Mrs Voorhees. The bitch was infecting the payphone the same way she'd attacked Glo's cell, only this time the girl wasn't going to be so easily panicked. She closed her eyes and did her utmost to shut the derision out of her mind. She tried to concentrate, to focus from one sentence to the next, but Pamela was growing stronger and soon the demented cackling was almost overwhelming.

Over by the counter, the waitress watched Glo with growing unease. She made a rule of never judging customers by their appearance but this little grunge dork was acting real strange.

"Earl!" she called anxiously.

A burly figure stepped out of the backroom. He had a balding head and a permanent five o' clock shadow, and his greasy apron as good as said he was the cook.

"What's wrong?" he asked.

The waitress nodded in Glo's direction; the girl was yelling into the phone and was beginning to upset the other patrons.

"Shut up, you bitch!" shouted Glo, her defiance crumbling.

"Hey!" Earl bustled out from behind the counter. "What's going on?"

Just then, Glo felt a hand grab her shoulder. She turned and saw the hockey mask of Jason Voorhees bearing down on her. This was the first time Glo had seen Jason in daylight, and the sheer force exuded by his decaying mass was almost beyond comprehension.

Glo screamed and snatched the backpack off the floor. Then, using her shortness to her advantage, she ducked under Jason's arms. The phone and the map slipped through her fingers as she scooted for the door, but Jason was too fast. He caught the girl's shoulder a second time and hauled her back into the room. Glo cringed as he raised his gleaming machete into the sunlight.

Brushing off her partner's hand, Kyler snatched the receiver up from the cradle and pressed it to her ear.

"This is Agent Kyler," she said with measured urgency. "Where is Jason Voorhees now? Hello? Please, if you can hear me, I need to know Jason's present location."

With her free hand, Kyler opened a drawer and took out a map of New Jersey. Crystal Lake was already circled with red ink, but now she highlighted both Reculver and the map reference Glo had given for the homicides.

"Hello," the agent tried again but the line was dead.

Tolleson breathed sharply, "Kyler, don't do this. You're on leave now."

But his words had about as much effect as Parental Advisory Warnings. Kyler pressed the Play button and listened to Glo's message a second time. Then a third. And a fourth, scribbling notes on each repeated playback.

"Michelle," Tolleson continued, "if you go anywhere near Crystal Lake, you'll be suspended."

"Only if Landau finds out," she answered, making a note of the incoming phone number.

"You think he won't?" Tolleson doubted.

"You said it yourself," answered Kyler. "I'm on leave. What I do in my spare time is my business."

She folded the map and dropped it into her brief-case.

"This puts me in a compromising position," said Tolleson, adopting a more formal posture.

"What does?" asked Kyler putting her notebook in with the map. "That before I left the building, I took a phone call? What's that to do with you?"

"You know what I mean. You're going to Crystal Lake."

Kyler stood up and snapped the case shut. "Then you need to do what's best for your career."

"That's below the belt," he frowned. "You know I wouldn't sell you out."

Kyler turned and studied his face. "Then, what are you going to do, Agent Tolleson?"

Cory didn't hesitate. "I'm coming with you."

"Out of the question." She lifted her briefcase and started to walk down the hall leading from the office.

"Look," muttered Tolleson, keeping pace beside her, "all I'm doing is paperwork on the Chapman case. I can spin it out so Landau won't reassign me till tomorrow afternoon."

"This isn't your concern." Kyler pushed straight ahead, nodding to Agent Fisher as she entered the reception area.

But Tolleson persisted.

"It'll take four or five hours to get to Crystal Lake, but we could still be through by tonight. That's plenty of time to prove it's a hoax."

"You mean like the zombies?" Kyler asked point-edly.

"Well—no," Tolleson back-pedaled. "What I meant to say is, *if* it's a hoax. And what if you run into local law enforcement? I can help with that. If they check your name, it'll come through to…"

"Still here, Agent Kyler?" came a voice from behind.

They turned and saw Landau walking along the corridor towards them.

Tolleson whispered, "I'll pick you up from your place in an hour." Then he stood back and said more loudly, "See you in a week, Agent Kyler."

It was obvious from Landau's expression that he was coming to see Kyler off the premises; it gave her just seconds to decide whether or not to accept Tolleson's offer. Cory had made a good point about the problems of working alone, but hadn't she just done that in Buffalo? Then again, what if Tolleson accidentally let slip she was working on an unauthorized case?

Kyler caught the rookie's eye and gave the slightest hint of a nod. Then she blanked her superior and marched out of the building.

Earl let go of Glo's leather jacket. He hoped she didn't try to go running off again before he had chance to explain.

"Hold on," he said. "You dropped this."

He held out the USGS map, but when Glo's eyes came to rest on the folded sheet she saw only a deadly blade. She retreated in horror as Jason stabbed the machete closer and closer towards her stomach, perversely entertaining himself with the foreplay of an assured kill.

"Go on, take it!"

Earl tried to put the map in Glo's hands, but she pressed her back against the door and did everything she could to avoid him.

"I think she's on drugs," said the waitress.

"What?" Glo hesitated long enough for Jason to bring the machete down across her right hand.

The girl winced, expecting the fire of amputation to burn through her wrist, but she felt nothing—no pain, no blood, no shock. And now there was a map resting in the palm of her hand.

A chuckle rippled through the depths of Glo's consciousness as Jason transformed into the disheveled cook.

"Get out of my head!" Glo shouted.

She could see the final curtain falling on her sanity. Her brain was awash with twisted laughter, a cruel backcloth for the most deranged hallucination yet:

"Kill her, Mommy. Kill her!"

Pamela was speaking in the voice of her drowned, retarded son.

Tears filled Glo's eyes and she knew that she was irredeemably lost. No treatment, no drug could save her. No method would ever bring her back from this cold, dark place of abandonment.

"Not now, Jason," spat Pamela. "We need this little slut to hold herself together."

Weeping at the horror of two voices—two murderous insanities—within her mind, Glo threw open the door and ran out onto the street. Earl watched as the girl careened down the sidewalk, tripped and fell onto the ground. The poor kid couldn't stop crying.

"I'm not taking you anywhere," she wept, but her words were broken and defeated.

"You don't understand, dear," said Pamela, throttling the girl's psyche to within an inch of its pathetic existence. "Jason's with the circus. They've got him trapped like he's *some kind of freak!*"

Glo rolled onto her back and stared up into the clear blue sky. And suddenly she was flying—flying away...

"Are you okay?" asked Earl, leaning into her vision.

"Why of course, dear," smiled Glo, rising easily to her feet. "I just wasn't feeling myself for a moment. Now tell me, isn't there a general store somewhere along here?"

Her question threw Earl off balance. "You've been here before?"

"Oh, not since the sixties, but I still know my way."

And with that Glo brushed herself down and strode confidently in the direction of the store.

The coke buzz had worn off over an hour ago, and Ross was in one shitstinger of a mood. In the good old days, he would have gone straight to hit number two, but Mama Marantez was running the dispensary now, and she had this crazy idea that they needed to cut down. She'd had some kind of religious conversion around the time Ross's bass player, Viktor Satanis, had shown up in an LA morgue covered in puke and nosebleeds. So that now left Ross only one course of action: close the blinds and watch more DVDs.

"Yeah—that's right," the huge plasma screen was filled by a close-up of one hell of a lived-in face. "I was the one who declared him dead."

"But he wasn't, was he?" the words came from an off-screen interviewer and were more a condemnation than a question.

The camera zoomed in even tighter on the old guy. His eyes flicked nervously towards the lens, "I was positive—absolutely positive Jason was dead."

"And that's what you told the medics?"

"Sure, but I was a medic myself—that's why I was there. I went into the barn, I checked the body and he was dead."

"Then how do you explain the fact that after Jason Voorhees was taken to the Wessex County Medical Center, he got up, killed two members of staff and went on the rampage for another forty-eight hours?"

"I—I don't have an explanation," stuttered the man. He raised a cigarette into shot and took a long pull, "Don't you think I feel bad about that?"

But the voice was remorseless, "You were fired, weren't you?"

"I quit," he took another puff of nicotine. "When I heard about Jason—those kids died because of me."

From across the room, Jaomi squealed with delight and stomped her sneakers on the polished hardwood floor.

Ross hit the pause button.

"Can I just point out," he called over, "that your noise is really starting to annoy me."

Whenever Ross tried to manage his anger, his voice took on a peculiar warbling quality, almost like one of his songs.

"But I've won." She smiled and she got up from behind her computer.

"Won what?" he asked irritably.

"I can't tell you," she smirked. "You said you didn't want to hear about ZingBid again."

"But I'm asking you."

"No, no. You can't do that," she stepped down into the pit and stood over him as he slouched across the sofa. "If I mention ZingBid, it'll break the cut-off."

"But I made the cut-off," Ross protested.

"So what?" she replied. "You can't break a cut-off just because it suits you, or the cut-off isn't a cut-off."

Ross slammed his hands on the leather cushions, "But it's my cut-off!"

"Is there a cut-off on ZingBid or not?" she demanded.

"Not!" he shouted. "Not, not, not, not, not! Now tell me what you fucking won!"

"Okay, okay," grinned Jaomi and she flapped her hands as if to steady her audience of one for a grand announcement. "I've won—some original silver spoons—from a dinner service—owned—by Napoleon Bonaparte."

There was a brief silence before Ross burst into laughter.

"And I'm sure they're really fucking genuine!" he howled. "Whoa Jaomi, and you're supposed to be the intelligent one."

"The spoons come with a certificate of authenticity," she insisted. She hated it when he poked fun at her.

"Signed by Napoleon himself," cracked Ross. "Just check it's not in fucking biro."

Suddenly, Jaomi snatched the remote from his hand and pressed the button that opened the shutters. Sunlight poured into the pit, blinding Ross and ruining the picture quality of the TV. He tried to steal the gadget back but his wife was too quick. She waggled the remote annoyingly close to his face and then ran across the room. Ross went after her and, one diving tackle later, the two of them were both laughing and rolling on the floor.

Ross lay on top of her and kissed her, "So how many's that now?"

"About eighty," she answered.

"You've won eighty auctions?" he sounded surprised. "Out of how many?"

Jaomi smiled, "Ohhh... about eighty."

"You mean, you haven't lost one?"

"Nope," she kissed his nose.

"With luck like that we should go to Vegas."

"Luck nothing," she scowled. "I've written a software program that blocks everyone else's bids. I just wait until half a minute from the end—it only works thirty seconds—then I run the blocker and put on the winning bid. Neat, huh?"

"Illegal," Ross smiled, shaking his head.

"Probably," she agreed. "But at the end of the day, I still have to pay for the stuff."

"Who pays?" Ross asked knowingly.

"Hey, I'm not exactly penniless," she sniggered, "though your multimillion dollar fortune is occasionally useful."

Ross kissed her again.

"Do you know," he commented, "I still don't get how an MIT computing graduate becomes a porn star."

"I just did the math," she explained. "A thousand times more money for a thousand times less work."

"And is there a scientific equation for you sucking my dick?" he teased.

"Well, I tried once," she snickered, "but I kept getting divide by zero errors."

Ross laughed. But like the 747 from LAX to Hong Kong, the joke had just flown straight over his head.

Alice tried to tell herself that the kid on the bike had only been spiteful, but his casual dismissal of the new Jason exhibit terrified her. She stared at the tableau, mentally role-playing every possible scenario of failure, and questioned for the thousandth time how her life had reached the point where all her dreams were hanging on the body of a serial killer.

"The boy was right," said Freely, sidling up to her. "It is shit."

Alice was wearing another of her mom's floral dresses but now her bare, tattooed shoulders were feeling exposed. She grabbed her coat—an old, brown fighter pilot's jacket she'd left near Jason's feet—and put it on.

Freely's eyes crawled up and down her body like a cum snake.

"You don't know how to run this show," he sneered. "Jason's no different from Dracula or any of this Halloween hogwash. It's all baloney."

Alice zipped up her jacket. "Kenton, you're like dog shit. I keep shaking my shoe and you're still there making a fucking stink."

Without warning, Freely grabbed a fistful of Alice's hair and dragged her in a spiral before throwing her to the ground. Alice yelped and tried to get up, but he swung his right foot into her ribs, knocking the wind clean out of her.

"I got a sweet thing going on around here," he swaggered. "You think I'd let a vinegar slut like you get in the way? Playtime's over, Alice. I'm in charge now."

"Over my dead body," she coughed.

"No," Kenton pointed a finger at Jason. "Over his dead body. Your old man, he's nothing, he's been under my thumb for years, but you—I've waited a long time for this."

Alice rolled onto her back and looked around for help, but Harper Field was now awash with theme park horror and all she could see were the exhibits: a corner of Victorian London for Jack the Ripper; a Transylvanian turret for Count Dracula; a graveyard dominated by a dreary manikin of the Frankenstein monster. There was a werewolf, an undersea humanoid, a flesh-eating zombie—all marauding through plasterboard simulacra of their mythological environments. But where the hell were the showmen?

Freely bent down, grabbed hold of Alice's collar and lifted her face up close to his. "I don't care if Goober's the real deal or not," he snapped, "but I'm betting he's not made of wax.".

Alice reached up and placed her nails on the dry flesh of Kenton's cheek. But before she could claw him, he pushed her back onto the ground and stepped away from her.

"Too slow," he smirked. "And before you try anything else, think about what you're gonna tell the cops. I mean it, Alice. I'm calling in the law unless…"

"Unless what?" Alice slowly got up.

Kenton smiled, "You know what I want. And you got until tonight to give it to me. If you don't, it's twenty years for you and twenty-five for the old man."

"You bastard," she cursed.

"Call me anything you want so long as you take a bath before we screw. You look a mess."

Alice raged and ran at him with both fists, but again she was denied. He grabbed her wrists and swung her around while laughing in her face.

"C'mon, Alice," he chuckled. "Why can't you be like your mom? Ellen was much more congenial."

"What do you mean?" snarled Alice.

Kenton spun her once more and then let go so abruptly that she went crashing back into the Crystal Lake display. She winced as her spine connected with the jutting slats of the boat dock.

"When I poked your mom," bragged Kenton, "she did all the running, not me."

"You never fucking touched her!" cried Alice.

"Sure I did. A few weeks before she died in her—accident," Freely spoke with an understatement that leant more truth to his words than any amount of hollering.

"Liar!" she roared.

"What's going on here?" Shawn Minter had seen the commotion and had rushed along to help. Alice only had to give the word and he would rip Freely limb from weasly limb.

But it was as if the big guy didn't even exist.

"Your mom was a lush," rattled Kenton. "She and George were always fighting—they hated each other. She was always getting loaded and screwing around, and your pop..." Kenton looked around at the displays. "I guess he had his toys. But then he went and hired me—young, handsome and available. And Ellen Witney couldn't wait to seduce my goddam ass."

Every muscle in Alice's body went numb. There was something so right about Kenton's story that she simply couldn't fight it. No histrionics. No denials. Like the bastard had said, "Playtime's over".

She turned and stormed in the direction of her RV.

Kenton laughed and called after her, "Don't forget, Alice. Put on something nice."

Minter grabbed Kenton's shoulder.

"If you do anything to hurt Alice—" he began.

But Freely brushed the burly man aside and shouted, "You mind your own business!" Then he strolled along in Alice's footsteps. He'd give her five minutes alone with George and then...

Round two.

Henshaw snipped a few more straggly hairs from behind the girl's left ear and then stood back. In all his thirty-two years as Reculver's only barber, he could honestly say he'd never had a customer like this one.

She'd come into the shop, bright and breezy as the day itself. His first thought was that she might be trouble because, for one, he didn't like the way

she looked, and for another, her manner was so
polite he thought she was making fun of him. But
no, the girl was genuine. She wanted some color
and she wanted a cut. And that's what he'd spent
half the morning doing.

"Your folks won't recognize you," he said, clipping away with his scissors.

When the girl had come into his shop, her hair
had been long and black; now, however, it was a
square of short blonde waves.

"Oh, he will," smiled Glo. "Jason's a very clever
boy."

Henshaw paused a moment and then continued
cutting. Once he got the collar straight, he'd be
done.

"Been in town long?" he asked.

"Just this morning. I was going to eat breakfast
at the diner but the food there is no good."

"Never had any problems," shrugged the barber.

Glo smiled, her eyes lethal, "But you wouldn't.
You're not a professional cook like I am, so you
wouldn't know when food's not been made properly."

"Suit yourself."

The gent made one final cut and then removed
the damp towel from around her neck.

"What do you think?" he asked, holding another
mirror behind her head.

"It's perfect!" beamed the girl and she stood up
to see how well her new hairstyle suited the
clothes she'd bought from the general store. Dark
pants, red checked shirt and a powder blue
sweater: other than her height, Gloria Sowici was
now the absolute double of Pamela Voorhees

when she was killed, twenty-five years ago on the shores of Crystal Lake.

"That'll be twenty-two fifty," said Henshaw, washing his hands.

Glo opened her backpack and, taking care not to expose the severed head, pulled out a couple of twenty dollar bills—she'd already ditched her old clothes in a trash can on Main Street.

"I'll get you some change," said the elderly barber and went into a backroom where he kept the money.

Glo admired herself in the mirror.

"Is there anywhere in town that sells hunting knives?" she called.

Henshaw replied through the curtained doorway, "There's a hardware store next to the chapel."

Glo frowned and muttered to herself, "I don't recall a hardware store. I guess I must have forgotten it."

"What's that?" asked Henshaw.

"Oh nothing," answered Glo. Then she sat back down in the chair and stared into the mirror. Deeper. Deeper. Her blonde hair. Her sharp eyes. The lunacy of her grin.

"Kill him, Mommy! Kill him! *Kill him! Kill—him!*"

CHAPTER TEN

Corning, Steuben County, was hardly the largest or most affluent city in New York State. But Kyler's downtown apartment was one of many buildings that had been refurbished in recent years, and it did just fine for her. It was somewhere she could sleep in between double and triple shifts, and that was all she needed, because family and leisure time were incompatible with Agent Kyler's personal agenda.

Lifting her briefcase from the passenger seat, Kyler got out of her blue Ford and walked across the gum-mottled sidewalk to her apartment building. Her place was on the second floor and, as the car alarm squawked in confirmation behind her, she glanced up at the living room window. Then she checked her watch: Tolleson wasn't due for another forty minutes.

"Ms Kyler!"

She froze.

The briefcase was in her left hand, but with her right she smoothly reached inside her jacket, her fingers coming to rest on the shoulder holster. She'd been required to leave her service handgun at the office but she always kept a spare hidden in the trunk of her car, and had rearmed even before leaving the parking lot.

"You won't need your weapon," said the voice.

Kyler could have kicked herself. With her back to the target, she could usually draw undetected. Nevertheless, she kept her hand where it was and turned very slowly to see a black limousine waiting in the road.

The limo had pulled up next to her Taurus and everything about the vehicle—from its gleaming hubs to the way it hugged the asphalt—was a lesson in implicit power. The chauffeur-driven occupant had lowered the rear window just enough for Kyler to hear him, while he remained hidden behind smoked glass.

"I wonder if you would be as kind as to join me." His manner was so polite that Kyler placed her fingertips on the GLOCK.

"Why would I want to do that?" she asked.

In answer, the rear door swung open to reveal an enormous backseat taken up by an equally king-sized figure; the man must have weighed at least three hundred and fifty pounds. He was aged around fifty-five, just shy of six foot and completely bald. However, his dress sense was impeccable. Everything about him was bespoke and expensive. His suit was hand-stitched, his white shirt made from specially imported cotton—even his fob watch was tastefully studded with diamonds.

"Ms Kyler," the man pointed to a stack of folders and documents resting beside him on the seat, "I think it's time you and I had a quiet talk about the Voorhees matter."

That magic word again.

Special Agent Kyler snatched a furtive look up and down the road, and then got inside the limo. Despite the man's colossal stature, the seat was so large he didn't have to budge. Instead, he just reached over, closed the door and signaled the chauffeur to drive.

Moments later, the sidewalk in front of Kyler's apartment was deserted.

With the exception of Kenton's pickup, the carnival vehicles were parked in their usual huddle: the Witney motorhome, the RV used by Sparx, Minter and Vincenzo, and the long eighteen-wheeler where Judge was now hard at work on his laptop. He noticed Alice walk by the open cab door and called down to her.

"Hey, Alice, I've got the new Jason page working. Wanna take a look?"

But the young woman was in no mood for cutesy computer crap and she ignored Judge completely.

"Bitch," he muttered. Then he closed the HTML editor and logged onto the internet. Much as he liked Alice, if she couldn't be bothered then he'd just surf NASCAR and screw her.

Inside the Witney truck, George sat fiddling with his flat cap, his nerves as shredded as the fabric he'd picked off the peak. He'd been watching Alice and Kenton through the window and had seen their fight. Any second now...

The door flew open.

"Did that weasel-faced bastard fuck Mom?" shouted Alice.

The old man expected to find tears in her eyes, but all he saw there was ice. He, on the other hand, had just been crushed by the words he'd hoped never to hear. He immediately started to cry.

"He promised," gulped the old man.

Alice was horrified, "Promised? Promised what?"

But the old man dropped his head in his hands and wept. Alice felt almost embarrassed to see him bawling like an infant. She stepped forward and shook him by the shoulders.

"Tell me!" she demanded.

Suddenly a shadow obscured the open doorway. Alice turned to see Kenton Freely.

"Aww, how touching," he mocked, sucking on a cancer stick.

"Fuck off!" she snapped.

"Kenton, please!" cried George. "You promised never to tell!"

"Tell what?" shouted Alice, only now her anger was focused on her father.

"I... I never forgave her," sobbed the old man.

So it was true. Alice had to steady herself against the wall. Kenton Freely had slept with her mom. And now her father couldn't cope because he'd not forgiven Ellen Witney before she'd died.

"I understand," murmured Alice, more than a little shell-shocked.

"Oh, I don't think you do," Kenton sneered.

George began to cough. "No, Kenton!" he trembled. But nothing and no one was going to stop Kenton Freely from hitting his home run.

"Ellen hated the show more than you do," he told Alice. "She was a grown woman. She had ambition—needs. But George, here, he didn't care who she fooled around with if it meant he could spend more time with his monster pals. Right, George?"

The old man stared at the wall in mournful silence.

"It got so bad, she hit the bottle," continued Freely. "But George was fine with that because then she shut up complaining about the money."

Alice ran to the kitchenette and picked up a carving knife. "Get out!" she yelled, coming forward with the blade.

"Or what?" snickered Freely. "You'll stick me like this old bastard stuck your mom?"

The floor lurched beneath Alice's feet and suddenly the whole room was spinning. But Kenton didn't let up.

"Your dad caught me and Ellen fooling around," he rapped. "Then he waited for her and stabbed her fourteen times. How else d'you think I wrapped the punk round my finger? I caught him and made it look like an accident."

"Please, Dad," said Alice feebly, "tell me he's lying."

But George Arthur Witney sank lower in his seat, his posture a confession of murder.

Alice thought she was going to faint. Her father was a murderer and Kenton had been blackmailing him. And now that Alice had killed Jason, she too would be under Freely's thumb—or would that be his dick?

Suddenly Kenton punched the door.

"Now listen up!" he snapped. "You two little faggots need to behave yourselves or you're both going to jail. Capeesh?"

George nodded weakly. "We'll do whatever you ask."

"I like that. You'll do whatever I athk," laughed Kenton, ridiculing the old man's impediment. "And what about you, Alice? Are you ready to play ball with Uncle Kenty?"

At that moment, Alice realized her entire life had been just another exhibit touring with the Carnival of Terrors. Now it was time to step outside the plasterboard and start living for real. She tightened her grip on the knife.

"You wanna see if I'm like my father?" she asked.

Kenton sucked in his cheeks and stepped back. There was no mistaking the look in the woman's eyes.

"Don't make me hurt you, sugar," he purred, fixing his eyes on the blade.

But Alice came another step closer. "Dad, if we don't get rid of this bastard now, we never will."

Her father stood up and wiped the tears from his eyes. He'd stopped coughing but didn't know how long his health would hold, especially given what he was about to do.

"Alice," he said, "put the knife down."

"What?" Alice couldn't believe what she was hearing. For the first time, tears crept into her eyes.

"I said put it away," the old man repeated sternly.

Alice looked at Kenton—at the parasitic grin smothering his lips—and then turned to her father in anguish.

"I know what's going on," she cried. "You let Freely push you around because you're using him as a shield. That way, you get to stay with the show and you don't feel guilty. But it's time to stand up..."

"Alice!" the old man shouted and slapped her across the face. "Be quiet!"

The blow was feeble, but the betrayal was as ruthless as the fourteen knife wounds in Ellen Witney's corpse.

"No one ever hits me like that," she said, her tone low, even.

"If you continue making a fuss," George lisped, "I'll hit you again. You're risking everything we have."

Alice chuckled, a dead sound suffused with anguish, "Because we've got so fucking much."

"With you, doll," laughed Freely, "I've got it all."

Alice ignored him and spoke directly to her father. "One last chance," she said. "Fire... Freely... now."

The old man stiffened and raised his head imperiously. "No."

"Now get out," snapped Freely. "Me and the old guy have got some business to attend to."

Alice looked at her father, looked at Freely, then threw the knife to the floor and thundered out of the motorhome.

The heat over Beverly Hills was a sweltering seventy degrees, the sun throwing out enough UV to obscure the entire LA weather map with one big warning triangle. Fortunately, most of the people swimming in their pools or reclining on their loungers were in no danger of melanoma, because at least eighty per cent of the rays were being absorbed by Luke Veranti's black suit.

Veranti pressed the doorbell outside Ross's mansion. A blast of apocalyptic classical music roared through the portico speakers. The oratorio was still booming when the door opened. Luke saw a dog-tired rock star standing before him. They waited as the mp3 reached its climax.

"I like that," nodded Veranti. "It's that Damien shit. Six, six, six and all that crap."

Ross groaned, "You know, Veranti, that's why I've always hated you. The music from *The Omen* was an original soundtrack written by Jerry Goldsmith but this," Ross thumped the doorbell and started the piece off all over, "is 'O Fortuna,' the opening section from *Carmina Burana* by Carl Orff."

"Sounds like fucking Damien to me," Luke insisted.

"So that's it, is it?" asked the singer, irritated. "Forget the fact the movie isn't called Damien. Forget the fact I chose this fucking music myself and I know it's *Carmina Burana*. You've decided it's Damian and that's it. And that's why you're such a lousy manager. You've got no eye for detail."

"Hey," Veranti cupped a hand against his ear. "You hear that?"

Ross listened but couldn't hear anything, "What?"

"Exactly," jibed the short guy. "When's the last time you heard a tour bus go by the end of the drive? I'll tell you when: when you shipped your new fucking album."

"Oh wow," Ross laughed, trying to suppress his anger. "If you've come back to ask for your job, this is an interesting way of apologizing."

"Apologize?" Now it was Luke's turn to laugh, with a sound like a skunk sticking a finger down its throat. "I think you're laboring under a serious misapprehension."

"Really? Then what's that?" Ross pointed at the high wall separating his estate from his neighbor's. Even in the blazing sunlight, a silvery glow was visible from over the other side.

"I don't know," squawked Veranti. "A fucking UFO. What do I care?"

"They're lights, Veranti, lights!" Ross stepped out of the porch and walked toward the wall, "My fucking airheaded bimbo of a neighbor is making a reality TV show!"

"Oh yeah—Kantayna Finwell. Two Academy Awards, three Emmys, a battle against breast cancer—*that* bimbo."

"Well how come I don't have a reality show?" whined Ross.

"I don't know. Ask your manager."

"If people saw my house, they'd freak. It's like—serial killer chic or something. She calls it *Kantayna of Joy*, for fuck's sake! But, hey, now that you're working for me again…"

"Stop right there." Veranti took an envelope out of his jacket. "I've not come back for your business, you prick. I'm here to serve you a writ for breach of contract." He slapped the envelope in Ross's hand, "Happy Eggday, you fuck." Then he turned and walked back to his Ferrari.

"You can't do that," shouted Ross. "You quit!"

"I bet you wish it was that simple," Luke called over his shoulder. He got in the car and hit the ignition.

Ross ran after him, "I want reality, Luke!"

Veranti turned the car around and lowered the window, "How about I stick my gun up your ass and blow your fucking balls off? Is that real enough for you?"

Ross tore the envelope into shreds, tossed the confetti into the air and then stomped back indoors.

Jaomi heard the door slam and came out of the living room.

"What's wrong, Ross?" she asked.

But the singer just stood there, shaking like a six foot dildo on the marble floor of the hallway. He could hear Luke's car speeding down the driveway.

"Get me my Jason costume," he seethed. "The good one."

"Which one's that?" Jaomi was almost too afraid to ask.

"The fucking good one!" he shouted. "The one with the lifts and the machete with the stage blood. Come on, Jaomi, you've got to know which one that is. KNB charged me a fortune for it."

"Ohhhhh," she clicked. "That one. I put it in the garage."

"You did what?!" Ross was not having a good day.

"Well, I found it in the third guestroom and it was making a mess. But don't worry, it's all in bags."

"Fuck the guestroom, fuck the bags and... fuck... you!"

Jaomi placed a tender hand on his chest, but he pushed her aside and went looking for the garage keys.

"If they want reality TV," he fumed, "I'll give them reality TV. Live. On air. I'm gonna go round and kill the motherfuckers. Jason Voorhees is taking Finwell down."

Kyler studied another crime scene photograph. It showed the body of a man—a cop—and he was lying in a small wooden boat with a steel dart buried in his forehead. Blood ran down his face but his eyes remained open in death. A badge showed the name Thornton.

"I've never seen this," she commented dryly.

"You won't have seen any of these documents before," replied the man, indicating the dozens of photos and reports spread along the backseat.

Kyler had been in the limo for approximately ten minutes and it had kept moving all that time. The driver was hidden on the other side of a solid screen, giving her and her mysterious contact total privacy. And now that she had spent some time

with the obese man, she found it hard to breathe
owing to the cologne he wore: it was expensive,
spicy and repugnant—reminding Kyler of some
moldy cinnamon bark she once forgot to throw
away.

"Okay," she said at last. "What's this about?"

The man started to gather up the paperwork,
putting all the documents back into their proper
folders.

"It's about a conspiracy," he said almost idly.
"I'm risking my life even by talking to you."

"That's not very original," she commented,
equally offhand.

"With all due respect, Ms Kyler, this is no place
for sarcasm. The Voorhees homicides are being
hushed up at the highest level of government.
How else do you explain why the official records
are confused? Is Jason alive or not? Didn't your
organization terminate him in 1993? Or did he
simply get up and walk out of the Youngstown
Morgue? None of it makes sense, Ms Kyler, and
that's because there are powerful interests in
Washington who don't want it to make sense."

"But why?" challenged Kyler. "Why would any
covert agency want to cover up a series of small
town murders?"

"That," the man paused dramatically, "is the
question I need answered."

Kyler looked out of the window; the car was still
circling round her neighborhood. "So why tell
me?"

"Oh come, Ms Kyler," the man reacted as if she
was trying to patronize him. "We both know
you're on enforced leave. We both know you have

a—shall we say—personal interest in the Voorhees murders. And we both know you're going to Crystal Lake this very afternoon."

Kyler reached into her jacket and pulled out her gun.

"Who are you?" she asked.

The man was unmoved by her show of arms, "I've been watching your career for some time, Ms Kyler, but I should warn you, you're in great danger."

"From you?" her grip tightened.

"No, no," chuckled the man humorlessly. "Within twenty-four hours you're going to be suspended from duty. You can't trust anyone, Ms Kyler, least of all your junior partner."

"Agent Tolleson?" her voice lilted with disbelief.

"Cory Tolleson is an informant," the man raised his voice to head off her protests. "He's been sent to spy on you and he will betray you."

"If this is an attempt to disrupt the Bureau..."

"I have no interest in your bureau," he interrupted, "or even in you. My only concern is the Voorhees matter. If you find anything—anything at all—when you go to Crystal Lake this afternoon, I want you to keep me informed."

Kyler kept the GLOCK pointed at his heart, "I don't know who you are or what your game is, but I don't owe you anything."

The man lifted an attaché case off the floor.

"I have something that may change your mind." He took a document out of the case and handed it to Kyler.

She read it. A police report dated 1987—three years after...

The man turned his head and sat facing the front of the car, as if leaving Kyler to read the sheet in private; in reality, however, he was keenly watching her through the corner of his eye.

"They've been playing you, Ms Kyler," he said.

A solitary tear rolled down Michelle's cheek, and she crushed the report until it was a crumpled mess in her hand. She put the GLOCK back in its holster.

"Can we hurt them?" she asked stonily.

"More than you can possibly imagine," he replied.

The hunting knife stabbed in and out of Swinburne's gut, each lunge widening and deepening the slit opened by the first blow. Blood spread in a Rorschach across his pale cotton shirt and flowed like lukewarm coffee over his clutching fingers. The storekeeper tried to cry out, but the knife was pulling the plug on his strength. Rationally, Swinburne had to accept he was going to die, and yet he felt no pain; there was something unreal about the maniacal laughter of the assassin and the leeching wounds that were sucking his soul into darkness.

The man fell, his body slapping like a fish on the floor of the hardware store; two gasps later and he was gone.

Glo bent down and wiped the jagged knife on the dead man's overall. Then she stood up and sliced and slashed at thin air, testing the weapon for weight and balance. She'd already seen how sharp the blade was, but she had very high standards when it came to murderware and needed to be absolutely positive this was the correct knife for her needs. After a few more strokes, she reached a decision.

"Perfect!" she smiled, slipping the blade into a sheath hanging from her left hip. "I'll take it."

Earlier that afternoon, Judge had been in a great mood. He'd asked Sparx to prepare a few graphics and got the new Jason page up and running in no time. Granted, there were no pictures of the Crystal Lake exhibit, but all the information was there and the whole thing didn't look bad. If Alice didn't appreciate the quality, she could have at least complimented the turnaround. But no, she didn't want to know. She'd just gone off on another of her flyers with Kenton, and had spent the last hour and a half draining the federal Jack Daniel's reserves. And now the ungrateful bitch was coming over to the semi.

"Judge!" she drawled.

Shit, she could barely walk in a straight line, and show time was just around three hours away.

"Hey, Alice," he mumbled, staring at the laptop.

"I just wanted to say I'm sorry." She took a swig from the bottle and hauled herself up into the cab.

"No problem," he answered dully.

"No, no," she insisted. "You see, I just found out my father—Doktor fucking Geistmann—is a killer and a coward. D'you know that?"

She leant forward and pushed her face close to his; her breath could have stripped the paint off a battleship. Judge squirmed in his seat and tried to pull away from her.

"Alice, don't."

"No, really," she dribbled onto his denim shirt. "He'd rather let his own daughter get raped by that ring-licking bastard, Freely—he'd rather do that than give up his toys."

She waved her arm vaguely in the direction of the exhibits, a motion that caused her to stumble back from where Judge was sitting.

"I don't know anything about that," murmured Judge, hitting the Enter key.

Alice steadied herself and tried to see what he was doing. "Is that what you wanted to show me?" she slurred.

"Nope. It's ZingBid."

"That's that auction thing, right?" She did her best to concentrate.

"That's the one," clipped Judge, making no effort to disguise his wish to be left alone.

"So what can you sell on there?"

"Anything."

"Anything at all?" she sounded doubtful. "Drugs?" He nodded.

"Booze? Guns?"

Two more nods, "Like it says: it's the world's most exclusive internet auction room. You can sell absolutely anything."

She squinted at the screen, "What if it's illegal?"

"Then make sure you sell it quickly and be careful who you deal with. I know a guy who went out one night—someone slipped him some Rohypnol and two weeks later, they sold his liver on ZingBid for three hundred dollars."

"That's bullshit," laughed Alice.

"No, Alice, that's fact," Judge was having a total humor failure.

"Well, whatever," her mood was turning dirty. "So how's it work?"

"FTFI."

"What's that? A program or something?"

"Follow The Fucking Instructions. Just click on the screen and do what it tells you."

She studied the computer with a perplexed expression. "But it's not even plugged in."

"That's because it's wireless and battery powered. Anything else?"

"Yeah…"

Alice smashed the whiskey bottle over Judge's head and grabbed his laptop from the table. Judge yelped and raised his arms to shield himself, but a second blow never came. When he opened his eyes, he saw Alice meandering across the field with the computer tucked under her arm.

"Alice!" he shouted.

"You wanna stay with the show?" she barked. "Then shut the fuck up!"

Judge glanced in the rearview. Luckily, he wasn't cut too bad, but there was glass and booze all over the floor and his head hurt like hell. He dabbed at the lump that was already starting to rise.

"Ow! Fucking bitch!"

He thumped the steering wheel in anger.

Out on Harper Field, Alice staggered in a drunken stupor over to where Jason was standing on the replica boat dock. Then she placed the laptop in front of his feet and tilted the LCD monitor so she could see it. The computer was still logged on to ZingBid.

"Okay, you piece of crap," she cussed. "Let's see how good you really are."

The black limousine crawled to a halt in front of Agent Kyler's apartment. Her meeting with the stranger had lasted almost thirty minutes, but now they had nothing more to say. She picked up her briefcase and got out of the car.

"Ms Kyler," said the man, "take this."

He placed a business card in her hand, and only then did she notice he'd been wearing gray cotton gloves throughout the entire encounter, so that there was no way of lifting prints.

Kyler looked at the card. Save for a printed phone number, it was blank.

"I still don't know your name," she remarked.

"If you need any help," he answered indirectly, "or if you find anything, call me at once. You're the only person who has that number, Ms Kyler, and I'm the only one who will answer it."

Kyler slipped the card in her jacket pocket. As far as she was concerned she hadn't made any deals with the man, so if she did contact him, it would be on a strictly need-to basis. The document he'd shown her had contained a terrible shock—something deeply personal and important—but she couldn't let it cloud her judgment; nor could she let him use it to put her in his debt. Against that, the well-spoken manipulator claimed to have vast resources at his disposal.

Suddenly she saw a familiar green Chrysler make a right turn on to the street. She glanced at her watch.

"Damn!" he was ten minutes early.

She stood back and watched as the black limousine drove away, only to have its exact spot filled by Cory Tolleson.

"Who was that?" he called, rolling alongside the curb.

Kyler replied without hesitation, "Someone wanted directions."

Tolleson studied her for a moment and then glanced at her clothes. "You ready?" he asked skeptically.

Kyler realized she looked exactly the same as when she'd left the office. But then weren't all her work clothes identical?

"I've been waiting ten minutes," she bluffed.

"Oh, I thought I was early," he laughed. Then he tilted his head in the direction of her briefcase. "So you're not planning on a stopover."

"No, I thought about what you said," she lied, reaching for the passenger door. "And you're right. It's probably a hoax."

"But you still want to go, right?"

Kyler thought again about the document the stranger had shown her: that police report from 1987.

"Crystal Lake's a long drive," she answered, climbing into the car, "so let's get started."

On another road in another state, a battered red van was choking up the asphalt through miles of rolling fields. The suspension of the Chevy was completely shot, causing the chassis to creak and thump over every tiny bump in the road. Glo tried giving the boneshaker more gas, but the heap of rust under the hood wouldn't cooperate. It didn't matter that she needed to get to Hunt Ridge in a hurry; there was nothing she could do to prod the needle over fifty.

She noticed the keys hanging from the ignition. They swayed with the rhythm of the engine and were streaked with blood.

The blood of the storekeeper.

It had been very considerate of Swinburne to keep his car keys in his pants, because now that Pamela had taken ownership of the delivery truck, she expected to find her son in no time at all. As for Glo, there was nothing left of the girl. Her clothes, her backpack, her belongings—they'd all been discarded. The only item that remained from her time with Trick and Z-Moll was the severed head sitting in the passenger seat.

Pamela looked down at the decayed relic.

"I've aged so well!" she smiled, when suddenly she heard the splashing of water and her expression fell blank.

"Help! Help, Mommy! Help! Help, Mommy! Mommy, help!"

"I'm coming, Jason!" Her eyes were staring into memory. "Don't worry, Mommy's coming! Mommy will make things better."

But no matter what she said, no matter what thoughts Pamela transmitted into the psychic abyss, the eleven year-old boy still kept drowning; his arms thrashing in Crystal Lake, his bald retarded head draped in weeds, howling as he sank lower and lower to his untimely death.

And Pamela crippled by the guilt.

* * *

Ross Feratu's bedroom was the stuff of Hollywood legend. It had seen more action than a hooker's crotch, stored drugs Timothy Leary couldn't even have spelled, and was kitted out like an S&M dungeon that got deleted from *Saturday Night Fever*. As one magazine commented:

"Think Gothic. Think Baron Frankenstein. Think Peter Cushing. Hold all those thoughts in your head and then add a mirrored ceiling and a four-poster bed with disco lights mounted in the bedposts."

In short, the Feratu inner sanctum wasn't famous for its sleaze—which was hardly unique to Beverly Hills—but because it was a laughing stock.

Jaomi sat at her dressing table. Between buffing her nails, she was searching through ZingBid on yet another of her Athlons, and was sick of listening to Ross crashing around inside the wardrobe—an adjacent walk-in larger than most people's living rooms. He still hadn't calmed down and now he was bitching about the state of his Jason costume, imagining damage that wasn't there.

"Did you polish the hockey mask?" he called through the open door.

"Why would I want to do that?" she asked wearily.

"You tell me," he huffed. "You're the one who put everything in bags. The hockey mask should look dirtier than this. Some of the grime's definitely been removed."

She clicked the mouse. "Maybe it fell off."

"Do you want to explain that?" Ross stepped into the bedroom and Jaomi nearly died.

"So when did Jason start looking like Stan Laurel?" she laughed.

But Ross was still stuck on her last point.

"Coffin dirt doesn't just fall off," he moaned. "You rubbed it off. I know how you work. You saw it in the guestroom, you wanted to put it in bags and you thought you'd do me a favor by giving it a quick clean. Well, don't do me favors. Okay?"

Then he went back into the dressing room.

Jaomi was about to answer him in no uncertain terms, because even with the lifts, the latex head-piece and all the tattered clothes, the guy still looked like a loser. But then a gentle tone rang from her PC, and a pop-up message alerted her to a new item that matched her default search terms. She clicked OK and waited to be redirected.

"Fucking techno-geek!" whined Ross. "How about lending me a hand?"

The page loaded.

Jaomi couldn't believe her eyes. Someone was actually claiming to have the body of Jason Voorhees for sale in a twenty-four hour auction. The seller's ID was "aliceinmonsterland."

"They should block this shit," she sighed, when a playful gleam suddenly entered her eyes. "Oh Ross," she called. "Guess what I've found?"

"Is it a ZingBid thing?" he asked.

"Yeah."

"Well, don't bother," he snapped. "I'm rein-stating the cut-off and it's absolutely non-negotiable. Now lend me a hand. I need to attack Finwell while she's still on air."

Jaomi groaned and turned off her computer. Ross was determined to go through with this reality thing. On no sleep and a head full of coke, he was hell-bent on going round to his neighbor's and making a complete fool of himself.

Just for a change.

Skyscrapers rose from the Manhattan bedrock like teeth on a witch's jaw. Some of the buildings—the Empire State, the Chrysler—were famous for being famous; while others, like the tower of plain glass dominating a corner of Midtown, thrived on sheer anonymity.

The black limousine signaled goodbye to the gridlock and made a left turn down a ramp, through an electronic gate into a private parking lot in the basement of the tower.

A woman was waiting for the vehicle's arrival. She was attractive, of average build and everything about her was tight. From the perfect angle of her stilettos to her scraped back hair, the woman was a model of black pinstriped severity. Her pencil skirt constrained her thighs as she opened the door and helped the gargantuan man out of the back seat.

"Thank you, Ms Jones," he puffed.

Then the two of them walked smartly over to an elevator large enough to accomodate the man seven times. Ms Jones stood aside to let him enter before her.

"The museum, please," he ordered.

She followed and pressed two buttons: one for the museum on the top floor and another for her office, five floors below. Her face remained impassive as the doors closed and the elevator began to rise, the mechanism so smooth that neither passenger felt momentum. Ms Jones was equally well oiled as she opened a wall compartment and took out a crystal tumbler, containing a measure of fifty year-old scotch. She placed the glass on a silver salver and offered it to her employer.

He accepted the drink without a word and sipped at the rich liquor as Ms Jones returned the tray and made her report.

"Special Agent Kyler is approaching Crystal Lake," her manner was crisp and monotonous. "She's been in transit approximately two hours."

"Excellent," confirmed the man. "She must have left instantly."

The next minute passed in silence until the elevator reached the first of its two stops and Ms Jones disembarked, leaving the man to continue alone. When the elevator finally reached the top floor, an automated voice requested, "Please enter your passcode or select another level."

Without pause, the man went to a keypad next to the main controls and entered: "1957." Then he waited as the door opened; it was a security door made from solid steel plate.

Four rows of lamps set high up in the ceiling sputtered into life and threw down yellow cones— islands of light in the unyielding darkness of a room that resembled an aircraft hangar. It seemed impossible that such a vast space could exist within the summit of the glass tower, but at this level the reflective exterior was merely a façade, cladding a vault of concrete and steel.

More astounding than the room itself, however, were its contents: dozens of cases made from bulletproof Perspex, each situated within its own pool of electric light and each containing one or more items from the man's private collection.

He had spent years putting this archive together. It had cost millions of dollars and he had had to use every means available to him—blackmail, bribery, theft, even murder—to gather all these priceless objects under one roof. The collection was all he lived for. It was his greatest pleasure. It was his obsession.

The man stepped out of the elevator and was comforted by the echoing of his shoes in this cavernous chamber, this dark and deathly womb.

Even from the bare semicircular entranceway, there was so much he could see. One case was full of assorted weapons: arrows, axes, a variety of knives, a poker, lengths of rope, two machetes—all pinned to a board. Another cabinet held a yellow, short-sleeved shirt with a mass of old bloodstains around the gut, and the words "Camp Crystal Lake" embroidered in black cotton on the left breast. A third container featured a stubby, cracked gravestone bearing the legend "Jason Voorhees," next to which stood an ornate pole torn from a cemetery railing that had been fashioned into a spear.

And then—heavens, he could barely control himself—he saw the case dedicated to two broken hockey masks, and a hood that was no more than a sack with a hole cut for the left eye. All evidence, all borrowed, bought or stolen from the authorities. And beyond that—the tanks, oh, the glorious, glorious tanks—bodies, remains, severed limbs, bleached and bloody dismemberment: victims of

Jason Voorhees floating in formaldehyde, their corpses disinterred, their rotting eyes replaced by white glass spheres giving them the semblance of butchered immortality.

But one case, one tall cabinet, stood alone. It had been brought to the front of the hall where it stood directly facing the elevator doors. And it was empty.

Nathaniel Morgas, the obese manipulator whose Voorhees museum was unique in the field of criminology, stared up at the vacant tank and took another sip of whiskey. Just one more relic—the ultimate relic—and his collection would be complete.

"I'm relying on you, Ms Kyler," he smirked, "you stupid, pathetic child."

A plaque at the base of the empty container read: "Jason Voorhees."

CHAPTER ELEVEN

It was well past six when the FBI agents reached Wessex County and an arboreal gloom was suffocating the headlamps of the Chrysler, forcing Tolleson to make heavy use of the GPS.

"We're almost there," he said, pointing at the navigator.

Kyler glanced at her map and saw they were less than a mile from the location specified in the Sowici message.

"We're losing the light," she commented.

"I'm more worried about the sheriff," added Tolleson. "D'you think he'll show?"

Kyler had phoned the local sheriff en route and had requested his assistance, only to be told that he was sick and tired of "Voorhees nonsense." Furthermore, the sheriff could state with absolute certainty that the message she'd received was a hoax, "just like the one I got last night." At which point, Kyler had forcefully reminded the sheriff of his duties.

"Look," Kyler angled her head towards the windshield and the squad car parked just ahead on the roadside, its lights in full swing.

Tolleson eased on the brakes and nosed the Chrysler close to the police vehicle.

"Okay," he said, straightening his back, "you're unofficial, remember, so let me handle the introductions."

Normally, as the senior agent, Kyler would have done the meeting and greeting, but her partner's suggestion made sense, and so she hung back as he got out and walked up to the sheriff.

"Thanks for coming out," said Tolleson, presenting his ID. "I'm Special Agent Tolleson and this," he pointed back at Michelle, "is Special Agent Kyler."

The sheriff tipped the brim of his hat, "John Haslip. Crystal Lake."

Kyler noticed the sheriff had come out alone, but, surprisingly, he wasn't displaying any hostility. Evidently he too was good at reading body language, because he immediately directed his comments in her direction.

"After you called," he started, "I ran a check on the number."

"It was a cellphone," Kyler interrupted, joining them, "registered in the name of Sowici."

"Half right," Haslip wasn't the least bit smug in his correction. "The owner's someone called Richard Willis."

Kyler turned to her partner, "Must be the boy she mentioned. Trick."

"He was one of the two kids I spoke to," said Haslip, frowning.

"Do you make a habit of ignoring emergency calls, Sheriff Haslip?" asked Kyler coolly.

The cop held his ground. "Only when they're fake. Listen, a carnival came through town last night and upset some of the residents. So I moved them on and within an hour I got the call. It's just their way of stirring up trouble."

Kyler stepped up to within a couple of feet of the sheriff.

"This morning," she said firmly, "I received a message from Gloria Sowici. She claims two of her friends were murdered near this position and that Jason Voorhees is responsible."

Haslip shook his head. "That's what I mean. Jason this, Jason that, always Jason. With all due respect, Agent Kyler, I've heard it a thousand times. Crystal Lake's a magnet for these freaks."

"So as far as you're concerned," said Kyler, her voice rising, "it's all just a sick joke?"

"That's right."

"And two kids weren't murdered out here, and you didn't even bother to check."

The sheriff stared blankly and let his silence do the talking.

Kyler turned to her partner. "Get a lamp and start searching over there," she indicated the trees on the northern side of the road.

Glad to be getting out of the heat, Tolleson went back to his car, took a flashlight out of the trunk and then went off into the woods.

Kyler watched her partner until he was out of sight, giving Haslip a chance to study her: plainly attractive, dark brown suit, no makeup, looking for a fight—there was something seductively powerful about Agent Kyler. Suddenly she turned, and the sheriff blurted out the first thing he could think of:

"So where's Sowici now?"

"She called from a diner in Reculver," answered Kyler, "but we haven't been able to reach her since."

"Well that clinches it," said the sheriff. "I sent the carnival that way myself. Boy, did I get that woman wrong."

"Woman?" Kyler caught the faint whiff of misconduct. "What woman?"

"Alice Witney," replied the sheriff. "She's the cause of all this. She couldn't get me riled by calling at the office, so now she's got you on my back."

Suddenly Kyler wasn't feeling so sure of herself. A potential suspect had just made an unexpected entrance, raising the possibility that both Kyler and her enigmatic ally in the black limousine had been fooled by a couple of dumb prank calls.

The agent was considering what to do next when Tolleson rushed out onto the road and threw up. His puke splashed and splattered on the asphalt and immediately galvanized the air with the cheesy stench of stomach acid.

"I... I think I just found Willis," he groaned before heaving more of his lunch onto the blacktop.

* * *

The news reporter crouched behind the wall as a further series of explosions went off in the distance. Despite the fact that he was wearing a flak jacket and had chosen to appear before camera wearing military style khakis, the unshaven young man was clearly terrified. He was also wrapping his report.

"One thing remains certain. Until the situation here in Baghdad is stabilized, more American lives will be lost. Ken Sears, LACA News, Iraq."

"Thanks Ken," said the anchorman, even though Sears had sent the recording in five hours ago.

"Now back to our top story: Shock Rock Legend Ross Feratu—Behind Bars. Earlier this afternoon, thousands of viewers saw the star arrested live on air when he gatecrashed daytime hit reality show, *Kantayna of Joy*. Wearing a costume based on the is-he-or-isn't-he-real serial killer, Jason Voorhees, Feratu ran in front of the cameras and attacked Ms Finwell with a prop machete. The Academy Award-winning actress escaped unharmed, but was drenched in stage blood, as not only her security staff but Feratu's own people fought to subdue him. Police then arrived to arrest the singer, who was handcuffed and taken to the local station. At the moment, it's unclear exactly what charges he's facing, but it's understood that eight separate misdemeanors are involved.

"Commentators are already dismissing the attack as a publicity stunt. Feratu's new album, *Making Krueger My Bitch*, was released just last week and is the first disc in the singer's spectacular career not to have entered the charts.

"Well, a few moments ago, reporter Sardice Winterton spoke to Ross Feratu's manager, Luke Veranti. Viewers are advised that this interview has been censored."

The camera held with the steadiness of a force ten gale as it buffeted up tight against the puffy, pale face and the dense black jacket and polo neck of the short media executive.

"I ain't that *BLEEP*'s *BLEEP*ing manager! You wanna speak to his manager? Go talk to that *BLEEP*ing *BLEEP* of a porn star. Now get that *BLEEP*ing piece of *BLEEP* outta my face, you dumb *BLEEP*."

The writing on the sign read "Hunt Ridge 4."

Just four more miles and Pamela would be reunited with her son. Even now, behind the wheel of the shaky old van, Pamela could hear Jason calling to her, his tormented wails drowning out that other voice—the voice of the girl Pamela had overpowered.

Glo looked at herself in the rearview and laughed.

"There's no point fighting, dear," she smiled. "Can't you see? You don't exist anymore. Not even your mother would recognize you now."

Suddenly her hands wrenched the steering wheel over to the left, aiming Swinburne's truck straight towards a wall of massive oak trees.

"I won't let you!" The vocal cords and the mind vibrating them both belonged to Gloria Sowici.

"Now now, dear," grimaced Pamela, struggling to bring the girl's body back under her influence.

"That's not very nice. That's not very nice at all. You know I'll have to punish you."

The tires kicked up dust from the shoulder before the truck veered and regained its rightful place along the center of the lane. Glo had failed in her attempt to defeat Pamela through suicide, and now she felt her dwindling life force being sucked into the maelstrom of Pamela's cruelty.

"I thought we might be friends," said Pamela with a hint of regret. "But I guess it's time to say goodbye. It's a pity. I don't get along with many people and I had to wait a long time before I found you. You're special."

Glo's failing life force tried to fight, to resist. She knew that, when Pamela finished speaking, her flame would be extinguished once and for all.

"Thanks to you," Pamela continued, "I'm going to find my son. You see, I've been away for far too long—Crystal Lake's become a mess. So I'm going to take Jason home and then we'll clear out all the trash. But first, I've got to make Jason better. He's sick, you know. That's why he hasn't killed those brutes at the carnival. But don't worry. I know how to fix Jason. By tomorrow, Jason won't need the silly old moon any more."

With that, Pamela tensed her stolen body and concentrated her willpower on one final task—a task that would stop the little bitch from interfering ever again. She could hear a recessed whisper in an alcove of her mind. She smiled. It was begging her for mercy. And then it fell silent.

Glo was dead.

* * *

Kyler watched as Trick was zipped up in a body bag. Then she rejoined Tolleson and Sheriff Haslip in the eye of the kind of 911 storm Crystal Lake hadn't seen in years. Squad cars, medics, photographers, floodlights, forensics teams—the forest was crawling with investigators, all working towards the one goal of identifying the killer.

"Sheriff!" a voice crackled over Haslip's radio. "We've found the other girl and there's a hut with three more bodies."

Kyler listened to the message intently.

"Please confirm," responded the sheriff.

"Two female civilians and a male police officer. The bodies look ten, twenty, maybe thirty years old."

"Jesus!" gasped Haslip. "What's going on?"

Kyler didn't hesitate to offer her opinion. "Sowici said she came searching for Voorhees artifacts. She didn't mention a hut but maybe that's where it all started. Maybe she found something there. Maybe even Jason."

"I don't have time for this," said the sheriff. He tried to pass by, but Kyler wouldn't budge.

"You didn't have time for their call either," she jibed.

Tolleson quickly stepped forward. "Look, sheriff, we're all on the same team here…"

"Then stop wasting my time with all this Jason crap," barked Haslip. "All right, I made a mistake—you can put that in your report if you want—but this is just a sick copycat. That's all."

And then he set off in the direction of the newly discovered bodies.

"Strong work," muttered Tolleson, but when he turned to look at Kyler he saw that she too had gone and was standing over by one of the forensics guys. The man was on his hands and knees and was pawing at a bare patch of dirt.

"What is it?" she asked.

"Three sets of prints," replied the investigator thoughtfully. "The boy's, another set... possibly female... and—"

"And?" prompted Kyler.

"Male. Size thirteen work boots in poor condition. Weight, three to four hundred pounds."

"What about height?" she asked.

The man rubbed his chin, "Difficult to tell, but... from the stride I'd say six five, six six, thereabouts."

"Some copycat," smiled Tolleson grimly. "Was there an audition?"

Kyler ignored the joke and grabbed the flashlight from Tolleson's hand. Then she directed the beam down onto the footprints and started to fight her way through the bushes.

"Hey!" called Tolleson. "Where are you going?"

Not wanting to be overheard, Kyler waved him over.

"The sheriff's so eager to get the bodies in front of the medical examiner, he's letting them walk all over the place before they've protected the prints. Look," she highlighted a clear set of indentations in the soil. "I think it's Sowici."

"Okay," Tolleson nodded. "You check this out and I'll go see what I can find out about the hut. That's if the sheriff will talk to me."

Kyler actually smiled, and then they split up.

Twenty paces on, she felt completely alone. All the floodlights, and all the voices and radio chatter, faded into nothing as she followed the prints through the trees around and back out onto the road. She was some fifty yards short of the emergency posse, but from the flashing lights she could see that the asphalt beneath her feet was a veritable Picasso of burnt rubber. She was surrounded by swirling tire marks, all from large vehicles like the trucks of a sideshow.

And there was something else.

A small object was glinting between the double yellows. It was hard, white, and had rough edges. Kyler went over for a closer look. It seemed impossible, but there was nothing else it could be. She bent down and picked up the broken piece of hockey mask.

Sheriff Haslip had seen enough. He made sure everyone knew what they had to do, then made his way back towards the road; there was coffee being served in one of the vans. But he'd barely had a second to himself when he saw Kyler rushing towards him.

"Sheriff!" she called, quickening her pace.

"We found three missing persons from the '84 incident," he said, anticipating her question. "What the hell were those kids doing here?"

But Kyler was coming from a completely different angle. "Sheriff, I need to know where you sent the carnival."

"What?" He looked at her as if she'd gone crazy. "You don't think they had anything to do with this?"

"No, but I think they might have picked up Sowici," she replied, not daring to tell him what she really thought.

"You serious?" he asked suspiciously.

"She's the only eyewitness," Kyler insisted. "We need her here."

Haslip shook his head. "I can't spare anyone. Maybe if I call ahead…"

"No," said Kyler a little too abruptly. "If she sees a uniform, it might scare her. But look, if I leave right now, I could have her back here in a few hours."

The sheriff considered her proposal.

"Well, okay," he said. "There's four trucks and an old man's in charge, Witney, seems a decent guy. But, and here's the thing, it's a horror show— Doctor Ghostman's Carnival of Terror. I told them to try their luck at Hunt Ridge. So if the girl's hitched up with them, that's where she'll be."

"Thanks," said Kyler, and she offered him her hand. "As soon as we find her, I'll let you know."

Haslip accepted her hand and shook it. "If I'm not here, call the office. You got my number, right?"

"I certainly have," she grimaced.

Despite the tragic setting, the sheriff had to laugh. He'd screwed up this case from day one, and here was a girl from the Bureau rubbing his face in his mess like a dog that needed house-training.

"Tolles…" she started to shout when she saw her partner emerge from the woods. He was holding his cellphone.

"I can't get a signal," he complained.

"It's the trees," explained Haslip. "Use my radio."

"We don't have time," interrupted Kyler, hustling her partner back towards the Chrysler.

"Hey!" he griped. "What's going on?"

"The girl's story was true," she whispered. "Now shut up and get in the car."

Sheriff Haslip drank his coffee but, as the agents prepared to leave, he couldn't decide if Kyler's departure was a cause for celebration or a matter for concern. Either way, it was going to be a long night.

George Witney opened the door of the motorhome and looked out on Harper Field. The show was due to commence at eight thirty, so that gave him twenty minutes to spare before putting on his Doktor Geistmann outfit. That's assuming they would actually have an audience tonight.

Normally, it was Kenton's duty to drum up publicity, but after Sparx and Vincenzo had built that accursed Voorhees display, it seemed that everyone had spent the afternoon either hiding or tearing one another apart. And yet—the show still had so many happy memories for the old man. He stepped down and enjoyed the stillness of the moment, among his beloved monsters.

The exhibits had all been arranged in a row along one end of the field, facing into the huge clearing where, hopefully, a crowd would be gathered. At the start of the evening, each tableau would be shrouded in darkness. But then, as the show progressed, Witney would present each item in turn, giving his spiel while his people operated the lights and special effects.

His eyes glistened as he relived the innocence of a vampire's bite. He longed to return to a time when the wolfbane bloomed and the villagers warned him not to go on to the castle. A life of flaming torches and grave robbers—with no bills, no blackmailing scoundrels, no sluts masquerading as wives and daughters, no human nature at all.

Gripping his cane, he hobbled in front of Camp Crystal Lake and shook a veined fist at Jason's dormant body.

"Damn you, Voorhees!" he cursed. "This is all your doing."

"No, George." Unknown to the old man, Freely had been keeping pace behind him. "It's your fault. Be a man for once in your life and take some responsibility."

George lifted his stick and pointed it at Jason. "I have half a mind to set fire to the thing."

"I wouldn't do that," Freely warned. "I hate to admit it, but your daughter's right. People will pay big bucks to see this jerk."

"Please, Kenton," begged the old man. "Don't make me present this monstrosity."

"Don't make me prethent thith monthrothity," laughed Freely. "George, what am I going to do with you?"

"What do you mean?"

Kenton's mood turned into venom. "If you don't pitch Voorhees tonight, I'll kill you myself, you stinking old bastard."

Witney cowered from the threat and bowed his head in resignation.

"All right," he intoned, "I'll do as you ask."

"Just make sure you do," warned Kenton.

The two of them sidled away, completely unaware that Alice had been listening to them from her hiding place beneath the facsimile boat dock. She was now on her second bottle of Jack and was getting shitfaced. A canvas travel bag lay on the ground beside her and, as she rested on her back, she patted the laptop tucked safely inside it.

"Freely," she slurred to no one in particular, "I don't use this word very often—Infact, I don't even like the word—but you are a total cunt."

And with that, she blew a kiss towards the bolted crotch of the unconscious, machete-wielding savior standing a mere couple of feet above her head, and then passed out.

It was Kyler who was now behind the wheel of the Chrysler. Tolleson couldn't help but flinch; she was thundering through the lake region as if all the Hounds of Hell were pursuing her.

"You really think we'll find Sowici in Hunt Ridge?" he asked, trying to relax.

"Nope," she replied. The sky had turned mazarine and Kyler could see a full moon rising over the hills.

"Then what—"

"I'm looking for Jason Voorhees," she cut in.

"I uh…" Tolleson cleared his throat, "I did a little research on that—before I came to your apartment."

"And?" she asked pointedly.

"Jason Voorhees was killed in a Bureau ambush in 1993. The coroner reported explosive trauma, third degree burns, multiple bullet—"

"Do you know what happened to that coroner?" she interrupted.

"As a matter of fact, I do. He... well, he ate some of Jason's remains and then killed over a dozen people. But it's because he was in collusion with Robert Campbell," he quickly added. "Either that or he was in the grip of some kind of hysteria."

"Very good," Kyler remarked. "You've got the official line down to a tee."

But Tolleson was undeterred. "All the evidence proved beyond doubt that every one of the murders in the week subsequent to the ambush was committed either by the coroner or by Campbell. Campbell was a nut. He was using the deaths to promote a TV show he was making."

"You need to go back and do your homework," Kyler answered stonily. "Diana Kimble, Sheriff Landis and Creighton Duke are just three victims I can think of whose deaths couldn't be attributed to either of the two main suspects."

"Kyler, come on. This is just more zombie talk."

Tolleson was walking a fine line between trying to reason with his partner and pissing her off.

"And that's Jason's most powerful defense," she replied. "He's killed hundreds of people, but the evidence is so confused we've got him filed somewhere between Father Christmas and the Tooth Fairy. In 1984, Ginny Field said in her statement that she'd found a hut containing three dead bodies, but there were doubts about her sanity and a police search turned up nothing. Now I'm positive that's the same hut. Three bodies—one of them a cop—Field said she thought the place was Jason's home. So Sowici and her friends come along, they find the place and now two of them are dead."

"But we've no evidence Jason's involved," argued Tolleson. "We don't know why Sowici said what she did. She's just a kid."

"Male—size thirteen work boots," Kyler was repeating the description of the killer's footprints, "three to four hundred pounds—six foot five."

"But that could be any big guy."

Tolleson was determined to keep his partner honest, but suddenly she wasn't listening to him. Because there was something else Field had said in her statement, about something she'd found in the shack…

A phone rang.

"Must have a signal," Cory observed.

He took the cell out of his jacket and answered the call, a terse conversation during which the young man did most of the listening. When it was over, he sat back in stunned silence.

"Can you talk about it?" Kyler tried to sound cool, but her ears were definitely burning.

"That was Landau," answered Tolleson with a gulp. "He knows you're here and he wants me to take your badge. You're to be suspended from duty immediately."

Kyler suddenly remembered the fat man's warning: "Within twenty-four hours you're going to be suspended from duty. You can't trust anyone, Ms Kyler, least of all your junior partner."

She kept her hands firmly on the wheel, but her grip on the situation was beginning to unravel.

* * *

Alice awoke to the familiar sound of a wolf howling over a crack of thunder and the ominous organ melody of Bach's *Toccata and Fugue in D Minor*. She was still lying in the crawlspace beneath the Voorhees display and it was completely dark, but she knew the drill well enough to realize that the show was about to start.

She felt inside the pocket of her pilot's jacket; good, the keys were still there. A few hours from now and she'd put Jason aboard the RV, take off and leave the dirty bastards to rot in hell.

Suddenly she heard voices. It was Freely.

"Have you seen Alice?"

"The fucking bitch stole my computer," whined Judge.

"All right," snapped Kenton, "I don't need your life story. Just make sure nothing goes wrong with the show."

The introductory tape had a couple more minutes left to run; but when the coffin creaked, a smoke bomb would go off, Doktor Geistmann would step out to greet the audience, and everyone would be tied up until the end of the performance.

Alice took a swig from the half-empty bottle and scuttled over to peek through a gap in the wooden base. She couldn't believe it: the field was full of people. Families, senior citizens, gangs of teenagers, children—it looked as if the whole town had come out.

"Good evening, ladies and gentleman," boomed a voice over the PA. "My name is Doktor Geistmann and I bid you welcome."

There was a loud cheer as two flash pots were ignited, and Alice decided it was time to go out and take a look. She grabbed the travel bag and got up from behind the Crystal Lake tableau, only to discover she was drunk as a fart. She sniggered and teetered out into the middle of the crowd. Rows of vehicles were parked along the far side of Harper Field, but Alice noticed a latecomer arriving in a beat-up old van: some writing on the side of the junk-heap read, "Swinburne's Hardware."

She drank some more Jack and then watched her father.

Seeing him standing there in the lights, wearing his ghoulish ringmaster's costume, she could have been seven years old again. God, he seemed so happy.

"Tonight, ladies and gentlemen," he was saying, "I will be unveiling the remains of the most notorious serial killer in the history of crime. I dare you! Look inside the hockey mask at the hideous face of the monster. And who among you will be brave enough to touch the machete that hacked one hundred bloody corpses into pieces?"

Just then Eli Brookes, a skinny ginger-haired boy standing near to Alice, started nudging his four friends.

"This blows major league chunks," he moaned. "There's no concessions, no merchandise and if you wanna take a leak, you gotta go in the corner of the frikking field. If these morons don't deliver some seriously awesome content, I'm going straight on the net."

"Let's trash the place," said one of the others excitedly.

A third teen put his hands to his mouth and hollered, "You suck!"

People started to laugh.

"I can see," Witney said raising his hands, "some of you are growing impatient. You're asking yourselves, 'Is it really true? Do they really have the body of the immortal Jason Voorhees?'"

"No!" shouted the ginger punk. "We're asking ourselves why we wasted our money on this shit!"

More laughs. The mood was turning ugly.

However, the old man hadn't been in the business over forty years without learning how to work an audience.

"Very well," he proclaimed. "I shall prove to the skeptics among you that the Crystal Lake killer is standing here on this very field. Prepare to witness the very first unveiling... *of Jason Voorhees!*"

A recording of a woman's scream ripped through the speakers, red lights came to life around Jason and then—nothing. The maniac merely stood there, posing in mid-slaughter like any other waxwork: the sense of anticlimax was almost palpable.

"What does he do?" heckled Eli.

"I'll show you," came a voice from the back. Glo lifted the head from the seat of the van and held it up into the eerie whitewash of the moon.

Jason burst into life and the crowd roared with delight.

"Finally," smiled the boy, "some action!"

The whiskey bottle fell from Alice's hand as she alone realized that the killer's violent eruption wasn't part of the act.

"Oh my God," she muttered. Alice ran forward through the tightly packed bodies, her eyes fixed on Jason as he broke free of the chain that was keeping him fastened to the upright. Sparx had posed the maniac using uncoiled wire hangers, and now Jason was plucking the twists of metal away from his joints, frustrated by the impediments.

"Dad, run!" cried Alice, but her father couldn't hear her above the delight of the audience. He was still facing the people and he seemed to have no idea that Jason had come alive behind him.

"Dad!"

Jason tried to bring the machete down on the back of Witney's head, but the blade had been wired to his wrist so it came loose and fell onto the boat dock. The noise brought George to his senses. He turned just as Jason reached out, pulled an entire window frame away from the wall of the fake cabin and brought it crashing down around the old man's head. The killer kept his hands on the wood and shook the window like a prospector panning for epileptic gold, ramming and splitting the shards of glass in and out of Witney's face. The old man screamed as the razor pane pierced his eyes, tore up his teeth and slashed into his arteries. His body juddered and stiffened as Jason transmitted the full force of his psychopathic wrath into the sheet of cracked glazing. Then Jason lifted the frame high above his head, the old man's feet kicking and twitching above the stage, and threw the window and George Witney into the front row of the audience.

The showman hit the ground in a shatter of mulched and heaving flesh.

Alice fell to her knees and screamed. And behind her, the flame-haired Brookes turned to his friends and shouted, "Cool!"

CHAPTER TWELVE

One last document was all that stood between Ross Feratu and freedom. He scanned the columns of cramped print—all the usual stuff about "aforementioned parties of the third part as defined in subsection 3.2"—before realizing he was hopelessly lost.

He looked up and whined, "Where do I sign?"

"Same as all the others," sighed Lieutenant Marshak, indicating the half dozen forms Ross had already scratched his moniker on. "The line at the bottom of the page."

The lieutenant and his officers, one female and one male, were doing their best not to laugh at Feratu's ridiculous outfit. The singer had got the replica hockey mask pushed high up on his forehead, revealing a sweaty, bewildered face framed within a balaclava of latex. His features were made even more absurd by two panda rings of greasepaint smeared around his eyes.

Ross looked up at Vonda Coles, his attorney, and waited for her to give him the nod. Then he signed the sheet, dropped the pen on the table and scraped back his chair. The room was so beige and Formica, it was practically Communist.

Lieutenant Marshak picked up the bail documents and started to go through them. Suddenly, he stopped on a page and smirked.

"Something funny?" pounced Ross.

The cop shook his head, cleared his throat and continued checking the rest of the papers.

"Go on," repeated the singer. "If you've got something to say, let's hear it."

"Ross," said Vonda, placing a hand on his shoulder. "We're done here."

Marshak looked up and addressed Coles directly. "The arraignment's set for the twentieth—"

"Whoa, whoa, whoa," interrupted Ross. "You haven't answered my question. Is it my handwriting? Is it funnier than other rock stars'?"

The lieutenant shuffled with mock self-restraint.

"Is it my name?" Ross persisted. "Does Dwayne Weintraub do it for you? Is that it?"

One of the other cops began to snigger.

"Well, no…" replied Marshak hesitantly. "It's just that under occupation you've put 'Musician.'"

Ross frowned. "So? What's funny about that?"

"Well, it's not that it's funny," Marshak explained. "But, well… you're not really a musician, are you?"

"What the fuck?" Ross was dumbstruck. "Of course I am!"

"Well, no, you're not," everything about the lieutenant stank of passive aggression. "You're more a celebrity."

Ross looked at his attorney. "Can you believe this guy?"

"Let's just go," she said. "Jaomi's waiting in the lobby."

"Fuck, Vonda! It's bad enough these guys have just taken fifty K off me. And now they're insulting me? Can they do that? I mean, legally?"

"Come on," Marshak argued. "You don't play anything. You're just a singer."

"That's where you're wrong, buddy," said Ross, turning from his attorney and jumping to his feet.

"Well, I've never seen you play," ventured one of the other cops sheepishly.

Ross kicked the chair.

"What is going on here?" he shouted. "Are you guys blind or something? I played guitar on the 'TJ's Gone Wild' video."

It was the third cop who spoke now.

"I've got a friend who plays guitar," she rattled, "and he says you definitely mimed in that video."

"Your friend!" shrieked Ross. "Who gives a shit?"

"So go on, then." The policewoman folded her arms as if digging in for a long battle. "How many hours a day do you practice?"

"What the fuck does that have to do with any-thing?"

"My friend's a musician," she persisted angrily, "a *real* musician, and he practices four hours a day,"

"Maybe he needs it," snapped Ross.

"So you must take a lot of singing practice, huh?" cracked Marshak.

The other policeman laughed, but the female officer was only just getting into her groove.

"This puppy don't even write his own songs," she howled. "He's written, sorry, *co-written* only five per cent of his entire catalog."

"What is it with you three?" Ross hollered. "Are you the new fucking LAPD Rapid Review Squad or something? A new show opens and you arm yourselves with typewriters?"

Silence.

"Now you listen," he shouted. "I've been to Ethiopia, okay. I've met starving children and they worship me. So don't tell me I'm not a real fucking musician!"

Coles had heard just about enough. She grabbed Ross by the frayed sleeves of his burlap jacket and hauled him out into the lobby where his wife was buffing her nails. When Ross saw Jaomi, he broke into tears.

"God," he cried, rushing to embrace her, "I thought I'd never see you again."

"It's only been an hour," she answered dryly.

"Those bastards," he wept. "If you could have seen what they just did to me. Seriously, Jaomi, forget Rodney King—it was that bad."

Vonda signed out at the front desk and called over to Ross, "I'll send you my bill." Then she asked the duty sergeant if there was another way out of the building and smartly made her exit.

Jaomi, on the other hand, led Ross to the front door where a rabid press pack was waiting. As soon as Ross stepped out, he was bombarded with questions and requests from photographers to "Look this way!"

The singer gawked disbelievingly at his wife, "What's going on?"

"They're here for you, hot stuff," she smiled. "Your attack on Finwell's been running all evening."

"You're shitting me?" his tears dried instantly, to be replaced by an expression of unbridled joy.

Jaomi shook her head and laughed, "You're big news, Ross."

"Rock and roll!" he shouted.

Then he pulled the hockey mask down over his face and, without wasting another second, began to pose for the paparazzi.

A journalist shoved a tape recorder under his nose. "Mister Feratu, will you be apologizing to Kantayna Finwell?"

"Apologize?" laughed Ross. "I've just sent her ratings through the roof."

"She's issued a statement," shouted another reporter, "accusing you of being mentally unstable."

"Hey, Osama," Ross jeered, "in case you haven't seen the news lately, the whole world's a carnival of maniacs. So who the hell will notice one more?"

The writing on the sign read "Hunt Ridge 4." Just four more miles and Kyler would know whether or not Jason Voorhees was real.

Logically, there was no guarantee the carnival had taken Sheriff Haslip's advice and gone to Hunt Ridge; nor was there any firm reason to believe that either Jason or Sowici was actually riding with the carnival. And yet somehow Kyler knew—just like she knew she couldn't trust the man in the limo—that events were rapidly drawing to a conclusion. At the moment, however, she had a more immediate problem to contend with.

"How did Landau find out?" she asked, slowing the Chrysler.

"What does it matter?" answered Tolleson. "If we don't turn back, you'll lose your job."

"You're the only person who knew," she said, keeping her eyes on the road.

"Maybe the sheriff..."

"We never told him which office we're from. Anyway, why would he? As far as he's concerned, we're here on official business."

"But you did piss him off," suggested Tolleson with an almost schoolyard levity.

"I don't buy that," Kyler fired back. "While you were off hiding in the woods, trying to get your cell to work, the sheriff and I came to an agreement."

"I was not hiding." Tolleson was clearly offended by her not-so-veiled accusation.

"Is that when you phoned Landau," she pushed, "or had you already tipped him off before we left Corning?"

Tolleson placed his back against the passenger door so that he could face his partner full on.

"Michelle, I swear. This has nothing to do with me."

"You've been opposed to this investigation from the start," she asserted, almost as if interrogating a suspect.

"Only because it's insane," he protested. "It's this crusade of yours. Landau's had it in for you for months. All these ghouls and zombies— they're killing your career. And now you're gonna throw it all away because of a suspect who doesn't even exist."

"There has never been a definitive solution to the Voorhees murders," she answered coolly. "Between 1984 and 2003 Jason's death was reported on nine separate occasions, and on each occasion there was a series of murders that either started or ended in the Crystal Lake area and each series used the same MO."

"Then the witnesses got it wrong." A hint of impatience was creeping into Tolleson's voice.

"Some of them were highly qualified medics," Kyler answered with equal impatience. "They were wholly reliable."

"Okay," said Tolleson, "then it's not Jason at all. It's a bunch of different people pretending to be Jason."

Kyler rejected this out of hand, "There's only one case on record of someone copying Jason. In 1987 a man named Roy..."

As she spoke, Tolleson shook his head with increasing annoyance until finally he'd heard enough.

"Every report describing Jason is different," he complained over the top of her. "I told you I did my homework. One minute he's got a sack on his head, the next it's a hockey mask. One person says the mask's cracked, another says there's no damage. And when they describe his face, they can't decide if he's rotted, melted or retarded! One girl says she can knock him down with a piece of wood while some guys say not even a shotgun will stop him—"

"All right!" Kyler raised her voice just south of an actual shout. "I admit there are some problems…"

"Problems?" Tolleson couldn't believe the understatement.

"But that's my whole point," she tried to explain. "There has never been a comprehensive explanation."

"I'm sorry, Kyler," Tolleson said, easing off a little, "but this is really starting to bother me. I don't want you to be pissed—really I don't—but maybe Landau has something. Maybe your judgment is foggy."

"But I just told you…"

"You just told me you need a vacation," he sighed.

"Thanks," she said, her voice falling.

"Michelle—"

"Don't call me Michelle." She was still managing to remain calm. The same breathing techniques she used in combat were just as valuable in personal relationships.

"Kyler, look, if you could just—I don't understand why you're so determined not to see the obvious."

She removed her right hand from the steering wheel and took a silver locket from around her neck. Then, without shifting her gaze from the road, she handed the pendant over to Tolleson.

"I've spent all my life searching for proof of life after death." Her partner delicately pressed the button that opened the trinket. "I need to know if Jason is real," she continued.

Tolleson leaned forward and held the locket close to the soft light of the dash. In one side of the case was a photo of a woman holding a baby girl, while in the other was a lock of that same woman's hair.

"Twenty years ago," said Kyler as her partner studied the locket, "Jason Voorhees murdered a woman named Martha Kyler."

Tolleson went cold.

"That's right," said Kyler. "Jason murdered my mother."

The crowd clapped and cheered as Jason held Sparx and Vincenzo up in the air. The killer had straightened the first two fingers of his hands into V shapes, plunging the left V into Vincenzo's eyes and the right V into Sparx's. Then he'd stood erect on the boat dock and lifted the bleeding victims off their feet in a murderous victory salute. Now he waited until the showmen finally stopped pissing and shitting themselves, and shook them off his hands.

Vincenzo went crashing into the cabin wall, bringing the whole façade down on his head, while Sparx landed in a snap of broken wood that used to be a paddle.

And still Eli Brookes didn't think he was getting his money's worth.

"Turn it up!" he shouted. "We can't hear anything!"

Alice looked up from where she was kneeling on the ground. "You fucking little bastard!" she screamed.

As she got up and started to rush towards Eli, every light in the carnival suddenly went out. The moon now held sway over Harper Field and panic went running through the crowd like a virus.

Jason grabbed the Camp Crystal Lake sign and broke one end of it into a mess of splintered teeth. Then he dropped down among the audience and thrust the puncture board in and out of their meat bags. Ravaging their faces, spilling their intestines, ending their lives—riding the horror like the charnel mongoloid reaper he was born to be.

Judge ran to the generator that stood behind the huge eighteen-wheeler. The diesel engine was still grinding away, but he was appalled to see that someone had severed all the power cables. Suddenly a sharp bang came from inside the trailer.

"Who's there?" he called.

The only answer he got was another loud crash.

He picked up a wrench lying next to the generator and crept forward, the screams from the crowd adding impossible tension.

"I'm warning you." He counted to three before raising the tool and jumping in front of the open trailer doors.

There was no one inside.

"Damn!" he gasped.

He turned to go back to the generator when Glo suddenly stabbed him through the stomach with her hunting knife. She laughed and came at him again and again, the sharp steel point cutting into his face, his chest, the hands he tried to shield himself with. He collapsed onto a stack of crates as she came tearing forward with laughter and the repeated downfall of the blade. Stabs of silver, shining in the moonlight, snatching at his flesh until all life faded from his eyes. And then she stabbed him in the throat.

And laughed.

Alice fought her way through the fleeing crowd. A couple of men with handguns tried to stop Jason, but managed only to wound and kill some of the other townsfolk. Everyone else was running for their vehicles, turning the far side of the field into a madhouse of horns, revving engines and crumpled metal.

Suddenly, a dead body hit the ground in front of her.

It had been tossed through the air by Jason, who was using an iron railing from the Jack the Ripper display as a spear.

Alice had to find a way to stop the maniac. The carnival was finished, but Jason Voorhees was still her meal ticket. If only she could... suddenly she saw the body of her father and a tunnel of sadness drew her towards his horribly violated remains. She didn't know if she was emboldened by liquor or numbed by grief, but she had started to move towards him, towards the chaos, when she was spun round and punched in the mouth.

"This is all your fault, you stupid bitch!"

She collapsed onto the dirt and saw Kenton Freely standing over her. He had a gun in his hand.

"You wanna say goodbye to the old bastard?" he snarled.

Then he hauled her to her feet, slapped her across the face and threw her down onto her father's body. Her hand fell on the window pane wrapped around the dead man's head and she screamed. Freely was out of control.

"Suck George's dick," he ranted, pointing the gun at her, "and I'll let you live."

"Are you fucking insane?" she cried.

Tears were flooding down Alice's face and her lips were thick with mucus. She could feel her father beneath her and was suddenly overcome by remorse at all their wasted years.

"Do it!" shouted Freely, as the diesel store exploded.

Clouds of flame, three stories high, rose behind the long storage truck. From short distance the heat wave was so intense, Kenton had to look away—which is why he didn't see Jason standing right behind him.

The cast-iron spear was rammed into Kenton's sphincter, pushed up into his bowels and then shoved out, in a shower of droplets, through his abdomen. He barely had time to scream before Jason took the pole in both hands and then hoisted his body up in the air like a banner.

"Arggh! For God's sakes!" shrieked Kenton, the gun falling from his hands. "Please! Help me!"

His limbs bobbed up and down, undulating with the killer's footsteps as Jason roamed unbound among the fleeing and the dead.

"Please!" cried Freely, gargling with bloody tracheal asphyxiation. "Help me!"

Alice climbed dizzily to her feet and tried to make sense of what was going on. Then she saw Kenton impaled on the end of the spear like a trophy puppet—and laughed.

"Alice!" he wailed, "Please! Help me! For God's sakes! *Please!*"

There was only one round left in the revolver and Jason was walking straight towards her. She took careful aim and...

"Argghhhhhhh!"

She shot Kenton in the balls.

Jason halted—the slug had gone straight through into his enormous chest—before tossing both the spear and Kenton onto the spreading fire. Freely screeched and yelped. He railed at every injustice he'd ever had to suffer at the hands of all those two-faced bastards who'd screwed up his life—people like Alice and her father—people like Jason. Kenton cursed every damn one of them as he writhed and blackened and dripped and melted and died.

Alice's laughter grew even more hysterical and was threatening to spill over into madness. Jason was coming for her now and she was completely and utterly defenseless.

"Jason!"

The killer stopped and looked to see who was calling him. Alice too managed to get a grip on her wits long enough to notice a short teenaged girl standing in front of the raging fire.

Backlit by the flame, exultant in the havoc she'd caused, Glo raised the severed head high into the moonlight and beckoned Jason forward with her bloody knife.

"That's it, Jason. Come on. Be a good boy. Come to Mommy!"

Alice was sole witness to this incredible rendezvous and, as the people of Hunt Ridge rushed

and hollered every which way over Harper Field,
she laughed with the needle-sharp dissonance of a
woman going insane.

High above the midtown traffic, but shielded from
the noise by the plate glass exterior, Nathaniel
Morgas sat waiting at his desk. Each piece of furniture in his office cost more than most of his staff
earned in a year. Combined, the décor and the
ornaments evoked the high-contrast minimalism
of a shark. Nathaniel Morgas was massive, and yet
the place where he conducted his business was
even bigger.

He remained perfectly still in his high-backed
leather chair, his eyes focused on the elevator
doors as they opened to admit his personal assistant. Her high heels rapped on the marble floor
with mechanical obedience.

"Thank you for being so prompt, Ms Jones," he
said.

She offered a curt bow, knowing that any
unwarranted speech would be classed as imperti-
nence.

"I wonder," asked Morgas gently, "if you'd be so
kind as to cast your mind back to a task I set you
five years ago."

Ms Jones immediately knew what her employer
was referring to.

"The Crystal Lake Millennium Project. Sep-
tember 2000."

"Precisely," he confirmed, sliding the word like
a snake of spit across his fat tongue. "I was given
to understand that your people had searched the
entire Crystal Lake area."

"Correct." She stared straight ahead like a military subordinate.

"And if I'm not mistaken," Morgas continued, "you submitted a budget based on the deployment of state-of-the-art surveillance and detection technology. Isn't that so?"

But of course he already knew the answer.

"Correct," she repeated, not showing a hint of nervousness.

In the absence of speech, the two of them could easily have been mistaken for the more tedious exhibits in Geistmann's carnival.

"Then would you please care to explain how your three-month search failed to uncover a makeshift dwelling containing: A, three bodies from the first tranche of the 1984 homicides, and B, a candlelit shrine possibly dedicated to Mrs Pamela Voorhees?"

For a fraction of a second, Ms Jones smoothed her lips together and her face turned ashen; but she regained her composure so fast that no one but Morgas would have noticed she'd even lost it.

"Crystal Lake," she began, "covers an area of hundreds of square—"

Morgas lifted his hand from under the desk and shot Ms Jones in the chest with a tidy steel revolver.

Blood spilled onto her chin as she collapsed to the floor in a tangle of stiletto shoes and crisp black stockings. She grabbed at the bullet wound and began to cough uncontrollably, as the air pockets in her lungs were flooded with internal pain.

Morgas stood up and looked on dispassionately, as the woman in the black pinstripe suit flailed around the floor like a squashed bug. Then he unloaded one of the remaining five shots into her face and the other four into her breasts.

Might as well mix business with pleasure.

He contemplated the corpse for a moment before returning the gun to the top drawer of his desk. The smell of cordite drifted past his nostrils, reminding him of the Fourth of July. Childhood. Taking a deep breath, he pressed the handsfree button on his phone.

"Is the tracking device still operational?" he asked.

"Yes, Mister Morgas," replied a female voice.

"Good," he soothed, and then more vigorously, "Excellent! Ms Cardella, if you'd be so kind, would you please come up. I have some good news for you."

"Yes, Mister Morgas," she answered, trying to mask her fear.

Morgas ended the call and looked out at the New York skyline.

"Jason's alive," he hissed. "I can feel it. Don't disappoint me, Ms Kyler. *Don't disappoint me!*"

Tolleson still couldn't bring himself to say anything. He just stared at the locket; at the photo of baby Kyler resting in her mother's arms.

"She was thirty-two when she died," said Kyler matter-of-factly. "I was still at school."

"Your father—" Tolleson began.

"Died of natural causes soon after I was born."

"I... I'm sorry."

Tolleson closed the locket and handed it back.

"You still haven't told me about Landau," she said, replacing the pendant around her neck. "How does he know I'm here?"

"Oh Christ, Miche—Kyler." Tolleson's whole body bent inwards, as if he was trying to convey sincerity through contortion. "I don't know what I can do to convince you, but I swear—I absolutely swear—I had nothing to do with it. I didn't tell Landau."

"Anyone else?" she asked.

"I told no one," he was emphatic. "Okay, I never wanted to come here—I admit that—and I'm real sorry about what happened to your mom. But Jason's dead, Kyler. He's gone!"

She took her foot off the gas and gently pushed on the brakes.

"What are you doing?" he asked, turning his gaze on the dark, empty forest two miles outside Hunt Ridge.

"After my mother was murdered," Kyler said coldly, "I swore I'd never let anything like that happen to me. I promised myself I'd never be a victim. I'd never let anyone use me or force me to do anything I don't want to."

The car stopped dead on the side of the road and she turned off the engine.

"Wh—why have you stopped?" he stuttered.

"I've built my whole life around that rule," Kyler turned and stared Tolleson in the eye. "No one gets in my way. No one. Understand?"

He nodded dumbly. His Adam's apple took one giant leap for mankind, followed by one colossal dive for cowardice.

Kyler unfastened her seat belt and started to get out the vehicle.

"Wait!" called Tolleson. "What are you doing? Wh—where are you going? You can't just walk out on me. Kyler!"

But Special Agent Kyler didn't respond; she just stood up on the grassy verge and slammed the door in her partner's face.

Alice Witney was drunk, terrified and heartbroken. Her father lay dead at her feet, the carnival vehicles were going up in smoke, she didn't know if any of the others were still alive, and now Jason—her only chance of a future—had turned his back on her and was walking out of her life. And with each step he took, the loss of everything she loved became more and more meaningless.

"You're not going anywhere!" she shouted.

She ran after him and tried to stop him, but he brushed her aside like the insubstantial and irrelevant victim she was.

"Good boy, Jason," smiled Glo, extending her arms in maternal embrace. "She's just a slut. She can't harm you. No one can. Now come to Mommy."

"No!" screamed Alice, scrabbling to her feet. "You're all I've got, you murdering fucking bastard!"

She rushed forward and jumped on his back, trying to pull him down, but he threw her over his head and she landed face down on the compacted soil. The impact knocked the wind out of her, and she was sure she'd broken a couple of ribs. Worse, she now lay helpless in front of the crazy blonde girl who, she now realized, was carrying a severed head.

Glo cackled, triumphant in the full moon.

"That's it Jason," she yelled ecstatically. "Mommy's here. Come give Mommy a great big hug."

Alice looked on as, at long last, Pamela Voorhees was about to be reunited with her son. But her fascination turned to horror when Jason pulled back his arm and punched Glo's head clean off her shoulders.

Blood pumped through the girl's open neck like a geyser. It sprayed into the air, squirted across Jason's white mask and poured deep red rain all over Alice. The teenager was still smiling when her head hit the grass, but her body fought against this impossible replay of that night, twenty-five years ago, when Pamela Voorhees was beheaded on the sands of Crystal Lake.

The decapitated corpse lashed out at Jason, slashing blindly with the hunting knife, before faltering and then collapsing at his feet. The severed head slipped from her fingers with slaughterhouse finality.

Just ten minutes had passed since Jason's reawakening and the carnival of terrors was all but destroyed.

CHAPTER THIRTEEN

The cleaning staff removed Ms Jones with such expertise that not even a top forensics team could have found evidence of her murder. Even the scratches on the marble floor, caused by two bullets passing through her body, had been smoothed and polished to perfection.

Nathaniel Morgas glanced at his fob watch, irritated. It was 8:47pm and the sanitation engineers were only just leaving the room. He made a mental note to have them all sent on a time management course.

Suddenly his phone rang and the LCD window displayed the caller he had been waiting all day and night to hear from.

"Ms Kyler," he said warmly. "How delightful."

Kyler's voice came through the speaker at such high quality that she could have been standing in the room.

"You were right," she said.

"About what, exactly?" A pulsing green light told him that the conversation was being recorded.

"I've been suspended," she answered with poker-playing evenness. "I don't suppose you had anything to do with that?"

"Heaven forbid!" Morgas blended outrage with bonhomie. "As I said in our meeting, Ms Kyler, the problem resides with your partner, Special Agent Tolleson. His sole purpose is to undermine your every move in the Voorhees matter."

"I don't accept that," she replied.

"Then you should anticipate more obstacles, Ms Kyler," he said, before asking, seemingly as an afterthought, "By the way, where are you?"

"So you're saying you had no involvement in my suspension?" she repeated, ignoring his question.

"I am not in the habit of lying, Ms Kyler," he answered curtly. "You have only to request my assistance and you shall have it."

"I get the feeling I've had the pleasure of your assistance already."

Morgas stiffened at the obvious slight.

"Don't forget the document I gave you," he reminded her. "Whatever you may think of my motives, Ms Kyler, we have common enemies. Now tell me, what progress have you made?"

The line went dead.

Kyler closed her cell and walked back to the Chrysler. Tolleson was standing by the passenger door but, even with the moonlight and the twin xenon beams, he failed to see her until she was only a few yards away.

"I thought you'd gone," he said, more like a child than a law enforcement officer.

"I had to make a call," she answered, returning the phone to her jacket.

"And you couldn't do that in front of me?" he accused.

"Someone told Landau about my unofficial investigation," she countered flatly.

"And you can't get it in your head I had nothing to do with it."

Tolleson seemed more hurt than angry. He came round the front of the car and stood toe to toe with her in the headlamps.

"Kyler, what do I have to say?" he pleaded. "After all the work we've done together!"

"You've been with the Bureau five months," she answered.

"Straight from Quantico," he pointed out.

"You're the only person who knew," she repeated. "So reverse the situation, Agent Tolleson. If you were in my place, what would you do?"

Cory rubbed the nascent stubble on his chin. They were rookie and mentor once more, and his senior partner was giving him a chance to shine. After a couple of minutes, however, he reached the only logical solution.

"You're right," he sighed. "Go on without me— you've got the car keys. I'll find my own way back. I'll tell Landau you lost me or something."

His face drooped in a hound-dog expression and he started to walk back along the way they'd just driven.

"Wait!" she called.

Tolleson stopped. "What?"

Kyler leaned into the vehicle and opened the hood. Then she took Tolleson's flashlight out of the backseat and shone it into the engine block.

"What are you doing?" asked Tolleson, not yet daring to rejoin her.

"Well," she said, rooting around the oily machinery, "if you're the only person who knew and you really haven't told anyone, then they must have another way of knowing."

"They?" Tolleson looked quizzical. "Who are 'they?'"

Kyler stood up.

"The people who put this in your car."

She held out a small, magnetic radio-transmitter. Tolleson's car had been bugged.

There were two heads lying on the ground at Harper Field. One of them was raw and sweet, but unfamiliar to Jason, while the other was old and withered and had once been the object of his devotion. That had been Pamela's mistake. In her fanaticism, she never once considered that Jason might recognize her severed head more readily than her persona. She'd been too eager, in her desire to be reunited with her son, to be mindful of the fact that she looked and sounded exactly like Gloria Sowici. As Jason was "special," it was only natural he might be confused. So Pamela only had herself to blame for losing her head once more.

Jason bent down and lifted Glo's corpse off the ground. Then, holding the body in a standing position, he picked up the decayed head of his

mother and dunked it on the wet scarlet disaster
of Glo's neck. When he was happy that Mommy
was good and fixed again—old head on a new
body—he let go of the girl's shoulder. Immediately
she folded at the knees and the head fell into a
pool of bloody mud.

Jason stared at the body parts. He turned and
looked left at Glo's body. He turned and looked
right at Pamela's head. He turned his head left
again. He turned his head right again...

Alice ran screaming up behind him and
smashed the Camp Crystal Lake sign—the self-
same board he had just used to claim dozens of
lives—across the back of his head. The wood
splintered into pieces, and numbing shock forced
Alice to drop what was left of the weapon. But
Jason stood his ground, completely unfazed.

He turned and started to walk towards her.

By now Alice was a picture of violence. Her long
dress, her hair and her pilot's jacket were all thick
with the red liquidity of Glo's destruction, and
even her skin was now so uniformly crimson as to
render her many tattoos invisible. She didn't
understand at all what had taken place between
Jason and the girl he'd just slaughtered, nor could
she work out why Jason seemed so interested in
the mummified head; but his intentions now were
unmistakable, and Alice ran for her life.

What the hell does someone do when forced to
flee from the person they need the most? Jason
wanted to kill her, she had no way of stopping
him, she was terrified of him. And yet she
needed him. Fuelled by alcohol and desperation,
she searched for a weapon or a solution, but

everywhere she looked there was only death—
the fire from the trucks; a field full of corpses.
Some casualties were still alive, and were begging her for help. Her boots felt even heavier as
she ran past them.

Suddenly Jason stopped in his tracks, and
moved back in the direction of the headless girl.

Alice laughed. No. She had to get a grip.
Laughter was dangerous. She'd been to that dark
place once already tonight, and couldn't afford to
mess with it again. Because if she surrendered to
the laughter—if she caterwauled at Jason playing
happy families with decapitated remains—then
she knew she would lose herself to madness.

"Come back, you bastard!" she screamed.

But Jason had only gone to fetch Glo's hunting
knife. He was ready to confront her now. The
hockey mask. The moonlight shining on the blade.
The hatred in his eye.

Ch-ch-ch. Ah-ah-ahhh.

Alice screamed and ran as fast as she could, the
beat of his footsteps never ceasing behind her. No
one else in the field seemed to matter anymore.
Jason was going to kill her.

She tried to hide among the exhibits, but it was
futile. No sooner did she take refuge in one of the
stands than Jason demolished it. One by one, he
plowed through them all: Dracula, Frankenstein,
the Wolfman—so much candle wax and firewood
in the path of the indomitable maniac.

Alice Witney was learning the hard way that it
was impossible to play cat and mouse with a bull-
dozer. Her lungs ached, her legs were failing, and
she was caught in the crossfire of one devastating

realization after another: she'd left Judge's laptop in the crawlspace of the Jason exhibit; her motorhome and all the other carnival trucks were ablaze, leaving her no means of escape; and she was exhausted, with not even enough strength left to save her own life.

She dropped to her knees and again had to fight back the unbalanced laughter, as she found herself staring at the two severed heads. She'd come back right to where she had started from. And if that wasn't the story of her whole damn life, nothing was.

Suddenly, Jason's pulverizing tread came to a halt. Alice looked over her shoulder and saw him getting ready to hurl the jagged knife deep into her skull.

She sniggered, beaten, "Go ahead, you bastard."

When a cloud passed in front of the moon and Jason froze.

Kyler dropped the tracking device on the ground and made sure it wouldn't be sending any more signals.

"Well, now we have our answer," she remarked, administering one final blow to the metal casing. "I'm under covert surveillance."

"It was in *my* car," Tolleson corrected her. "It's not even a pool car. It's my own. Why would anyone want to keep tabs on me?"

"I'm sorry to disappoint you," said Kyler, "but this is about me. They probably have a listening device somewhere in the office. So when they heard you were coming to pick me up, your car was the obvious choice."

Tolleson watched as Kyler proceeded to search the rest of the vehicle.

"I don't understand," he groaned. "If this gets out, Landau's finished. Even he can't do this. It's totally against Bureau protocol."

Kyler lay down on the road and ran the flashlight underneath the vehicle.

"It's not just Landau," she said, checking the rear axle. "There's a conspiracy."

Tolleson kicked the smashed radio-transmitter into the underbrush of the surrounding forest.

"Oh no, Kyler," he whined. "Please don't. I don't want to hear this, I'm doing my best to understand. The least you can do is treat it seriously."

Kyler stood up and dusted herself.

"I am serious," she said, wiping her hands. "An informant warned me I was going to be suspended."

"But, Kyler, anyone from the office could have told you that. I even warned you myself." Tolleson was close to tearing out his hair.

"Then how do you explain the tracking device?" she asked defensively.

Tolleson threw his hands in the air and shrugged.

Kyler finished searching the Chrysler's bodywork and now turned her attention to the interior.

"I have concrete proof," she said, groping under the steering wheel, "that someone is trying to eradicate all evidence connected to the Voorhees homicides."

"I don't suppose there's anything you can show me?" he prompted meekly.

She got up out of the car. "I told you Jason killed my mother?"

"How could I forget?"

Kyler took a crumpled sheet of paper out of her pocket and gave it to her partner. Then she held the flashlight up to help him see.

"What's this," he started, "an old police report?"

"Just read it," she answered.

A moment later and Tolleson could hardly speak.

"Oh—my—God," he gasped. "Is it true? They actually opened her grave?"

Kyler nodded.

He quickly scanned the key points a second time, but the print remained unchanged and unequivocal. Six years ago, someone had broken into the Winter Green Cemetery in Wisconsin and had stolen Martha Kyler's body.

Harper Field changed from black to silver as the moon was released. Jason aimed his knife a second time. But he was already too late. Alice had observed his immobility and her natural cunning was filling in the blanks.

She remembered Glo calling from the back of the crowd just before Jason came alive. Then she saw how the girl had emerged from the diesel blast holding the severed head in the moonlight. And then there was Jason—he'd tried to attach the decrepit head to the dead girl's neck.

The head. It always came back to the head.

Alice took off her leather jacket and threw it down over Pamela's remains. A rush of excitement coursed through her body as Jason was paralyzed once more. This could be the million-dollar miracle she'd been hoping for. But first she had to be certain.

She bent down and turned up a corner of her coat; moonlight touched the exposed ground. Slowly, she peeled her jacket off the grass and watched as the cold wash inched its way towards the severed head, until...

Jason flailed in confusion and snapped his gaze in Alice's direction. Immediately he pounded forwards, but she threw the jacket down again, locking the killer in mid-stride; and the knife fell out of his hand.

"Yes!" she roared and suddenly she was laughing, only this time her hysterics were a release of the ultimate anxiety.

"You ugly motherfucker!" she howled, and started to dance among the dead.

Laughing, singing, whooping like a lottery winner, she sashayed over to Jason, placed both hands on his chest and pushed him over.

"Timber, you fucker, timber!"

Jason toppled and crashed onto the flat of his back.

Dozens of corpses were strewn across Harper Field, but Alice felt like she was walking on air. Screw the carnival, screw Freely, screw everyone! She was calling the shots now.

Tolleson folded up the police report and gave it back to Kyler.

"When I woke up this morning," he remarked absently, "I thought today was going to be like any other."

"And now?" she asked, putting the document away.

"The theft of your mom's body does not prove a conspiracy," he answered quietly. "And it doesn't prove Voorhees is real. I understand how you feel about Jason and your mom, but you can't bring him back just because you need closure."

Her head whipped in his direction.

"Is that what you think this is?" she snapped. "You think it's my mother who's clouding my judgment? You think I don't mind how many people Jason kills so long as I get a shot at revenge?"

Tolleson was about to answer, when she raised a hand for silence.

"What's that?" she frowned, listening.

Her partner looked all around. "I don't hear anything."

But gradually he became aware of a wall of sirens, and suddenly the dark forest road burst into a Vegas of speeding lights. One, two, three squad cars. An ambulance. Two more patrol cars. Another ambulance. The emergency convoy came hurtling past Tolleson's Chrysler like an arrow fired by an angel of mercy.

"Quick," shouted Kyler, hurrying round to the driver's seat. "Get in the car!"

"But—"

"I don't have time for your doubts, Agent Tolleson. There's an emergency situation in progress and we both know who's responsible. Now get in the car or I *will* leave you."

Tolleson was still fumbling with his safety belt when the G force kicked him back in his seat. The tires squealed as Kyler set off in pursuit of the red and blue lights, and Tolleson was almost frightened by her determination.

It had always annoyed the other showmen that Freely would never park with them, but today Alice could have kissed him for it. Freely's pickup was the only truck that hadn't been touched by the fire. Even better, the idiot always kept a spare set of keys taped under the wheel arch.

She clambered up onto the eight-foot rear bed and started tossing Kenton's garbage over the side. Tools, boxes, food, even booze—it all had to go. She kept a watchful eye on Jason as she emptied the trailer; but the severed head remained wrapped in her jacket, and it never left her side.

When she was done, she jumped down and began to make her way over to the Crystal Lake platform.

"Alice! You're alive!"

It was Minter. The big guy was in one piece, but he was horrified to see her soaked with blood. He didn't know that the two and a half pints had come from Glo.

"Mint," Alice drawled, suddenly remembering just how drunk she was.

He ran forward and put his arms round her. "My God, are you all right? Are you okay to walk?"

"I need something from the truck," she pointed at the open door.

"I'll go get it for you. Just wait here." He turned and went over to the cab.

Behind him, Alice quietly picked up a spade she'd thrown down earlier. Then she tiptoed up to Minter and bashed him on the back of the head.

"Wh—what are you doing?" he cried, horrified.

He tried to grab her but she leapt out of his way and swung the flat of the spade into his face. Minter fell onto his knees and tried to brace his thighs so that he could get up again. But Alice stood over him and beat him around the head until he was senseless. One final blow and he was out cold.

"Sorry, Mint," she dropped the spade on the ground and ran across to the mangled ruin of Crystal Lake.

Sparx and Vincenzo looked awful, but what did she care? She crawled under the boat dock, grabbed the travel bag with the computer, and struggled back out to begin the most difficult task of them all: dragging Jason's body to the pickup truck.

The last time she and her father had tried to lift the monster, the strain had been unbearable. But now, Alice was amazed to find that moving him was almost too easy. She didn't know if it was alcohol, adrenaline or fate, but she just hooked her hands under his shoulders and pulled him backwards along the ground. The hardest part was getting him up on the bed, and even that succumbed to her determination. Just touching the bastard made her want to throw up, but she was a desperate woman.

Quickly, she stuffed the severed head in the travel bag and dropped the bag next to Jason in the back of the truck. Then she locked the gate and took one last look at the carnival: it was a flaming, bleeding scene of mass murder.

Minter was out cold and her father—was dead.

Suddenly she could hear sirens. The police were coming.

"Shit!"

She ran into the truck and turned the ignition. There was plenty of gas in the tank, but how could she get away if the road was filled with cops?

Suddenly she remembered the dirt track on the far side of the field. It ran up into the surrounding hills and looked a bitch to drive, especially at night, but what choice did she have? If the police caught her, they'd see Jason and the severed head, they'd find out Alice was with the carnival, and then she'd spend the rest of her life answering questions. No, she was too close to give up now. Jason was going to make her rich and she couldn't let anybody prevent that from happening, not even the authorities.

She shifted the truck into gear and rolled forward; some of the bodies she bumped over were still alive before they were crushed under her wheels.

"Better hurry, dear. They're coming for you."

Alice shook her head.

She guessed she must be going crazy after all; she could have sworn she'd just heard a woman's voice in her head.

There was hardly a guy in the civilized world who would have refused a blow job from Jaomi Marantez. But as her moist, natural lips brought Ross closer to the money shot, he couldn't help but wonder about her dental hygiene.

Suddenly—*kashuga!*—the Mount Etna of Beverly Hills lived up to his reputation and Jaomi whooped at how high he fired.

"God, you should enter that thing in the Olympics," she giggled, spoiling the fourth quarter. Then she rolled over and took a line of blow from the nightstand. Ross joined her.

"What a day," he snorted. "The phone's not stopped ringing."

"I told you Veranti was no good," she said, white-lining equally as fast. "He'd never have got you this publicity."

"What's that?" Ross frowned.

"Well, I've been your manager one day and look what's happened."

"But you had nothing to do with it," Ross protested. "Attacking Finwell was my idea. It was just something I did. You didn't arrange it."

"But I'm your manager," she restated.

"So—what—you get credit for everything now? I have a thought and suddenly you own it like you've got psychic powers or something?"

Jaomi laughed. "Dwayne, don't be childish. That's not it at all."

Ross helped himself to a second hit.

"Shit," he said, aligning his nostril. "At least Veranti only took my money."

"Come on," she said persuasively. "Don't spoil the mood. Just think about all the calls."

"Damn right," said Feratu proudly. "Most of them said I look more like Jason than Jason does. How cool is that?"

"Well, I bet you look more real than that stupid body on ZingBid," she said casually.

Ross froze, "That—what?"

"Oh shit," she held up her hands defensively. "Sorry. I completely forgot about the cut-off."

"No, no," fired Ross. "What's this about a body?"

"Hey, if this is a test," she answered, laughing, "I just passed."

"Jaomi!" Ross shouted, throwing the cocaine salver across the room. "For fuck's sake, just tell me!"

But the "adult" model was used to his tantrums by now, and she refused to take him seriously.

"The cut-off's non-negotiable," she said.

"Fuck the cut-off!" he shouted. "Just tell me about the fucking body!"

"Non-*fucking*-negotiable."

Ross jumped out of the bed and walked down the hall to his wife's office, where a PC was always online. Normally Ross got on with computers about as well as Dracula got on with garlic, but the screen was already on ZingBid and a little box in the corner read, "Search."

A few fumbled, nervous seconds later and there it was:

ITEM: Jason Voorhees.

DURATION: 24 hours.

DELIVERY: Buyer to collect in person.

PAYMENT METHOD: Cash only. To be paid on collection.

DESCRIPTION: The body of the world's most famous serial killer. This is 100% genuine. If you've got the money, it's yours. No time wasters. Buyer accepts all risk.

CURRENT BID: $18.00.

CONDITION: Poor.

"It's a scam," said Jaomi, looking over his shoulder. "There isn't even a photograph."

Ross hadn't noticed she'd followed him into the room. He just gazed at the screen with near religious fervor.

"I've gotta have it," he said.

"If you bid on that dog," she warned, "the only thing you'll win is a hole in your pocket."

Ross stared back at her. "If I don't win, I'm giving you a divorce."

"All right," she sighed. "But if you're determined to go through with this, let's do it properly."

"What do you mean?" he asked, worried she was about to trick him.

Jaomi ignored him and looked at the screen, and suddenly she was the one giving the orders.

"Okay, the current bid's eighteen dollars. You don't bid. You don't touch a thing. Then, thirty seconds from the end, I'll run my bid blocker and whatever the last bid is, you add a dollar and the body's yours."

"That easy?" asked Ross hopefully.

"That easy," she confirmed.

Ross smiled and took her hand. "Then why don't you go put on your Jason costume and let me fuck you up the ass?"

It was time for the rock star to get some sweet hockey-mask lurve.

CHAPTER FOURTEEN

The narrow track leading down to Harper Field was
deluged with fleeing casualties. People were running and screaming. They banged on the windows
of Tolleson's Chrysler and cried for help. Some of
them had terrible burns, others were pouring with
blood; Kyler saw a child of nine clutching a ragged
stump where her right hand used to be. And everywhere there was blind panic.

"My God, it's a nightmare," murmured Tolleson.

But his partner said nothing as she carefully followed the rescue party to the bottom of the asphalt
lane: to the site of mass murder.

The fire Pamela had set in motion was still eating
through Witney's beloved monsters, casting a
satanic glow over the carpet of the slain. Police officers and paramedics were already rushing through
the scattered victims, seeing who was dead and
who might be saved. Two groups of patrolmen had

drawn their guns and were searching the scene for the perpetrator. Kyler prayed for their sakes they weren't successful.

Tolleson pointed through the windshield.

"There!" he said excitedly.

It was so black outside that Kyler could see nothing but the grass illuminated in her headlamps; so she slowed down and cut the lights. And then she saw it.

Two tiny taillights were climbing behind a fan of white light into the hills on the far side of the clearing. Even though it was hard to make out in the dark, Kyler guessed that the mountain trail would be slow and hazardous, and it was in completely the opposite direction from where everyone else was fleeing. In short, someone was trying to escape.

Kyler checked to see if any of the squad cars were giving chase, but no one except the agents had even spotted the lone vehicle. She looked at Tolleson. He stared back at her.

"Do it," he said decisively.

Kyler thrashed the gas pedal and the Chrysler went steaming in pursuit.

The engine of the pickup wheezed and whined as Alice forced the vehicle up an even steeper grade. Dirt slipped from under the doubled rear tires, and Jason's body slid down the smooth metal of the flat bed; his feet slamming against the tailgate, followed soon after by a more muted thud. Suddenly Alice realized she'd left the travel bag—with the severed head and the laptop—in the back of the truck.

"Damn!"

She banged the palm of her hand against the steering wheel and looked ahead for somewhere more level where she could park. But the trail continued to climb as far as she could see. Worse, it was gradually bearing right, towards the sheer side of the hill.

"Oh you can't stop now, dear," said a voice up close. "They're right behind you."

Alice was imagining that woman again. But although she seriously feared for her own sanity, she instinctively glanced into the mirrors and saw a set of headlamps quickly gaining on her. And that's not all she saw. Because smiling at her in the glass, with lineaments thin and spectral in the moonlight, was the arrogant face of Pamela Voorhees.

"You know," said Pamela idly, "I've never cared much for 'Alice.' It's a horrible name."

"Shut up!" shouted Alice, punching the rearview.

The glass cracked and her knuckles bled, but the mocking face remained in the mirror.

"It's seen us," hollered Tolleson as the truck picked up speed in front of them, kicking dust in its wake.

"They'll have to do better than that," answered Kyler grimly.

She put the headlamps on high beam and fed even more power to the transmission. Tolleson's Chrysler wasn't built for steep, unpaved trails like this, and yet they were having no trouble reeling in Kenton's pickup.

Kyler pounded the horn and flashed her lights, but the truck wouldn't stop; if anything, it moved even faster. If this had been a Bureau vehicle rather than Tolleson's personal car, Kyler would have used the siren to let whoever it was know they were being pursued by law enforcement officers. Maybe then they wouldn't be so eager to go offroad racing.

"Hold on," she warned her partner.

The car surged forwards as Kyler revved it into an overtaking position; but the pickup swung wide, anticipating the maneuver and killing it before it had even begun.

Kyler's top lip peeled back above her teeth and her brows pitched forward as she cut right, then left, jammed the car forwards, but then abruptly pulled back. The trail was just too damned steep and uneven for Kyler to build up enough speed to get by the truck.

"Hey, take it easy!" warbled Tolleson, white as a sheet.

But Kyler was stopping for no man.

She gunned the Chrysler straight into an impossible space and the two vehicles connected.

Wham!

The agents were rocked back in their seats as the saloon rebounded off the rear side of the pickup. Kyler swung in for a second blow, and again they glanced off the heavy metal bodywork. The right headlamp went out in a ricochet of broken glass.

"Kyler!" shouted Tolleson, bracing himself.

They had only one beam working now, but that was all the light Kyler needed to slam the fender into the back of the truck. Two, three times—each impact was like a nail in the coffin of Satan, but still the pickup climbed the hill in front of her.

Kyler eased off in preparation for one final attempt. Then she stabbed forward and crashed all two hundred horsepower dead center on the license plate. The rear gate of the pickup crumpled with the collision, and Kyler came off the gas only to realize that her car had been snagged by the pickup's tow hook.

This was her chance.

She stamped on the brakes and Tolleson saw with horror that she was about to reach for the gear shift.

"What the hell are you doing?" he hollered.

The Chrysler skidded and buckled as its locking wheels fought to drag the pickup to a halt. Kyler could feel resistance mounting through the very fabric of the vehicle as the driver of the truck pressed equally hard on the gas.

Then Kyler wrenched the gears into reverse.

The car screamed. It was being subjected to impossible forces and the cross-directional power was mechanical torture. The truck strained to climb up the hill while the car labored to pull it back down. It was an insane tug of war, crawling up the dirt track and sliding in a zigzag that could only end in roadkill.

Suddenly the whole back of the pickup—the tow hook, the fender and the bent rear gate—all broke free and came spinning towards the windshield. Tolleson raised his arms in front of his face, and Kyler lowered her head just in time, as the tailstorm smashed the glass into a thousand prismatic fragments and then rebounded onto the roadside.

Kyler struggled to get the vehicle back under control, but she could barely see the trail and was aware at any moment they could go careening over the side of the hill. Tolleson took out his gun and used the handle to punch a hole in the crystal cobweb. Smoke was rising from under the hood. The car went hurtling up the bumpy track and was sideswiping every rock and tree along the way.

"Look!" shouted Tolleson, his eyes watering with the rush of air.

Kyler squinted forward and saw a pair of feet resting on the bed of the truck. There was a body in the back of the vehicle. And now that the rear gate was gone, the body was sliding forwards out onto the road.

No more than five yards in front, Alice Witney was frantic. Somebody was trying to kill her. At first she thought it might be the cops, but there were no sirens, no lights, and the crazy bastards had tried to run her off the road. When their vehicles had got snarled up, and they'd tried to haul her back, she'd thought the pickup was going to explode—the engine was making that much noise. But somehow, she'd broken free and now she was driving out of her skin. She knew she was good behind the wheel, but Jesus shit...

"My son!" shouted her new multiple personality disorder. "You're losing my son."

Thanks to Alice's punch, the rearview was no good. She glanced over her shoulder and was horrified to see both Jason and the travel bag sliding out of the truck.

"I can't stop!" she cried, the headlamps of the Chrysler sticking to her tire marks.

"You must!" snarled Pamela. "They can't have Jason."

"If I stop, they'll kill me," Alice shouted.

"Not if I kill you first, you little slut."

Suddenly Alice's hands were no longer her own; they seesawed left and right over the steering wheel in an ectoplasmic effort to turn the truck around.

Alice stared out of the window and screamed.

The instant the pickup veered out of control, Jason shot out of the vehicle like a human missile. His feet, his legs and his body all slid onto the dirt in swift succession, only for his hockey mask to get caught on a jutting piece of metal where the fender used to be. And suddenly he was being dragged full length behind the truck. His limbs shook and thrashed over each bump and hole in the road. Sparks flew up from the heels of his boots, columns of dust mushroomed all around him, and his twitching, juddering frame was center stage in Kyler's one good headlamp.

Her eyes widened and her mouth fell open. At long last she had found the man who had killed her mother: Jason Voorhees was real.

"Watch out!" cried Tolleson.

But the sight of Jason had distracted Kyler long enough for her to miss the sharp right bend. She wrenched at the wheel but the car was already committed. The pickup disappeared round the corner of the hillside, pulling Jason with it like a hogtied bandit, but the Chrysler went flying over the edge. All four wheels left the ground and the FBI agents found themselves falling towards a slope of dense pinewood.

Back up on the road, the sudden turn had caused the rear of the pickup to yank sideways, and had sent the travel bag spinning past Jason's head. The fabric carrier tumbled in the red glow of the receding taillights and bounced along the dirt

before catching on a stray branch and ripping wide
open.

Tolleson screamed as the automobile rolled over
to meet the serried treetops of the forest. Pine needles lashed through the windshield, his body was
jostled by the pinball descent. From the moment
they'd left the road, his life had turned into a game
of cards: and until the vehicle stopped moving, he
wouldn't know if he was pulling twenty-one or
bust.

Sitting in the open bag, the head of Pamela
Voorhees was bathed in glorious moonlight...

And Jason was no longer the rag doll in the
exhaust. His body stiffened and he frantically
reached round for whatever it was that was holding
onto his mask. He lifted his legs and tried to run
with the scrolling of the road, but his boots slipped
on the sandy earth and his lower body swayed in
an outstretched wave like a sidewinder with a V8
engine up its ass. And yet slowly, ever so slowly, he
raised his arms and clamped them on the top of the
bed. Then, almost as if he were bench pressing
three hundred and fifty pounds *behind* his head, he
raised himself just enough to unhook the mask
from the twisted shard. The feat seemed impossible, yet Jason continued to defy possibility.

Next he placed one hand on the side of the truck
and then climbed up onto the trailer. For all the distance he'd just been dragged, and for all the jolts
that would have broken any other man's neck,
Jason stood victorious on the back of Freely's
pickup, seemingly unaffected by the vehicle's
lurching, haphazard motion.

He turned his ungodly stare at the cabin.

He had some unfinished business to attend to.

Out of the darkness came pain. Out of the pain came awareness. Snapping back to full consciousness, Kyler saw her partner slumped dead or unconscious beside her. Blood was trickling from a deep cut in his forehead and the two of them were sitting upside down, the roof of the car an imploded stalactite mere inches from her face.

"Cory," she called gently.

She reached over and felt for a pulse. He was still alive.

"Agent Tolleson," she said louder.

After the fury of the chase, everything seemed unnaturally quiet. The car creaked and hissed as it settled into scrap, but other than that, Kyler could hardly hear a thing. Carefully, she unhooked her seat belt and lowered herself onto the roof of the vehicle. The side window was already smashed but it took a few additional blows to make it safe to crawl through.

She climbed groggily to her feet on the forest floor and slowly set about examining herself. She was covered in minor wounds but, miraculously, didn't feel as if she'd broken any bones. No internal injuries. Not even mild concussion.

Satisfied with her status, Kyler went round to the passenger side of the Chrysler and saw Tolleson hanging there. Her initial reaction was to reach for the door handle, but then a more urgent thought tore through her mind.

"Jason!"

Kyler quickly ran her eyes over the automobile: there didn't seem to be any immediate danger. Then she checked her cell, but there was no signal. Again she looked at Tolleson, bleeding and upside down. But the truck carrying Jason had to be stopped.

Aching and tired, she took one last look at the Chrysler and then began a long and arduous climb back up the rise.

Alice didn't know what was happening to her. She'd seen that sharp right on the edge of the hill and had thought she was finished. But somehow she'd regained control of her hands, and was able to make the turn with a few feet to spare. Judging from the sudden quiet, she guessed her pursuers hadn't been so lucky. The last few minutes had gone without a single crash, a flash of headlamps or anything; which meant she had escaped. Problem was, she'd also lost Jason.

It seemed to Alice she would always be cursed to have either freedom or hope, but never both.

She heard the engine straining and realized she had cramp in her foot from treading so hard on the gas. The trail here was still ascending, and the truck rocked from side to side as it lumbered over the uneven ground, but Alice was no longer in any real peril. Jason and her pursuers were all gone, and when she sobered up the voice in her head would be gone as well.

Alice counted to ten and forced herself to ease off the pedal. Then she breathed deeply and told herself to calm down and stop taking risks with the road. It was all over now. She had to relax. It was finished. Over.

The rear window exploded behind her as Jason reached both arms into the cab and placed them

round her head like a vise. Alice screamed, the van
swerved and the bastard squeezed harder.

The gradient was never so steep that Kyler had to
use her hands, nor was the hill so high that she got
out of breath; but the one thing the climb did kill
was time. When she regained the spot where her
car had left the road, the pickup was long gone.

"Damn!"

In the light of the full moon, the tire marks told
an obvious story—one that was no use to Kyler,
because she'd already read the last page. She took
her cell out and checked for a signal. It was weak,
but she definitely had one.

But who to call? Every police officer for miles
around would be down on Harper Field, dealing
with the aftermath of Jason's atrocities. And the
FBI—well, she was their public enemy number
one. Suddenly another idea crossed her mind. It
was a long shot, but she lifted the keypad—before
she saw something odd lying by the side of the
road.

The object was partially hidden in the under-
brush, and Kyler couldn't quite make out what it
was. But the presence of *any* unusual object here
was cause for concern. She went over for a closer
look.

The head of Mrs Voorhees was malevolent in the
moonlight. Kyler had found the travel bag.

No matter how violently Alice turned the wheel,
Jason wouldn't let go of her. She'd tried pulling his
hands away but he was too strong. She'd dug her
nails into his skin—skin that had died long ago—but

that had proven equally futile. So now she was trying to shake him off by swerving the pickup. But Jason wouldn't release her and she was starting to feel an unnatural pain; an organic movement in the stem of her neck that said he was ripping her head off.

The pain pushed her beyond reason. Jason was causing irreversible damage to her cells. She was separating. And suddenly she was screaming. Now was the time for piteous, instinctive thrashing—the five flailing legs of the fly after one has just been pulled off.

She punched Jason's mask and tried to bite him, but his movement through the broken window was erratic and his fingers were all over her.

Alice Witney was finished.

Kyler felt as if someone had just walked across her grave. A shiver of prescience palpitated through her heart as she stared at the cadaver eyes:

Mrs Pamela Voorhees, born 1930, died 1980, murderess and mother of one Jason Voorhees.

For Kyler, this was the final piece of the jigsaw puzzle.

The kids from Seattle had gone to Crystal Lake and discovered the shack mentioned in 1984 by Ginny Field. That was where they'd found the severed head, and that's what had set Jason into motion. Either beacuse they'd removed the head, or Jason didn't want them to see it or because of some pathological mother-son dynamic, Jason had gone on the offensive. And then he'd been hit by the carnival trucks and brought to Hunt Ridge.

Even so, who was driving the pickup truck? And what were they doing with Jason's body—why not hand him over to the police? And what about Jason himself, after he'd been dragged along the road? Was he dead?

It seemed to Kyler that someone had just thrown another thousand pieces into the jigsaw box. Still, if nothing else came from this debacle of an investigation, she'd at least obtained an invaluable source of DNA.

She put the head back in the bag and closed it.

Speeding wildly out of control, the pickup somehow emerged onto smooth asphalt: the trail had ended on the high mountain road a few miles north of Hunt Ridge. But that was no consolation to the dying woman.

Blood streamed from her nose as tiny holes were torn like Swiss cheese into the sinews of her neck. She fought and screamed and bunched up her shoulders, trying to resist the unavoidable separation of muscle.

"What's taking you so long?" she shouted. "Why don't you just fucking kill me?"

The pickup veered over onto the oncoming lane and bore straight into the path of a gigantic haulage truck. The huge trailer flashed its headlamps and sounded its horn, urging Alice to get out of the way. Two rows of lights burst into life along the top and center of the high chromium cab, blinding Alice, making her feel closer to heaven, and she begged her father for understanding—just as Jason let go.

Choking with snot and blood, her mouth filling with a clear, viscous fluid that tasted of damage,

Alice heaved and spat but somehow managed to pull the pickup out of the way of disaster.

The vehicle skidded and turned one-eighty on the sandy verge, before slapping against the side of the hill and then scraping to a dead stop. Alice threw up all over her dress as the gleaming trailer went roaring past, the trucker signaling his anger with the unrelenting drone of his horn.

Alice tried to look back through the rear window of the cab, but her neck was in agony and she couldn't move it at all. Carefully, she turned her whole body and saw Jason lying flat out on the bed. He was dormant once more. But for how long?

How long?

She reached over to the glove box—the movement causing her to cry with pain—and took out a bottle of Jack Daniel's. But she'd barely started to unwrap the top when she booted open the door and threw the bottle to the ground. It smashed, flooding the soil with band-aid comfort.

"Oh—God…"

Alice was hurt, angry, frightened, she'd been almost killed. She tried to hold back the tears but it was impossible. Her father. Jason. If she could just hold it together for another few hours—but Christ, her neck hurt.

She slumped forward against the steering wheel and broke down, sobbing with every ache of her heart.

CHAPTER FIFTEEN

As much as Jaomi was addicted to ZingBid, her idea of a great evening was not spending hours in front of the computer, reloading the same damn page over and over and—*yawn*—over again.

"Ross, this is a total waste of time," she grouched. "The auction's not due for another nineteen hours."

"I know," he said appreciatively. "But just do it one more."

The two of them were huddled in Jaomi's office, a pink purgatory festooned with posters of such direct-to-video classics as *The Maltese Hard-on*, and *A Nice Pair on Elm Street*. A fresh pot of coffee was percolating on a table by the door.

Jaomi sighed and clicked the mouse.

"I can't believe I agreed to this," she moaned as the data reloaded. "Eight bids and forty-seven dollars. Same as the last two hours."

"Maybe we should send another email," suggested Ross; the singer was now showing and smelling of his previous all-nighter spent watching DVDs.

"Ross, we've sent thirty already and the seller hasn't replied to any of them," Jaomi complained.

"The next one'll be different," Ross insisted. "I can feel it."

"But what's the point?" she asked. "No matter how many questions you ask, he won't admit it's a hoax."

"Is that what you think this is?" Ross was amazed by his wife's lack of understanding. "You think I'm trying to catch him out?"

"Well, aren't you?" she asked, stopping to look at him.

"Come on! I wanna know who the seller is and how he found Jason. I wanna know what Jason looks like, you know? The details. I wanna get excited about this thing! Come on! Join in!"

Jaomi's chin slumped onto her breast.

"Ross," she began, "the only question you should ask is how much these guys are gonna sting you for."

"Hey," he pushed away from the desk, "you promised to help, remember?"

"I know, but…"

"Just send the damn message!" he yelled. Suddenly there was a bad feeling in the room. Jaomi bit her tongue and switched grudgingly to the mail program as Ross got up off his chair.

"You know, Jaomi," he said, "sometimes I think you don't know me at all."

"No. You don't know me," she corrected, resending the same mail for the thirty-first pointless time.

"Oh, I know you all right," Ross shook. "It's you who doesn't know me. If you did, you'd know how important this is to me. All this—it's not a hoax. If it was, there'd be special effects, photos—the whole nine yards. But there's nothing. That's how I know it's real."

"Great," she nodded. "You know it's real because there's nothing there."

"You don't have to shout if you're the man."

"Like your brain—"

"It's only the little people who jump, Jaomi."

"Just a big, big space—"

"But this guy's not jumping at all. He's just sitting there. With Jason. Typing in the dark."

"You're not listening to me at all, are you?"

"I've waited all my life for this moment. It's Jason Voorhees. Jason fucking Voorhees. I've gotta have him."

Now it was Jaomi's turn to stand up.

"Fine," she said, heading for the door. "I'll come back thirty seconds from the end and use my blocker."

Ross stepped in her way. "Wait, where are you going?"

"Bed," she answered, flicking back her hair. "I'm tired and I'm bored."

"But I need you here in case something goes wrong. You're my manager now, remember? So from now on you do as I say."

"Oh, is that right?"

Jaomi smiled, but she was seriously pissed, and the cattiness of her voice was not lost on Ross.

"It is, if you want to keep your job," he told her.

"Err, excuse me?" Jaomi angled her head in ersatz confusion. "Correct me if I'm wrong, but wasn't your relationship with Veranti mostly him telling you to fuck off?"

Now it was Ross's turn to feel angry.

"Was that how it looked to you?" he seethed, quaking with buttoned-up petulance.

"Well yes, now you come to ask, it did. Veranti called and you ran—that's exactly how it looked. And I don't see why that has to change. If you guys had a system, I can run with that."

At which point, Ross wanted to kill her. But instead he gave her a simple ultimatum.

"I'm serious. If you leave this room, you're fired."

She left the room.

Gripping the travel bag, Special Agent Kyler walked back to where her car had left the trail. From that viewpoint it seemed impossible she'd survived; the initial drop was almost vertical, and the Chrysler must have plummeted forty or fifty feet before hitting the tops of the pine trees. She could see a dark crater where the vehicle had entered the forest and where, down below, her partner lay unconscious.

Quickly, she retraced the footprints she'd made on her previous ascent. She didn't have a flashlight, so following her own tracks seemed like the safest and fastest method for getting back to the car. But she had barely begun to put her feet over the edge when the sound of an explosion caused her to throw herself flat on the ground.

Kyler read the blast immediately. It was distant enough not to harm her, but close enough to say she was involved. She rolled over onto her back and looked out as a towering pillar of flame confirmed her worst fears.

"Tolleson..."

The Chrysler had exploded.

She pitched forward over the side of the hill and took every knock and scratch that was coming to her. She ran, clawed, stumbled, dived, grabbed on to branches and swung—anything to get to the bottom of the slope as quickly as possible. But as the ground started to level, the fire came out to meet her. The blaze was spreading through the forest with terrifying speed, and Kyler soon found she had to navigate a tortuous route through a maze of conflagration. Smoke entered her lungs and the heat on her exposed skin was almost unbearable; but she pressed forward, determined to rescue her partner, when finally she saw the Chrysler.

Upside down, blackened, bent out of all recognition by the accidental igniting of the fuel tank. The automobile was lost in the white heat of a raging fireball.

Kyler tried to get closer, but it was impossible.

Cory Tolleson was dead.

Floodlights threw harsh relief over the scattered body parts, disentangling them from the wash of blood and dirt they first appeared to be. The last time Frank Lynch had seen anything like Harper Field was when a 737 had come down in the Catskills. Granted, he wasn't a cop, but he'd been a firefighter long enough to disregard the rumors that just one man could have been responsible for all this carnage.

He looked down on a spill of internal organs, following their glistening trail back to the smiling face of the young woman they were still attached to. Her parents were standing nearby, weeping and clinging to each other in their misery, but Frank didn't know what to say to them.

Despite every effort to cordon off the area, too many townsfolk had been affected by this tragedy. They'd all returned to see if their loved ones had escaped. Mostly they hadn't.

Further on, a dead boy was still holding hands with his dead father. It looked as if the man had been trying to use his body to shield the boy, but both of them had ended their lives in torment. The child's face was streaked with dry tears and there was blood all over his clothes.

Elsewhere, a couple of paramedics were struggling to sedate a man who'd just found his wife stabbed through the mouth with a wooden stake. And beyond them, Frank could see body bags strewn across the field like maggots waiting to be harvested by morgue attendants.

The fire had been put out long ago, but Frank had stayed behind to help with the rescue operation. He'd been with the service over twelve years and he thought he was used to death by now; he'd seen his fair share of burned and suffocated bodies, and he'd had to meet with Lord knows how many grieving parents. But there was something about what happened here at Hunt Ridge that made him feel sick to the stomach.

The stench of ruined lives was everywhere. Frank Lynch was beginning to wonder just how long this damned night was going to last.

"Okay, now we're just getting reports of over two hundred casualties. That's significantly up on the previous estimate of eighty to ninety…"

The news broadcast sounded tiny and remote in the vastness of the Voorhees archive, and yet the transmission was sufficiently clear to hold Morgas's attention as he strolled through his collection of homicidal treasures. He sipped on a glass of single malt, weighing up the significance of each word, when suddenly the anchorman went live to a reporter in Hunt Ridge.

"According to eyewitnesses," said the on-the-spot man, "the attacks started quite bizarrely with a sideshow that's more than lived up to its name. A waxworks called Doktor Geistmann's Carnival of Terror…"

The reporter mispronounced the name *Geestman*, instead of the correct *iced man* with a hard *G*. And the rest of his report was a catalog of guesswork and scaremongering; anything to pump up the ratings. But the mere mention of Hunt Ridge—the town the FBI agents had been heading towards when the surveillance device was deactivated—was enough to tell Morgas everything he needed to know.

He finished his drink and walked back to the semicircular entranceway in front of the elevator. Normally, this part of the museum was kept clear so as to give the owner-curator a grand view of all four aisles each time he entered. Now, however, he'd had one of the items in his collection brought forward and placed into the center. He had special plans for this particular artifact; he looked at it adoringly. It was a tank filled with liquid and...

The collector listened as the newscast continued.

"I spoke to one man who told me the suspect was wearing a hockey mask. Now for anyone who's been living in New Jersey over the last twenty years, that's sure to stir up memories of the Crystal Lake Massacre..."

Morgas's eyes narrowed with each amplified syllable. "There's something you're not telling me, Ms Kyler," he said.

He stood back and looked admiringly at the object floating in the tank.

"But then," he said with a self-satisfied sneer, "there's something I'm not telling you."

Aching and worn out, Kyler sat at the foot of the slope. Two more explosions had torn the vehicle apart before she'd given up any hope of freeing her partner, and the inferno was now raging unchecked.

She looked at herself in the orange glow and was depressed by what she saw. There wasn't a part of her that wasn't either scratched or cut or dirty or torn or streaked with smoke. All in all, she was an absolute mess.

She breathed deeply and thought of Tolleson. Then she thought of Jason and her mother. And then she hefted the travel bag in her right hand and stood up. Michelle Kyler had a hill to climb.

Three hours had passed, and Freely's pickup was still parked where Alice had nearly crashed it on the side of the road. The lights and the engine were off; Jason lay motionless on the rear bed. Alice's door hung open as she bent over the wheel and sobbed.

She cried, she kicked, she twisted in her seat and cursed. She didn't know if it was anger, guilt or grief she was feeling—it seemed like all three, and she couldn't deal with it. Her confused mind couldn't see beyond the fact of her father's death, and the loss only grew more painful until drunkenness and exhaustion dragged her into the abyss of a deep sleep.

It was almost five in the morning and Ross was wired. He'd lost track of how many black coffees he'd had, and the pink carpet around Jaomi's desk was a polka dot of foil from all the gum and amphetamines he'd unwrapped.

There were now over fifty bids on Jason's body, but the current high was a laughable two hundred and seventy dollars—this against a man who owned millions.

"Come on, Ross."

Jaomi's voice was quiet and soothing, but Ross was so focused on the computer that he jumped in his seat. He looked up and saw her standing in the doorway; she had never been a pajama person and was completely naked.

"Get some sleep," she implored him.

He could feel his pecker hardening and the lure of a soft mattress was almost irresistible, but this was his hour. This moment, in the dead of night, was the testing of Dwayne Weintraub—and by God, he would prove superior to the challenge.

"You said all you had to say when you quit." For some inexplicable reason, Ross was speaking in a Texan accent. "In less than thirteen hours, I'm gonna be the man who owns Jason Voorhees. So you, Morgas, that loser Veranti—all of you—I'm gonna show you all."

"Oh, Ross, baby. I'm sorry."

Jaomi came forward and rested his head on her breasts. She stroked his hair, knowing that any form of scalp action was his Achilles heel.

"I know it's important," she said, trying to make up for earlier.

"But I really wanted you with me for this," he sulked, sounding Californian again.

"Well, if you still want," she smiled, "I'll stay up with you."

A childlike smile crossed his face. "Will you?" he asked excitedly.

Jaomi nodded and kissed him on the brow.

Ross had known his wife too long to care much about the silicone hooters bouncing in his face. Instead, he just placed his arms around her and they hugged.

Then he looked again at the monitor, he looked into his wife's gleaming face, he looked at the stack of the drugs he hadn't taken yet, and he punched his fist into the air.

"Yeah!" he shouted. "Whoever said it's always darkest before dawn is talking bullshit!"

The time was 5:00am.

The date: Friday The 13th.

CHAPTER SIXTEEN

Sheriff Haslip poured two cups of water from the cooler and walked back over to the interview room—a dreary, windowless box off of the main office. He'd been kept up half the night, initially by the double homicide, but later by the fallout from Hunt Ridge. The people there had heard about the murders of Trick and Z-Moll, and had come swarming over Crystal Lake—until, at about 5:30am, the entire investigation had been taken over by some big shot from Newark who'd also helped himself to most of Haslip's staff. Which was why the office was now deserted, and why a seriously pissed sheriff hadn't told anyone about the phone call he'd received a few hours ago—a call that just might turn things around in his favor.

He nudged the door open and placed the cups down on the interview room table. Both drinks were for his seated guest, and she wasted no time in sinking one of them.

"Thanks for coming out," said Kyler, wiping her lips.

"Hey," smiled the sheriff ruefully, "the last time I ignored a phone call, someone got killed."

"You couldn't have reached them in time."

Kyler's remark was an unquestionable fact, but the sheriff dismissed it as a lame effort to reassure him. "All the same," he commented, "it's not a mistake I intend to repeat."

Kyler tried a change of approach.

"How's the investigation progressing?" she asked, unaware she was now prodding an even more painful nerve.

"It's not," replied the sheriff tersely. "You saw what happened at Hunt Ridge. They followed it back here and now it's out of my hands. The only part I don't understand is where you fit in."

Her eyes flicked up and were met by a stare waiting in ambush.

"What do you mean?" she asked.

"Well, look at you. You've been burned, beat up, you walked miles till you found a phone. Why aren't you back at Hunt Ridge with your people?"

"The Bureau are there?" she frowned.

"Sure. But what happened to your car? And where's your partner? You still haven't told me everything…"

"Jason," she said flatly.

Haslip sighed. "I've just spent half the night listening to a dozen senior officers bend over backwards not to use that name."

"It was Jason," she repeated.

"So I guess you don't know anything about your Sowici friend going crazy with a knife in Reculver?"

Kyler reeled in her seat, "What?"

"Or eyewitnesses saying they saw Sowici at the carnival?"

But if Haslip thought this new evidence was going to test Kyler's resolve, he was sorely mistaken.

"I saw Jason with my own eyes," she stated.

"You saw an impostor."

"Jason, an impostor, whoever. I saw him dragged from the back of this pickup truck."

Kyler handed the sheriff a piece of note paper. He looked at it and saw she'd written the full details of a suspect vehicle.

"Find that truck," she said, "and you'll find the killer."

Jason wrapped his hands around Alice's throat and squeezed. Tighter... tighter... he coiled his fingers about her neck and drilled his thumbs into her windpipe. She tried to scream, but her cries escaped as bubbles through the bloody holes in her throat. Holes like the black pits of Jason's emotionless mask.

And then she woke up.

Alice started in her seat, before realizing it was a quiet, sunny morning and she was perfectly safe. Jason was immobile in the back of the truck, and there was no traffic anywhere along the mountain road. But then she noticed the clock.

"Shit!"

Of all the problems Alice had faced these last few days, the obstinate display face reading 11:37 still managed to depress her; she'd been asleep nearly twelve hours. Worse, the auction was due to end some time after five, and she needed to be ready long before then.

Wondering if anyone had placed any bids, Alice jumped out of the cab and ran round to the back of the truck, her boots scuffing the dirt as she eagerly went in search of the laptop. For a moment, the mere sight of Jason—the bastard who'd tried to tear her head off—was enough to deter her from climbing up onto the bed, but Alice swallowed her fear and...

The travel bag was gone.

At first she thought she was just missing it somehow. But after she'd rolled Jason over and searched every inch of the vehicle four times, she had to accept that the bag must have fallen out during the car chase.

"Fuck," she whispered.

And suddenly she was fighting panic. Her hands shook and she started to bite her thumb nail. The travel bag was somewhere on the road behind her, but how far back? Surely, after what had happened at Harper Field, the cops would be everywhere by now? What if they already had the bag? What if she went looking for it and they caught her? Her truck was a mess, so she was hardly inconspicuous.

"Come on, Alice, think. If you get rid of Jason before sunset, you won't need the head anymore. So what do you need the laptop for? To sell Jason."

She raised her forearm and saw the ZingBid ID and password written on the back of her hand.

"That's it!" she gasped. "You just need a computer. You just need a fucking computer!"

She clenched her fist and hollered—the mountains seemed so much more beautiful in the daylight—but then she heard a distant helicopter and remembered that Jason was lying fully exposed on the flatbed.

Quickly, she got back in the truck and turned the ignition. Just six more hours and this would all be over.

A miniature black hole had materialized inside the hallway of Ross Feratu's mansion. It floated behind one of the security guards and its intense gravity was sucking every particle of goodwill out of the atmosphere.

"Where is the skuzzy-headed prick?" asked Veranti, as the tall assistant led him through the upstairs corridor.

The guard said nothing, choosing instead to motion Luke through an open door into Jaomi's office. Ross was still glued to the monitor on his wife's desk, and now the whole room was ringing with the funk of his crevices.

Veranti looked around at the pink walls, the pink carpet, the pink furniture.

"I never been here before," he commented, ogling one of Jaomi's lurid video posters. "It's like sitting inside a fucking pussy."

"I can't leave the computer," offered Ross pathetically.

"So I had to come all the way out here because you're stuck in a fucking porn cycle?" Luke's head started to bob with irritation and it reminded Ross of the good old days.

"Is that what you think this is?" asked the singer.

"You tell me," snapped Veranti. "You're the guy who needs that clickety fucking click shoving up your ass."

Ross took his hand off the mouse.

"All right, listen," he began. "I don't have time to explain right now, but I need you back on the team…"

The black piranha still hadn't taken a seat. He caught sight of himself in the mirror and smartly adjusted his jacket and roll neck.

"What team's that?" he rasped, straightening his cuffs. "The fucking Egg Squad, is that what it is? Team fucking Yoko Up My Ass? Team Screw Your Manager And Get Arrested on TV?"

"Luke, I'm serious," said Ross as earnestly as his tired voice could manage. "I totally regret everything I said before, okay? I apologize. I screwed up."

Veranti was unmoved.

"Too right you did," he rattled. "Now stop wasting my time. Either cough up the termination fee or get yourself a good fucking lawyer."

Ross decided it was time to put his cards on the table.

"I want you to get me a slot on *The Hardest Rock on Earth*," he announced plainly. "Tonight. Live. I want to perform 'Frightday 13.'"

"Awww," Veranti snickered. "Now I get it. You got me confused with Siegfried and Roy."

"I've got something awesome lined up but it can't wait." Ross came out from behind the desk, the PC momentarily forgotten in his urgency. "It'll put me right back on the map"

"Go ask your new manager," sniped Luke, making for the door.

"Oh, that's bullshit!" shouted Ross. "The whole thing with Jaomi, it was just—I was freaked by the sales figures."

Veranti stopped and glanced over his shoulder, "And where is Countess Benedict?"

"She's out shopping or something—how the hell do I know?"

Ross had hated sending Jaomi away from the computer, even for only half an hour, but he knew what would have happened if she'd caught Veranti visiting with him.

"Do you know how tough it is to get on *Hardest Rock*?" said Luke. "Everyone in town wants that. And they don't have their own facility, so you need a studio, a crew, set design, a feed—and that's before you even talk a deal. And you want it all by twenty-three hundred? Are you serious?"

"Pull it off," replied the singer, "and I'll pay you four times the termination fee. In cash."

Veranti bobbed his head. "This egg shit's killing you, you know that?"

"Just do it," said Ross, offering his hand for a shake and make up, "and if business still sucks after seven days of the show, I'll give you the termination fee as well as the one-off payment and I'll tear up the contract myself."

Luke thought about it. For the first time today, Ross was starting to make some sense.

"On one condition," said Veranti finally.

"What's that?"

"I get four hours in the sack with your wife."

Ross almost died.

"What?"

"Four hours of uphill grind with Jaomi."

"Oh, come on, I can't ask her that!" Ross hollered. "You know she hates you. If I told her she was part of the deal, she'd kill me. Come on Veranti! That's totally out of the question."

"Two," haggled the manager. "It's my final offer."

"Done."

And both men shook hands, closing the deal over Jaomi's porn star body. Ross had no idea how he was going to break it to her, but he sure as shit wasn't going to mention it before the end of the auction.

If Kyler had been able to get any closer to the Chrysler, what would she have seen? Would Tolleson have been charred and barbecued? Would he have been ash? Or would he have been screaming and struggling to crawl out through the window while his body blistered and seared?

The door opened and Sheriff Haslip entered the interview room.

Kyler had spent all afternoon sitting alone, so she thought he might have some news for her. But if anything, the cop seemed reluctant to speak at all.

"How are you feeling?" he mumbled.

"I don't know," she answered pensively. "Part of me wants to be out there but the other half just wants to rest."

"I can understand that," he murmured. "Have you had any sleep?"

"Not really, maybe if…"

"I've been in touch with the Bureau," he said, talking over her in a now-or-never outburst.

Kyler tensed immediately. "You called them?"

"No," he answered uncomfortably. "I put a call out for the truck, like you asked, and one thing led to another and…"

"It's okay," she yawned.

"They're sending someone to pick you up. They want you to stay here until they arrive."

Kyler nodded but made no reply.

"Okay then," shrugged Haslip. "I have some work to do. But if you need anything—"

"I'll be all right," she said, finishing the thought for him.

Haslip smiled and shuffled out of the room. He closed the door again, but Kyler tried not to read anything sinister into it. She yawned and started to cross her legs, when her shoe kicked something beneath the table. In her exhaustion, she'd completely forgotten about the travel bag; presumably she would have to submit it as evidence.

Despondently, she put the bag up on the table, took out the head of Mrs Voorhees—and saw the laptop. It was just lying there in the bottom of the case. Kyler couldn't believe she hadn't found it sooner.

Keeping an ear open for the sheriff, she placed the computer next to the head and switched on the power. She watched impatiently as the PC chugged through its loading routine. Fortunately, it wasn't password protected, and in less than a minute the software was up and running.

As far as Kyler could tell, the computer was owned by someone called Judge, and his most frequently used program was the internet browser. She opened the browser and searched through Judge's list of recently visited websites. After wading through masses of autosports material, she found a series of offline pages cached from an auction site called ZingBid. There were over thirty auctions on the list, but the agent diligently worked through each one until she found the most impossible sale of all time: Jason Voorhees.

Jaomi was beginning to resent the fact that Ross had taken up residence in her private office. There were dozens of computers all over the house, but he'd as much as told her he was afraid that if he moved from one machine to another, he'd somehow break his connection with the auction and lose everything. The moron.

"I heard Veranti came by earlier," Jaomi tried to sound casual, as if the comment was of no conse-quence.

Ross looked up and saw her standing in the doorway. She was wearing her fitness baggies and hefting a pair of one-kilo dumbbells like the dumb cliché she was.

"He came back to beg for his job," the singer lied outrageously.

Ross really was looking terrible now. After one night in front of the plasma, one night screwing Jaomi and watching the auction, this was his third afternoon in a row without sleep.

"You told him to take a hike, right?" Jaomi wasn't asking, she was telling.

But Ross was slow to offer confirmation. In fact, he didn't give her any confirmation at all.

"Tell me about Jerry," he said, dodging the issue. "Did you tell him to take the jet to New Jersey, like I asked?"

"Yeah, I did," she answered. "But I still don't know why."

Ross nodded at the screen, "It's Jason. I need him back here tonight."

"But why New Jersey?" she panted.

"Because that's where he'll be. That's where Jason always is."

Jaomi seemed skeptical, but decided the course of least resistance was to humor the stinky son-of-a-tard.

"So what's the price now?" she asked.

The tendons in Ross's hand pleaded for mercy, but he gripped the mouse and refreshed the screen yet again.

"Three eighty-five," he laughed. "And there's only an hour to go."

Jaomi increased the speed of her reps. "I wouldn't be surprised if you weren't bidding for one of your old robots. Every time you make a video one of them gets stolen."

"They're animatronics, not robots," Ross insisted pettily.

"Frankly, Ross, I could care less if they were clothes store dummies."

"Listen!" shouted the singer. "You just make sure you're ready with that bid blocker thing. Okay?"

"Oh, I'm ready," she fumed. "Then maybe we can get this over with and go back to normal."

And she used the word "normal" without any sense of irony.

All across America and around the world, people were settling down in front of their monitors and strapping themselves in for the main event. Housewives checked their credit limits, doctors called their telephone banking services. A trained criminologist, an ex-cop in Detroit, hundreds of kids and heavy metal freaks, an accountant, a school teacher, even an Italian priest—regardless of local time, they were all logging onto ZingBid and getting ready for the countdown.

Word of the unbelievable sale had spread across the internet grapevine, leaping from seedy forum to illegal chat room in a matter of hours. No one who could have stopped the sale knew it was even happening, and the media were equally in the dark, as the anonymous denizens of the digital underworld—seemingly harmless citizens living double lives—swarmed like rats towards the auction site.

So far potential buyers had been playing it cool, keeping the price low by not submitting any early bids. In the final ten minutes, however, the wires would go crazy, with everyone either trying to out-muscle the competition, or using the Russian roulette approach of trying to be the last person to click a successful bid before the clock ran to zero.

The body of Jason Voorhees was the greatest collectable of a lifetime. Hundreds of greedy little fingers hovered over their mouse buttons in anticipation. Online gambling had nothing on this thrill. For the next thirty minutes or so, the world's most notorious serial killer was public property; anyone could buy him if they had the cash. But once the auction was up, he would be lost to everyone except the winner.

There were less than fifteen minutes to go before the end of the auction. Kyler worked feverishly on the laptop. She'd found Judge's web site for the carnival, and the information it contained was invaluable: particularly the History page, which featured a biography for every member of the show. Judge was there, and so was a woman named Alice Witney.

Last night, when Kyler had first met Sheriff Haslip, he'd mentioned Alice Witney as a suspect. And the seller's ZingBid ID was "aliceinmonsterland." So although she was certain the computer belonged to Judge, Kyler was convinced that Alice was the one who'd driven the pickup out of Hunt Ridge. It was Alice Witney who had Jason now.

The wireless connection was already in operation, so Kyler skated her finger over the touchpad and reloaded the ZingBid page—Jason's current value was set at four hundred dollars, which seemed an awful lot just to get killed. Kyler selected the link for sending questions to the seller and then, hoping that Alice would have some other means of checking her email, typed a message stating in no uncertain terms that Alice Jane Witney was under arrest, and that she had to surrender Jason's body to the FBI immediately.

Kyler was about to send the message when the battery expired and the PC shut down right in front of her face.

"No!"

She frantically tried to restart it, but each time the laptop commenced its boot sequence, it automatically closed back down until eventually it didn't respond to the power button at all. Kyler searched the travel bag, but there was no sign of a power cord. She even checked the severed head—maybe a cable was hidden inside—but the ragged parchment of Pamela's skin was unbroken, save for where a piece of vertebra poked through the plane of her neck.

Putting the head back on the table, Kyler tiptoed over to the door and pressed her ear to the frosted glass window. Hearing nothing, she peeked into the main office; there was no sign of Haslip or any of his men—and the computer on his desk was unattended.

She crept over and started it up.

"Damn!"

The computer wanted a password.

Kyler turned the PC back off and looked for a cord that might fit the laptop. She went rummaging through drawers, cupboards—anywhere that wasn't locked—but the office was too big and the auction had less than ten minutes remaining. Desperate, she ran outside onto the main street, her heart sinking when she saw only a diner and a convenience store.

Eight minutes.

She hurried back indoors. Haslip still wasn't around, so she couldn't ask his help even if she'd been willing to take the risk. All along, her plan had been to bid in the auction with the sole aim of securing access to Jason. But now time was running out and she couldn't even get online.

Kyler realized she had no choice but to call someone for help.

Her cell was broken, but there were phones all over the sheriff's office; there was even one in the interview room.

Seven minutes.

Kyler rushed back to her bland guestroom, checked the head and laptop were okay, and then picked up the phone. She didn't have many options: no one would believe her story about Jason; the FBI were coming out practically to arrest her; Haslip was doing everything he could to avoid her, and it would take hours to stop the auction through normal channels—by which time Jason would have completely vanished. No, there was only one person who could help her now.

Kyler took the business card out of her pocket. The card was blank save for a phone number. She hesitated.

Six minutes.

She had no choice.

Nathaniel Morgas took a moment to compose himself. He let the phone ring two more times and then picked up.

"Ahh, the elusive Ms Kyler," he declared grandly. "And how may I be of assistance?"

A map of Wessex County was spread across his desk, with small flags pinned into Hunt Ridge, Crystal Lake and all the other places Tolleson's car had passed through. Opposite the desk, three huge screens ran endless news reports of the bloodbath at Harper Field. Morgas knew Special Agent Kyler was somehow involved, and yet it had taken her twenty-one hours before she'd deigned to contact him.

Indeed, if Morgas didn't have one more ace up his sleeve, he'd probably have been feeling rather angry by now.

In Sometown USA—she was too tired to give a damn what the berg was called—Alice coughed up some metal for a coffee and went and sat over by the window. Lettering on the pane read, "Mackie's Internet Café." Her hangover was still killing her, and it didn't help that she hadn't eaten all day and had been driving north for hours.

She chose a workstation positioned so that she could see the truck parked out on the street. A figure was slumped in the passenger seat with Alice's leather jacket thrown over its head, as if trying to grab some shuteye. That was the only way she could think of hiding Jason, while she herself had dived fully dressed into a lake before reaching town, to get rid of Glo's blood and all the puke.

Now she sat with bated breath in front of the computer. The auction was going to end in just five minutes, and she had visions of six-figure sums escalating in front of her astonished eyes. Other than the staff, there were only two other people in the café and they were slurping their lattes, completely oblivious to what Alice was doing. Nevertheless, she maneuvered her body to hide the screen and then logged onto ZingBid as aliceinmonsterland.

A pop-up window announced, "You have 234 new messages."

Alice clicked OK and went straight to the auction page; with two hundred and thirty-four enquiries in just one day, Jason had to be worth a fortune. Her hands were shaking, so she took another hit of espresso as the sale page assembled on the screen. And there it was:

"CURRENT BID: $702.00."

Not even enough to get the pickup fixed.

"Damn you, Dad," she whispered, her whole life crashing down to this one moment of colossal failure. "Damn you to fucking hell!"

CHAPTER SEVENTEEN

Ten slimy slugs wriggled on the keyboard. The peripheral was exotic: handmade, brushed chrome, the perfect bed for two writhing hands—sweating, sexual, leaving the grease and filth of obsession on every sordid key they punished.

"Of course you've done the right thing, Ms Kyler," said Morgas, typing on his computer. "I offered you unlimited assistance."

The obese collector was doing his utmost to sound leisurely, but inside he was burning with excitement. He knew how little Kyler trusted him, so for her to call, the stakes must have been considerable.

"Where would you like me to look?" he asked.

As before, Kyler's voice came through the phone with breathtaking clarity: "Go to ZingBid dot com."

"A moment please."

He dragged his slugs across the keys and, in a few seconds, the page was displayed on his monitor.

"Now what?" he asked her.

"Find the search box and—" She stopped.

"And what, Ms Kyler?"

Silence.

Morgas sensed that this was the moment of truth. Once Kyler told him what she knew, there would be no going back: the balance of power would shift irrevocably in his favor. But would she do it? Would she open Pandora's box?

"Ms Kyler?" he prompted.

"Type Jason Voorhees," she said hurriedly.

Now it was Morgas's turn to hesitate—only it wasn't reluctance that was holding him, it was doubt. It didn't seem possible that he would find Jason here on this tawdry auction site; and yet the only other explanation was that Kyler had found out what Morgas really wanted, and the cruel bitch was toying with him.

His rational mind was still deadlocked—desperate but not daring to look—while the slugs typed with a will of their own: JASON VOORHEES.

Click.

And then a single word spilled from his lips.

"Heavens…"

"Can you see it?" asked Michelle through the line.

At that precise juncture, Nathaniel Morgas could see nothing else. There, in 1024 by 768 pixels, was the Holy Grail of Jasonalia. The one remaining treasure. The only thing Morgas needed to make his life complete.

"Are you still there?" she asked. "There's less than three minutes. You've got to make a bid—put on any amount. If someone else wins, we'll never find Jason again. Do you understand? It's the only way we'll recover Jason's body. You must win the auction."

Morgas, however, was in the grip of a physiological condition he had never experienced before. He was speechless.

Ross Feratu, however, was screaming his lungs out. No sleep for three days, a bucket of drugs and shouting at the top of his voice: it was just like being on the road.

"Shit, Jaomi, shit!" he cried, slamming some uppers into his mouth, quickly followed by a lo-fat, hi-caff triple cola.

"Don't panic," she grouched. "It's under control."

"But it's just hit two and a half," he pointed at the screen, "and there's three minutes left."

"Quit whining!"

Jaomi had gone to fetch another chair and was now firmly in the driving seat. Ross remained center monitor, but Jaomi held the mouse, and even getting that off the dillweed had been a trial; she'd had to drop one of her dumbbells in his nuts before he'd even considered surrendering.

"Are you sure your blocker thing'll work?" he asked nervously.

"Ross!" Jaomi's coding pride was momentarily offended. "I use it all the time. Don't worry."

"So why don't you use it now, just in case?"

"Because," she sighed, "it only lasts thirty seconds."

"So?"

She wanted to strangle him. "So! There's two minutes left. If I use it now, everyone'll have a minute and a half to beat you."

"Oh, I get it," he nodded. "Okay."

"All you have to do," she explained, "is make sure you've got enough money to beat the last real bid."

"Like that'll be a problem," Ross jeered.

Famous last words.

Jaomi refreshed the screen and the current bid changed from three thousand, two hundred to... one... million... dollars.

Ross fell off his chair and screamed.

"It's that fucking asstool Morgas! It's gotta be. Nathaniel fucking Morgas!"

From pole to pole, the million dollar bid came down like a giant hammer and smashed all the wannabes into pieces.

The kids who'd pooled their allowances; the low-budget moviemaker who'd redirected a couple of cash buckets from his latest project; the Chicago syndicate who agreed Jason might constitute a high risk investment package; the internet addict who'd staked all his disabled mom's savings; the trauma therapist who secretly masturbated over photos of real murders, when not at work counseling victims of crime; the Norwegian paranoiac who was convinced he was bidding on the body of Elvis—as one, they united in their disappointment, and a collective groan traveled through the time zones like a Mexican wave of frustration.

In particular, Kevan Rey of Utah thought that such a high bid was "totally against the spirit of ZingBid," and had already started angrily typing an email of complaint to the site administrator.

Nathaniel Morgas, however, was perfectly content. It had taken him longer to create an account, using one of his aliases, than it had to enter the winning amount. Now he sat alone in his office with a radiance that was sickening. A million meant nothing to him. Indeed, one million dollars was practically vulgar—it was the kind of figure that got the little people excited.

"Have no worries, Ms Kyler," he said aloud. "Everything is under control."

"Have you won?" she asked sharply.

"In a moment, Ms Kyler, in a—"

Two million dollars appeared on the screen.

"What the hell did you do that for?" hollered Jaomi.

She didn't know what annoyed her more: that Ross had snatched the mouse off of her, or that he was wasting his money like a total retard. But the singer was unrepentant. He stared at the monitor with the concentration of someone whose prehistoric hunter-gatherer instincts, so long dormant, had been reawakened.

"I can't let him beat me," he announced determinedly.

"What is wrong with you? You don't bid until I start the blocker. If you just leave it alone, you could have got it for a million. Now it's going to cost at least two, and if someone raises…"

"I'm not gonna let that bastard win. Not this time."

"But you don't—need—to bid!" she screamed point blank in his face.

There was a minute and ten remaining.

Ross refreshed the data, saw it was still two million, and looked directly into his wife's beautiful eyes.

"Jaomi, you're either with me or against me."

"Do you know something?" she said, unflinching in the heat of both his hardass act and his unwashed breath. "You're a total dick."

"No. I've got everything lined up," he said, ignoring her. "I've got Jerry in New Jersey waiting to bring Jason here. I've got Veranti setting up a live broadcast for eleven thirty—"

Jaomi pounced on Ross's careless remark.

"Tell me I didn't hear that," she crossed her arms and sat back.

"Say what?" Ross regarded her as if she'd just spoken in Martian.

"You and that spunk-nut..." she began. "Don't tell me you've gone behind my back. Because if you need a TV appearance, let me handle it. My pedicurist knows someone who works on *Jimmy Kimmel*..."

"Oh yeah, 'cause Kimmel's so funny," boomed Ross, completely beyond patience. "Gimme a fucking break."

"Well, you're not working with Veranti again. That's not something I see as a possibility."

Suddenly Ross yelled, "Forty seconds! Shut up and get ready."

"Give me that," Jaomi wrenched the mouse out of his hands and moved the cursor over her bid blocker.

Kyler felt utterly frustrated. She had seen Jason for only a few tantalizing seconds before he'd been taken from her, and now it felt as if he was moving further out of reach. The only hope she had was this last minute phone call to her sinister ally, a man whose name and motives remained a mystery—and who had just given a throttled cry not unlike the exclamation of a cardiac arrest.

"Is something wrong?" asked Kyler.

Instinctively, she clutched at the phone as if trying to wring Jason out of the plastic.

"Hello?" she called again. "What's your current status? Are you still the highest bidder? Hello!"

Suddenly the line went dead.

Kyler immediately replaced the handset, lifted it up and—nothing. No dial tone, no ring tone—just silence. She punched some of the buttons and hit the studs a few times but nothing worked.

"Damn!"

Confident that no one else was around, she turned to go out into the main office. Suddenly she heard a voice.

"You're wasting your time, dear. No one can help you now."

It didn't seem possible; the words had come from behind her in the small, empty interview room—a cramped space with no windows and no other doors. Kyler whipped out her GLOCK and spun in the direction of the voice.

Her barrel came to rest on the head of Pamela Voorhees.

* * *

Thirty-five seconds remained until the end of the auction and the price had ping-ponged up to five million.

"See!" shouted Jaomi. "I warned you. You fucking moron!"

But Ross only had eyes for the flat panel. "Twenty nine seconds!" he shrieked. "Go! Go! Go!"

The MIT graduate, who also possessed a diploma in blow jobs, swung smoothly yet swiftly into action. She double-clicked her clipart icon and a bright pink window opened in the center of the screen. The bid-blocker was now in operation.

"Go on!" shouted Ross. "Put the bid in."

The singer was so close to pissing his pants that it just wasn't funny. But Jaomi was unflappable; she typed fluidly with all ten fingers, not making a single mistake as she keyed a series of commands into her program, followed by the most crucial entry of all:

"$5,000,001"

ENTER.

A scrolling heap of hexadecimal numbers ran down one side of the bid-blocker, as it operated at lightning speed to head off any rival submissions. What Jaomi was doing was purely illegal, but no one had found her out so far, so why should they do so now?

A pop-up message appeared on the monitor:

"You are now bidder number one! Please refresh your screen to check for higher bids."

As if Ross needed telling twice.

He cheered with excitement and gave his wife a peck on the cheek. Her bid-blocker had another nineteen seconds left while the auction had only fourteen.

If their convulsive flailing was any measure, the ten slugs had just been dipped in acid. Morgas banged on the numerical keys, hit return, clicked OK, thrashed in six more zeroes but nothing— nothing!—would work.

"Ms Kyler!" His usual quiet eloquence had tightened into a piercing whimper. "Are you there? Please. Speak to me."

He typed six million dollars for the sixth frantic time, but still some cretin named jamantez63 was shown as the highest bidder with only five million—there had to be a fault with the website. Morgas banged his fist on the desk.

"Ms Kyler!" he bellowed, screwing his mouth up into a snarl.

The snarl became a wordless roar as he pushed another button on his phone, "Ms Cardella, come see me at once!"

His recently promoted assistant had no time to answer before Morgas switched back.

"Ms Kyler! This is your fault!"

He saw the monitor. Five seconds left.

"Ms Kyler!"

Four.

"I'll kill you for this."

Three.

"*Raggghh!*" he grabbed the flat panel and threw it across the room.

Two.

He dashed the keyboard sideways onto the marble floor.

One.

"No!"

Zero.

He stood up and toppled the entire desk. The phone, the lamp, the antique crystal paperweight: they all crashed against the floor in an arc of petty destruction. By the time Ms Cardella entered the room, her employer had wrecked everything— even the Whistler landscape and the Shirayamadani vase; nothing had escaped his vandalism.

"H—how can I help you, sir?"

Ms Cardella could barely bring herself to speak, and when her employer turned she almost fainted. The bald, sweaty tyrant had foam on his lips and was ranting like a maniac.

"Get in touch with ZingBid," he raved. "Find out who their top people are and fire them. I don't care how much it costs, just do it. Kill them if you have to. I want that auction overturned."

Ms Cardella hadn't a clue what her employer was talking about, but she didn't dare interrupt him.

"And contact jamantez63," he bellowed. "Find out who he is, retrieve Jason's body and kill him. Do you hear me?"

Cardella tilted her head in terrified obedience.

"I want them all killed," he went on, his hands grasping the air, reaching impulsively for something else to break. "I don't care what you do. Use their families if necessary, but just bring me that body!"

* * *

Though she remained convinced the auction was a hoax, Jaomi couldn't help but get swept along with Ross's happiness. The last time she'd seen him party like this was the time he'd discovered his name in an encyclopedia he'd once bought. He'd picked up *The Ultimate Crystal Lake Massacre Sourcebook*, just to add to his collection, and had been amazed to find himself listed for all the Jason Voorhees references in his music.

Just like then, Ross was now dancing and cheering. He was sticking cocaine up his nose and champagne down his throat, and Jaomi was suddenly the most fantastic woman on the planet. He kissed her from every angle and kept telling her how much he loved her.

"I don't fucking believe it!" he yelled, but every time he looked at the computer the text remained the same:

"CONGRATULATIONS—YOU ARE THE WINNER OF THIS AUCTION!"

"I just hope you don't regret it," said Jaomi maternally.

She didn't want to piss on her man's parade, but Ross had to prepare himself for the worst. He was about to blow five million on a fraud, and when the shit finally hit the fan, who would he come crying to? For now though, Jaomi had to smile. Ross was jumping around like a little boy.

"Who da man?" he shouted in triumph. "Quick, send a message to the seller. Tell him we'll do everything he asks. Cash, no questions asked. We'll pick it up right now. Call Jerry. Ask him—"

Ross was interrupted by a gentle ring from the computer. Jaomi sat down in her chair—it was unpleasantly warm—and swapped to her mail program. She'd just received a message from aliceinmonsterland.

Alice suddenly realized that everyone in the café was staring at her. The two other customers both had quizzical smiles on their faces and were looking at her expectantly—waiting for her to share—while the serving staff were watching her for signs of trouble. None of them knew she had just seen the auction finish on five million, and that she was going a happy version of postal.

She wept, she cheered—her first cry had made one guy choke on his cappuccino—she clapped her hands and wrapped her arms around herself. She stood up and sat down again. She looked a mess. She was torn with conflicting emotions: her dead father, Kenton Freely and his attempts to use her, the carnage at Harper Field, the road chase, Jason Voorhees alive and killing, five million dollars—none of it seemed real. Five million—just numbers on a screen. It meant nothing. Yet.

"I'm sorry," she mumbled, smiling at the bewildered and slightly nervous onlookers. "I'm not a nut. Honest."

She burst out laughing.

"Okay," said one of the men behind the counter. "I'm going to have to ask you to respect the rules of this establishment."

"Respect?" giggled Alice. "If you don't shut your fucking mouth, I'm gonna buy this dump. Now where's the nearest bar?"

* * *

Kyler had barely had time to react to the voice when she heard the front door to the sheriff's office open and close; someone must have entered from the street outside.

"Sheriff, is that you?" she called.

She waited a moment, but there was no response. Quickly, she holstered her handgun and made for the door—only to find she couldn't move.

"Not so fast, dear." It was that voice again. "You're going to help me find my son."

Suddenly, Kyler felt as if her whole face had been injected with Novocain. Her legs refused to budge, and images of murder filtered into her desire. But unlike Glo and Alice before her, Kyler immediately understood that the life force of Pamela Voorhees had lived on inside that shriveled skull, and was now creeping like ivy through her soul.

"This is not... going... to happen," she gasped, fighting the possession.

"But it's already happened, dear," laughed Pamela as she forced the agent to take a step back towards the table.

Kyler recalled the speech she'd given Tolleson; the same speech she'd uttered many times since childhood, about not letting anyone use her, or make her into a victim...

"Mom!"

"Yes, dear?" answered Pamela.

Summoning all her willpower, Kyler reached inside her blouse for the sole remaining keepsake of her murdered mother. As soon as her fingers touched the locket, Pamela grunted like a wounded pig and was ejected from her mind.

"It's not possible!" cursed Voorhees. "You're too strong!"

Kyler staggered forward with the sudden release of exorcism. She almost crashed into the table as all feeling and power were restored to her.

"You're no longer a credible threat, Mrs Voorhees," she panted.

"If you don't let me in…" Pamela began to threaten.

"You've failed."

"Please!" begged the disembodied killer. "You must let me in. Jason needs me."

Kyler arched an eyebrow. "You know where he is?"

"How could I not?" gasped Pamela. "I'm his mother. All I've wanted all along is to join my boy."

"But if you're such a good mother," Kyler observed harshly, "why doesn't he come to you?"

If anyone else could have heard this other-worldly dialog, they would have sensed the rage fermenting beneath Pamela's reply.

"It's not that simple," she boiled.

Suddenly, Kyler remembered seeing Jason being dragged behind the pickup: he wasn't moving at all. And how could Alice sell Jason on ZingBid? And why hadn't Jason killed anyone until Glo and her friends had found the cabin?

"There's something wrong with him," she realized. "That's why Jason can't come to you. He's in some kind of dormant condition."

Pamela sniggered, "Oh and I suppose all those people at the carnival just fell to pieces?"

"Then it's only at certain times," guessed Kyler, and she knew from the turmoil in her mind that she'd just hit pay dirt. "That's it. Jason can't come to you because he's immobile, except under specific conditions."

"You don't know what you're talking about."

Kyler drew her GLOCK and shoved the muzzle into Pamela's left eye.

"Tell me how it works," she demanded, "or I'll give you more holes than Jason's hockey mask."

She squeezed the trigger and there was a faint click, as the first of the three automatic safeties disengaged.

"All right!" said Pamela. "Take me to him and I'll tell you."

The FBI agent didn't trust Pamela one bit, but she was in no doubt that the maternal maniac would lead her to her son; finding Jason had always been Kyler's primary objective.

"Okay, Mrs Voorhees, it's a deal. Now where is he?"

Kyler returned the gun to its holster.

"Do you think I'd fall for a stupid trick like that?" spat Pamela. "I said I'll take you to him."

Michelle sighed. Her mistake had been unintentional, but she still needed proof that Pamela would honor the agreement—at least until the inevitable double-cross. So she chose her next question very carefully.

"Tell me Jason's secret," she asked. "Why isn't he active?"

Pamela replied without hesitation.

"When Jason's hurt, he takes time to get better—and the more he's hurt, the longer it takes. But last time, he took such a horrible beating that it was too much for the poor boy! He needs my help."

"But at the carnival he seemed fine."

Pamela chuckled.

"Frankly dear, I don't really understand it myself. But when I see a full moon, I can give him some of my strength. And when I can't, he falls asleep again."

Kyler was suddenly dizzy with the possibilities. She already owned Pamela's head, so if she could find Jason...

"That's incredible," she murmured.

"Yes," agreed Pamela. "Jason's having an awful time. But don't worry. Mommy knows how to fix him."

Kyler reacted sharply. "What do you mean?"

"He's just sick," Pamela explained. "But we can cure him, don't you see? If we help Jason kill someone on the same day that he died, he'll be in the pink again. Then he won't need the moon anymore."

"Friday the 13th," muttered Kyler. "But that's today!"

"And that's why we need to find him," said Pamela silkily. "Now let... me... in..."

Kyler experienced the rapid numbing of consciousness which told her that Pamela was trying to possess her. She stroked the locket—her connection with her own mother was even stronger.

"I don't understand!" cried Pamela, denied. "We made a bargain."

"Oh, I'll take you," said Kyler, ignoring the killer's nail-on-chalkboard wrath, "but you're staying in here."

She lifted the severed head and returned it, along with the laptop, to Alice Witney's travel bag. Even out of sight, the remnant was close enough to speak into Kyler's mind.

"How will we get there?" asked Mrs Voorhees.

The agent zipped up the bag and sneaked over to the door. She waited a moment and listened. Ever since the sheriff had returned to the office, he hadn't made a sound—or maybe she'd been too preoccupied to notice.

"Well, it's not standard procedure," whispered Kyler, "but I'm going to steal the sheriff's car."

"Why, what a clever girl you are," said Pamela approvingly.

"Be quiet."

Kyler gently opened the door, but was confused to find the room empty. No sheriff, no deputies—the place was deserted. Better still, Haslip's car keys were lying on his desk. The agent took them and made for the rear exit, an alley where the patrol cars were parked. With the sheriff himself gone, Kyler was worried his vehicle might also be missing. But when she stepped out into the evening air, she saw the car standing exactly where he'd left it after driving her back.

She went round to the driver's side, opened the door, and Haslip's body fell out. There was a bullet hole between his eyes. Kyler took out her gun, but had only just started to scan the alley for possible targets before a figure came up behind her.

"Tolleson!"

She couldn't believe it. Her partner was standing there, smiling. He was alive.

Cory Tolleson stepped forward to greet her.

"Hey there," he said.

But instead of embracing her, he expertly delivered a blow to the base of her skull with a PR-24 nightstick.

CHAPTER EIGHTEEN

"Tonight, on *The Hardest Rock on Earth*, shock rocker Ross Feratu will be performing his new single, 'Frightday 13,' with a guest star you won't believe! For the first time ever on TV, Ross Feratu will appear LIVE with Jason Voorhees! Don't miss it: Ross Feratu and the legendary maniac from hell, Jason Voorhees, together on one telecast. 'Frightday 13,' LIVE on *The Hardest Rock On Earth*, tonight at eleven thirty PST. *The Hardest Rock On Earth*: the only TV show that can be heard from space."

Kyler was in slow-motion freefall, following a gray sheen of words she never seemed able to reach through her fractured overload of pain.

"Welcome back, Ms Kyler."

The man's voice seemed familiar. Kyler tried to rub her aching head but her hand wouldn't move.

"Where am I?" she murmured, her lips dry.

"Where you've always been," answered the voice. "That is to say, you're exactly where I want you."

The obvious threat acted like a pail of icy water. Kyler snapped open her eyes and found she was tied to a dentist's chair. Plasticuffs held her wrists and ankles, while a single lamp shone over her head, making her the star attraction in this grim theater of abduction. The walls of the room were lost in darkness, but echoes suggested a massive chamber.

"Just who are you?" she drawled, her voice thick with fatigue.

Other than the chair and the marble floor, the only thing Kyler could see was...

"Nathaniel Morgas," he replied with dramatic understatement.

"Who?" Kyler's ignorance was genuine.

"Ah, you wound me, Ms Kyler. With your comprehensive knowledge of the Voorhees crimes, I should have thought my name would have at least meant something to you."

His smooth tongue was met by a blank stare.

"I see I am in error," he continued. "Never mind. The only thing you need concern yourself with is that you have been a pet project of mine for many years. I have long believed that if anyone would be able to find Jason Voorhees, it was you. And yet you disappoint me."

Kyler looked at her bonds and realized it would be futile to struggle. Better to conserve her strength until the right opportunity came along.

"What exactly do you want?" she asked.

In response, the room was flooded with light, revealing the entire collection of murder memorabilia. The weapons, the masks, the Crystal Lake paraphernalia, even the bodies in formaldehyde—everything was put on show for the delectation of Morgas's prisoner.

One display case stood much closer than the rest and was hidden beneath heavy drapes. But it was to a tall, empty cabinet further back that Morgas now drew Kyler's attention. She read the nameplate attached to the bottom.

"Jason?" she slurred.

"That's right, Ms Kyler, the only gap in my collection. You were to secure him for me and you failed. However, I should thank you for bringing a bonus item to my attention."

A man walked forward from behind Kyler's chair and placed the severed head of Pamela Voorhees on a carbon fiber lectern, a yard or so in front of the captured agent. Then the assistant turned so that Kyler could see his face.

"Tolleson!" she gasped. Concussion had made her completely forget the blow of betrayal.

Her partner bowed but said nothing, leaving all conversation to his employer.

"I told you Tolleson was a spy, Ms Kyler," said Morgas. "Unfortunately, I neglected to indicate he was spying for me. I've been playing you all along."

"Do you think you'll get away with this?" she rattled.

"I am not in the business of trading empty threats, Ms Kyler."

He took out his small, shiny revolver and fired a slug into her right kneecap. Kyler coiled in her seat and tried not to scream.

"You have seriously inconvenienced me, Ms Kyler. In less than—" he glanced at his watch; it was thirty-eight minutes after midnight "—two hours, Jason is going to be paraded before the world in a ludicrous rock video. That cannot be allowed to happen."

Cold sweat poured down Kyler's brow. Her body arced and heaved against its restraints. The pain coursing through her leg was excruciating.

"Now the problem I have," Morgas continued, "is that there is simply not enough time to search every studio in Los Angeles before the outrage takes place. Therefore, if I cannot find Jason, Jason must come to me. And I think you know how to bring that about."

Kyler struggled to retrieve her wits from the ache of the gunshot. "I don't know what you're talking about."

"Oh, but you do, Ms Kyler. My employee, Mr Tolleson here, is of the firm opinion that this remarkable lady," he indicated the severed head, "has told you Jason's secret. Regrettably, Mr Tolleson was able to hear only your side of the conversation."

"Just listen to yourself," spat Kyler. She was regaining more composure by the second.

Morgas sighed, "I had an inkling you were going to be tedious."

Without waiting for a cue, Tolleson went to fetch a medical trolley full to capacity with surgical equipment, hardware tools, and unfamiliar appli-

ances custom-built for the purpose of human torture. He rolled the barbaric workstation into
position, next to Kyler's chair, and picked up a
cordless power drill. Two pulls at the trigger confirmed the device was in working order.

"I'll leave you two to catch up on old times,"
said Morgas idly.

Then he strolled out of the room, taking a mod-
icum of pleasure from the first of Michelle Kyler's
many screams.

The replica of Camp Crystal Lake was so convincing, Ross had to pinch himself to make sure
he wasn't dreaming. The water, the sandy lake-
side, the bushes and the trees, even the stars in
the sky—it all seemed so real. Only the presence
of the scurrying crew dented the illusion.

It was 9:38pm. They were two hours from transmission and Ross had to admit Veranti had
worked a miracle. In just one day, the grumpy
little eight ball had secured a slot on *The Hardest
Rock on Earth*, located a vacant soundstage in the
San Pornando Valley, assembled a top team, hired
a satellite link and recalled Ross's band. And, to
top it all—thanks to the three-hour time difference and Jerry's lightning-fast work—Jason's
body had arrived just after nine and was totally
awesome.

The singer didn't need makeup for another hour,
so it left him free to explore the pseudo stalking
ground like a kid in Santa's grotto. At least until
he saw Jaomi enter the soundstage.

She was wearing a black spray-on dress and
moved through the studio like an eyeball magnet.

"I've had another forty emails from Morgas," she said through frosted pink lips. "They're sending one every five minutes."

"Oh, I'm heartbroken," laughed Ross.

"But who is he?" she asked. "I mean, where does he get his money? Is it inherited, is he a businessman, the mafia or what?"

"What difference does it make?" boomed Ross. "He's just rich, that's all. He's just a pain in the ass."

"Well, he's offered thirty million if we give him Jason."

Jaomi didn't want to push the issue, but she hoped Ross would see sense and agree to offload the useless fake ASAP.

"Thirty million?" he whooped. "What a moron!"

"But we could be twenty-five million up on the deal," she protested.

The singer marched over to an upright cargo crate standing in a corner of the set. The box was made from battered wooden boards and had been stenciled with a label that read, "Urgent— Crystal Lake to Hollywood—Hazardous Materials."

"I keep telling you, Jaomi!" he shouted. "This isn't about the money."

"No, it's not," she agreed, moving over to join him. "Morgas has said he'll kill you if you don't sell."

Ross patted the crate.

"Oh, he's just smarting because I've beaten him. For all his shitty collection, what's it worth if I've got *The Mona Lisa*?"

Jaomi stared at the tall wooden box and sighed.

The killer had been brought to the studio wrapped in tarpaulin, but had quickly been nailed inside the crate as part of the staging for tonight's unique event. She and Ross must have seen Jason for no more than ten seconds.

"Jerry says he's less convincing than one of your robots," she commented absent-mindedly.

"Animatronics," Ross corrected her.

"Whatever. Jerry thinks this Jason is shit."

"Well, thanks for sharing that with me," the singer nodded. "Now listen. Go find the producer and tell him I want news footage from the real homicides mixed into the video."

"I already gave him the DVD."

"Okay, well tell him I want copies of the original newspapers pasted all over the trees. Tell him I want front pages..."

"Shit," Jaomi started chewing her lip.

"What's wrong?"

"I left the papers in the car," she mumbled.

Ross really didn't need any eleventh hour disasters. "Well fuck it, Jaomi. Go get 'em."

He watched as she wriggled her skinny, high-heeled ass out of the room and back along the corridor, where she had the misfortune to bump into that total eclipse of a suit known as Luke Veranti. Now that Veranti was Ross's manager again, Jaomi wanted to kill him.

"So," said Luke, swaggering over to the singer, "you're gonna unmask this egg fuck live on air. Then what?"

The question caught Ross off balance.

"What do you mean?"

"Well, what happens then? Is he gonna dance? Sing? You gonna beat him into a giant fucking omelet?"

Ross tried to stay calm.

"What's going to happen," he said, pointing at a tool lying in the dirt, "is that I'm going to pick up that crowbar. Then I'm going to rip this crate open, take off Jason's mask, see his face for the very first time, and a hundred million kids are gonna go wild."

Luke raised a hand.

"Wait a second," he squawked. "Rewind that for me. What do you mean, 'For the very first time?' Haven't you seen him already?"

Ross scrunched his face dismissively.

"Heck no! When I take off his hockey mask, I want the kids to see a real reaction."

"Oh, they'll get a reaction when you lift that white piece of shit and he looks like Humpty fucking Dumpty…"

The singer tried to interrupt, but Veranti was in full flow.

"I don't know why I let you do this to me. I go out of my way to put this shit together for you and you take me right up the fucking ass. I'm telling you, Ross, when this goes out on air and everybody sees it's some prick in a rubber mask, we'll be finished."

"No, no. I swear to God," Ross placed a hand on Luke's shoulder. "It's the real deal. Honest. It's Jason Voorhees."

Veranti pushed the hand away.

"That's fucking crazy talk. Who'd you buy it from, anyhow?"

"I didn't meet her myself—"

"That's wonderful." Luke could feel his temperature rising.

"But Jerry told me she was terrified. He said she was about thirty but looked sixty, and he told me she had bloodstains on her. That's gotta count for something."

"Well, what's her name?"

"She didn't go into details—that was part of the deal. She just delivered Jason, took the cash and drove off."

"Cash?"

Ross hesitated before muttering, "Five mil."

Luke's chin began to tremble. Then his whole head started to bob. Ross tried to see through Luke's sunglasses, but the lenses had been coated with an extra layer of inscrutability.

"Turn around," said Veranti suddenly.

Ross was confused. "What for?"

"So I can see the big fucking target painted on your back, you fucking Coco the money-wasting clown prick. You moron, you've been taken for a fucking ride."

"Well, well, well," said Jaomi returning with the old newspapers Ross had asked for. "We finally agree on something, Veranti."

"Well, well, well," he sneered, patting her on the tush. "If it ain't little Miss Dealclincher."

Jaomi looked at Ross. "What's that supposed to mean?"

Ross buried his head in his hands.

Red fire scraping in blackness, eternal, grating on bone and wrenching each spurting vein in mortal

suffering. Could there be hope? So much was
screaming from the wall of death. Her mind huddled in the corner of a car crash, a frightened child,
every twitch of the flesh an act of sadism. Finding
the next exposed nerve. *Snip.* The cruel laughter of
the traitor. Michelle Kyler was lost: real and unreal,
the extremities of torture. Surely there had to be an
end to it?

"You're not looking too good, dear."

Did Kyler imagine it, or was Pamela speaking to
her again?

Black mounds of swelling obscured Kyler's left
eye. Teeth had been broken and extracted. Two
steel pins jutted from holes hammered into her
knees. Her neck was a tracery of hyenic scalpel
slicing. Her smart brown suit and white blouse
were now no more than tattered cerements.

She grunted.

As Tolleson continued to work her over—
twisting a corkscrew into bleeding, raw flesh—the
voice spoke a second time.

"My, what have they been doing to you?"

Kyler tried to answer, but her jaw had been dislocated and was now spilling black berries of
damage down the length of her neck; the severe
beating reduced her language to a Morse code of
desolation.

"Don't try to talk, dear," said Pamela. "Just think
the words in your mind. I'll hear them."

Tolleson stood back to take a look at his handi-
work.

"You know something, Michelle?" he said,
pleased with the results. "I got real sick of listening
to your self-aggrandizing bullshit. Michelle Kyler:

the woman who put the big frigging I in FBI. You were so easy."

He picked up a tiny steel mallet and set about fracturing every bone in her left hand; methodically, one by one, starting with the pinky.

"All I had to say was, 'Michelle, don't go,' and off you ran like a total knee-jerk. You didn't even notice my screw-ups. I mean, come on, Trick's body? I thought I'd gone way too far with the rookie act—you know, putting my fingers down my throat to make myself hurl? The kid had choked on a phone for Christ's sake! There wasn't even any blood."

Kyler heard the elevator door open behind her as Morgas re-entered the room.

"Is she ready to talk?" he asked.

"Ask her yourself," answered Tolleson, his earlier mocking tone now replaced by calm detachment.

Morgas came forward, betraying no sign of emotion at the dehumanized, broken piece of human shit before him. Nor did he care about the mess— the blood on the floor, the strips of skin and soft tissue on the torture chair. Instead he turned his attention to the agent's personal effects, which now lay scattered along the top shelf of the surgical trolley.

Passing over the GLOCK, the damaged cell and various other insignificant items, Morgas promptly rifled through her wallet.

Nothing.

"Well, Ms Kyler?" he said, dropping the leather holder to the floor.

Her one good eye crawled up to look at the scheming bastard. A series of moist rasps escaped from her chest and Morgas realized she was laughing at him. Hiding his anger, he looked again at the trolley and picked up Kyler's locket.

He opened it.

"Ahh, the unfortunate Martha Kyler. You never did find out what happened to her body, did you?"

From the moment Kyler saw Morgas touch the pendant, she began to struggle against the cable ties binding her to the seat. But it was in vain.

"B... stards... too... k... it," she swallowed.

"No, Ms Kyler, the bastards didn't take it," he proclaimed, his voice getting louder. "I did! She's in my museum, Ms Kyler!"

Morgas punched a button on his remote control, and the velvet drapes hiding the display case right in front of Kyler started to rise. Four lamps had been specially positioned to trap the Perspex tank of formaldehyde in a perfect X of light, leaving no room for doubt as the contents were slowly unveiled.

Inch by inch, Kyler beheld the horror of her personal tragedy: the ragged diagonal of sewn, naked flesh that ran from right hip to left breast—the torso and legs completely gone; the flailing arms whose fingernails had grown uncut; her breasts, blue and seamed with static veins; hair that drifted like the snakes of a dying Medusa; and the eyes—balls of opaque, white glass shoved into the sockets of a bleached and sagging face.

Kyler didn't need to read the brass plaque to know what it said.

"Martha Kyler: 1952-1984."

The lock of hair fell from the pendant in Morgas's hand. But he didn't even notice it as he walked across to the grisly display cabinet, his right foot trampling the precious strands into the floor.

"What a touching reunion," he smirked. "Sadly, my collection of Jason's victims is only thirty-five per cent complete. However, I guessed you'd find this entry of particular merit."

Kyler fell back in her seat.

She wanted to cry but the tears just wouldn't come.

In LA, everything was ready. The set was finished, the technical guys were in place, and Ross was hopping about in full costume like a vampire who needed a comfort break. Friday the 13th was shaping up to be the best day of the singer's life, and not even Luke and Jaomi could spoil his excitement.

"You dick me?" hollered Jaomi. "I'd rather kill myself first."

"Don't worry," Veranti yelled. "After I've dicked you, I'll kill you myself."

Although the two of them stuck close to Ross, he had become deaf to their yelling. He smiled and waved at the band—four guys on lead, bass, drums and keys. *Hardest Rock* was starting in ten minutes and "Frightday 13" was due to be one of the first tracks on the show.

"Ross!" barked Jaomi. "Are you listening? You can't legally oblige me to jump this spunk-nut. It's slavery."

Luke retched with derisory laughter.

"Oh, so you can take Johnny Cumquat's cock in your mouth—"

"That's my career!" she shouted.

"Oh yeah, you and your dumb fucking videos. What was that one where you broke the world record for hand-jobs?"

"*A Round of Pearls in Eighty Days* was a legitimate—"

"You whacked off over a thousand fucking strangers!" Luke yelled over her. "So what's the big deal with sucking my balls?"

The eternal struggle faded from Ross's attention as he took another look at the packing crate, wondering at the hero inside. Suddenly the producer's voice cut through the sound monitors.

"Final places, everyone."

Ross felt a lump rise in his throat. In less than ten minutes, he was going to see the face of his idol: Jason Voorhees.

A TV was now standing next to the bloody trolley. There was something hideously domesticated about the way in which Tolleson went about setting it up for his employer.

"We've got a direct live feed from LA," Tolleson remarked, before resuming his post behind Kyler's chair. "It starts in ten minutes."

"Do you hear that, Ms Kyler?"

Morgas stared at his prisoner with growing impatience. Since the presentation of her mother, Special Agent Kyler had become completely unresponsive. He took a step closer and shouted with such force that he showered her with spittle.

"I demand to know Jason's secret!" he raged. "I know that once he is able, he will return here for his mother's head. But how do we revive him, Ms Kyler? Tell me!"

Blood trickled over Kyler's lip and fell onto her torn blouse.

"Tell me!" Morgas bellowed.

He waited a few seconds, hoping to see some break in the monotony of her resistance; but there was none. Suddenly he bundled forwards, curled his hands into fists and rested them, not on the arms of the chair, but on Kyler's broken wrists. And as Morgas ground her shattered bones, Tolleson looped a coil of razor wire over her head and pulled it tight around her throat. Kyler's head slammed back against the chair and, even in the remoteness of her damage, she felt herself start to choke.

"Tell me, Ms Kyler! TELL ME!"

Morgas hurled his fury against her tense form like a battering ram. Her wrists pinned, her head pulled back, blood rising in her windpipe, a wave of twitching spread through her muscles like an epileptic spasm. And then a whimper of abandonment stole from her lips.

"You're dying, Ms Kyler!" said Morgas with overbearing certainty. "No matter what you say or do, I will kill you. But tell me Jason's secret and I will order an immediate end to your suffering."

Crimson torpor fastened its invisible burden onto Kyler, and she could feel her anatomy being drawn into the abyss.

"Don't listen to them, dear," said Pamela, her voice a beacon through the pain.

"But if you remain silent," threatened Morgas, "Mr Tolleson will continue your agonies for days."

Pamela tut-tutted.

"That's no way to treat a mother," she said. "Floating in all that dirty water. They should be ashamed of themselves."

Kyler saw the saturated corpse of her own mother; trapped in a case beyond the squat, rabid head of her enemy. She tried to open her lips. Morgas saw it instantly and placed his ear close so he could listen.

"H... h... hel... p—" she whispered.

"I'm trying," gasped Morgas, unaware that he was not the one Kyler was speaking to. "But you must help yourself."

The agent shut out the noise in her ears and listened with her mind for the answer she wanted.

"You know they're killing you, don't you?" asked Pamela.

Kyler tried to nod in the affirmative.

"Well, tell me!" demanded Morgas, misunderstanding the gesture.

"And all because of my poor boy," said Mrs Voorhees. "My Jason."

The wire had cut clean through the skin, flesh and muscle, and had now made contact with Kyler's trachea. Quickly, Morgas let go of her wrists. Then he snatched a hot soldering iron off the trolley and thrust it into her ribcage.

"TELL ME!"

The band had been standing in front of the moonlit lake for almost a quarter of an hour, and the playback of "Frightday 13" still hadn't started. Ross looked at the floor clock. It was a quarter of midnight: *The Hardest Rock On Earth* had been on air fifteen minutes.

"What's going on?" he hollered.

The air was so thick with dry ice, Ross could hardly see anyone—not even Jaomi, and he knew she was definitely around someplace. He thought about quitting the stage—even though the producer had told him not to leave his mark under any circumstances—but then Veranti came strutting forward through the mist.

"There's been a problem with the link," he confirmed. "But it's fixed now. You'll be going on in ten minutes."

Ross glanced at the clock a second time.

"But that's five to midnight," he complained.

"So? That's good, right? I thought you and the egg man were into all that witches' hour bullshit."

"Well, it better not be any later because if this goes out after midnight, I'll miss Friday the 13th. And you know what that means."

"It'll be Saturday the Fourteenth," said Veranti plainly.

The singer shook his head in dismay. It seemed that no one but him understood just how important this moment was. But then Ross didn't fully appreciate how important it was either. Only Michelle Kyler knew—and she wasn't telling anyone.

Morgas and Tolleson continued their butchery; breaking, gouging, manipulating the agent's battered form any way they pleased. And with each inventive new act of cruelty, Morgas demanded Jason's secret.

"Tell me!" he raved.

Michelle Kyler was riding an express bound for her destruction; a train with only one broken window left open.

"Oh, I can help you," said Pamela, the only person Kyler could still hear with any clarity. "We still have a deal, remember. We still have to find my boy. But unless we do something, you'll soon be gone."

Kyler didn't understand.

"Give me your body," said Pamela.

No.

"Give me your body and you won't just live, you'll be able to fight back."

Tolleson continued to tighten the noose around her neck, but Nathaniel Morgas stood back and loaded his revolver.

"We can kill them," urged Pamela.

But Kyler knew that fully surrendering her body to Pamela was irreversible; her soul would cease to exist, just as if Tolleson and Morgas had killed her. She also knew that Pamela would already have possessed her had it not been for the presence of her own mother's remains—a power many times greater than the locket.

"Look what they did to your mother," spat Pamela furiously. "Don't you want to make them pay? Look what they did to her! Look what they did to her!"

Kyler recalled that it was Jason who killed her mother. It was Pamela's precious son who was ultimately responsible for the mutilated remains floating in the formaldehyde. Once again Kyler rejected her.

"No!" wailed Pamela. "You don't understand. Jason didn't kill your mother..."

Morgas jammed the barrel of his gun against Kyler's forehead, Tolleson tugged harder on the strangle-cord, and from deep within her nightmare, Kyler found the strength to pull the string that operated her voice.

She coughed, spat blood, and gasped, "Moonlight."

"Ah, the survival instinct is a wonderful thing, Ms Kyler."

Morgas lifted the revolver from her forehead and motioned Tolleson to keep the garrote in place, but not to tighten it any further.

"We've tortured you beyond recognition," he expounded, "you've endured unimaginable pain, and yet all it took to make you talk was a simple gun to the head, along with your recognition of the fact that I would not hesitate to use it. And so you've bought yourself a few extra seconds of that most precious commodity: life."

Tolleson let go of one of the wire handles and pointed at the TV.

"It's starting," he said, drawing his employer's attention to the opening bars of "Frightday 13."

"Well, Ms Kyler?" Morgas sneered, tapping her left temple with the muzzle. "What about the moonlight?"

It was 11:58pm PST and, now that the link had been fixed, the telecast was well underway. The false moon was bright, the night air was thick with mist, and Ross growled and haunted his way through the artificial woodland. Historic images of the Crystal Lake Massacre bled across the screen as he bent forward over a blood red lamp.

"Hack the motherfuckers
Fuck the motherhackers
Hack the motherfuckers
Yeah. Yeahhhh!"

Ross was miming to the playback like the bastard son of a devil-whore. In his mind, he really was The Vampire and this really was Crystal Lake. There were only two minutes of Friday the 13th remaining, and in just a few more bars, the guitar solo would start and Ross would tear the lid off the cargo crate.

"Frightday 13, thirteen die.
Hey yeah, there's blood in your eye."

He lifted the crowbar and stomp-danced his way to the tall wooden box. Out of the corner of his eye, he could see Veranti and Jaomi bickering. The two people he loved most and they weren't even watching.

"First you're gonna run, then you're gonna cry.
Frightday 13... DIE!"

With immaculate timing, the lead guitar screamed like a digital banshee over a news report about another set of bodies found near Crystal Lake, and Ross jammed the crowbar into the crate.

It was one minute to midnight.

Still holding the gun to Kyler's head, Morgas took the open locket with his other hand and dangled it in front of her face; the picture of her mother spun round and round.

"Come now, Ms Kyler, the sooner you tell me everything, the sooner you and your mother will be reunited. Your corpse will make an excellent sidebar to my collection."

Kyler desperately wanted to speak, but the dual sight of her mother—the bloodstained photo in the foreground and the jigsaw body in the background—found a part of her that had almost been buried by the torture; the part that was still an FBI special agent. Tough, resilient and defiant.

Sensing the change, Pamela seized the opportunity to speak to Michelle one last time.

"If you tell them, they'll kill you," she shouted. "And then we'll all become part of this blasphemous freak show. You, me, Jason, your poor mother—we'll be their playthings until the end of time."

Again, Kyler recalled that Jason killed her mother.

"But that's what I'm trying to tell you," gasped Pamela. "Jason didn't kill your mother. It was Francis Grissom. Look!"

Pamela Voorhees opened a funereal gate into the past and, as if in a dream, Kyler relived the night when Francis Grissom found a woman he called "stinky-slut" caught in one of his mantraps. It was dark, she was afraid, and she begged Grissom for help. In return, he beat her about the head and cut her body in half with an axe. He was going to take her home for meat, but some of stinky-slut's friends showed up and he had to "do a leggy." Martha Kyler had been no more than a common victim of humankind's endemic self-hatred.

At long last, Kyler's one unbroken eye flooded with tears. They crawled down her face, fell from her dislocated jaw and splashed upon the locket.

Drip—a lachrymose crown exploded on the surface of her mother's smiling face.

"I'm losing my patience, Ms Kyler," growled
Morgas. "Now tell me. What's the secret of the
moonlight?"

Kyler could feel the last seconds of her life were
approaching.

Tolleson kept a firm grip on the garrote, but he
was watching Ross Feratu on the TV; the wooden
crate had just begun to splinter, the lid would
come away at any moment. A bright light was
pointed at Ross's head, simulating the moon, and
suddenly every answer tumbled into place.

"I've got it!" he shouted.

"What?" Morgas asked impatiently.

Tolleson let go of the wire, the groove in Kyler's
neck holding it in place, and rushed over to the
lectern. Then he snatched up Pamela's head and
ran across to a tiny window high in the wall of the
vast chamber: a slender pole of moonlight shone
through the aperture.

"Kill the lights!" he called.

But Morgas wasn't in the habit of taking orders
from anyone, "What are you talking about, Mr
Tolleson?"

"The moonlight needs to fall on Pamela's head,"
said Tolleson excitedly.

"Heavens!" whispered Morgas.

Kyler's heartbeat stuttered: her next ragged
breath would be her last. She saw her mother in
the Perspex tank, she felt Pamela begging to be
given control of her body, she saw Tolleson about
to throw the kill switch, and then there was
Morgas—the one who had beaten them all—a

monster set against whom Jason was truly a child.

As her pulse crawled to zero, Michelle Kyler spilled one last tear and made her silent deal.

The museum was plunged into darkness and Cory Tolleson held the head aloft, breaking the thin shaft of light that was falling towards the floor…

Jason erupted from the cargo crate. Shards of wood flew across the soundstage as he snatched the crowbar out of Ross's hand and hurled it with crossbow precision into the face of the cameraman. The TV image went crazy, the cracked lens spinning in a vertigo of violence, barely making sense of the sight of Jason bringing an arc lamp down over the bass player's head. The musician staggered across the room in a shower of sparks, his improvised helmet shooting flares in all directions, before he collapsed among the trees and set the makeshift forest on fire.

"Frightday 13" continued to pound through the speakers, even though the remaining members of the band had stopped miming to the music and were now looking at one another, wondering what the hell was going on. The lead guitarist guessed it was Ross, pulling another lame stunt. He was about to confront the singer, when Jason snatched a hi-hat off the drum kit and tossed it like a Frisbee into his neck. The guitarist puked blood and died, his corpse hitting the deck mere seconds before the drummer, who Jason hauled off a stool and repeatedly choke-slammed into the floor, beating his head into neck butter.

"Holy shit!" cried the keyboard player.

He tried to run but Jason seized him in a head-lock. The killer held him fast, as he pulled an audio cable out of the rear of the synthesizer and then jammed the metal jack plug so hard into the keyboardist's eye that it punched straight through into the brain. In their recording days, Ross had never let the guy add backing vocals to any of his albums because he had always sounded tone deaf; now, however, the keyboard player screamed in perfect pitch. Jason gouged deeper into his cerebrum and screwed the pin with such force that juice spat onto his hands. When the body stopped shaking—and the long black cord was plugged into its skull—Jason hurled it at the dry ice machine.

The dead musician crashed into the special effects apparatus and sent the system into overload. Chemical mist threw a shroud over the soundstage. With the bloodshed and the fire, the chaos was complete.

"Ross!" Luke called from a corner of the room. His voice was barely audible over the rock music playback. "What the fuck is this? One of your fucking egg muppets?"

Jaomi called over too. She was standing close to Luke, but kept a little behind him just in case Jason came their way.

"Dwayne, this has gone too far. Either you stop this or I'm leaving!"

But the singer was frozen in amazement. He'd been watching Jason go about his deadly business, passing from one murder to the next, with a feeling akin to ecstasy. Each inventive homicide was proof not only that Jason Voorhees was real, but that he'd always been real. So there was no guilt in Ross's pleasure, only the delight of a dream come true.

Over on the other side of the soundstage, the director, the second cameraman, the sound girl and two other crew members had only just realized that none of this was a hoax.

"We gotta get outta here, guys!" the director urged.

But no sooner did the team start to run across the studio than the sprinkler system kicked belatedly into life. Gallons of water poured from the ceiling, turning the polished floor into an ice rink. The makeup woman went skidding towards the exit—the only door out of the soundstage—only to find Jason waiting for her.

The showers were having no effect on the fire whatsoever; worse, when the droplets of cold water hit the blazing trees, great swathes of smoke arose, adding confusion to the already impenetrable dry ice.

Veranti couldn't see what was happening by the exit but, by the sound of it, it wasn't too pretty. Jason was killing the entire crew using their own equipment as weapons. Suddenly the assistant producer lurched forward through the mist. His headphones had been wound so tightly around his neck that his head looked like the top half of an hourglass ready to burst. The guy couldn't breathe—but a few seconds later he didn't need to.

The producer of the video shoot was furious. From the moment Jason had killed the first camera operator, the pictures running in the production booth had been a complete mess.

"What the fuck is he doing?" the producer moaned, his eyes flicking from monitor to monitor. "He's ruined the entire broadcast."

Without waiting for an answer from his two colleagues in the booth, he got up and marched across the room. The soundstage was just a short walk along the corridor, but when the producer threw open the door he saw Jason standing in his way.

"Ross, you crazy bastard!" he shouted. "People told me not to work with you. I was warned. They said, 'Stay away from that crazy motherfucker,' but did I listen? No. And now you've gone and screwed up everything!"

It hadn't occurred to the producer that Ross didn't have time to change from his vampire costume into such a perfect Jason outfit. He just kept unloading at the hockey mask, shouting louder and louder, until Jason punched him in the stomach, ripped out his intestines and gagged the noisy bastard with his own innards.

Incredibly, the producer was still alive as his tongue savored the offal-like flavor of his colon. He retched at the serving suggestion of disembowelment, but remained conscious as Jason grabbed his shoulders and drove him backwards into the mixing console. The entire panel shorted, the producer danced with electric shock and the satellite link to the studio was terminated—just like the two assistants cowering in the corner of the booth.

Across the corridor, the last surviving crew members were enjoying the catering, unaware of the devastation unfolding just a few doors away. But when the production desk shorted, the music abruptly stopped. One second, "Frightday 13" was echoing at full volume around the building; the next second, nothing.

"I'll go see if everything's okay," offered one of the rigging engineers.

But no one else seemed particularly interested. They carried on chatting and eating until Jason burst into the room. He was holding the producer's liver and was soaked in blood.

The engineer held out a bottle. "Wanna beer?"

Jason shut the door—and then the screaming started.

"He's alive!" laughed Morgas, fascinated by the NTSC flicker that was made even more vivid now that the lights had been extinguished. His ear was almost touching Kyler's lips.

"Don't you see?" he boomed. "He's alive! Alive!"

Kyler craned forward, sank her teeth in the soft folds of Morgas's neck, and tore open a crater that sprayed jets of blood all over the collector's face. He screamed and stumbled, only to witness Kyler break free from her restraints as if they were made of tissue. The garrote slipped from her throat, giving Morgas just enough time to crap into his thousand-dollar pants before Kyler stood up and snatched the pistol from his hand.

Tolleson turned to see what was happening, inadvertently stepping into the moonlight; the shaft of silver was now pointing like a laser at his heart.

One—two—three—four—five—six. Each of Kyler's bullets found its ventricular target, knocking Tolleson off his feet, dealing with him dispassionately and decisively. His body slammed against the marble with a squelch, the four-chambered meat pump doing its best to supply the dead man with redundant corpuscles. The severed head fell with him and rolled beyond the moonbeams.

"Pleeaase," whined Morgas. He was crawling on all fours in a pig sty of his own shit and blood. "Help me," he cried, as he reached forward to kiss Kyler's feet.

Michelle rose to her full height above him.

"It's judgment day, Mr Morgas," she smiled.

Then she reached for the trolley full of torture tools and began to exact her revenge. It would take all her skill and know-how to cause maximum pain before the bleating hog bled to death. She had a minute at the most. But a lot could happen in sixty seconds.

The studio clock flipped to 00:00, but Jason had already claimed enough victims never to have to rely on Mommy again. Of all the people working in the studio, only three remained alive, and now every corner of the soundstage was on fire.

"Please, Ross!" Jaomi cried. "We have to leave before Jason comes back."

But the singer was beyond reach. While Luke and Jaomi edged towards the door, Ross chose to stand in the middle of the room. The building was starting to collapse about him, but he was in no danger; not when he could stare at the carnage of Crystal Lake with the certain knowledge that Jason would come back for him. He was no longer imagining or reading about the Crystal Lake Murders; he was living them.

"This is your fault!" snapped Veranti. "If you hadn't bought Humpty on the internet..."

"You set this up!" shouted Jaomi. "You're the manager!"

Even now, with dismembered bodies lying all around, the two of them couldn't see beyond personal recriminations.

"Where d'you find him?" barked Luke. "Whackos-R-Us? Lastmaniac dot com? You fucking porn star prick!"

"Veranti!" she screamed.

"How many times do I have to tell you?" he said, oblivious to the fear in her eyes. "It's Veranti, rhymes with panty, not fucking monty."

Jason rammed the microphone stand into Veranti's back. The spear continued and plunged through Jaomi's gut in a double impalement, before finally embedding in the wall, holding the two of them on their feet like a Beverly Hills kebab.

Veranti stared up into the black eyes of the hockey mask.

"Goo goo, g'joob," he exhaled, sarcastic to the very end.

Viewers at home had seen their screens go from predictable to chaotic to blank, and they'd changed channels in their millions while everyone in the studio was being killed.

Now only Ross was left.

"Jason?" he called.

Loose wires buzzed and crackled, and the singer recoiled from a burst of flame. But he could see Jason, with his back to him, studying the skewered corpses of Luke and Jaomi. Jason turned and Ross cried with joy.

"I'd do anything for you. You know that, don't you?" wept Ross.

The icon—the legend—was real, and he loomed over the singer with calm menace, impassive and powerful, a monument to the point where childish fantasy and adult reality meet as a horrible misunderstanding.

Jason took off his hockey mask and placed it over the singer's face.

Ross cried even harder. Jason was giving him his mask. It was as if Jason Voorhees understood. He knew that Ross was his biggest fan, and he was giving the singer his most personal and precious belonging. For a moment, Ross thought he was in heaven. But then he looked through the eyes of the mask and saw Jason's awful features. And then he felt him press down. Jason wasn't giving him the hockey mask—he was killing him with it.

"No, Jason. No!"

The killer forced the mask into Ross's skin, the circular holes forming red wheals that soon became cuts.

"Agggh!"

Ross clawed at the sheer white plastic, his nails splintering as the mask drove into him with the unstoppable force of a meat grinder. Cylinders of flesh oozed through the holes, but still the singer would not die—not until Jason braced his elbows and plunged the mask into the cracked bones of his skull.

Dwayne Weintraub fell screaming to his death, and only now did he find out what it meant to meet the real Jason Voorhees.

EPILOGUE

The open-topped convertible cruised at a steady fifty down the long, lonely freeway. It was late afternoon and the vehicle was on cruise control, giving the driver a chance to relax with the radio.

"It's unlucky thirteen, but posthumous album sales are going through the roof," announced the newscaster. "Following the commercial and critical failure of his latest album, increasingly erratic behavior, and a bizarre arrest on Kantayna Finwell's reality TV show, international rock star Ross Feratu committed suicide on live television last week after murdering his wife, his manager and members of his former band. Viewers watching…"

Kyler turned the radio off and checked herself in the mirror. Her face was bruised and she needed some dental work, but she'd healed remarkably well over the last seven days; in fact, her recovery seemed positively unnatural. She was delighted with her new look. Gone were the boring brown business suit and the white blouse, replaced by jeans, a checked shirt and a powder blue sweater. She'd also found time to have her hair done and now had a blonde permanent wave in place of her former shoulder-length brunette. And she wore a hunting knife in a leather sheath hanging off her belt.

"Don't worry, Jason," she whispered. "Mommy's coming. Mommy will make it better."

Staring through the windshield at the endless miles of farmland, she pushed harder on the gas and went speeding along the road. She didn't know where Jason was or what he was doing, but she knew that each mile she traveled was another mile closer to him.

A mother just knows these things.

Smoke rose from the wrecked Greyhound bus. The vehicle had crashed off the side of the Arizona desert road and all the passengers were dead. However, only two of them had been killed by the accident itself; everyone else had been torn into body parts by the passenger they should never have stopped to pick up.

Jason walked from the debris, oblivious to the tree of grief he'd just planted. He'd crushed the driver's head and massacred everybody on board, as soon as he boarded the bus. Now he was back on foot, trudging north-east in a pitiless diagonal of death.

Because Jason wanted to get back home.

Home to Crystal Lake.

* * *

"Can I get you another cocktail, ma'am?"

The waiter couldn't help but admire the beauty of the woman lying full-stretch on the beach. He'd been working at the exclusive Caribbean resort for more than seven years, so he was way past the novelty of seeing fantastically rich bitches lolling around in swimsuits. After a while, they'd all looked the same: great hair, tanned bodies, perfect nails, trim physique, tight butts, Botox, implants—all the usual. But this woman was unique, and in the few days since she'd checked in, the waiter had really taken a shine to her.

Personality wise, she was a diamond in the rough. But body wise, she was covered in tattoos and didn't care a goddamn who saw her. She just paraded in a series of tiny bikinis and, without even trying, got the guys staring at her all day long.

The woman checked her martini glass; it was almost empty.

"I'll have another vodka boatman," she smiled, revealing two rows of gleaming new crowns.

"Sure," said the waiter, returning the grin as he headed back across the sand.

The woman propped herself up on her elbows and gazed lovingly at the water. The aquamarine waves were crested by just the right amount of pure white foam—she didn't think she'd ever seen a sea so beautiful.

Suddenly, the book she'd been reading fell off her chest and dropped into the sand. She picked it up, dusted it down and carried on reading from where she'd just left off. The book was called *My Life of Hell: One Man's Fight against Jason*

Voorhees, and it was written by someone called Thomas Jarvis.

"What a loser," she murmured.

Multimillionaire Alice Jane Witney read another couple of pages of this whiny piece of garbage, finished off her drink, and laughed, and laughed, and laughed...

ABOUT THE AUTHOR

Stephen Hand is the author of six books and has also written for *Fear*, *Edge*, *Prediction* and *Develop* magazines. He has designed five board games including *Chainsaw Warrior*, *Fury of Dracula* and *Star Wars: Escape From The Death Star*, he is the producer of over twenty video games, among them the international million-seller blockbuster *Grand Prix 2*, and in the late 1990s he worked as Director of European Product Development for Californian publisher, MicroProse. He has previously contributed to Black Flame with *Freddy vs Jason* and *The Texas Chainsaw Massacre*. Stephen lives in the south-west of England with his wife, Mandy. You can write to him at: *stephenhand.books@btopenworld.com.*